LOVE MYSTIFIES

Beguiling love stories of mystery, magic and suspense

Carolee Joy
Tami D. Cowden
Betsy Norman

Susan D. Brooks
Su Kopil
Charlotte Shreck Burns

To: Patti,
Wishing you
magic,
Carolee Joy
12/6/2000

Fusion Press

Published by Dream Street Prose,
In cooperation with Fusion Press,
A publishing service of Authorlink
(http://www.authorlink.com)
3720 Millswood Dr.
Irving, Texas 75062, USA

First published by Dream Street Prose
In cooperation with Fusion Press,
A publishing service of Authorlink
First Printing, September, 2000

Printed in the United States of America

ISBN 1 928704 81 6

Dedicated to all those who believe
in the mystery and magic called love.

Author's Notes

TABLE OF CONTENTS

* These stories are rated "R" for adult sexual situations

HAUNTED DREAMS

Carolee Joy

The house beckoned her.

During the day, thoughts of the beautiful house she'd discovered nibbled at the edges of her mind. At night, Julia dreamed of the peace she would find within its walls.

Finally, not sure she was making the right decision, but unable to bear living in the house she had shared with her ex-husband until he'd run off with their Sunday School teacher, she stuck a For Sale sign in the yard and began to pack.

One month later, she was unloading boxes in the charming house her realtor friend, Donna, described as "Texas Country."

Donna stopped by at sunset with a bottle of wine to see how she was doing. "You really got a deal on this place, Julia. I hope you won't be disappointed." She took the chair opposite Julia on the side patio.

"Why would I be?" She waved her hand towards the pond and admired the pink and purple streaked sky beyond it.

"Well," Donna hesitated and took a slow sip of white zinfandel. "That graveyard on the other side of the empty lot. I try to be very honest when I'm selling people a house, and most people were too put off by it to think of anything else."

Julia nibbled on a wheat cracker spread with dill and cream cheese. "I think it's fascinating. Imagine, a little bit of Texas history practically in my back yard."

"Think you'll see any ghosts?" Donna laughed.

Julia finished her cracker and dusted crumbs off her fingers. "I hope so. Wouldn't that be an incredible way to overcome this writer's block I've had?"

Donna finished her wine and set the glass on the white wrought-iron table. "Honey, you don't have writer's block. What you have is just plain old-fashioned emotional exhaustion."

"Maybe. Restless spirits could be a good basis for a story, though." She offered her friend another splash of wine, but Donna shook her head.

"Have to show a house this evening. What do you mean?"

"The alleged horse thief who was buried there first. I mean, what if he wasn't even guilty? Maybe the McAllens just wanted an excuse to start a family burial ground. Although why they'd want to start with a stranger is pretty interesting."

Donna wrinkled her nose. "You have the most morbid curiosity. Don't tell me you actually walked to the graveyard and read that old historical marker before you've even had a chance to unpack your dishes."

Julia smiled. "Research always comes first. I did check it out, and obviously you have too, or you wouldn't know what I'm talking about."

Donna waved away the significance. "Purely professional information gathering. I had no idea when I took the listing that this gorgeous new house would be an albatross. After several deals fell through, I figured I better find out why."

"So what did you find out?"

Donna shrugged. "Nothing more than what the marker says. The last McAllen was buried there more than fifty years ago. And since our horse thief was buried 100 years before that, it's impossible that anyone would have any information about it. If the McAllens did, then it died with old Gussie."

Julia shivered, whether from the chill settling in or from the tug twilight always gave her imagination, she wasn't sure. "Wasn't there a story going around about the McAllens being cursed? I heard Gussie died penniless because she couldn't find a buyer for the land."

"Maybe she was just too stubborn to know when to subdivide. But it doesn't matter now."

They both rose, and Donna enfolded Julia in a hug. "I hope you'll be happy here, sweetie. Fill up this place with some brand new memories and never mind about that old horse thief."

Julia watched her friend drive away in her shiny new Mercedes sedan. Success agreed with Donna, and she'd always enjoyed the things money could buy. Until now, Julia hadn't thought much about money one way or another. Buying this house would definitely strain her budget, but every instinct she had told her it would be well worth it. The house spoke to her on some level she didn't know how to analyze.

Exhausted from the move and months of turmoil, she fell asleep the moment her head touched the feather pillow.

Only you can save me, Julia.

A man's voice filtered past her consciousness, stole into her dreams and changed their direction. She twirled across a wooden dance floor, the starched skirt of her gingham dress flaring out around her. From across the room, she felt Brett's gaze touch her until her skin burned with the sensation, and a fire ignited in the pit of her belly.

"You look a little flushed, Miss Julia." The cowboy leading her through the Virginia Reel authoritatively escorted her from the floor, further away from Brett, and over to the huge trestle table laden with food and drinks. One thing was for certain, her father knew how to throw a party.

Too bad he thought he knew what kind of man his only daughter should marry. She edged away from Adam. Something about her father's slick ranch foreman made her skin creep, made her yank her hand from his the moment she could do so without making a scene. It had been his double talk that had made her father fire Brett.

She looked past the cowboy to see Brett less than ten steps away. The cowboy's image faded into insignificance as she stretched her hand out towards the handsome man with the tawny hair and caramel colored eyes. He reached for her. Her heart pounded with anticipation and exhilaration. He'd defied her father's orders to be with her, and the thought filled her with a curious sense of awe and power.

Only you can save me, Julia.

Instead of Brett's warm hand, her fingers brushed something cold and damp. Julia bolted upright in bed.

Moonlight streamed through her open bedroom window and pooled on the floor. Trembling and chilled to the bone, she pressed her hand to her heart and tried to draw a calming breath. A dream. It was only a dream.

Julia, the voice beckoned with a mixture of seduction and sadness.

She tried to dismiss the sound as the wind sighing through the trees. Then she realized her shades were up and the windows open. Fear crawled through her.

She'd closed them all before going to sleep.

Scrambling from the bed, she grabbed her robe and wrapped it around herself, then hurried to the windows and quickly shut them. Her hands hesitated on the last one as something pulled her gaze toward the cemetery.

Across the vacant lot, through the stands of post oaks, shadows shifted and moved in the moonlight. Wisps floated, reaching long tendrils towards her, pulling, luring.

She closed her eyes and shook her head to clear the visions. Ground fog. That's all it was, not at all unusual for this time of year. Ignoring the plea that reached into her heart, she slammed down the window and let the pleated shade roll down. Then she jumped back into bed and pulled the covers over her head.

Save me, Julia. You're the only one who can.

The voice persisted long after she found the courage to close her eyes and seek sleep. But she didn't find any until the first rays of sunrise lighted the rectangular windows and the mourning doves began their own plaintive calling.

When she awoke shortly before noon, she had made her decision. Unpacked boxes and crates be damned, she was going to find out the real story behind the McAllen's horse thief. Somehow she knew she wouldn't get a good night's sleep until she did. Besides, the writer in her couldn't let such a golden opportunity for a story slip away. Maybe this was just the kind of excitement she needed to get the creative juices flowing again. Her agent had been pestering her to contribute something to a Texas author's anthology. This might be the material she needed to make that happen.

After a quick shower, she grabbed her car keys and headed for the library.

Three days of research and two restless nights later, the sketchy information she'd found only confirmed that Brett Williams, next of kin unknown, had been hanged for horse thievery and buried on the McAllen property.

The only other interesting bit of information was that Julia McAllen, the daughter who would have been seventeen at the time, had died an old maid. The direct line of McAllens had died when she did. Gussie McAllen Kimball, the last descendent buried in the family plot, had been a great-great-grand niece of Julia McAllen's father.

Julia slowly closed the aging family record book which had been donated to the historical society. That was it then. Anything else she wanted to believe about the story, she'd have to make up. How strange that she shared a name with one of the long dead McAllens.

That night, Julia tossed restlessly, her dreams filled with unfamiliar longings.

Save me, Julia. Don't give up.

Turning to her side, she glanced at the bedside clock. Two a.m. The air seemed heavy with expectancy. Moonlight backlit the shades and turned the oaks outside her bedroom window into a dancing, writhing silhouette of movement and shadow. She threw back the covers and slid from the bed, every movement taking a supreme effort, like moving through pudding. A long cotton gown cascaded past her knees and swirled around her ankles. How peculiar, yet how right it felt. She hadn't owned a nightgown since she was a teenager.

She drew up the shade and let her gaze drift to the cemetery. Low shrubs pirouetted in the breeze, sending a shower of small white blossoms to the ground in a trail that seemed to point toward her house.

To her.

Not sure where she was going or why, she let the intense feelings overpower her and moved to the patio door. Her fingers shook slightly and hesitated on the lock. The next thing she knew she stood beneath towering trees, grass silky beneath her bare feet.

She should be cold, standing in a cemetery on a chilly April night, but she saw herself as if from a long way off as the years peeled away, and she became a seventeen-year-old girl with a desperate secret.

"Brett," she whispered softly, half afraid he was hiding behind the stand of blackjack trees just beyond the porch, more afraid he wasn't. She twisted the end of her braided hair and cast a nervous glance at the ranch house. If Daddy caught her out in the middle of the night in her nightgown, he'd pack her off to that boarding school out East he kept threatening her with.

Or worse, marry her off to that awful Adam.

Brett's work roughened hand over her mouth muffled her

shriek of surprise.

"You shouldn't be out here." His warm breath tickled her neck as she relaxed against him. "But I'm glad you are."

Turning, she flung her arms around him and buried her face against his chest. "Oh, Brett. You came back."

His soft laugh stole her remaining tension.

"Don't you know by now that I will never leave you?"

Taking her by the hand, he led her further away from the house, and she went willingly. Eagerly. Not even a slight hesitation slowed her footsteps. Just deep enough into the thicket to be shielded from the revealing rays of moonlight, Brett's horse stood quietly, tethered and waiting patiently. He pulled a rolled blanket off the saddle and continued on. Still gripping her hand tightly, he stopped, spread the blanket and motioned for her to sit.

"We need to talk."

Tugging on his hand, she pulled him down beside her. "I love you, Brett," she blurted, before common sense could still her reckless tongue. Yet she didn't regret telling him. Because if she didn't love him, then why did she feel both hot and cold at the same time? Why did her skin feel too tight over her bones? Why else did she have a strange achy sensation in places she'd never thought about before?

"Lord, Julia," he groaned, tumbling her on the blanket and pressing kisses against her throat. "If your father were to find us—"

"Shh." She placed her fingers against his lips, thrilling at the sensation when he sucked gently on her fingertips. Then hot kisses stole her breath and robbed her of any remaining reason she might have had.

His hands roamed down over her gown and drew her against his denim and leather clad body. "Julia, Julia. How can you expect me to act like a gentleman when you're not dressed like a proper young lady?"

"I don't want to be a proper young lady." She feathered kisses over the sand-papery texture of his face. "I want to be your—" She hesitated, swallowed, and set the words free. "Wife. Take me with you, Brett. Take me now." Heart fluttering like the wind-tossed trees, she undid his belt and worked at the buttons on his shirt. Somehow, she knew she needed to bind herself to him or else in the clear light of day, he might put aside promises he made in the dark.

He brought her hand to his lips and pressed kisses in her palm. "We'll leave tomorrow night. Meet me here before the moon rises."

She pushed his shirt down his strongly muscled arms, their plan making her bolder than she'd ever been before. "I wish we could leave now."

"One more day. I've been doing some work at that ranch down the road a piece. He promised to have my pay ready tomorrow. We can wait that long to go. But I'm not sure I can wait to have you."

She closed her eyes on a sigh as he eased her gown up past her waist and pulled it off over her head. His mouth came down warm and coaxing on her breast. "I don't want you to wait," she breathed, lacing her fingers through his thick hair and holding him close against her skin. His tongue burned a path down her abdomen, then touched her in an intimate way that shocked her to her soul even as it sent her arching towards him, begging for more. Her breath caught in her throat as he undressed, then hovered over her, seeking her gaze in the shadows.

"I want to please you," he murmured, his body hot and hard against hers. Teasing. Tempting.

She trembled with a mixture of fear, anticipation and desperate need. "Tell me you love me." She knew he must to risk her father's wrath, yet she needed to hear the words.

"I do love you, Julia. Enough to risk everything."

Then he entered her, and the sense of rightness overwhelmed her. Caught up in his rhythm, a breathless feeling, as if her chest would burst with happiness, thrummed through her, turning her blood into a raging torrent that sang in her veins and pounded in her ears. His buttocks flexed beneath her fingers, her name ripped from his lips in a hoarse cry, and the joy burst within her as he claimed her heart for all eternity.

Julia woke and threw the covers off her sweat-drenched body. Slowly, she eased to a sitting position. A cool breeze filtered through the open window, pebbling her skin. She touched her mouth with trembling fingers. What a vivid dream. Her lips felt tender from kisses, her face tingled. A damp gown clung to her.

The white, ruffled gown from her dream. Stifling a cry, she leaped from the bed and stumbled into the bathroom. Peering into the mirror, she examined her face. She must have burrowed against the pillow, that was all. That was the reason it looked as if she had a case of whisker burn.

But where had the gown come from? Why didn't she remember putting it on? Why did her body feel sensitized, yet utterly sated?

And why were dried leaves stuck in her hair?

She spent the next day trying to reason out what had happened. Several times, she nearly called Donna, but how could she explain the inexplicable to her pragmatic friend?

That night she lay awake for a long time watching patterns dance across the ceiling, fearful of falling asleep, even more terrified of never again knowing the dream feelings of total completion. Maybe it had been a mistake to buy this house, and her imagination was just letting her know what her mind was too stressed to see.

Against her will, her eyes drifted shut.

Her footsteps again led her to the wooded area where the graveyard now stood. Where in a long ago time, another Julia crept silently from a darkened house, dodging creaky boards on the wooden porch, tiptoeing down the steps until her stockinged feet touched cool grass.

Then she ran, heedless of the stones digging into her feet, unmindful of the dark, the wind and everything save one thought:

Brett waited nearby. For her! *Please let him be there*, she prayed.

When she reached the thicket, she found only flattened grass where Brett's blanket had lain the night before. The wind moaned through the post oaks. She waited quietly, one long moment stretching out into another, the thudding of her heart nearly drowning out the sound of hoofbeats drawing nearer.

Too many hoofbeats.

Nearer. Filling her with fear, killing her hopes.

The clearing became a blaze of torchlight and angry men. Brett, face bruised and battered, hands tied in front of him, slumped in the saddle of her chestnut mare. Julia's father, eyes wild with fury, tossed one end of a long rope to the ranch foreman. Adam seemed only too happy to comply with her father's order to anchor it around a thick branch in the tallest oak.

"Daddy! What are you doing?" Horror rose in her throat, threatening to choke her as she spied the other end of the rope.

Around Brett's neck.

The wind ripped her shriek of anguish away, making her protest as insignificant as the moon playing hide and seek with the clouds roiling across the night sky. "Nooo, Daddy, no! Please!"

"See why I warned you to stay away from this trash, daughter?"

"Damn drifter's nothing but a horse thief, sir!" Adam's eyes gleamed with a savage light. "Caught him red-handed."

Ignoring Julia's hands clutching at his pants leg as he sat astride his black stallion, her father turned to Brett. "Don't know where you're from, boy, but I know where you're going."

Screams filled her ears, her own screams, unheeded by the half dozen men following her father's orders. Driven by a misguided lust for revenge, no one listened to her pleas, no one saw fit to hear her story of how Brett wasn't stealing her horse, just—

Helping her run away.

Every word further sounded Brett's death sentence. Julia fell to her knees, sobbing, pleading with all the powers of heaven and hell not to take her love away from her.

Lightning crackled across the sky, the wind rose to a wild frenzy. The stallion reared. Julia looked up. A sharp pain cracked across her skull.

Then darkness descended and plunged her into blessed oblivion.

Dawn came, sending feeble tendrils of light across the patchwork quilt. Julia touched tentative fingertips to her temple and winced.

Silence pressed around her. She eased up and tiptoed to the window. Crows cawed from the thicket beyond the house. Scavenger birds, come to further desecrate her beloved. She wouldn't allow it.

Ignoring the pain in her head, she made her way to the barn, then dragged the shovel to the thicket which only yesterday had held memories of love and hope.

Now it held the stench of death and betrayal. Julia wept, soft, silent tears as she cut the rope and struggled to carefully lower Brett down from the oak tree which had once sheltered them and given them refuge. The shovel picked feebly at the hard ground, but she refused to give up. She hadn't been able to save him, the least she could do was see he was buried properly.

"What do you think you're doing, girl?"

Her father's harsh voice finally penetrated her exhausted mind. She ignored him.

His hand clamped down on her shoulder, forced her to face him. She met his hard gaze with her own cold fury.

"I won't let him be left to rot in the trees."

"Leave it be, daughter."

"No." She shrugged off his hand and returned to her digging.

"He doesn't deserve a burial."

She leveled a look of disgust on him. How could the father she'd idolized turn into such a heartless monster? She pressed one hand to her abdomen. If fate held any kindness, then what she hoped for would soon prove to be a reality.

"That's no way to speak of the father of your grandchild."

Without warning, he raised his hand and struck her hard across the mouth. Julia met his gaze with weariness and an inner rage she knew would never go away. She shrugged.

"He wasn't stealing my horse, Daddy. He was bringing her to me so that we could go and get married." Tears filled her eyes and spilled down her cheeks until she could barely see her father's shocked gaze through the shimmer.

"Brett loved me. I'm going to have his child. Just wait and see. There's nothing you can do about it."

Shaken to her soul, Julia pulled herself from the dream and raced to her office. At last, she had the answers to the bizarre beginning of the McAllen family burial ground. The long forgotten cowboy had been no horse thief.

He'd been the answer to a young woman's earnest prayers.

She didn't understand how she knew what had happened was more than some stress-induced dream.

She just knew it was the truth.

By the time she had the story written for *True Texas Tales*, her fingers tingled with exhaustion. She proofed and printed out a final copy, sealed it in an envelope addressed to her agent and set it out in the mailbox for the mail carrier.

Then she showered, heated some soup for her supper and fell into bed.

Just as pink began to streak the sky with early morning

light, Julia woke to the familiar sensation of cool breezes caressing her skin. Slowly, she opened her eyes and turned her head toward the window.

Amongst the shadow shapes of the trees stood a darker form.

Brett.

He sat astride a roan stallion who danced nervously several inches above the brilliant pinks of the petunias beneath her window. What would happen if she tried to touch him? Would he vanish like mist before the slowly rising sun? Had she merely dreamed what happened or had he in some way really touched her? Loved her?

Not sure where the dream Julia started and her real self ended, Julia rose to her side and began to swing her legs to the floor.

Brett smiled, swept his hat from his head and bowed low, his gratitude as real as if he'd spoken his thanks. Then the horse wheeled and began to gallop towards the graveyard.

Julia threw open the door and raced out behind him. "Wait!" she called, although she wasn't sure why. *He isn't really there*, some part of her mind protested even as her legs pumped in long strides, as if she had even the slightest chance of catching up to him.

As if she weren't trying to run after some kind of phantom.

The stallion hesitated a moment, then sailed over the low shrubs. With one last tip of his hat, Brett turned and grinned, eyes dancing with some kind of mischief before he vanished into the fog.

Julia stumbled to a halt, her breath coming in short gasps.

"Ma'am?" The sound of a man's voice startled her, made her whirl in a mixture of fear and curiosity.

From amidst the trees and brush on the empty lot next door, a man started toward her. This was the first time she'd noticed anyone there, and although when she bought her house, she'd wondered how long it would be before the noise of bulldozers and carpenters disturbed her early mornings, seeing him now took her completely by surprise.

Funny how she hadn't noticed his presence before. Even stranger how his eyes were the color of caramel candy.

"Are you all right?" He stepped closer, concern apparent on his tanned face.

Julia wrapped her arms around herself, as much in protection from the bite of the early morning air as from the realization that she was standing face to face with a strange man who seemed like someone she was intimately acquainted with. And she was wearing only shortie pajamas and what must be a very foolish expression.

"I'm fine. Just enjoying the sunrise." She turned toward the graveyard where not so much as a wisp of fog remained beneath the approaching warmth of the sun.

"It's a beautiful morning, at that." He extended his hand. "Mac Williams. I'm the building contractor."

"Mac?" Why did his name touch a cord in her?

He grinned ruefully. "Short for McAllen. It's a family name."

McAllen. Warm fingers grasped her cold ones. "As in *the* McAllens?" She gestured with her free hand towards the graveyard. *Williams as in Brett Williams?*

He chuckled, his hand lingering on hers for a long moment before he released her. "Possibly. Family lore has it that my great-great granddaddy was born on the wrong side of the blanket."

She pondered that for a moment as a slow smile spread across her face. So Julia really had been pregnant, just as she had told her father she was. And she had let her baby carry Brett's family name, rather than her own. "Are you building this house for you and your wife?"

"Yes and no." At her quizzical look, he smiled and continued. "I'm not married. And you know how builders are. This house is slated to be mine, unless I get a better offer somewhere along the way."

A thousand nerve endings crying out to her in recognition, Julia came to a quick decision. "Well, how does a cup of coffee sound? I was just going to put on a pot." She glanced down at her attire and laughed. "After I put on some clothes, that is. You can tell me about your plans."

He studied her for a long moment, his perusal lingering on her lips, making hers tingle, before he raised his gaze to hers again.

"You're Julia." His voice tinged with awe, he said it as a statement rather than a question. His hand cupped her cheek with a touch as light as the breeze. "My God. You're Julia."

"Yes," she whispered, leaning into his palm.

Warmth flared in his gaze, overpowering the bemused look on his face. "Oh, yeah. We need to talk about plans."

She smiled, letting the solid and very real man beside her override the phantom lingering at the edges of her mind. "And after that, maybe some dreams?"

His gaze skipped over her face, as if he sought answers to perplexing questions. Finally, he grinned as if satisfied he'd found what he sought. When he took her hand again and then brought it to his lips, it seemed like the most natural, right thing in the world. His fingers wrapped around hers as they made their way back to Julia's house.

"Yeah," he said softly. "We most definitely should talk about the dreams."

IMAGINE

Betsy Norman

"Reassignment request denied." The secretary for the IFN, Imaginary Friends Network, thumped Scott's request with a large rubber stamp marked DENIED in red letters and shoved it back into his hands. "Next—"

"But she needs me," Scott insisted. "I can feel her wishing for me, conjuring my image in her mind." He hadn't slept all night because of the restless dreams of his former human playmate, and he spent two hours that morning waiting outside the office to open at eight o'clock.

"I'm sorry, sir, but Imaginary Friends are reserved for children only. You know the rules. It is impossible for an IF to remain after their assigned human's eighteenth birthday. An IF can only exist in their assigned human's imagination when called upon and under no circumstance deviate or originate play or appearance. An IF's sensory system is strictly limited to their assigned human's experiences or memories and inoperable otherwise. An IF can not problem solve or reveal homework answers for their assigned human—"

"I know, I know. I know all the rules." *And did my best to break them, too,* but revealing that wouldn't help his case. Scott's mind raced for a solution. He missed Lizzie Cortnay desperately since she matured into adulthood. His chest ached with the pull of her unconscious beckoning. "What about her daughter, Gina? Isn't she due for an Imaginary Friend? How about it, huh? I was her mother's IF for years. Can't we keep it in the family? Please?" He assembled his best pleading expression and added a snitch of groveling. Anything, anything, to get close to Lizzie again.

"You know that's not allowed. Humans must conjure up their own IF. Little Gina has to choose for herself who—"

"What's to choose? She's four years old. She loves the zoo. Poof! I could pop into her head as a monkey, and that would be it—"

"Absolutely forbidden."

Scott slammed his fist on the high marble countertop. "Then I demand an application for human status." All heads turned simultaneously in his direction with a gasp. What made him say that? His Adam's apple convulsed on a dry swallow, but he held his head up in determination.

If he could be human, he could be with Lizzie. Touch her, *really* touch her. Feel her creamy skin. Smell her, taste her, know more than just her thoughts and emotions, but how she really felt. He'd never longed for the full sensory experience denied Imaginary Friends until he met Lizzie. He wanted to touch *her*, not have her images of how *he* should feel projected into his mind.

"Do you *really* know what you're asking for?" The IFN secretary hissed.

Did he? Sure, when they were kids the world was fun and games and clouds and rainbows. He was Lizzie's friend when she needed one, but her needs were different now. Her search wasn't for a playmate, no sirree, but a soul mate. Someone to love and share her life. To change the stuff dreams were made of into reality. Could he step into that dimension and be all that? Could he be human?

"Lizzie needs me." Scott stared down the gaping onlookers. Swiping a hand through his hair, he leaned in closer. "And I need her. Just get me the application," he snarled, dipping his brows low and menacing. His long, black hair fell forward again over his cheekbones.

The secretary's posture stiffened. Rising in the same ramrod position, she did a militant heel-turn and strode purposefully toward the back of the room. Scott hurdled the counter and followed.

The sling of metal keys rounding the mammoth ring at her hip echoed through the breathless silence in the air. She scavenged for an archaic and intricately wrought key buried near the end of the loop and stuck it into the lock of the last file on the left. In the very bottom drawer, in the very last folder, she puffed away the dust and retrieved a withered and rolled up piece of parchment.

Scott pulled up short when she turned and glared at him.

"You must complete the questionnaire in its entirety," she told him. "Leave nothing unanswered or you will not be granted an audience. Present yourself to the Board of Elders for an interview at the next Gathering. They will take it into consideration and make a decision only if your sincerity is genuine."

"That doesn't sound so hard. I'm as sincere as they come." Scott raised an eyebrow and gave her a smug look, rounding a glance over the crowd as well. They nodded their heads in affirmation, bolstering his confidence. "I don't know why it's such a big deal."

Nudging him back to his place behind the counter, she undid the ribbon, held one end and flapped the twenty-foot long scroll out over his outstretched hand and down along the floor.

Scott shivered and mentally shook himself. Inspecting the list, his eyes bulged at question two thousand and forty one, which was only halfway down the document. How many questions were there?

Scott gulped. "When's the next Gathering?"

"Tomorrow at two o'clock." Her skinny nostrils flared with a prim snort of rebuttal. "The next one isn't for twelve years."

"WHAT?" Scott paced back and forth, snatching up the scroll in a tangled skein of loops over one forearm. "I can't possibly answer all these questions by tomorrow!" He flailed the arm and the scroll unraveled back onto the floor. "Twelve years?" He gasped in horror. "What if she finds someone else?"

Tugging at the hair at his temple, Scott moaned. "Nooooo... She loves me. I can't let her grow old alone. There has to be another way."

"There's no other way. Fill out the form and wait for the Board. NEXT!" The IFN secretary bellowed.

Scott scrambled to collect the rest of the scroll. His mind tripped over the impossible interrogation he had to complete within the next.... He glanced at the bald-faced clock on the wall. Twenty-nine and a half hours!

Trailing the looping parchment behind him, he grabbed a handful of pencils off of the counter and thrust them into the hands of the startled onlookers. "Help me," his throaty entreaty sounded foreign in his own ears. "Please. I love her. She loves me, too. I know she does. I need help."

Liz Cortnay tucked her daughter into bed, snuggling the comforter tightly around the little girl's shoulders. Only four books read tonight before Gina's eyes drooped. The day at the zoo must have tuckered her out. "Goodnight pun'kin," she whispered and placed a kiss on Gina's sleepy soft cheek. "Sweet dreams."

"Night mama. Night Teddy." She hugged her ever-present stuffed bear tighter.

Even with the divorce three years behind her, this was always the hardest part of the day. A house too quiet without her four year-old's fanfare, with too many empty rooms.

Liz sat on the edge of the bed watching her daughter sleep. She didn't want Gina to be like her. Divorced parents and no siblings to play with made her cautious and shy. Liz had depended on an overactive imagination to compensate for her isolation, but she didn't want her daughter to have to rely on the same. Imaginary friends tended to be too perfect and accommodating, perhaps leaving one unprepared for the reality of fickle human emotions.

As an adult, Liz thought marriage would replace the imaginary friends she created, liberate her from the feelings of loneliness and abandonment.

Too bad her ex-husband's version of playmates were flesh and blood, not to mention blond and coed. Her first clue should have been his increased teaching docket of night classes. Maybe a raised suspicion or two could have spared her the half-nude clinch she walked in on when she thought to surprise him with a late night picnic.

Rubbing her temple, she blew out an exhausted breath and rose carefully so as not to wake Gina. Hindsight was useless to her now. Better to focus on loving her daughter and making her feel loved to break any cycle of introversion Gina may have inherited. Despite Liz's best efforts at playgroups and days out, she knew she couldn't stifle her daughter's future creative instincts to animate the inanimate and bring friends to life when there were none.

Heading down to the kitchen for a cup of herbal tea, Liz smiled ruefully. She couldn't outright deny the benefits of having her own personal friend to confide in. Someone no one else could see, or hear, or know about, to share her secrets and sorrow.

Liz created her imaginary friend when she was about Gina's age. Scott Tupple, she called him, because he'd often multiply himself so they could play house appropriately to their individual standards. Each bit part acted out by Scott.

"No home is complete without the mommy, the daddy and the baby," she'd told him in her best authoritative preschooler voice. Even though her imagined playmate was a few years older, she was still the boss.

"But what about the dog and the cat and goldfish?" he'd add, bouncing from one corner of her room to the next. "And there's always the mailman and the milkman and the Culligan man to consider." Spouting off a dozen more important cast members, he'd immediately take up the supporting roles and entertain her with a series of scenarios. Often their little "family" took trips to the park or the zoo. Scott played the zookeeper as well as the menagerie of animals.

They'd pretend for hours. She never tired of him. At bedtime, he'd shrink to teddy bear size so she could hold him through the night. Loneliness fled away in Scott's presence, replaced by unconditional love and acceptance.

Why couldn't real life be that way? Growing up, her separated parents were rarely around to complete her idyllic version of home, and now divorce left an empty hole in her own marriage and family. Whatever happened to the mommy, the daddy and the baby to complete her life?

At thirteen, she was yoked with braces and a training bra, with no date for the first official boy-girl skating party. She couldn't concentrate on the test answers Scott was trying to get her to memorize. Eventually, Scott flumped his gangling adolescent limbs into the window seat of her bedroom and mirrored her glum expression.

"You don't even know how to skate," he said. "So why do you wanna go sweaty hand-holding at the roller rink with Jim Larrick, the barbaric, anyway? He's a jerk-joke-jock." He rolled his eyes and shook his head. "You think if you get him dizzy, he'll kiss you or something?" He glared out at the rain, tracing jagged edges in the condensation with his hand.

Liz fidgeted with her stubby fingernails. "No. Who'd wanna kiss a flat-chested metal-mouth?" She hadn't told him about her humiliation earlier in the day and how Jim's jeering remark made her run to the girl's bathroom in tears.

Scott's sharp glance made her face grow hot. She dropped her hands into her lap and tore at a cuticle to hide the renewed moisture in her eyes.

"I might."

Her hands stilled.

Scott was beside her in an instant. "Jerk-joke-jock doesn't know squat. Doesn't know you, Lizzie."

A soft touch at her chin tilted her face toward him. She looked into his chocolate brown eyes, fringed in black. As she aged, so had Scott. His image was a mixture of all she admired in teen idols until settling into his own look. Uniquely Scott, and the handsomest boy alive. Because, to her, he was alive. At some point, the things he did had deviated from her imagination, and he took on his own personality and actions.

"Jerk-joke-jock sees the outside," he whispered. "I see the inside." He tapped her forehead with one finger. The dramatic black brows he could use to strike any expression drew together tight. "I might." Pausing, he swallowed, and his seriousness made Liz hold her breath. "I might kiss you."

They stared at each other, nose to nose, his warm breath fanning the tingling fear and anticipation thrumming in her throat and temples.

"When?" Liz was afraid if she continued to hold her breath, she'd turn blue and pass out before her first kiss.

"Maybe now." He stroked a lock of her hair, concentrating on separating the strands and fingering the texture. Moving closer, his cheek rubbed hers like a cat's greeting gesture. Scott inhaled deeply, the corner of his mouth hovering close to hers.

Liz closed her eyes and tried hard to imagine what kissing a boy should feel like. The faint tang of a cologne she liked from the department store at the mall filled her senses. His skin felt smooth, like Bobby Gibson's when they did the orange pass in gym. She sat very still, opening her eyes just a crack the way they did on TV before kissing.

Scott withdrew an inch, his expression crumpling into a frustrated frown. With a graveled sound low in his throat, he popped off the bed to throw himself back into window seat. "Maybe not."

What had she done wrong? Liz remembered being crushed by his rejection, never knowing the true reason why he hadn't kissed her until years later.

The braces came off, and while she still had remained boyishly thin, the boob fairy did visit sometime around her sophomore year. A date here and there, junior prom, senior homecoming, left little time for cloistered imaginary games once real life stepped in. She grew up. Scott grew scarce. At times she felt his presence strongly, watching from his perch in the window, only to turn and find no one there.

Nights she'd wake from dreaming of him, not the boys in her class, imagining herself embraced by his lean limbs, his cheek against hers. Except now, like her, he was grown. His cheeks tainted with the stubble of manhood. Most times he'd be by her side when her eyes opened, a sad smile on his face. Liz knew as a teenager she should surrender her imaginary friend as easily as she'd packed up her toys, but Scott meant so much more. He was a part of her she couldn't let go.

She got engaged on the eve of her eighteenth birthday to the son of one of her mother's friends. A teaching assistant at Harvard Liz had been specifically urged to date and now marry. The wedding was set for the day after graduation. She was unsure if it were love or loneliness or duty that made her say yes.

She lay wide-awake in bed that same night watching the clock creep toward midnight. Afraid to approach the final milestone alone that marked the end of her childhood, Liz wished hard for Scott to appear and comfort her.

"I'm here, Lizzie," he whispered, silhouetted in the window seat; clad in black so only the glint of his eyes reflected the moonlight. "But I can't stay once you turn eighteen. Want to. Can't. Tick-tock, twelve o'clock and it's pumpkin time for me."

"Will I ever see you again?"

"No." He sounded harsh, terse, hidden. Abandoned.

"Please?"

"It's against the rules. You need to go play house for real now. You don't need me to play the daddy anymore."

"Will it be like us?"

Scott let out a low groan, bowing his head forward, his hand tugged at the hair at his temple. "No," he rasped. "It will never be like us. It will be for real. Real touch. Real sensation. Real love."

Liz was confused. He'd always been real to her. "Scott?"

"Don't forget me, Lizzie, because I'll never forget you. Never."

"I won't. Scott?" She had to tell him, had to know. "My love for you *is* real. Don't you feel the same way?"

He leapt from the window seat, skidding to fall on his knees next to her bed, and gathered up her hands. "Oh, but I do. I do love you. For real. I always have, Lizzie. I always will. Don't forget. Don't forget. I am your first love. Aren't I? Say it!" He gave a panicked glance toward the clock. Eleven fifty-five.

His black hair fell long at the collar, lean face animated with the passion in his eyes. How could she not love this man? Her heart ached at the pain in his voice, the pain of his leaving. "Scott Tupple, I have loved you since I was a little girl. You were made from a piece of my heart. I could never forget you."

The lines of his face softened, colored his expression with a regret she couldn't decipher. He raised her hands to her own face, his palms gently cradling the outside of her fingers while tears formed in his eyes. She'd never seen him cry before.

"Tell me, Lizzie, please before I go. Tell me what *your* skin feels like. Imagine the texture, the scent, so I can take those memories with me. Please?"

"You mean you don't know?"

He shook his head. "I can only feel what you feel."

The breath left her lungs in realization. "That's why you didn't kiss me. All this time I thought—"

"It's almost midnight, Lizzie," he pleaded.

She closed her eyes and concentrated, touching her face and mentally projecting the supple contours of her cheekbones and the moist bow of her mouth to him. Scott's breath gasped and halted, his hands trembling against hers. Liz hesitated, both fascinated and afraid of his strong reaction.

"Keep going," he sobbed. "Don't stop." His hands guided hers to thread through her hair. The silken strands fanned like a golden waterfall through their combined fingers. He bowed his head, kneeling before her, sucking in an emotion she knew she hadn't imagined. "Oh, cripes, you can't even know what this means to me. Quick. Let me smell you, too. I want to know all of you, want to take that with me—"

The grandfather clock in the hall began to chime the midnight hour. Scott's head snapped up, teeth gritted, eyes wild. Liz brought her wrist to her nose and inhaled deeply, the scent of rose and powder commingled with soap and skin swirled into her mind. The gesture calmed him, his eyes sliding closed in serenity.

Bong. Six. *Bong.* Seven. *Bong.* Eight.

Liz hugged him around the shoulders, squeezed tighter when his arms surrounded her in return. He couldn't leave if she didn't let go. "I'll love you forever, Scott. Kiss me."

"Remember my love is real," he murmured, brushing full, firm lips to hers. Lips like she'd never felt before. Real lips. His lips, his kiss.

Bong. Twelve o'clock. Her arms fell empty to her lap in a rush of expelled air. Liz clapped her hand over her mouth with a sob. She had turned eighteen. Scott was gone forever.

He never came to her again, no matter how hard she tried to conjure him up. Wedding, husband, and baby happened so fast, eventually she had stopped trying. Even after the divorce, the despair and guilt occupying her mind and spirit kept her from reaching out.

Liz took a sip from her cup of now cold tea and realized she was crying. The memories she'd kept locked preciously in her heart overflowed freely for the first time in six years. She missed Scott. She still loved him. How foolish to love a man no one else could see.

But he was real, her subconscious chastised. *To me.*

"Oh, Scott." She dismayed aloud. "You were wrong. Real 'house' was nothing like us. Real touch, real sensation, real love. You gave that to me, not him. If only you could be a real man. The mommy, the daddy, and the baby. How I want that with you so much."

She felt like a foolish child, wishing for the moon. Burying adult pain and reverting to childish comfort to avoid dealing with her loneliness. Was she finally having a mental breakdown? A woman in love with an imaginary man, unable, unwilling to seek the companionship of a real man for fear he'd never live up to the standards of the one she'd created for herself?

The unique fantasy world she lived in growing up was not like those experienced by others. When the subject of imaginary friends came up, the women in her social group laughed. They'd all done that route. None spoke with reverence or longing. An uneventful phase, they said. Over long before elementary school.

Scott was never a "phase" to Liz. He was her confidante, her shoulder to cry on, her best friend. Her soul mate.

You really are crazy, Liz.

Scott's legs jitterbugged while he sat on the bench outside the Hall of Elders. All night long he felt Liz's despair while he barked out answers to the questions. His fellow Imaginary Friends rallied together, a dozen of them alternating between asking the next one and jotting down the last one.

He checked and double-checked. Triple checked even. Each number had his answer. Enough questions bent on forcing one to toss his hands up altogether and quit.

"No way, no way," he muttered to himself, his hands working the scroll tighter and tighter. "Lizzie needs me. I need her. They can ask me a trillion questions, and I'd answer them all."

"Scott Tupple." An IFN official called his name.

Scott vaulted off the bench to land in front of the uniformed man, saluting him. "At your service!"

The official leaned away from him, eyes dropping over Scott suspiciously. "They're ready to see you now."

"And boy am I ever ready for them. Carry on!" He bowed and gestured for the man to precede him. His twitchy body sidled up close behind, peeking over one shoulder first, then the other, to catch a glimpse of the Board.

A row of eleven stern faces stared back at him.

Scott gulped, and tugged the hair back from his face. Fingering his tight collar one last time, he forced himself to relax his shallow breathing. The official retreated to his perch on one side of the Board.

The Eldest Elder, a gray-haired woman whose tight bun warred against gravity to stretch her sagging skin back into place, spoke. "The scroll, please."

"Yes, of course, your illustrious eminence ladyship, sir, I mean ma'am." He skittered up and presented the scroll with a courtly bow. "Every question answered correctly, right to the very last. Scout's honor. Can I be human now? I'm kind of in a hurry." He pasted on a gracious smile.

The horned-owl brows of the Eldest Elder swooped together. "This is a very serious request, not to be taken lightly. Human status hasn't been granted to an IF in centuries. We must evaluate the questionnaire first, which takes a great deal of time. We will grant you a reply at the next Gathering."

"But that's *twelve years from now!*" Shouting, Scott

dragged a hand through his hair, circling in small steps. "No, no, NO. That won't do. I need an answer NOW!" Hands splayed on the table, he crouched face-to-face before the Elder. "You asked your questions. I answered them all. I'm in love with Lizzie Cortnay. She's in love with me. What more do you need to know?"

"That's not enough." The Elder slapped her gavel, causing Scott to jump to attention. "Of course she loves you. That's the point. Imaginary Friends are like teddy bears to children. We are specifically designed to be loved by humans. To make them feel loved."

"I was much more than that to Liz. It went way beyond stuffed animals for us. Sure, I *played* animals on occasion, but I was first and foremost much, much more. I stayed with her through high school."

"You broke the rules?" Her shocked and accusing stare dominoed through the rest of the Elders.

"Yeah. No. Maybe. Sure, I broke some rules." Capering back and forth in front of the Board, Scott launched his defense. "I wasn't just a soft cuddly teddy bear. Oh, no. I was the Daddy to her Mommy. Her homework partner. I was the one who almost gave Lizzie her first kiss. I was there in the night even when she didn't call for me. Watching her breathe, and knowing it was *me* she was dreaming of. We grew up together. I loved her so much, seeing her grow into a teenager killed me because our time was nearly over."

"Nearly? You should have left her in grade school."

"She didn't want me to go. *I* didn't want to go."

Another Elder spoke up. "Surely you didn't break the sacred IFN rule. You did leave when she turned into a woman?"

Scott scrubbed his face with his hands, his throat convulsed. That was the one rule he couldn't break. "Yes, I left," he croaked. "But I'll never forget the night she turned eighteen. Never so long as I live." Which meant forever to the Imagined.

"What happened?" Two or three Elders leaned in to listen. "She let me touch her," he whispered. "I told her I loved her. Even if I wasn't real, my love was." He closed his eyes and sucked in a lip remembering, the rampant emotions returning with a thundering shudder. "My Lizzie told me I'd always been real to her." He smiled, a sorrowful laugh escaping him. "Made from a piece of her heart, she said. She loved me too."

"What do you mean she let you touch her?"

"Touch her. Feel her. Smell her. What part don't you get? That night, for the first time she projected her own image into *my* mind."

"Impossible," the Elder snorted.

"Oh yes it is. I felt her." He mentally wrapped himself around Lizzie in his heart. The scent of roses and powder permeated his mind, supple skin and moist mouth leaving a tactile impression against his own. "I can feel her now."

"That's impossible. No human ever recorded has cared enough beyond their own needs being met by an IF to do such a thing. You are mistaken."

"No." Scott shook his head slowly. "You're the mistaken one. Feel for yourself." Placing his hands against the Eldest Elder's face, he imagined touching Lizzie instead.

She sucked in a gasp and placed her hands over his. "How are you doing that?" A smile of delight spread across her aged features. "My skin feels so young. Like a girl again."

A clatter of scraping chairs and outraged voices filled the room.

"Preposterous!"

"It's a trick!"

"No Imagined can project thoughts in such a manner."

"It can't be done!"

An IFN official placed an arm across Scott's chest and moved him a safe distance from the Board. Chaos and shouts rang through the room. Half of the Elders jumped to their feet, shaking a fist and arguing with the other half.

"Please!" Scott tried to roar above the crowd. "Let me be human," he begged. "I want to be with Lizzie!"

The crack of a gavel brought the cacophony to a halt.

"Silence. Sit down," The Eldest Elder commanded. "You there." She pointed to the official. "Release him."

Scott shrugged off the hammy fists and dusted the front of his vest, tossing a glare at the man.

"Approach the bench, Mr. Tupple."

Swallowing, he stepped forward, his confidence flagging after the outburst. "Please. I'll do anything. My heart isn't into playing IF to other children anymore. Not when it belongs solely to Lizzie. I'm no good to the IFN. Please. Please let me be a human. I want to be real."

"You'd sacrifice immortality for this woman?"

"In a heartbeat. I'm dying inside, anyway."

The Eldest Elder considered him at length. Scott adjusted his collar and smoothed back his disheveled hair, trying very hard to stand still beneath her scrutiny. Maybe if he behaved, she'd think him worthy and approve.

"The Board cannot grant your request."

The air left his lungs in a vacuum. Scott fell to his knees, slumping over with his hands covering his face in abject misery. "Nooooooo," he moaned.

"Hear me out, Mr. Tupple."

He stopped wailing and peeked out at her between two fingers. Was there still hope?

"Do you realize what you've done?"

"Been denied my heart's desire?" he snapped, thinking she intended to punish him now. He no longer cared. "Cut to the quick? Lost my will to live? Crucified my soul—"

"You've done something only humans can do."

Scott went silent.

"You willed your thoughts and emotions into me, opened your mind and made me feel what you felt. For a brief moment, I was your Lizzie and knew your great love for her and hers for you."

"I did?" He dropped his hands. "I did! So why can't I be granted human status?" Jumping to his feet, Scott didn't understand. She knew. She knew how he felt and yet did nothing. "Why? Why won't you make me real?" he demanded, one fist pummeling the table.

"Because your Lizzie has already made you so, Scott Tupple."

Another week, another Saturday, and Liz Cortnay held her daughter's hand as they strolled through the zoo. Gina named each animal as they passed the habitats. The little girl's passion was evident in her exuberant chatter. Liz loved bringing her here. Since leaving the house she grew up in, she felt closest to Scott when they went to the zoo. So much like their imagined trips, except the real animals were no match for his antics.

"Excuse me, miss, but there's a new cougar cub exhibit in the children's zoo your little girl might be especially interested in," a familiar voice behind her said.

Liz froze.

"Soft, fuzzy, rumbly, tumbly and striped around the ears. She'll love 'em. You can't help but want to snug 'em."

Her neck unthawed only enough to turn to look out of the corner of her eye at who was speaking. "You. You're—"

"It's me, Lizzie. It's *really* me." Scott's smile beamed larger than his face could contain. Seeing him dressed in his old zookeeper's uniform, she nearly lost control and flung herself at him.

What would Gina think? She glanced at her daughter. "But I thought you couldn't—"

"Can we go see the cougar cubs, Mama? Like the zookeeper said? Can we, please?" Gina tugged at Liz's skirt while accepting Scott's outstretched hand to lead her to the children's zoo.

Gina could see Scott?

"Oh." A warped Peter Pan scenario flitted through her

head. "You're here for Gina, aren't you?" Numb and disappointed, her shoulders slumped.

"Oh no, Lizzie." Scott shook his head. "I'm here for you. Because of you."

"You know my mama?" Gina asked.

"Yes, my darling little poppet." He hefted Gina into his arms, bouncing her around in a circle while the little girl squealed. "I've known your mama since we were your age."

"You're funny." Gina giggled. "I like him, Mama."

Liz followed in a daze while he took them to see the cubs. This couldn't be happening. Passersby were smiling, laughing at the infectious joy Gina and Scott were creating with their chatter. How? They couldn't see him. Only she could. And now, Gina, too.

"Mr. Tupple?" An employee of the zoo jogged up to them. This normally wouldn't have been a strange occurrence, given Scott's penchant for a cast of thousands. With one exception. This man looked nothing like Scott.

"Yes, Peter." Scott put Gina down. She ran over to admire the baby animals.

"There's a delivery of hay I need your signature for."

Scott twirled his finger and the man turned around so he could use Peter's back to scribble his name across the invoice. "There you be."

"Thanks. Sorry to bother you."

"Not at all. I absolutely *adore* every single one of my duties around here." Scott saluted the man smartly and Peter jogged off, laughing.

"Scott?" Liz reached out and touched him, smoothed her hand over the chest of his khaki uniform. He leaned into her fingers, head bowed, pressing her palm flat. Beneath her hand, his heart pounded. She'd never noticed a heartbeat before. "Are you—"

"Real?" He studied her, the black brows high, teasing, adoring. "What do you think?"

"I think I've gone crazy." Trepidation and exhilaration

seeped from her fingertips into her soul. "I think I've loved you and missed you so much, I've finally lost my mind."

"Exactly the opposite," he whispered, lifting her fingertips to his lips, kissing them. His breath seized like it did the eve of her eighteenth birthday. "Your love, your gift of touch, has made me real."

"Real?" She didn't dare believe. "All these people can see you? You really do work here?"

"Yes." He kissed her knuckles. "Yes." Then her palm. "And yes." Then finally, her wrist. Each time his eyelids hooded further downward in rapture.

Liz glanced around, noting the people smiling at their obvious affection, greeting the new zookeeper and nodding their welcome.

"Oh, Scott." She threw herself into his waiting arms, kissing his face, basking in the resonant burrs of pleasure he made each time she did.

"Don't stop. Don't stop. Don't let go." His hands clutched into her hair, his mouth chasing hers. "I've waited a lifetime for this. Your lifetime, and now mine."

"Mr. Tupple! Really," an older woman chided. "This *is* the children's zoo, after all. What's the occasion?"

Scott licked his lips and blushed apologetically but never once released her. Liz reveled in his possessive embrace.

"The occasion?" he crowed. "The occasion? I'll tell you the occasion." One arm swept wide to encompass everyone in his announcement. "I am about to ask," he dropped to one knee in front of Liz, gathering her hands in his. "This amazing, miracle performing woman, *love of my life!* My Lizzie." He stared directly into her eyes. She wanted to melt into the chocolate warmth. "To become my wife." Lowering his voice, he repeated the question. "Please, Lizzie? Be my wife? What other purpose could there be for my being here?"

"Oh, Scott!" Tears blurred her vision. Could this really be true? "Yes, yes!"

Everyone applauded and offered congratulations. Scott

swooped her into his arms again, cheering along with the crowd.

"Does this mean we get to live at the zoo?" Gina chimed in, tugging at both of them.

"Oh, sweetheart," Liz laughed, breathless. "No, but we can visit whenever we want."

Scott scooped Gina up, too, forming a circle with the three of them. "The mommy, and the daddy, and the baby. *Lots* of babies," he added, his gaze lingering on Liz's mouth before sliding back upwards. "Lots of babies. Right away, if you please."

Liz mouthed "I love you" to Scott just before he kissed her. She thrilled in the sensation of his warm, firm mouth pressed to hers, tasting her with a voraciousness she knew she'd never tire of.

"Is it true you're going to marry him, Mama? Is it for *real?*" Gina demanded an answer to her question between squeals as Scott tickled her.

"Yes," Liz finally managed to say. "It's for real."

MEANT TO BE

Tami D. Cowden

"Stand and deliver!"

Nick Wentworth jerked awake at the bellow. Confused yells, accompanied by the neighs of frightened horses, assaulted his ears. A gunshot caused a wince as the sound reverberated in his aching head. Blearily looking through the gray darkness, he groped for the television remote to turn off the costume drama.

Instead of the nubby fabric of his sofa, soft moss met his searching hand. He rolled to his stomach. Pebbles pressed against his palms as he pushed himself to his feet. The acrid smell of gunpowder filled his nostrils. Leaning against a tree, he tried to focus on the moonlit scene revealed though the branches of the weeping willow hiding him from view.

An old-fashioned coach listed across the crown of a narrow road. One man sat on the coach box with both arms stretched straight up. His compatriot held only one hand high, struggling to hold the reins of four restless horses with the other. The left forward horse reared up. The coach jerked, and a high-pitched scream, quickly stifled, came from within the coach.

Nick started toward the sound, but stopped as suddenly as the implications of what he was seeing swept across him.

He'd traveled in time. Wouldn't Uncle Zack be thrilled that his invention actually worked? Now he only had to find the Wentworth stables, and get to the horse before it broke its leg and was destroyed, and he could rebuild his family's reputation. Meanwhile, to avoid upsetting the future, he knew he should not interfere in any way with events taking place. He forced himself to watch as the terrified carriage horse was calmed.

"'Ere now, you keep 'old of them 'orses." The stern command came from a caped and masked figure on a horse in front of the coach and four. A dull metallic gleam in his hand suggested a weapon, explaining the attempts of the men sitting upon the coach to touch the sky. "And keep yer dabblers where I can see 'em, Mister Guard."

Another cloaked rider moved his horse to within only a few feet of Nick's tree. Laughing coarsely, the bandit said, "Such high spirited mounts must belong to someone well able to pay the tolls. Come out, gentle folk." No cockney accent evident in this voice. To Nick's untrained ears, the voice sounded rather educated. Not at all what he'd have expected from a common highway robber.

"Come out, I say. Let us poor highwaymen see you." Mockery filled the unpleasant words.

The shade on the coach door was thrust up and a head appeared in the dark opening. Nick's jaw dropped as the moonlight revealed hair shinier than spun gold, surrounding a face more beautiful than a Botticelli. But no heaven-sent serenity filled this woman's expression. Flashing eyes showed her fury.

"You need not keep up this pretense, Wentworth. I recognize your voice."

Wentworth? Good God, was the robber his ancestor? Nick blinked at the revelation of the lady's acquaintance with the robber. But his heart was lightened by the news. Any interference from him might upset the whole course of history. But if this lady knew the "highwayman," then this was just some kind of romantic escapade, not a vicious crime. If his calculations had been correct, the year was 1814. The English aristocracy at that time was given to foolish wagers and dramatic pranks. Was this Wentworth fellow trying to win a bet?

If the highwayman had hoped to win the lady, he had clearly miscalculated. The thought gave Nick a certain satisfaction.

"Your mistake, my lady, you do not know me." Menace dripped from the voice now. Nick's relief fled.

"Not know you? I only wish it were true." The woman, not much more than a girl as far as Nick could tell, opened the door and jumped down. She stood by the head of the highwayman's horse and nodded. "Even if I didn't know your croaking tone, I'd recognize the blaze on Sinbad."

Sinbad? Nick's attention was drawn to the noble lines of the horse. Yes, definitely the right breed. He would have to watch for his chance to grab him. But the lady was continuing her disdainful speech. Forgetting the object of his quest, he turned his attention back to her.

"I don't know what your game is now, Wentworth, but I find it as boring as your proposals. Ride on and leave us to do the same." She turned back toward the coach.

"It is a pity, Lady Jess, that you are so observant. I will now have to make sure there are no witnesses." Wentworth motioned to his partner. Another shot was fired. The carriage guard who'd so obediently kept his hands high fell from the coach. Lady Jess screamed and ran to the fallen man. Her coachman, taking advantage of the confusion, put his horses to, quickly whipping them to a frenzied pace. As it flew by, another woman leaned out of the coach, shrieking.

"Damn you, after them!" Wentworth shouted to his henchman. The gunman raced after the coach.

Nick clutched branches of willow in his fist. Bile rose in

his throat. *I cannot interfere. I cannot interfere.*

"He's dead! You murderer!" Tears streamed down her face as she looked up at Wentworth from her place at the victim's side. "You can't mean to kill poor John Coachman and my aunt—your aunt!—too?"

"But it is your own fault, dear cousin. Had you not identified me to your servants, they might have lived with my goodwill. Indeed, I preferred to have witnesses to your abduction. So much better for my own planned alibi." He shrugged. "But one must make do, after all. And now that leaves us. All alone."

The icy threat in the tone sent chills down Nick's back. He had never heard such cold bloodedness in his time. And this guy was a member of his family?

The lady stood. "I do not understand you. You cannot think I'll ever marry you now."

The woman was magnificent. Her contemptuous defiance in the face of this bastard was impressive, particularly since even from where Nick stood, he could see a telltale shake of the lady's hand.

Wentworth merely laughed. "I don't think it. I've long given up on that possibility." He laughed shortly. "I confess, I preferred marriage to this distasteful course of action, but one way or another, sweet cousin, I must have your fortune. So, in due time, some honest soul will stumble upon your poor, violated body—"

A shocked gasp broke from her at this evidence of his intent. Nick swallowed his own choking protest. The branch in his right fist snapped free of the tree, but the lack of reaction from the two indicated only he heard the sound.

"Yes, as I said, your violated body will be found in the forest, the latest victim of the lawless miscreants who plague our highways. And as your closest relative, I shall inherit one hundred thousand pounds, safely invested in the Funds." Wentworth began to dismount as Lady Jess backed away.

Without conscious thought, Nick jumped forward. His

hand lifted the length of willow branch high and came down on Sinbad's rump with a slashing whip. Terrified by this unexpected assault, the horse reared with Wentworth half out of his saddle. The aristocratic robber fell heavily to the ground, cursing loudly. He tried to rise, but his cape tangled in his feet, bringing him to the ground with another oath.

Grabbing hold of the flying reins, Nick charged toward Lady Jess, who stood rooted to the spot at the sight of this unexpected rescue. Catching her about the waist, he flung her over the horse and half climbed, half jumped behind her. Sinbad wheeled and tried to buck, but Nick pulled hard on the bit, unmindful of injury to his prize, unthinking of anything except saving this lady.

A quick look over his shoulder told him Wentworth was aiming a small pistol at them. Holding Lady Jess down with a hand on her back, he kicked his heel into the mount's sides and headed for the trees. A bullet whistled close to his ear.

Then the forest enveloped them.

Jessica Alverstoke's heartfelt relief at her timely rescue was short-lived. This mad careening through the thick forest could not long continue without mishap. The forest floor was barely visible in the scant moonlight trickling through the trees. A rabbit hole or tree root would send them all crashing down to broken limbs or necks.

Besides, the pounding of the saddle into her stomach that accompanied every hoof beat was becoming quite painful.

"Stop!" Her first command going unheeded, she shouted again. "Stop, I say!"

"We have to get out of here!"

She tried to twist to see her Galahad, but a large hand pressed her flatter against the pommel. Grabbing a firm masculine thigh covered in a strange fabric, she dug in her nails. "Stop before we come to grief!"

"Ouch! Hey!" The pounding into her middle slowed as Sinbad's speed decreased to a trot. If anything, the slower pace was more painful. Through gritted teeth, she said, "He's miles behind us—if he dares to follow us at all, he follows on foot. Now, stop."

The jarring ended, and the hand holding her against the horse lifted. With a sigh, she slid down the horse's front leg, collapsing onto the ground in a small clearing. Leaning on one arm, and holding the other to her bruised stomach, she watched as first one booted foot and then the other appeared beside her. The boots, mostly hidden by the odd pantaloons, were of a strange leather, the squarish pattern making them look rather like the skin of an exotic snake. Her gaze shifted up the legs, stopping briefly at a large oval ornament at the man's waist. A coat with a fringe along the arms covered a soft-looking checked shirt. Her eyes widened at the sight of his open collar, where a hint of darkness suggested a generous sprinkling of chest hair.

Continuing her inspection, she found a firm jaw untouched by a razor for a day or two. A strong nose added character to a face that might otherwise have been a bit boyish. Two gray eyes, beneath heavy black brows, stared solemnly back at her. His head, free of any covering, was topped with tousled jet hair.

His suit of armor was most unusual, but otherwise she had no complaints regarding this rescuing knight's appearance.

He knelt beside her. "Are you okay?"

"Okay?" His accent was strange, unlike any she had ever heard.

"Are you hurt?" He cocked his head at her, his eyes filled with concern.

"No. Not really." Her stomach was sore, but she was not injured. Amazing, all things considered. "Thanks to you."

A shadow fell across his face. Pulling her to her feet, he shook his head. "I interfered. I shouldn't have done it, but I had to. I couldn't just stand there and watch him kill you."

Should not have done it? Despite her gratitude, a bubble of indignation rose in her throat. Was her hero mad? "Well, sir, I for one am most glad you overcame your scruples," she said, unable to keep the asperity from her voice.

She brushed at the satin skirt of her ball gown. Now streaked with mud and torn from the branches during their mad dash through the wood, it no longer shimmered as it had earlier in the evening. She sighed. No gown had ever become her so well, and now it was certainly ruined. But time enough to worry about her wardrobe when she was safely home. She thrust her chin forward and rubbed her hands together briskly. "We must find the magistrate."

"No." The single syllable was flat, but emphatic.

"No? Murder was committed on the King's highway. Of course, we must inform the magistrate."

Her hero thrust a hand through his thick hair. It seemed he could not meet her eye. "You don't understand. That man—"

"Wentworth, my worthless cousin," she interposed, one toe tapping against the tree root at her feet.

"Uh, yeah. Well, the thing is, if I hadn't interfered, he would have, well, succeeded in his plan." A lock of the blackest hair she'd ever seen fell over his eyes as he stared down at the ground between them.

Lady Jess resisted the urge to smooth the straying lock back into place. Was her handsome knight trying to gather the courage to ask for a reward? She'd put his mercenary heart at ease. Her lip curled. "Indeed, sir, I am aware. You need not worry that I shall be ungrateful. Escort me to the magistrate, and I shall see you handsomely rewarded."

A blaze of gray fire shot from beneath black brows. "I don't want a reward!"

She could not help but be intrigued at his indignation. "Well, then, what worries you?"

"Who knows what havoc I may have caused by saving you? The whole timeline could be changed." He paced around her, one hand running through his hair as he thought. "So little is known about temporal mechanics."

"Temporal what?" She had been half hoping this had all

been a dream, but somehow she didn't think she would have dreamed so odd a conversation.

"Temporal mechanics. Time travel." He stopped his pacing and frowned at her. "No one knows whether a time travel can change events. Some theorize that everything that happens, even any seeming interference by a time traveler, was always meant to be. If I knew for sure that theory was true, then we wouldn't have a problem."

Time travel? Jess backed up a bit. The man truly was mad. For a wild moment, she wished she were back in the clutches of her cousin. At least he was a devil she knew.

On the other hand, those touched in the upper works could be quite harmless when humored. Taking a deep breath, she put on her brightest smile. "Oh, I am sure that this... theory is correct, sir. Only consider the fortuity of your coming to this particular time, just when you were most needed." Noticing the hint of modesty crossing her mad hero's face, she decided a little flattery probably couldn't hurt. She reached out to touch his strong, well formed hand.

A tremor swept through her at the contact with his warm flesh. "Such a daring rescue. Clearly our meeting was meant to be." As she spoke the words, she realized with a shock she believed them.

He clasped her hand, gazing back at her. The look of wonder in his eyes matched that filling her heart. But then a shadow passed over his eyes. "But you see, others, in fact, the *majority* of time theorists, believe that a time traveler can change events. That if even the slightest change is made to the timeline, the future as we know it can alter completely." Still holding her hand, he leaned back against a tree, staring up at the sky. "By saving you, I may have created a shift in the timeline. I might be responsible for terrible wars or— who knows what?"

She plucked her hand back, ignoring the feeling of loss that filled her. "So are you saying you must deliver me back to my cousin?" She spoke sarcastically, but the pain that filled his eyes caused her to back away from him. Her blood drummed painfully in her ears as she looked wildly around the forest for an avenue of escape.

"No, wait! Of course, the perfect solution!" Relief filled his features, and the feral beating of her own heart slowed to a more moderate pace.

He slipped one hand into the pocket of his shirt coat with one hand, and pulled out a large pocket watch. After flicking the case open, he poked against the glass face of the timepiece. He placed one hand on Sinbad's withers. Then with a reassuring smile, he held out his hand to her.

Uncertain of the cause of her willingness to trust him, Jessica placed her hand in his again. The now familiar warmth spread rapidly from her hand to the rest of her limbs, to her very core.

Before she had time to examine her strange reaction to this stranger's touch, a brilliant flash of light blinded her. The ground beneath her feet fell away, and a whirlwind snatched her up. The bright light faded in an instant, and darkness enveloped her. Air rushed out of her lungs as she was spun around, the only solid contact left to her the feel of her rescuers strong grasp on her hand. Sinbad's frenzied whinny rent the air. Only the firm squeeze against her fingers kept her from releasing the scream that welled in her throat.

And then, all sensation ended.

A velvety nose nudged against her cheek

"Easy, Sinbad. I'll wake her." The voice, strangely familiar, sounded very distant. A warm hand replaced the nose and smoothed against her jawbone. "Lady Jessica? Wake up, Lady Jess."

The sound of her name pulled her completely from the deep sleep embracing her. As consciousness slowly returned, she became aware of the hard surface beneath her. Her eyelids fluttered open, only to close immediately against the harsh light that assaulted her eyes. Warily, she squinted, allowing herself time to grow accustomed to the brightness.

The briefest of glances was enough to tell her she was no longer in the forest. Odors drifting around her were reassuringly familiar—hay, horse, dung, and straw, but the room in which she lay was unlike any stable she had ever seen. High windows allowed in some sunshine, but these were not the source of the room's brightness. Instead, long poles suspended from the ceiling seemed to glow as though filled with a thousand candles. But surely no candles would be placed so close to the roof of a stable?

"Lady Jess? Let me help you up.

She turned toward the voice. The man who had rescued her from her cousin knelt next to her, concern filling his face. She accepted the offer of his hands and climbed unsteadily to her feet. Turning slowly around, she absorbed both the alien wonders and the familiar sights surrounding her.

Definitely a stable. The top halves of doors were open to reveal the proud occupants of the rows of stalls extending before her. Here and there, a curious nose extended high over the top of the door, displaying the large blunt nostrils and sturdy lines of high quality draft horses. A rack containing shovels and rakes hung near a door. Buckets were stacked nearby, as were bales of straw.

But in one corner stood a shiny green contraption, with huge black wheels, but no place to harness the horses. And everywhere she looked, she saw items, large and small, in every shape imaginable, the purpose of which she could only guess, constructed of materials she had never seen before. Swallowing hard, she accepted the truth of her rescuer's earlier statements. He was, indeed, from another time.

But, apparently, it was she who was now from another time. She pushed her heart back down her throat, and called upon all the social resources the daughter of an Earl might have in reserve. Turning toward the man who had first rescued her, and now kidnapped her, she noted the wary look in his eyes. She held out her hand. "I think, sir, that because we are unlikely to have mutual acquaintances, we had best introduce ourselves. I am Lady Jessica Alverstoke, of Alverstoke Hall."

He grinned back at her, relief adding even more charm to his smile. "Nick Wentworth, Ma'am. It is a pleasure."

She recoiled. "Wentworth?"

"Yes, Ma'am. I, well, I don't know if that fellow was a relative, but I guess I have reason to think he was. I'm real sorry." He massaged the back of his neck with one hand as he looked down at her. "Now, I can tell you that no one in my family has committed any crimes since then, unless you count my Uncle Zack getting a ticket when he caused an explosion out in the north forty and scared the daylights out of Mrs. Borwin down the road."

Speech evaded her for several minutes. Finally, she managed, "Lucius Wentworth. That is his full name."

He brightened a bit. "There's no Lucius in the family Bible. But it only starts with my five times great granddaddy. Nicholas, like me. "

Nicholas? "Lucius has a son named Nicholas." Looking at the progeny of her enemy proved too difficult. But as she stared down at her hands, she realized she was being unreasonable. After all, this man was not responsible for his ancestor's crimes. Indeed, he had saved her from a dreadful fate. And he stirred emotions in her that no man had ever roused before.

She looked up. "Actually, it is not so terrible to think of you as Nicky's great-great and so on grandson. He has been in the care of his maternal grandparents since his mother died in childbirth. He is a very nice little boy, most unlike his father." The incongruity of her statement struck her and a laugh passed her lips. "What year is it, if you please?"

"2001." Mr. Wentworth was watching her carefully. "Do you want a drink or something?"

She shook her head at his offer, unable to form any words. At least the social niceties were completed. A new millennium, even. She continued her survey of her environment. Sinbad nudged her elbow, and she absently patted the thoroughbred's delicate nose. Tears started to her eyes as she realized the only friend from her own time left to her was this horse who had been her father's pride. How typical of Wentworth to make free with her stables.

But this thought begged a question. "I understand from your explanation of theories why you brought me here, Mr. Wentworth. But why Sinbad, as well?"

A sheepish look fell over the face even more handsome in the abundant light. "Ah, well, actually, Sinbad was the reason I went to your time."

She felt her jaw drop. "You traveled through time to steal a horse?" Vaguely, she supposed the how was more important than the why, yet his purpose seemed so extraordinary she had to know the answer.

"I suppose it is stealing technically, but I knew Wentworth would not suffer because of it. Sinbad was going to be destroyed that very night."

"Sinbad destroyed? But why?"

"Broken leg. In fact, maybe it happened somehow when Wentwoth was, well, you know when you were to struggle with him." Nick's voice trailed off and a hard look entered his eyes. "I would have liked to have taken that guy apart after what he did. What he planned to do. "

Her stomach did a small flip-flop at this sign of a protective urge, even as the reality of what had occurred began to sink in. "So you saved Sinbad's life as well as mine." Lady Jess spoke quietly. "But I don't understand why you would want a horse from another time."

"For stud, of course." He waved his hand at the horses in the stalls. "All of these horses carry the blood of Sinbad's colt, Gallant Lord. Champion thoroughbreds, the entire line. In fact, all of Sinbad's progeny were champions. For generations. At least, until about ten years ago." He raked a hand through the waves of dark hair covering his head. "The line is weakening. We haven't produced a winner for years. My family's legacy is disappearing. By bringing Sinbad here, I could build the bloodline again, eliminating the dilutions of the past centuries."

Lady Jess peered at the horse closest to her for a moment. A suspicion formed in her mind. "How did you know he was to be put down?"

"We obtained the English Wentworth Stables bloodstock records on microfiche. They noted that Sinbad was destroyed after breaking his leg just one day after he covered Gallant Lord's dam."

Ignoring the reference to micro-something, her eyes narrowed. The Wentworth bloodstock records? "You mean the Alverstoke, not the Wentworth stables? My cousin has made free to ride Sinbad, but the horse belongs to me. My cousin has no horses of his own."

"Err, no. The first champion was Gallant Lord, born in 1814, owned by the Wentworth stables."

Her stables, in Wentworth hands. Bitterness filled her heart. "I see. So my cousin truly did succeed in his plan and inherited my property." But then the import of the rest of his words hit her. "Wait a moment. This colt was born in 1814?" At his nod, she covered her mouth with one hand, and waved the other toward the stalls. "Mr. Wentworth, I beg you, take a closer look at your 'thoroughbreds.'"

He shot a puzzled look her way, then glanced toward the nearest horse. "Why do you—" A profane exclamation burst from his lips as he strode toward the stall and looked at the horse shaking its head at him. "Clydesdale? This horse is a Clydesdale." He ran from stall to stall, checking the breed of each of the horses. By the time he reached the final stall, he had slowed to a walk. For a moment, he leaned against the door, one hand ruffling the mane of a huge horse that nuzzled against his shoulder. Then he walked with measured steps back to her and slumped down on a bale of straw. "The barn is the same. Everything else is the same as it was. So I guess maybe my family was every bit as successful hauling beer for Budweiser as it was breeding racehorses."

She did not understand this cryptic remark, but understood his devastation at the changes that had occurred. She sat beside him on the straw. Her thigh pressed against his, causing shivers of warmth to spread across her limbs. She did her best to ignore the unaccustomed feelings, and patted the hand he rested on his knee. "I'm so very sorry."

"It's not your fault." He straightened and forced a smile. "My uncle warned me before he died that using the time travel watch was too dangerous. He was kind of a mad professor, you know, but he never used half his inventions. Always said they were too dangerous." He shook his head. "But, I made my choice, and I don't regret it. I couldn't stand there and watch that bastard rape and murder you." His hand turned under hers and grasped tightly. "Saving you was worth it."

He turned to her and placed his arm around her shoulders. Pulling her toward him until their faces were but inches apart, he spoke in a tone so low she had to strain to hear him. "What you said, back there, about our meeting being meant to be? I know you only said it because you were humoring me, but I really believe it."

She released a breath she had not known she'd held and returned the pressure of his fingers. "I believe it to be true as well, Mr. Wentworth."

"Nick," he whispered, moments before his lips met hers.

Lady Jess felt none of the faint revulsion she had felt on the other occasions gentlemen had dared to press a kiss upon her. Instead, the warm, languorous feeling that spread over her at his every touch now threatened to overwhelm her completely. Entirely of its own accord, her mouth opened under his and warmth turned to fiery heat. Several minutes passed before she recalled her surroundings and gently pushed him away.

"Mr. Went—Nick!" Her use of his first name earned her

another kiss. Laughing, she pulled away again. "Nick, listen to me. History did not change because you saved me."

He shook his head. "It doesn't matter. What's done is done."

"It does matter. It matters to me. My father's stables were the best in all of England. Sinbad was my father's pride and joy—but all that is changed. We should put it right." He shook his head at her, but she stood and leaned over him. "I know what went wrong. You came too soon. Sinbad has not yet sired the colt."

"But the records! They were clear—unmistakable."

"Oh, I don't doubt the accuracy of the records. But the year you came to was 1812."

"1812?" He jumped to his feet. "No, I made the calculation. June 6, 1814, the very day Sinbad covered Lady's Delight."

"I assure you, the date was June 6, 1812. At any rate, Nick, since my father's death, I have had complete oversight of my father's stables. Sinbad has not yet been put to stud." She grasped his forearms and looked up into his slate eyes. "We must take Sinbad back to 1812." And deliver my cousin to justice, she added silently, even as she feared what her revenge might wreak on Nick's present.

And her future with him.

Nick awoke to chill dampness against his cheek. After a moment's disorientation, he realized he was once again face down on a bed of moss. A quick glance around in the faint dawn light showed he'd returned to the same spot as the first time he traveled across the centuries. A low whinny brought him to his feet to capture Sinbad's reins. Tying them quickly to a small bush, he then knelt next to Lady Jess.

For a moment, he simply gazed at her. Long silky lashes rested against her alabaster cheeks as she slumbered from the effects of the journey, and her mouth formed a sweet pink rosebud. Two days had passed since he had first traveled in

time and met his own destiny. In that short time, he had
shown her the wonders of the 21st century, eager to persuade
her she could be happy with him in his time.

He'd brought her with him against his better judgment.
She'd be much safer back at his ranch in Nevada. But she
insisted on returning with him, fearing their future together
would always be overshadowed by the question of whether
he would have realized the mistaken year if he had not
rescued her. Without her knowledge of the countryside, he
might be unable to return the horse to Alverstoke land so
Sinbad could fulfill his destiny.

For Nick's part, he no longer cared. He made a choice
when he interfered; in that moment, acting from instinct,
he'd realized that truth was the here and now—wherever and
whenever that here and now was. Cupid's dart had been right
on target—he knew he wanted Jessica from the moment he
saw her; he knew he loved her after her steadfast bravery.
Saving her was the only choice he could have lived with for
the rest of his life.

Bringing her to his time had been a way to keep her near
him, not to protect the future. And the change hadn't been
that great. No disasters, wars or plagues. The Wentworths
had simply begun breeding other horses. He was the only
one impacted, after all. The rest of the family was gone now.

But making Jessica happy was now his first priority. So
here they were, in a forest, with her homicidal cousin
perhaps still lurking while she gave a convincing portrayal of
sleeping beauty. He stroked his thumb across her full lips
before leaning down to wake her with his kiss.

"Mmm." Her eyes fluttered open. A smile curved her lips
as she saw him. "The journey starts out so ferociously, but it
seems to end in a very relaxing manner. Why is that?"

He shrugged. "I'm just glad it isn't painful." He pulled her
to her feet, and placed a kiss on her brow. "We don't have to
do this. It's so dangerous. We could just go back now."

"No, we must put things right." She reached out to stroke

his cheek. Her satiny fingers left trails of fire along his skin. "You know we must do it."

He sensed an undercurrent in her words, some greater meaning, but a sudden noise prevented him from questioning her. He pushed her behind him, and peered into the trees, pulling from his waistband the heavy pistol he'd brought along. A flash of brown fur shot past them, and the tension eased from his shoulders.

"Just a rabbit." He turned back to find tears streaming down her face. "Jess, why are you crying?"

She shook her head and hugged him. Feeling confused, he returned the embrace. "I guess women haven't changed much in the past 200 years. Tell me. Are you happy or sad?"

She shook under his arm, but raised a laughing, if watery, gaze to his. "Your weapon. You are no longer concerned about changing the future?"

He glanced at the gun. "Well, I would be if anyone found it. But if we meet up with Wentworth, I'm not taking any chances with you. You mean everything to me."

"Thank you." She said the words simply, but with heartfelt sincerity shining in her eyes. He pulled her close again, then lifted her onto Sinbad's back.

Faint color rose in her cheeks. "I've not ridden astride since I was a young girl."

"Well, get used to it, Jess, unless you want to bring a sidesaddle back with us. I doubt we could find one anywhere back home." Home. He liked the sound of being home with Jess. As soon as they got the horse back to his stable, they'd head back to the safety of his time.

Reins gathered in his fist, he looked up. "Which way?"

Jess pointed the down the road. She guessed they were but a mile or two from Alverstoke land. As Nick kept his eyes peeled for any locals abroad so early in the morning, she slipped the note she had written between the saddle and the blanket. In it, she had written an account of her cousin's attack and his plans to ravish and murder her. Her grooms would find the paper and deliver it to the magistrate. She hoped that gentleman would assume she had managed to write the note before Wentworth committed his foul deed, but that the villain had succeeded. He would be brought to justice for the murder of the guard.

Jess bit her lip as she wondered if Wentworth had also succeeded in murdering their aunt and the driver. If not, her note would not be needed, but if so, then it was crucial Sinbad, with the evidence of Wentworth's guilt, be returned to her land. The horse could not simply be set free. There could be no guarantee that a chance traveler would be honest enough to report so valuable a stray. Indeed, she was determined to get as close to the stables as they could risk without being seen.

Of course, another problem weighed upon her. She did not know the laws of inheritance well enough. After Wentworth, little Nicky would be her heir. If he inherited, then history would surely continue much as it had, and Nick's family would prosper as it had. But what if exposure of Lucius' crime resulted in an innocent boy's disinheritance? Would Nick forgive her?

She roused herself from her thoughts to note their location. "Nick, there is a break in the hedge just ahead. We should pass through there and cut across the fields."

"Okay. Then what? How close is close enough?"

"My gamekeeper has a cottage just at the edge of the woods. He is visiting his mother in Norfolk this week, so we should be able to release Sinbad nearby without discovery. He'll certainly find his way home from so close a spot."

Nick turned back to her and grinned. "And then we'll find our way home, too." His smile sent shivers of promise down her spine. She had become reconciled to her own need to disappear from this time. In truth, it was no sacrifice. While they had spent only two days together, she knew she would follow Nick to the ends of time. A mere two centuries forward was nothing in comparison. She could not deny the feeling of rightness, of certain belonging she felt in his arms.

They walked on in silence, finally reaching the cottage. Nick lifted her down and tied Sinbad's reins to the saddle so the horse would not trip. He slapped the horse lightly on the rump to send it on its way.

"You!"

Jess spun around toward the cottage at the sound of her cousin's voice. Lucius loomed in the doorway, unshaven and haggard, his once dandified clothing dirty and disheveled. She stepped back a few paces at the sight of her would-be murderer, standing only a few yards away.

Hatred poured from her cousin's eyes as he raised a gun. His teeth bared in a horrific grin, Lucius spat, "I had the perfect plan, and you, you bitch, ruined everything. Aunt Mary has roused the countryside, and I'm a hunted man."

Without warning, a loud report issued from his weapon, just as Nick sprang in front of Jessica. The force of the bullet pushed him back into Jess, knocking her down into an inelegant sprawl. A brief glance at her cousin showed him striding toward her, yet more murder in his eyes. She pulled the gun from Nick's waistband and fired without hesitation at her cousin just a few feet away. Lucius fell back against the cottage wall before slowly sliding down to the ground. A scarlet stain spread across the dingy white of his loose shirt.

Not sparing her cousin another glance, Jess laid Nick to the ground, frantically searching for evidence of his wound. A blackened hole showed in the pocket above his heart, but no blood flowed. "Nick, Nick? Can you hear me, my love?"

His eyes opened, and he blinked. "You're not hurt?"

"Me? No!"

"Good." His eyes closed again.

"Nick, stay awake. I'll get help." She looked around. Sinbad had fled at the gunshots and was probably already nearly home. She jumped up to follow, but stopped. In just two days time, the miracles performed in the 21st century had been borne upon her time and again. Medical care would be much better there surely. She threw herself to her knees beside him again.

"Nick! Nick, you must tell me where the watch is!"

"Jess." His eyes opened again. He started to sit.

"No, don't get up. Just tell me where the watch is."

He continued to a sitting position and reached for his shirt pocket. "Uh, oh." Reaching a hand into the torn pocket, he pulled the watch out. A small lead ball was lodged in the center of the case. When he opened the case, bits of glass and tiny springs fell into his lap.

Jess' heart went into her throat. The watch had saved his life but condemned him to stay in her time. "Nick, I'm so sorry," she whispered.

He sat silently for a moment, and shook his head. A slow smile turned up the corners of his mouth. "I'm not." He climbed to his feet, and pulled her up after him.

"But, but, Nick, don't you see? We can't go to your time."

"Yes, I see, Jess. Now we know which theory is correct. What is meant to be, is meant to be." He hugged her until she could barely breathe, but she did not mind.

Wonder caught in her throat as his meaning sank in. "And we were meant to be. In this time."

"Always. That is, if you'll marry me?"

Her eyes swam with tears, but she could see well enough to throw her arms around him. She frowned as a thought occurred to her and pulled away. "Nick, do you realize what this means? Nicky never inherited my estate. You are your own great-great and so on grandfather!"

He shot her the cocky grin she had so quickly grown to cherish. "I hope so. After all, my fondest dream has always been to rejuvenate the Wentworth bloodline."

THE RETURN

Susan D. Brooks

"I'm seventy nine years old and this is the first time anyone has wanted to interview me." Marge Smith leaned back in her ivory brocade wing chair, eyeing the reporter. "I can't imagine what it is you want to know. I've lived my whole life right here in Niagara Falls."

"Yes, I realize that." The young man, seated on the other side of the oak coffee table, smiled. "That's why I'm here."

She watched him remove a small, black tape recorder from his black canvas briefcase and set it between them. Her gaze lingered on his long, slender fingers and wide palms.

An artist's hand.

The thought pleased her. She liked artists as a rule. Their work helped her to see life through different prisms, helped her to see beauty where she thought none existed.

"Are you sure I can't get you something to drink? Coffee? A beer?" She motioned with her glass, making the ice clink against the crystal. "Scotch?"

"No, thank you." He pulled a bottle of name-brand water out of his attaché. "I always carry my own. You'd be surprised how the tap water varies from place to place."

He's cute, she thought, as he slipped a tape into the recorder. Sexy smile, nose a bit wobbly, maybe broken once, but giving him a touch of the rascal. What did he say his name was? She glanced at the business card he'd given her. Jonathan D. Kulak. Photojournalist.

"As I mentioned on the phone," he said, "the local historical society wants to document life in the Niagara area during World War II and the mayor suggested talking to you." He quirked an eyebrow, a gesture that changed the shape of his eyes and made them oddly familiar. "He said you're a storehouse of knowledge."

"I'll bet he did," Marge sniffed, "he never could resist the opportunity to schmooze a voter." She put her glass on a marble-top end table, then folded her hands. "Where shall we start?"

"How about with your job at Bell Aircraft?"

"How did you know I worked there?" Intrigued, she thought a moment. "Did the mayor tell you?"

"No, I did a little research before I came." He shrugged and offered her an engaging smile. "I was counting on getting this interview. I wanted to know a few things first in order to ask the right questions. Get the ball rolling, so to speak."

"Fair enough." She took another tiny sip of scotch. "But if I'm telling you something you already know, stop me. Don't let me prattle on like some old fool."

"I promise." Kulak flipped through pages of notes, and paused to read. "You worked at Bell for thirty-three years. When you left you were the assistant Head of Human Resources. But you didn't start in that department." He looked at her for confirmation.

"I started as a mail clerk a week before Pearl Harbor was bombed." She could still see the haunted eyes of the workers in the aftermath of the announcement. Engineers huddled together, talking in low urgent voices; line workers tense and silent. Many would enlist, many would not return.

"Mail clerk?" Jonathan's voice broke into the daydream. "You must have known everyone in the plant."

"Well, eventually I at least knew everyone's name. It was a big place. People came and went."

"Did you ever meet the Russian pilot, Darius Kozlov? He was in Niagara…."

The rest of Jonathan's words faded as shards of Marge's past tumbled into the present; memories she'd put into her own mental storage room. Darius. Her Darius.

"…an ace pilot. We'd like to mention him in the story, but there isn't much information available." Kulak looked up.

"No one has spoken his name in years," Marge stammered, hand automatically reaching for her scotch.

"Then you did know him." Jonathan's demeanor changed slightly. He leaned toward her, eyes intent, the pen now reversed in his hand, the tip resting against the sleeve of his blue button-down shirt. A small ink stain appeared. "Did you know him well?"

"Yes, I did." Marge clasped her moist palms. "The Russian government sent him to test Bell's Air Cobra fighter plane. We saw each other frequently."

"Did he speak English?"

"Some, he was a quick learner, but we used all sorts of ways to communicate. A look, a laugh… a touch."

"Pencil drawings?" Jonathan lifted an eyebrow in question.

Marge stared at the man for a full minute. Her throat constricted. How could he know about those?

Jonathan scratched his chin. "Did I say something wrong?"

"No, no." Marge's thoughts whirled in confusion. "I'm surprised that you know about them. The sketches, I mean."

"He documented his whole life with them." Jonathan's voice rose with excitement. "His family in Russia have over one hundred that he drew before he left to serve in the military."

"Oh." Marge wiped her damp palms on her thighs. "Have you seen them?"

"A few. He was a gifted artist." Jonathan noticed his pen and the stain. With a soft oath, he turned the pen around and drew a Kleenex from his trouser pocket to dab at the stain. "How did you two meet?"

"Oh, all the girls at Bell knew Darius," she said distractedly. "He was very friendly and very handsome. I don't remember ever being introduced, but somehow he knew my name and I knew his."

"So, you were friends? Did you date?" The question, asked in a matter-of-fact tone, caught her off guard.

"Date?" The word seemed so inadequate for what happened on those magical nights. "Yes, we did."

"Did your father meet him?" asked Kulak. "Any of your brothers or sisters?"

"No!" Marge burst out laughing. "Dad never let me date military men. Only good Catholic boys from the city. Darius and I met on the sly." She smiled. "My friends thought it was so romantic."

"Would you tell me about your first date?" Kulak flashed his winning smile again.

"I suppose most people wouldn't consider it a date, but there was a night that brought us together. I was on Luna Island, standing next to Bridal Veil Falls. I went there a lot in those days just to be alone. The city was dark with another blackout.

"I was almost ready to leave when I heard a plane. He came in from the east, down low, close to the water. If the moon hadn't been out, I never would have seen him because he was flying without lights."

Jonathan's eyes widened. "Kozlov flew over the cataracts without lights?"

"He was a bit of a daredevil."

"Go on," Kulak urged.

"At first, I was scared. I thought the Germans were

attacking, but when the plane turned, I realized it was an Air Cobra. One of ours.

"He circled around and, just as the air raid siren sounded the All Clear, the lights on the island came back on. When he passed, I waved to him. He rocked his wings and flew off into the night. On my desk at work the next morning, I found a pencil sketch of me waving from Luna Island." She felt a thrill remembering the discovery. "It was exquisite.

"Anyway, that afternoon he stopped by my desk to talk. He told me he was the pilot from the night before and had drawn the picture.

"He asked me to dinner. We went to Luna Island with pizza and wine." She laughed. "We talked in a combination of pantomime and mispronounced words, but it was wonderful."

The reporter sat very still, listening, a soft smile curling his lips.

"We met as often as we could over the next six months. Darius wanted to go everywhere, do everything. He was so full of energy, so full of life. My hometown looked very different through his eyes.

"Then he was gone; called home unexpectedly." Marge lifted the crystal glass, hand trembling. "I received a dozen letters, heavily censored, of course. My last to him was returned marked as undeliverable. That was almost a year after he left Niagara. I don't know what happened to him."

As the last words left her lips, she caught her breath. *My God. Maybe this man knows.*

The idea of knowing the truth after all this time seared her mind; rendered her speechless. She looked at Kulak.

He cleared his throat, stroked his chin, then said, "He never returned home after the war."

The gently spoken words hit like ice water, waking her to the unpleasant reality. Somehow, a tiny part of her thought Darius had survived. Broken, perhaps, and unable to return to her, but alive.

The understanding in Kulak's eyes touched something deep in her heart. She stood, suddenly eager to share her treasures with this young reporter. "Let me show you something."

Marge led the way down a hallway to the back of the house. In a small room she flipped on a light. Rows of framed sketches hung eye-level around the room. Jonathan stepped close to study an image.

"This was the first." Marge touched the picture nearest the door. "They're in the order he drew them."

Kulak nodded, already engaged in the story unfolding around the room. She watched him smile at the image of a young Marge looking up and waving from Luna Island, laughing on the deck of the Maid of the Mist tour boat, of Darius with their rented bicycles, them together standing on the bastion at Fort Niagara, and other vignettes that captured tiny moments of time.

"Your whole relationship is here, in these pictures." His words, taut with emotion, sounded loud in the small room.

"Much of it." She stared at one of the images, remembering the rainy day spent climbing down into the gorge. Darius told her that he loved her while standing there by the turbulent water. He promised to return. He promised to marry her.

Marge led the reporter back to the living room and talked a while longer. Marge forced herself to focus on his questions and give him thoughtful answers, but memories crept in; her voice faded. Her attention wandered. Finally, Jonathan shut off the recorder.

"I have enough to work with." He stuffed his paper, pens, and recorder into his briefcase. Standing, he offered his hand. "Thank you. You've helped me a great deal."

"If you ever find out about Darius, could you… would you please let me know?" She fought for calm.

Eyes sympathetic, Kulak smiled and nodded. Marge saw him out and went upstairs to lie down.

A week later, a parcel delivery truck stopped in front of Marge's house and left a long cardboard tube on the porch. The return address, a town in New York, was not familiar. Puzzled, Marge removed the end cover and pulled out a roll of paper and an envelope with her name on it. Inside was a note.

Dear Ms. Smith,

I thank you again for your help with the article about Niagara's history, but I do owe you an apology. I deliberately deceived you.

Darius Kozlov was my great uncle. Although I never knew him, I do know a great deal about him. His plane was shot down by Germans and he was captured. After sixteen months as a prisoner of war, he was shot while trying to escape. His remains are in an unmarked grave in Germany.

When you see the contents of this package, you'll see that he never stopped loving you, a fact that may bring some comfort. A fellow prisoner carried them out of the camp at the end of the war and brought them to my great grandfather's house in Russia. Your name and address were on the back of each drawing.

When my grandfather died last spring, the sketches were found rolled up in oilcloth, stored in his attic. My mother begged me to try to find you and, after I got this assignment, I agreed. The moment you opened the front door, I recognized you as the woman in the pictures. There is no doubt that these belong to you.

Respectfully,
Jonathan Darius Kulak

Marge unrolled the papers. Her heart pounded and her fingers trembled as she turned them over, one by one. They led her through a life she had only dreamed of: Darius and her as bride and groom, in front of a picketed Cape Cod, pushing two young children on swings, then gray-haired, holding hands on Luna Island. And one more of him standing before a faceless German soldier, eyes despairing, body thin, uniform in rags.

Tears formed and rolled, unchecked, down her cheeks. She clutched the papers to her chest. He'd kept his promises the only way he could.

That night, after all the tourists had returned to their hotels, Marge crossed the tiny bridge to Luna Island. By the railing next to Bridal Veil Falls, she closed her eyes. Crisp air signaled autumn's approach, but the smell of summer still lingered in the whiff of fresh-cut grass. She drew in a deep breath and let memories, some vivid, some faded, carry her back through time. Her hands moved over the rolled up sketch, removing the rubber band to let it unfurl. Slowly, she tore the sketch of Darius behind the prison barrier into tiny squares.

When the moon came out from behind a silvery cloud, Marge opened her eyes, held her hand over the railing, and unclenched her fist. A gust of wind scattered the pieces over the precipice to the rocks below. Instantly, the atmosphere changed, growing heavy with an unknown tension. Around her, an indigo veil fell across the night, obscuring the hotels and restaurants. Across the river, the lights of Canada faded.

Heart racing, Marge backed away from the railing. Darkness penetrated every crevice, but objects remained outlined in pale ivory. She turned to climb the path to Goat Island when she heard the sound.

Faint at first, Marge stopped and cocked her head to listen. A moment later, she recognized the hum as that of an airplane engine. Through the dark she watched a shadow skim the upper rivers surface then shoot out over the gorge.

She ran back to the fence. Her hands gripped the cool metal and she leaned as far forward as she could. Mist rose from the falls, coating her face. She blinked. Where was the plane?

It returned to circle once and in a faint light glowing from the wings, she recognized an Air Cobra.

Flying with no lights.

Marge felt her heart pound and a shiver started in her legs. She squinted at the apparition, willing the pilot to reveal himself in the cockpit window, but the darkness prevailed.

She watched, breathless, as he soared past. How could it be? Darius?

Waves of elation rolled over her, lifting her soul to heights she hadn't known in years. His voice rang in her ears. His touch lingered on her lips.

"I love you!" she shouted to the phantom Air Cobra. The pilot rocked the wings in response.

Peace replaced elation. Her knees gave way, and she sank to the ground. Eyes now blurry with tears, she watched as the small fighter climbed straight into the sky. And vanished.

A LOVE THROUGH TIME

Su Kopil

Cassie Scott ran her hand over the worn wood of the antique desk she had purchased at auction earlier in the week. It would make a nice addition to her small shop already brimming with pieces from various periods.

"If that'll be all, Miss Scott. I've got a full truck to deliver today. We thought it best to drop off your desk first thing." The deliveryman handed her his clipboard.

She signed the bill and gave him the tip money she'd taken from the register before he arrived. "Thanks Stan. I appreciate your stopping here first."

"No problem. See you next week." She walked him to the door, then locked it after he left.

Before she opened the shop for the day, she wanted a chance to examine the desk more carefully. She still couldn't believe she found a piece so similar to the one in her dreams. She probably paid too much for it considering the nicks and the dark stain marring the surface, but something about this piece beckoned to her. It was almost as if she'd seen it, touched it before, and not only in her dreams.

"Ridiculous." She spoke aloud, shaking off the feelings of

déjà vu that nagged at her.

But she couldn't turn away.

Instead she sat in the matching wooden chair, feeling as though she'd done so a hundred times before, and opened each drawer in turn. Each slid smoothly towards her revealing its emptiness. All but the top left drawer with the narrow keyhole. Without thinking her actions through, Cassie reached beneath the desk, her fingers connecting with a thin slat of wood. She slid the wood towards her. Something cold and hard fell into her palm.

A tarnished gold skeleton key. A chill swept through her. How had she known it was there?

Fingers trembling, she fit the key into the lock, turning it until the tumblers clicked. Like the others, the drawer opened smoothly to reveal a wooden bottom. Her shoulders sagged. What made her think she would find anything?

She'd spent her whole life searching for that elusive something that always remained just out of reach. Her practical parents called her a dreamer, but they were gone now. Aunt Clara, on her mother's side, whom she'd never met, was her only relation. Instead of closing the drawer and getting on with opening the shop as her father would have done, she pulled the drawer open farther causing the front end to angle down. In the back left corner, sat a square white box, yellowed with age.

A tingle of excitement raced along her spine. Part of her wanted to forget the box and rebel against the mysterious pull luring her away from her work. Daddy had always opened the shop promptly at nine. But a stronger part of her needed to know what lay hidden within its tiny walls.

Drawing a deep breath, she lifted out the box and carefully opened the lid. Nestled in the black velvet lining lay a round gold case attached to a stone set pendant.

Cassie felt a flush of heat sweep through her. Her skin grew clammy so that she had to wipe her palm on her jeans before removing the piece from the box. The weight of it in her hand surprised her. No doubt the casing was made of steel and plated gold. Sturdy, yet beautiful.

With a gentle touch, the casing opened to reveal a white enamel dial with black Roman numerals. The gilt hands had suspended time at a quarter to four.

A surge of emotion overwhelmed Cassie. Her heart pounded. The image of a man, tall with a brawny build, hair the color of obsidian with eyes to match, left her breathless and stunned. Lord Nicholas Grayson. Though his manner of dress depicted a different era, she knew him. Just as she knew this timepiece of a hundred years or more once belonged to her. But how was that possible?

Turning the piece over in her hand, she knew the engraving would be there before she ever saw it. Etched in the gold were the same words that had echoed through her heart longer than a lifetime—"A love through time."

Cassie traced the delicate lettering with her fingers allowing the emotions that came unbidden free reign. A deep and abiding sorrow threatened to crush her heart if it were not for the overwhelming sense of love that surrounded her. They were the same emotions that left her throat dry and her heart pounding on those nights when her dream woke her. In daylight, the images grew fuzzy, fading before her mind could fully grasp the outcome. The only things that remained clear were the desk and the man.

On impulse, she retrieved the tiny key she'd spotted within the folds of dark velvet and used it to wind the watch. A tremor erupted along her fingertips, traveled up her arm, and spread through her body. A wave of dizziness caught her offguard. Grabbing the desk for support, she closed her eyes and drew in deep calming breaths. But she couldn't erase the feeling of spiraling backwards, down, down…. Like a dream gone awry, she lost sense of herself.

Time was irrelevant.

What seemed like hours, Cassie knew could only have been minutes. She opened her eyes not quite sure what had just happened. The watch still ticked in her hands. But now the gilt hands read a quarter past twelve.

The first thing she noticed was the desk. Although the wood was still smooth and cool to her touch, the dark stain on the upper right side no longer marred the surface. No nicks. No scratches. Instead an inkwell and pen sat there. A small oil lamp sat in the left hand corner.

A flash of recognition rocked Cassie. This was her desk, her room. Pivoting in her chair, she glanced at the lavishly furnished bedroom decorated in the palest of lavender and lace. Directly to her left stood a wash stand with a porcelain pitcher and basin. Perhaps cool water on her face would help her nerves. She stood, the rough material brushing her skin bringing her attention to the wool riding skirt she wore and beyond that to the sparkling diamond on her left hand.

A sharp knock brought her head up sharply. Before she could answer, the door opened. A man's broad form filled the doorway. But it was not his size or the tight breeches fitted over muscular legs that caused her to catch her breath. It was his gaze, dark and hungry, brimming with a love that knew no boundaries. This was her dream come to life.

"Nicholas," she whispered, her hand stilled on the handle of the pitcher.

He was by her side in a second. "My love," his voice rumbled in her ear. "What is it?"

His warm breath on her cheek, the pressure of his hand on the small of her back, comforted her. His familiar touch brought her a sense of peace so that she no longer feared this strange reversal in time. Cassie knew without a doubt this man, her lover, her husband, her friend, was what she'd been seeking her whole life. Something had pulled them irrevocably apart and now, for some inexplicable reason, they were being given a second chance.

"Are you ill, Cassandra? Perhaps we should cancel our ride today." Concern drew his brows to a vee.

The urge to smooth away his concern pulled at her. She

resisted. Riding. Yes, they were to go riding as they did every afternoon when business didn't call Nicholas away.

"I'm fine. Truly." She smiled. "You know how much I look forward to our rides." Anticipation quickened her pulse, and she knew the truth of her statement.

"Are you pleased with your anniversary present? Did you like the inscription?" he asked.

Her present. The watch. Fragments of her dream mixed with memories streaked across her mind. He'd given it to her at their one year anniversary party the night before.

"Oh, yes, a love through time."

"Our love will always endure, Cassandra. Not even death will separate us."

"Not even death," she whispered. He stood before her so sure, so strong. She held the timepiece out to him. "Would you pin it on for me?"

His fingers touched hers as he lifted the piece from her hand, leaving her yearning to feel his arms around her.

"Now you have no excuse for returning late when riding alone." He chuckled.

He moved to place the pin on her left side. Instantly, she knew that was wrong. Why, she couldn't say. But she couldn't quell the panic bubbling inside of her.

"No!" She cried out.

He pulled back as though he'd stuck her with the pin. "Did I hurt you? My darling, I'm—"

"No, I'm sorry." She felt foolish. "I'm fine. Could you pin it on my right side please. It… it looks better there."

He frowned but didn't say anything as his fingers deftly worked the pin into place. She studied his face, noting his strong jawline and generous mouth, the worry lines along his brow. She knew and loved every inch of this man. What had happened to them? Why had she ended up in twentieth century America, a time and place she never fully embraced, experiencing dreams of a nineteenth century lord—a man she couldn't relinquish.

She could feel it even now. An unnamed menace looming over their love. Whatever it was, Cassie knew it would make itself known soon. She vowed to be ready for it this time. Forty minutes later, they had left the manor and the evil lurking in the shadows far behind. Birds twittered in the trees around them. Cassie and Nicholas dismounted on a lush patch of green grass that sloped towards a wide meadow sprinkled with yellow and pink wildflowers.

Nicholas spread a checkered quilt on the ground, then retrieved the basket from his horse's saddle. While the animals grazed quietly, Cassie laid out Cook's offerings. Three cheeses, cold chicken, a crusty loaf of bread, and a jar of cool mint tea.

They ate their fill, happy and content in each other's company. When they finished, Nicholas moved to sit beside her. He removed the pins from her hair and stroked the long tresses; his gentle touch a balm on her soul.

"I leave for London in the morning. Will you miss me, darling?" His breath tickled her ear.

"Like a bee without honey."

He laughed and kissed her neck. "Are you saying I am your sustenance? Do you hunger for me as I do you?"

Her body heated with desire. "Always."

He pulled her closer, his eyes darkening, and she knew his desire matched her own. She leaned forward anticipating his kiss. She reveled in the silky touch of his tongue tracing her lips, teasing, parrying with her own until the need of him consumed her.

With the ease born of a year's worth of practice, they quickly shed their clothing. His heated skin upon hers caused a throbbing ache in her center. Even the cool breeze couldn't quench the fire between them. Cassie knew nothing in the world mattered except her love for Nicholas. Whatever nameless menace came before, she would not allow it to rip them apart again.

With their desire sated for the moment, Nicholas helped

her dress, then quickly donned his own clothes. Cassie repinned her hair as best she could, then checked to make sure her timepiece was still in place. Opening the casement, she saw the gilt hands read five to three. A feeling of dread washed over her leaving a heavy weight on her heart.

"Cassandra?" Nicholas's dark eyes watched her.

She tried to shake the feeling and offered him a tremulous smile. "I wish you weren't leaving tomorrow."

"I'll be back soon, a week or two at the most."

Cassie gathered the used dishes and left over food and placed them in the basket.

"Besides, Geoff will be here should you need anything while I'm gone."

Her stomach clenched, and she dropped the jar of tea, spilling what was left on the quilt. "It must have slipped." She grabbed a napkin and frantically dabbed at the wet spot.

He stilled her hand with his own. "It will dry. Does my brother's being here worry you?"

"No." She allowed him to take the wet napkin and pack the rest of their things. Why had she reacted so violently to Geoff's name and why had she lied to Nicholas about her feelings? Whatever danger awaited them, she somehow knew that Nicholas' brother was involved.

They returned to the house, Nicholas going to his office in the library and Cassie to her room after claiming a need to rest before dinner. The house was empty save for the servants who scurried quietly about their business, and Geoff, who she now knew lurked somewhere on the grounds.

She needed time to think. It no longer mattered why she and Nicholas were being given this miraculous opportunity, only that this time they must survive whatever had rent them in two the first time.

Reaching for the sheet of stationary that lay at the end of the desk, she sat down, uncapped the inkwell, and dipped her pen into the well. Writing had always helped her to clear her thoughts, perhaps it would help her now.

Staring at the blank sheet, she wrote the letters G... E... O... F. She was about to redip her pen when her bedroom door burst open. Startled, her hand knocked over the inkwell, spilling a small pool of black liquid before she could right it. "Ah, Cassandra, my dear, would that my presence always excited you so." Geoff's voice was a higher timbre than Nicholas'. Everything about him was a paler imitation of his older brother.

He closed the door and advanced towards her. The feelings of déjà vu hit her like a tidal wave. And she knew without a doubt that he was their nemesis.

She stood, the back of her leg hitting the chair in her haste. "What do you want, Geoff? Why did you close the door? You know it is not proper to—"

"Proper?" He scoffed.

She could smell his sour breath. He'd been drinking again, or more likely had never stopped. Images flashed through her mind of Geoff, drunk, pawing at her, forcing his attentions on her, turning violent and ugly when she refused him. Then the threats began.

"What do you know of being proper? You, who cavorts with my sainted brother in the fields for all to see."

"You watched us?" The thought horrified her.

He ignored her. His gaze fell to the paper on the desk. "What's this? Perhaps you are not so immune to my attentions after all." He grabbed her by the back of the neck, pulling her towards him. His head lowered.

She shoved at his chest, trying vainly to twist away.

He laughed and captured her mouth in a bruising kiss.

She bit down hard on his lip, ignoring the taste of blood.

He yelped in pain and stepped away from her. "Bitch!" His tone was flat, but his eyes were wild. "You will pay for that. I've had enough of your games." He swiped at the blood dribbling down his chin.

"You are the one who will pay. I will see to it that Nicholas—"

"Nicholas be damned!" He spat. "Mark my words, you will be mine by morning." With that, he stormed out. Cassie dropped into the chair, willing her trembling body to calm down. What did he mean, she'll be his by morning? Did he think because Nicholas was leaving there would be no one to protect her? If only she could remember how her dream ended. Or—Her gaze fell on the dark stain now marring the desk's surface. Or, did his words hold a deeper meaning. Evil tainted his soul, darkening it like the ink stained the wood, indelibly, forever. Then, suddenly, in a burst of insight, she knew.

Geoff intended to kill Nicholas.

"No!" she cried. This was the horror that had torn them apart! Geoff's insane jealousy of his brother. Everything he had been denied as the younger sibling, he craved.

Bolting out of her room, she ran down the stairs, ignoring the wide-eyed stare of the servant girl carrying fresh linens. Racing through the hallway toward the rear of the house, she burst into the library.

"Cassandra!" Nicholas rose from his chair.

She saw the alarm in his face and tried to calm her rapid breathing. Her gaze darted around the room taking in the shelves lined with books, the leather furnishing, the closed door leading onto the terrace. No Geoff. Had she been mistaken?

She allowed Nicholas to lead her to one of the leather chairs. Urging her to sit, he brought her a glass half filled with brandy. He knelt beside her watching as she took a sip of the amber liquid. It burned a trail to her stomach leaving a calm in its wake.

"Now, tell me what is wrong." Nicholas took her free hand in his, rubbing her palm.

What could she say? She thought his brother wanted to kill him? He wouldn't believe her. She wasn't sure she believed it herself. Geoff had been angry, yes, but was he foolish enough to attempt murder? Foolish or insane?

A shudder swept through her.

"Tell me," Nicholas said.

"It's Geoff."

"My brother?"

"Yes. He is not right, Nicholas. There is something wrong with him." She saw the stubborn tightening of his lips and knew she was on delicate ground. Nicholas' loyalty to his brother was almost as obsessive as Geoff's jealousy. They'd had this argument before. Only this time she had to make him believe.

"He is jealous of you. He always has been."

"Ridiculous. Where are you getting these notions?"

"He wants what you have—the estate, your title, your... wife."

Anger flashed in his eyes. He stood abruptly, pacing the floor with short quick steps. "Absurd! Why do you say these things? I see to it Geoff has everything he needs. He wants for nothing."

"You're wrong." She stood, blocking his path so that he must face her, face the truth. "He wants your life." She had to convince him. Nothing else mattered. Especially not the shell of a life she had left in the twentieth century. Nicholas was all she ever wanted. She could not fail him again.

"Bravo, bravo, wonderful performance, my dear."

They both turned to see Geoff enter the room through the terrace door. He stopped several feet into the room, hands in his jacket pockets as he leaned against the paneled wall.

"But why don't you tell him the truth, my dear?"

"What truth?" Nicholas looked from one to the other.

"Simply that your... wife," Geoff turned his glazed gaze on her, "wants to leave you for me."

"Liar!" she shouted. "Nicholas, what he says is not true. I love you." But he had turned away to stare at his brother.

"Who would you believe? Your devoted brother or some whore you picked up in London in a moment of weakness?"

Cassie saw Nicholas stiffen with rage. He started towards

Geoff. From the corner of her eye, she saw a flash of silver. Suddenly, she knew the end of her dream.

"No!" she screamed. Everything moved as if in slow motion. She saw the small derringer in Geoff's hand. She heard the hammer click and smelled the burnt powder a second later. In another moment, she would be ripped apart from Nicholas forever. It had been her choice that fateful night to take the bullet meant for her beloved. How could she not do the same thing now? There was no choice, no second chance. Some cruel twist of fate had brought her to the same nightmare all over again.

Dropping the glass of brandy, she leaped in front of Nicholas, pushing him to the floor. She felt a force strike her chest, then a sharp heated pain. She felt herself falling. In the distance she heard Nicholas cry out. There was a scurrying about her, arms lifting her, voices talking. Then nothing.

The first thing she felt when she awoke was a dull ache in her chest. "Nicholas?"

"I'm here, darling." He sat at the edge of her bed. The lamp on her desk lent a soft glow to the darkening room.

"What happened? Am I—" She tried to sit up.

"You're fine. You took the bullet that Geoff meant for me, my brave sweet girl." He pressed a light kiss to her lips.

"But…." Her head throbbed, and she couldn't seem to remember anything past their afternoon ride earlier or was it the day before? "How?"

"It's a miracle." She heard the awe in his voice. "The bullet struck your pendant. If you hadn't told me to pin it to your right side…." His voice broke. He cleared his throat before continuing. "I'm afraid it's destroyed." He held up the damaged timepiece. "The doctor said it saved your life. You'll have some bruising, but you're going to be fine."

"And Geoff?"

Nicholas shook his head. "He's gone. Took off. The authorities are looking for him, but he won't dare set foot on this property again. You're safe. We're both safe."

She smiled, reaching for him.

He took her in his arms, holding her close, so that she heard the beating of his heart. "My love," he whispered, "I thought I'd lost you."

"Never." She caressed his cheek. "Nothing will ever separate us, Nicholas. Not ever."

Stan double-checked the address again before bringing his shipment through the front door. "Hello," he called. "I'm looking for a Clara Scott."

"I'm Clara." A woman in her fifties came out of the back room. "Oh, wonderful, my desk is here. You can leave it right in that corner. Thank you."

Stan did as she asked and handed her the work order. "Wasn't sure I had the right address at first. I haven't delivered here in awhile. What happened to Mr. Scott?"

"My poor dear brother passed on some time ago. Such a tragedy," she sniffed. "Never did get over losing his wife last year. If only they'd been able to have children things might have been different...." her voice trailed off.

Stan nodded sagely, taking back his clipboard. "Will you be running the shop now?"

"Yes, I've always loved antiques. I helped my brother out from time to time with the buying, especially the last few years. Like this desk. Isn't it a beauty?" She lifted the protective blanket and ran her hand along the polished wood surface. "What do you think?"

Stan glanced at the worn wood and nicked edges. He never did understand why people wanted old junk when they could buy new, but the old gal seemed pleased with her find. Who was he to argue? He shrugged. "Nice piece, too bad there's a stain in the right corner."

Clara's fingers traced the dark blotch. "Doesn't that make it interesting? One can only imagine the stories this desk could tell."

ON THE NIGHT WE WERE WED

Charlotte Schreck Burns

She left the Katy Freeway, merged into traffic on I-45 and headed north, away from Houston, away from the scene of the crime. He'd accepted a home-cooked steak dinner and her killer salad which was followed by chocolate soufflé with raspberry cream, then he'd collected more than kisses before saying, "Mara, darling, I hope this hasn't gone too far—I hope you weren't misled about things."

She'd kept a smile frozen on her face while waiting for him to explain why they couldn't keep their appointment at the little chapel she'd reserved, why he wasn't enthusiastic about the wedding dress she'd retrieved from the seamstress that afternoon.

"I'd marry you if I could," he said, "if I didn't already have a wife."

His excuse was so much more definitive than, "I don't know if I'm ready for marriage—can we take some time to think about it?" or, "Why spoil a good thing? Can't we go on the way we are?" She'd thrown him out, grabbed the suitcase already packed to take on their honeymoon, and begun driving, her only purpose to distance herself from him and from the parody of bliss they'd shared.

In the dark, she switched radio stations when signals faded, bought a cup of bitter coffee from a drive-through, pushed the speed limit until lights from southbound Dallas traffic intensified her headache. She left the interstate for a county road and drove west, hoping to find a motel before turning back to Houston the next day.

She was on Beltline Road through the small town of Wilmer, past the train tracks, when heavy fog dropped to shroud the winding road. Mara glanced at the doors to make sure they were locked.

She crept along, sensing rather than seeing the edge of the shoulder. Minutes later she made out the words on a sign that hung from a post—Bed and Breakfast—and turned in at the long drive, bringing her car to rest under a giant tree. An ancient farmhouse floated in the night mist, a diaphanous moon glowing, then retreating behind clouds above the roof of the second story. Mara grabbed her purse and a tote and walked up the steps onto the wide front porch.

Chains on a wood swing creaked above the sound of footsteps inside the house. The door opened.

"Come in," said an old woman. She wore a red checked apron, and her gray hair was pulled into a bun. "I'm Mrs. Breedlove. You look as though you've been driving a while. I'll just show you to your room."

"I don't have reserva—"

"You don't need them. I've put you upstairs in the Sweetheart Room. Your bath is just down the hall. I'll see you in the morning for breakfast, about eight-thirty."

Taken aback, but too tired to question her host, Mara followed Mrs. Breedlove up the stairs, past vintage photos and wall tapestries. The woman pointed to a small table on the landing.

"You'll find muffins and coffee there when you wake." She opened a bedroom door and handed Mara a set of keys.

Well, thought Mara, *it will do for the night*. She opened her purse, wondering which form of payment was preferred, but when she turned around, she found herself alone. A sense of déjà vu overwhelmed her. She'd seen the rosebud wallpaper somewhere, had slept high off the floor in that same inviting tester bed, could almost remember the pictures on the wall. The room seemed enchanted, comforting, as if it were a sentient being in sympathy with the hurt she'd suffered.

She dressed in one of her new negligees and climbed into bed, wanting to let loose a flood of tears, to wallow in self-pity. So stupid, so cheap, Mara chided herself. He used me, and I never saw it coming. Remorse filled her. She longed for someone of depth—a gentle, trustworthy man whose loving would be tender and passionate. If he existed, she wanted to find him soon.

She slept deeply with not a single dream and woke early. She felt at peace, but a kaleidoscope of memories she didn't yet have teased her mind, revealed the tiniest glimmer of a divine motif as though she were being readied for a great adventure.

The scent of baked apple-cinnamon muffins drew her to the table outside her room. The fog had lifted, but not the dark. She stepped through a door onto a porch which overlooked the front gardens. Through the glow of her window, she found a wicker chair, dropped into it, and sat to drink Mrs. Breedlove's dark coffee.

A rustling startled her, and she turned to see a man lay his newspaper aside and smile. "Hope you don't mind if I share your aerie."

She hugged her silken robe close, remembering how much of her body it disclosed. "Aerie? It isn't mine, I'm sure."

"I'm Robert," he said. "I'm in the Lancaster Room downstairs, but I wanted to see the sunrise from up here."

I know. She almost spoke aloud, wondering how such knowledge had come to her, marveling that she found his presence as welcome as snow on Christmas trees.

"Come watch." He took her hand, and she let him, as if it were the most natural reaction, as though she'd known him forever. A sense of inevitability quieted the astonishment she felt at her own response but did not slow her pulse. She held her breath as a rosy tint colored the horizon.

"Do you believe in love at first sight?" he asked.

She looked at him, followed the lines around his mouth to the crinkles enlivening his dark eyes. There was strength and honesty there. She was sure they'd never met, surer still she could trust him.

"I didn't before," she told him, surrendering to the magic.

"I have a good job in the aerospace industry in Houston. I lost my wife last year. We never had children. I'm a registered Democrat who usually votes Republican. I drink mint juleps on Derby Day, and beer with barbecue." He paused, a blush deepening his ruddy complexion.

"Go on, please, Robert"

"I couldn't stop myself if I tried. Do you mind that I like John Wayne movies and baseball? I go to church six or eight times a year, whether I need to or not. And I don't know why I'm so sure you were meant to be my love… my wife… I think something mystical is happening. I hope it's not a long engagement."

Her eyes were moist, her breath caught in her throat. "Let's have breakfast first. Then I'll see if I can find the courage to give you my history."

Downstairs Mrs. Breedlove presided over a table laden with fresh fruit and egg casseroles. "The courthouse opens at nine," she told them.

"The courthouse?"

"If you get your marriage license now, you can have the wedding by Thursday."

"Thursday," said Mara, knowing it was all the time they needed in this charmed house where days and nights revolved in other dimensions, where music wafted from metal discs spun in a giant music box and the old radio played cassettes of *Green Hornet* and *Fred Allen*, and where—in Mrs. Breedlove's B&B—time could be mastered. By day they walked along the creek bank and skipped stones across the water. They ate hamburgers at a little joint on the town square. In the evening they found a candlelit café close by and silently pledged their love as an off-key lounge crooner sang "The Anniversary Song." At night they sat chastely on the upstairs porch, searched their hearts, and found homes for their souls.

The day of the wedding, Mrs. Breedlove placed baskets of sweetheart roses around the downstairs parlor. The "Wedding March" announced the beginning of the ceremony, and Mara glided down the stairs in her dress of white satin. They repeated their vows before a preacher they'd met on the sidewalk outside his church. And then Robert moved his suitcase upstairs to her room.

In the twenty years they were married, she never tired of Robert, never ceased to marvel at the blessings that came her way. But when their son was eighteen, Robert suffered a heart attack and drove his car through a barrier and into a deep ravine. Mara was inconsolable, love for her son supplying her only reason for marking the days.

"I need to get away," she told her boy, because she did not want to spend her wedding anniversary weeping in front of him. "Will you be okay for a few days without me?"

"Sure," he said. "Just leave plenty of beer in the fridge and two or three credit cards. Where are you going?"

"I'm not," said Mara. "Changed my mind."

He put his hands on her shoulders and fixed his gaze on her face. He looked so much like his dad, she was simultaneously comforted and distraught. "Mom, go. I'll be fine—no booze, no chicks, no dope. I'm my old man's son, you know."

She did know. She reached up and kissed his forehead, then packed a battered tote. She headed north on I-45 looking for something she couldn't possibly find again. And at Wilmer, she turned west.

There was no fog this time, and August light streaked the hot western skies. But Mrs. Breedlove, a little plumper, a little grayer, welcomed her as before. "You know where your room is. And I'll see you in the morning, child." Suddenly she gathered Mara in her arms and let her sob until she was exhausted.

"I'm so sorry… it's just that…."

"I know, dear. He was a fine man. I know."

Upstairs Mara undressed in the bathroom down the hall and let the stream from the shower head flow until her skin buzzed. She wrapped up in her terry robe and walked to the Sweetheart Room. An open guest book rested on the washstand. Robert's signature on the page startled her. He'd written, "Somehow we found each other in this special place, and the joy of true love. I shall forever be grateful." *Mrs. Breedlove must have thought it would comfort me*, thought Mara.

She stepped from her room and went outside onto the upstairs porch. From the music box downstairs, "The Anniversary Song" echoed eerily, making her heart ache. A soft breeze sighed through the ancient pecan tree and made shadows on the wooden floor.

She heard the door open behind her. "I'm okay, Mrs. Breedlove. I mean, I will be okay."

The air turned cool—too cool for August, and a blue haze settled about the world. "It's me, Mara."

She turned to stare. "Robert!" she gasped.

"Don't be afraid, Mara. Nothing is real."

She touched his arm. It was solid and very real.

"In a little while I will go. We have just this moment."

"But the accident—you've already left me. How—"

"Shh," he said, and smothered her lips in a deep kiss, then swept her into his arms and carried her to the bedroom as easily as if they moved through waters of a warm lake.

Sometime in the dark hours she woke. Stars fell outside the bedroom window. She reached for Robert, but he was gone.

Days later, traveling with her son on their way to enroll him at the university, they detoured on Beltline Road so she could show him the place she'd married his father.

They found the lot with a large pecan tree shading only weeds and a tangle of vines. The phone book had no listing for a B&B. Neither City Hall, nor the Chamber of Commerce had any knowledge of such an establishment. No one had heard of Mrs. Breedlove.

All that was real was her twenty year marriage, her beautiful college-bound son, and another child within her, conceived in a place that never was.

WHAT MIGHT HAVE BEEN

Carolee Joy

"So throw me into the dungeon. I don't like antiques."
Sabrina reluctantly slowed as her grandmother ignored her
complaint and headed for the door of the antique shop.
"Granny, can't we please have lunch on the way back to
Austin instead?"

"They have a tea room." Grandmother grinned
mischievously over her shoulder. "And my guess would be
that whatever they serve will be much better than the slop at
the Burger Boy down the highway."

"I hate small towns," Sabrina muttered as she followed
her inside. She didn't really, but Walker, her fiancé,
absolutely refused to even consider living more than a short
drive away from a major airport.

The bell on the door chimed to announce their presence,
but the shop appeared empty.

"Doesn't it smell yummy?" Granny inhaled dramatically.

Sabrina sneezed. "Delicious. Just like a dust bowl."

"Oh, it does not. Incense, baked ham, and history, that's
what it smells like. You'd do well to have a better
appreciation of times gone by." Grandmother began the

methodical perusal she always employed in antique stores: look at everything. Slowly. More than once. "Doesn't it make you think of when you and your mother would come visit me on a Sunday afternoon?"

She hoped it wouldn't. Now there was a sure way to cement the bad mood she felt herself falling into, especially since she'd be seeing Mother and the rest of the family at the family reunion that weekend. Somehow Granny had aligned the family in her anti-Walker campaign, but it didn't matter. Tonight Sabrina would tell him she had decided to accept his proposal. "Must we continue this stroll down antiquity lane? I'm meeting Walker for dinner."

Granny's hands lingered on a wedding ring quilt. "So you're really going to marry your *cute* guy."

"Yes, Granny." Sabrina held in a huff of impatience. Gran had never liked Walker, but money and looks didn't make a person evil, did it?

"He didn't buy you a big enough diamond." Granny had already expressed her opinion on the quarter carat diamond ring Walker had purchased.

"That sounds so mercenary." Sabrina straightened a stray curl on a porcelain doll sitting on a small dresser. Besides, she didn't care what kind of ring she had, the important thing was the feelings it represented. She ignored the little voice that refused to let her relinquish her doubts. She was very fond of Walker. She—loved him, didn't she?

"Never trust a man who's stingy with his money, dear. Later, he'll be just as mean-spirited with his love."

Despite her efforts to ignore the barb, Gran's words unsettled her and made her wonder if she was making the right decision to marry Walker Bennington. True, he didn't spend as much time with her as she would like, but building up a successful business took a lot of time and effort. He was working for their future, he liked to say.

Gran sighed. "I wish you would have let me introduce you to Violet's son."

She had always been more than a little intrigued about Violet's mysterious grandson but had never wanted to give her meddling grandmother that kind of ammunition. She assumed a nonchalant tone. "Too late now. Or it will be once I tell Walker my decision."

Gran's expression brightened. "So you haven't told him yet."

"No, that's why I have to be back to Austin in time for dinner." Sabrina trailed along as Gran stopped in front of a display of antique clothes.

"Oh, my. Just look at these hats. Aren't they fabulous?" Granny picked up a wide brimmed bonnet trimmed with fading flowers and ribbons. "I bet this dusty rose was once a vibrant red." She placed it on her head and preened before the wavy mirror on a scarred dresser. "How do I look?"

"Elegant." Sabrina gave her an affectionate smile, then chose a hat in green satin and velvet and carefully put it on. "How about me?"

"It brings out the color of your eyes." The deep voice behind them made Sabrina jump guiltily.

They probably weren't supposed to actually wear the bonnets. She started to remove it and turned to find a man moving towards them. Tall, with honey blonde hair slightly shaggy as if it had been some time since he'd remembered to get a haircut, he smiled. Her hand hesitated on the brim.

"No, no, don't take it off." The man moved swiftly through the aisle crowded with small end tables, vases, and ornately trimmed mirrors until he stood beside her. "But the ribbon should be tied like this." His fingers hovered over hers.

Warmth shot up her arm and quickly spread through her as he expertly retied the sash and adjusted the bow to frame the side of her face.

"Like that." He stepped back and winked at Granny. "Hello, Rachel. How are you?"

"Don't you just love that Scarlet O'Hara look," Granny

murmured, her eyes alight with appreciation. "I'm going to buy it for you."

"Oh, no, Granny. What on earth would I do with a hat like this?" Sabrina reached up to untie the sash but hesitated when the man gave her a smile that paralyzed her breathing.

Granny's eyes continued to sparkle. "You could keep it as a souvenir of the afternoon. I'm going to the car to get my pocketbook."

Before Sabrina could protest again, Granny had scurried off through a maze of antique chairs and umbrella stands and disappeared out the door.

"She's just as feisty as ever." The man smiled and shook his head. "And you must be Sabrina."

"Excuse me?" Sabrina was immediately drawn by the warmth in his eyes. "How do you know who I am?"

"I'm Will Talbert." He extended his hand.

Sabrina let her fingers be swallowed up in his slightly callused palm. She felt her jaw drop. "You're Violet's—"

"Grandson. And if you smell something fishy, it's not from the tea room. We've been set up by a pair of wonderful, conniving, grandmothers."

"Oh." She felt heat rise in her face again. How embarrassing! And how utterly unnecessary and, and ridiculous! She was going to marry Walker, and it didn't matter who Granny threw in her path, she'd make up her own mind! She already *had* made up her mind.

"Look, Will—" she stopped, not certain what to say.

"Hey, I don't like this any more than you do. Not," he rushed on, apparently noting her quick intake of breath, "that I don't think you are a beautiful lady and obviously very caring and intelligent. I just don't need to be foisted on someone whose attentions are already taken."

She relaxed despite the tiny frisson of disappointment that took her by surprise. So he didn't want to be manipulated either. *That was good.* She thought. "They mean well, I guess."

He smiled, making little friendly crinkles around his intense blue eyes. "Yeah, they do. So while Rachel hides out and waits, why don't you try on this other creation? If you're going to get stuck with one, it might as well be the one with the magic." He picked up the hat Gran had admired earlier.

Sabrina untied the sash on her bonnet, removed it, and set it aside. "Magic, you say? What does it do?"

Will placed the hat on her head and adjusted the fading roses. Then, his hands warm on her shoulders, he guided her before the cloudy mirror. "You tell me."

Sabrina glanced over her shoulder at him. His face was set and very serious. She looked away and caught his gaze in the mirror, then the room faded away into a haze of twilight grays and blacks. The present spun away into a past not her own.

Rachel was never going to speak to Hubert Talbert again! Never! Her chest ached as if it would explode with unshed tears and anger. She knew this was the right decision, but her heart refused to accept it.

Hubert did, however. All too easily. As if her anger meant nothing to him. As if he had the right to behave recklessly, and she was supposed to go right along with it. Well, that just proved how shallow his love was.

Rachel tore off the wide-brimmed hat and tossed it onto the bed. Imagine him spending the money they'd been saving, scrimping along and sacrificing so that they could put a down payment on a house only to have him throw the whole thing away on that miserable little mercantile. And for what! No way was this little town ever going to be able to support a store like that.

Hubert might think his own shop would provide a living for the family they both wanted, but Rachel knew better. Just pie in the sky, she'd told him.

Oh, he'd tried to sweet talk her into believing old Mr. Manning's offer to sell the business to Hubert was a good deal, a dream come true. All she saw were years of helping him run the store, managing a household, and raising children. By the time she was thirty, she'd be an old woman, worn out with work and worry.

She flopped down on the bed, crushing the hat beneath her. She pulled it out and tried to smooth the flattened red roses adorning the brim. Hubert had given her the hat for Valentine's Day, even though buying it went contrary to their careful plan of watching every penny until the day when they would be wed, just three months away.

It didn't matter now. No way was she going to weave her future with someone as irresponsible as Hubert Talbert.

As if watching years roll by in a slow motion video, Sabrina saw her grandmother's heartache when Hubert refused to come after her and try to make amends. She watched as Granny, face as solemn as if she were at a funeral, descended the staircase of her father's house to take the arm of the man she married instead, a solid, financially secure banker named Randolf Pitts. Sabrina's grandfather.

Granny's life rolled by, safe, secure, and secretly miserable as she struggled to raise her family with only her love for her children and a polite respect for her husband to sustain her. Hubert's wife, Violet, became Granny's best friend. The little shop evolved into one of the area's most respected sources for antiques, and while it probably earned only a modest living, Granny had always talked about how happy the Talbert family seemed.

Sabrina's heart ached as she saw how her grandmother struggled to hide her undying love for Hubert. They each raised their own families, until he left his wife a widow when his heart failed him at age fifty.

Sabrina wondered if it had been as difficult for him and suspected that it had. Had he ultimately died from a broken heart?

From a long way off, Will's voice drifted through her

consciousness. "He never stopped loving her. Seeing Rachel with my grandmother made him so sad."

Granny's words drifted to her over the confused swirl of place and time she found herself in. "Don't marry a man just because it seems like the comfortable thing to do. Listen to your heart."

Sabrina shook off a wave of dizziness, closed her eyes and felt herself fall.

Sometime later, she awoke to find herself stretched out on an antique poster bed. One of Will's strong hands enfolded hers, while he dabbed a cold cloth to her face with the other.

"Are you okay?"

When she tried to rise, he pressed her shoulder and urged her to stay still. She gave him a weak smile. "I think so."

Granny leaned over her and clucked softly. "Gave us quite a scare, you did. Luckily, Will was here to keep you from hitting your head when you swooned."

She rose to her elbow. "What are you talking about? It was that hat. One minute I was looking in the mirror, the next I was watching your life parade by me."

"Must have been some dream." Will slid an arm behind her shoulders and helped her sit on the edge of the bed.

"It wasn't a dream. You were talking to me. Did you see it too?"

He shook his head, but something in his gaze tugged at her, made it impossible for her to look away. He has his grandfather's eyes, she remembered Granny saying. Now at last she understood why that had mattered so much to her grandmother.

He smiled. "I'd like to hear all about it. If you're free for dinner tonight."

"I'm supposed to be in Austin this evening."

Again, Will shook his head. "I wouldn't advise making the drive. Granny Rachel has already booked you into a B&B. You can head home in the morning."

Granny straightened and gave them a brilliant smile.
"That's settled, then. I'm going to dinner at the B&B. You
young folks have a lovely time. Oh! I almost forgot." She
brandished Sabrina's cell phone and handed it to her.
"Walker called. He said he had to fly to Phoenix for the
weekend, that you two could talk when he returns. Maybe
you'll have a different answer for him by then." She waved,
then wove her way through the store and out the door.

Sabrina stood and rubbed her temples with her fingers. So
Walker had left again. After assuring her that nothing was
more important to him than meeting with her, he had gone
chasing another business deal.

She didn't care. Like a blast of cold air, reality slapped
away the lukewarm feelings she'd been trying to convince
herself were the real deal. How could she expect to make a
marriage work with a man who never had time for her before
they were even married?

"Sabrina." Will stuffed his hands in the pockets of his
jeans and stared at the floor. "I have a confession to make."

"What?" Heart pounding, she waited for him to continue.

"I put your grandmother up to bringing you here today."

"You? Why?" She reached out and touched his arm. The
warmth of his skin seeped through his tee shirt and into her
palm, made her wonder what it would feel like to be
wrapped in his strong arms.

"I've wanted to meet you for ages. Somehow, I just felt
like we would have a lot in common. Must be from all the
stories I heard about Rachel, you, and your family whenever
I visited Gramps."

Funny, she'd felt the same way, but some sort of silly
stubbornness had always made her balk whenever Granny
had suggested bringing her to meet Violet and Hubert's
grandson. Too bad she'd wasted all this time when she could
have spent it getting to know him better.

"Now you *have* met me." She smiled, encouraged when
he lifted his gaze and grinned. "Was it worth the wait?"

Slowly his hands came up to cradle her face. Then his mouth descended to hers in a soft, gentle kiss that filled her with yearning and promise.

"Oh, yeah," he said slowly. "Definitely worth the wait."

Feeling suddenly shy, Sabrina moved away and touched the hat lying on the bed. The youthful image of her grandmother rushed back at her. Now she knew why the rose was so crumpled. She carefully straightened the curling petals. The look of hopefulness in Granny's face when she saw her with Will filled her mind. Would it happen again if she put the hat back on? Did it matter? She now knew clearly what she was meant to do. Fate was offering her and Will the chance their grandparents had lost. A chance to find true love and a lifetime of happiness.

She picked the hat up, but before she could raise it to her head, it crumpled into powdery dust.

"Oh, Will! I'm so sorry." She glanced at her hands. How could that have happened?

Will just smiled and took her hand. "It's okay, Sabrina. It wasn't really a magic hat."

Oh, yes it was, she wanted to say, but smiled at him instead as he led her from the shop.

Feeling cherished by the warmth of his smile in a way she never had before, she let his pace lull her into a feeling of rightness and anticipation. "I just realized something."

"What's that?" He tucked her hand in the crook of his arm as they walked slowly down the cobblestones towards a small café at the end of the quiet street.

She rested her head against his shoulder and watched the evening star wink a promise. "When you're offered a chance to follow your heart, you should take it. That way you'll never have to wonder about what might have been."

MOON DANCE

Betsy Norman

For the fourth night in a row, Gareth dreamed of the Selkie maiden. She slipped from her sealskin in a mesmerizing moon dance on the craggy shoreline below the lighthouse. He watched, entranced by the ritual, his body aching for an invitation to join her.

In his dreams, he woke to her wailing call that crashed over the tide. His limbs, heavy and slumber-drugged, moved of their own accord to the window. Once there, he swayed in time to her wraithlike choreography, hypnotized, only to wake alone. Alone, always alone, he mourned.

Legends passed down for generations told of the Selkie. She was bound as bride to the human who captured her sealskin pelt and hid it successfully from her seeking eyes. A cruelty, in his opinion. One couldn't imprison love no matter how desperately one desired it. Love came of free will, not coercion.

Still, he coveted the creature who visited his dreams, questioning her presence. Was she real? Or merely a conjured lover to temper his forlorn heart.

On the fifth night he devised a plan. He would feign sleep

and wait. Gareth forced himself to stay alert and not let her bewitching spell immobilize him.

Tonight he would dance beneath the full moon with her.

The Selkie's keening cry rose along the shore, summoning him at midnight. Gareth sprinted down the beach, sand splaying at his eagerness. She waited for him in the briny mist, arms outstretched in welcome as if she knew he would come. He swirled her about like a tidal whirlpool, her arms held fast about his shoulders.

She had the eyes of the sea, restless and froth, green in shade and blue in moonlight. Black hair hung in ropes down her back, lashing about his wrists.

"Dance with me, Selkie. Show me the way."

Her limbs wound about him, drawing Gareth into the ebb and flow of the waves. Their bodies danced as the surf's reflection became an elliptical stage.

No longer mute in the suspended animation of dreams, he murmured his passion against the shell of her ear.

"Tell me your name. Why do you come? Love me... love me...."

She replied with the song of the ocean, ageless wisdom and immeasurable depth. A soulful dirge of vast loneliness.

Gareth knew her isolation. Recognized it. "Please, stay."

But she was a wild thing, uninitiated to the shackles of humanity. Her freedom lay within the glistening pelt upon the rocks. He could take it, he knew. Gareth stood, his hands poised to snatch the sealskin. By claiming her as his bride, he would force her to stay.

His conscience pricked him. She'd come to him willingly. After his betrayal, she'd never do so again. Only as his captive. He wanted her love but couldn't bring himself to steal it.

Clouds drew like a curtain across the stars. The Selkie shook her head in fear, quickly donning the pelt to escape his contemplated deed. The tide receded, and she along with it. The black grief of her seal's eyes haunted him. He knew he'd destroyed her trust even though he hadn't acted on his selfish desires.

"Come back… come back…."

Gareth's entreaty for the Selkie's return drowned in the churning waters.

His heartache glowed brighter than the relentless lighthouse torch. He felt the burning void of his soul alone could navigate seafarers around the treacherous cove. Weeks passed, each night devoid of the Selkie maiden's call. Gareth thrashed upon his spartan pillow in anguish. The blank staring eye of the full moon rose again. Memories of how he'd danced beneath the last one with the Selkie maiden taunted him.

Gareth cursed it and shook his fist. An all-encompassing rage forced him to confront the mute disk in the sky. On the beach, he paced and demanded retribution. Injustice! He had not acted on his moment's consideration of selfish love but desired her come to him freely. He bid her accept his love and return it in kind.

"I am not guilty of this crime!"

An eerie melody rode the current. Soft at first, then gradually increasing with each influx of the tide. Gareth's tirade halted. His ears strained to catch the notes. A glint of moonlit motion bobbed along the surface. He dashed back and forth along the wet sand tracking the movement.

The lithe seal ascended from the sea, her pelt sliding downward to reveal the Selkie maiden. Gareth's breath lurched at her ethereal beauty. The desire to run to her tore at him. He craved her touch, her song, to make him whole.

"Punish me no longer, Selkie. Your freedom costs me my heart."

She came to Gareth, draping her pelt like a regal cloak before him on the sand. Taking his hand, they knelt. A loving sea-song filled his mind and dictated his pulse to its rhythm. Her salty kiss forgave him and begged forgiveness in kind.

With the full moon as witness, Gareth and the Selkie pledged their vows to one another.

He brought her back to his lighthouse, and the Selkie hung her pelt openly on a peg for the night. At dawn, Gareth stroked the sleek coat in farewell as she swam back out to sea. Just as she had trusted him, he knew in turn her song would beckon him again.

On the next rise of the moon.

BY THE LIGHT
OF THE SILVERY MOON

Tami D. Cowden

Sylvia rested her forehead against the coolness of the window as she gazed out at the seemingly endless night. The stars twinkled through her reflection, mocking her own melancholy mood.

What had seemed like the dream assignment, the culmination of all her professional aspirations, was rapidly becoming her worst nightmare.

All because of him.

She finally had the opportunity to participate in crucial scientific experiments, but instead, she found herself focusing on her partner. If only he were not here, she would be able to concentrate on her job. Instead, she concentrated far too much on Roger.

The object of her musings sat less than ten feet away, busily engaged in front of the computer monitor. His rapid fire clicking on the keyboard drew her attention.

Glancing at his profile, she sucked in a breath at the heat that immediately formed in the pit of her stomach. Just the sight of him caused that reaction in her every time. Her temperature fluctuations would probably drive a doctor to drink.

He was a vision of a man with all the right stuff. A lock of his rich brown hair tumbled down his brow. A faint hint of stubble darkened his chin, and mahogany eyes danced in the pale glow given off by the monitor.

As she watched, he let out a deep breath and pushed his chair back.

"Finished!" He laughed and shook his head. "I didn't think I'd ever get those calculations done. I am no mathematical whiz like you." Standing, he stretched, his muscles straining the fabric across his shoulders.

Sylvia tensed, imagining the feel of that taut physique beneath her exploring hands.

His fingers massaged the back of his neck, and she wished it were her neck, her skin, feeling his touch. "I don't know how much more I can take of this," she muttered.

"Yeah, these late nights are getting a little rough." His eyes met hers for a moment, and then he glanced away. "Hey, I know what we both need! A brisk walk!"

A few steps brought him next to her by the wide window. "Admiring those stars, eh? They take my breath away every time I see them."

"Yeah, I know the feeling." She inhaled his crisp, clean scent, and struggled to keep from taking deep heady gulps.

"It's gorgeous out there." Waggling his eyebrows, he grinned down at her. "Whaddyasay? Wanna take a walk by the light of the silvery moon?"

How like him. Romantic suggestions accompanied by happy "we're just friends" smiles were his specialty.

For another six months, she and he would be alone here together, observing, studying, and reporting back their findings. And somehow, she didn't think the bosses wanted her observations of the effects of unrequited love on a scientist's ability to do her job. That kind of data was a little too personal.

But she really could not resist a moonlight walk with him by her side.

"Sure, why not?" She forced the eagerness out of her voice as she answered. She couldn't bear it if he ever found out about how much he attracted her. It would surely strain their camaraderie if he knew he starred in her wildest fantasies.

Working with him after that would be impossible.

Almost as impossible as not working with him.

They pulled on their outer gear silently, then went outside. Without speaking, they both headed for a rocky ledge that had become a favorite spot for meditation and observation. Stillness enveloped them as they trekked across the unforgiving landscape.

It had been more than six weeks since Sylvia had first seen it, but she could still barely believe the harsh yet dramatic scene. The profiles of outcroppings were silhouetted against the deep blue-black of the universe that surrounded them. The moon glowed brightly, its craggy surface fully revealed in all its beauty.

"You never get used to it, do you?" Roger spoke the words with reverence.

"It's incredibly romantic." Damn! The words left her mouth before she could stop them. Now he'd think she was a total sap.

"Yes, it is."

Nervously, she glanced his way, fearing she'd see a mocking smirk pasted on his face. Instead she saw a trace of a smile, matched with a tender look.

Or was that just wishful thinking?

She attempted to recover. Pulling her best school teacher's tone out of her hat, she intoned, "You know, the moon has inspired a large number of romantic poems and stories. Songs, too. It is really quite interesting, the way the moon has contributed to cult—" she broke off as Roger suddenly took her gloved hand in both of his.

"Sylvia, I don't think I can hold this in any longer. Especially since we are going to be working here together for months." He stopped. "I've, well, I don't know how to say this. These past weeks, working here, with you... the two of us, together." He broke off, clearly searching for words.

Hope soared within her.

Roger started again. "I know we're alone here, and you don't need to worry. I've tried to keep things on a professional plane, but I can't ignore what I feel any longer. If you don't have feelings for me, I won't be a pest, but—"

This time, she stopped him, giving him a grin wider than any he'd ever given her.

Apparently her smile gave him the courage he needed. "Sylvia, I want us to be more than lab partners. I want us to be life partners, too."

Looking into his eyes in blue-gray light, she saw her own love warmly reflected back. She moved into his embrace. For a long moment, they stood together, basking in the ethereal glow of the moon on which they stood. Finally, they turned back toward the station, walking hand in hand.

Perhaps NASA would be interested in some personal data, after all.

BELIEVE

Susan D. Brooks

"Either this is magic or you are one lucky woman."

"What do you mean?" Tessa McCormick looked up. Marie, her sales clerk, stood in the doorway between the office and the gift shop.

"Wait until you see what Joe found." Marie stepped aside as Tessa's other clerk stepped into the room, a cardboard box cradled against his barrel chest. Affection washed over her as she smiled at the older man. Since walking into her store four years ago looking for a part time job, he'd become an important part of her life as surrogate father and close friend. His eyes sparkled as he set the package down and gestured for her to look inside.

"What is it, Joe? Did you win the lottery and buy all the almond cookies at the bakery?" She started to laugh, then noticed the intense excitement in his eyes.

"Oh, Joe, please tell me you found it," she said, reaching for the bag with eager hands.

He grinned and waited for her reaction.

Tessa peeked inside. Wrapped in an original display box and cushioned with Styrofoam packing peanuts, lay the one porcelain gift item she hadn't been able to locate in the last three weeks. Told by the manufacturer that the item had been discontinued, she'd contacted other stores, surfed the Internet, and called everyone in her Rolodex. Nothing. And now Joe had found one.

Tessa gingerly lifted the figurine out. Requested by a woman as a gift for her sick son, the musical porcelain piece was of a Golden Retriever holding a Frisbee in his mouth. Tessa turned the key on the bottom and the first notes of "We Are the Champions" floated into the room.

A lump formed in her throat. The woman, a long-time customer, told Tessa that her youngest son was undergoing chemotherapy for leukemia. For the last four years, he and his Golden Retriever placed first in the state Frisbee championships. His mother wanted him to have this as a reminder of what he had to look forward to when the treatments were done.

"Oh Joe," she sighed. "You've worked another miracle."

"Nah, just weaving a little magic," he said, but his lined face glowed with satisfaction. "I'll go open the register."

Marie shook her head, a look of wonder on her face. "You know, good things always happen when he's around."

"I know." Tessa chuckled. "Sometimes I feel like he's my good luck charm."

"Or a wizard of some sort." Marie took a key from the rack. "We ready to open?"

"All set." Tessa grinned. "Let the shopping masses in."

Marie laughed and headed into the showroom to unlock the front door. Tessa tried to turn her attention back to her accounts payable invoices, but she kept thinking about Joe.

Good things always did happen when Joe was around, that was true. Tessa's unreliable old car would always start one more time if he turned the ignition key. When she wanted to open her own shop, Joe put her in touch with a friend of his who just happened to have the perfect place at the perfect price. And, when they all worked late doing inventory, the numbers always reconciled and the pizza never arrived cold.

"Tessa, Trent somebody is out here to see you." Marie reappeared in the doorway, grinned, and wiggled her eyebrows. "He's good looking. Put on some lipstick."

"Trent somebody?" Tessa ignored the oft-repeated makeup advice and looked at her calendar. She didn't recognize the name and had no appointments scheduled. "Is he a sales rep? Do you know what company he's with?"

"No. Sorry." Marie snapped her gum. She tipped her head to one side. "But he's not wearing a wedding ring."

"Well, thanks for that bit of helpful information." Tessa shook her head in mock despair. Marie could sell an extension ladder to an acrophobic, but her office skills, especially when combined with an intent to play Cupid, left a lot to be desired.

Tessa glanced at her watch, stood, and reached for her cardigan sweater.

"You won't need that." Marie gestured to the sweater. "Why do you want to hide that pretty outfit?"

"I'm not hiding anything. I get chilled easily."

"Hmmm." Marie pursed her lips and tilted her head. "Don't forget the lipstick." She winked and returned to the showroom.

Tessa chuckled. When would her friend stop trying to play Cupid? Happily married with four sons, Marie believed everyone should experience the bliss of family life.

"Family makes life worth living," she chirped time and again. And honestly, Tessa couldn't agree more, but finding a mate wasn't that simple.

Heck, if I thought a man would be interested, I'd give her free reign to find someone for me. She shook her head. *But I'm not the type of woman that attracts men.*

Since junior high Tessa had struggled to overcome shyness, to tame her curly elbow-length hair, and gain back the self-confidence she lost when her height shot up to five feet, ten inches. Although she finally conquered the recalcitrant tresses and discovered many guys who liked tall women, her bashfulness still kept her from being able to connect with members of the opposite sex.

But I have friends, relatives, and a fun job. And that is so much more than many people have.

Tessa lifted her chin, smoothed her hair, and walked out into the store. She caught a glimpse of her haughty posture in a mirrored display case and almost laughed.

Relax, Tessa. You have nothing to prove. Find out what he wants, then make a fresh pot of coffee and post yesterday's sales numbers.

Beside the check out counter stood a tall dark-haired man, his back to the room. She instinctively appreciated the perfect fit of his jacket across broad shoulders and the fashionable cut of the trousers on long legs.

Nice.

He turned, his gaze locking with hers. She noted blue eyes over classic facial features, a dimple, and an amazing smile.

He wasn't one of her vendors. She wouldn't have forgotten him.

And she didn't recognize him as one of her father's acquaintances. He wouldn't have let her forget him.

So, why was he here? She made herself look him in the eye as she felt the most common words fly out of her head.

"Lee Trenton with Treewalk Village," he said, crossing the few feet with his right hand extended.

"Lee Trenton?" She shook his hand and threw an annoyed look at Marie who shrugged, eyes wide.

"Tessa McCormick," she said. "I'm glad to meet you. Lilly Trenton's always been the one to visit my store."

"Lilly is my mother. She's recovering from an illness so I'll be taking her place."

"I'm sorry to hear that," Tessa said, then hastily added, "I mean I'm sorry to hear Lilly's been sick."

"She'll be fine with a little less responsibility on her plate." Lee nodded solemnly as his eyes twinkled. He glanced around the shop. "You've got a nice store. Lots of light. Lots of room."

"Thanks. I'm pleased with how it's turning out."

"You say that like it isn't finished." He tilted his head in question.

Delighted with his thoughtful observation, she found herself opening up. "The shop won't ever be finished, not in the formal sense of the word. I think customers like to make discoveries so, I move things around and introduce new products every month. They keep coming back to see the latest pieces."

He looked around as four ladies entered the shop. Marie greeted them by name and an exuberant conversation ensued.

Tessa lowered her voice and said, "They are some of my more loyal customers. It's a rare week when they don't stop in and even more rare when they don't buy something."

Marie came from behind the cash register and led the group to a display of ceramic village accessory pieces.

Lee stared after them, paying close attention to what items caught their attention. Tessa pretended to do the same, but she kept stealing glances at him out of the corner of her eye. He seemed so relaxed and comfortable that he put her at ease.

Maybe a touch of lip-gloss wouldn't have hurt. She caught herself and winced. Agitated with her train of thought, she shifted her feet, causing her shoulder to bump a display of wind chimes. Loud, merry notes rang throughout the store. Everyone turned to look at Tessa. Marie's mouth curled into a knowing smile.

"I'm sorry," she stammered, catching the tubes to silence them. "I'm so clumsy…."

With a smile, Lee helped her still the ringing chimes. When quiet was restored, he turned to her. "Have you got a few minutes? I have something I'd like to talk to you about."

"Certainly." Tessa, glad to have the attention diverted, gestured toward the back of the store.

She led the way, aware of his footsteps behind her. Was her blouse tucked in? Was her hair in place? Was he even looking?

Good grief, Tessa. She felt a blush rise on her cheeks. "Please, make yourself comfortable." She waved him into a leather wing back chair. "There's tea if you'd like." She sat in a chair across from him and plucked at the arm.

"No, thank you." He laid his briefcase across his thighs and snapped open the latches. "Even though my mother won't be involved with the retail side of the business, she will continue to design new pieces." He lifted the attaché's cover and rummaged through the items inside. After a few moments, he gave her a sheepish glance. "I have to admit, this all happened so fast, I'm a little unorganized. Please bear with me."

Tessa smiled and shrugged one shoulder. She tried to recall what Mrs. Trenton told her about her only son, but remembered little except that he'd started his own company in Florida several years ago.

"There they are." Lee pulled out a brochure. "I studied our sales records before coming here today. Our pieces sell very well in your store. In fact, you've had top sales figures for us the past six years. We're very happy with your success."

"Your designs are easy to sell." Tessa tapped an uncompleted Treewalk order form. "They're very popular. No one does interior and exterior detail like Treewalk."

"My mom will be delighted to hear that." His brows drew together. "Unfortunately, Treewalk isn't catching on anywhere but here."

"That's surprising." Tessa leaned back in her chair, folding her hands on her lap. A curious little knot formed in her stomach as she looked across the desk at Lee. Oh, yes, he had handsome features, but she detected no sign of the arrogance that she often associated with classic good looks. His tanned face and trim, athletic body suggested a life of tennis and golf, not a desk-bound career.

"We're surprised at the poor sales, too, and that's why I wanted to talk to you." He handed her the pamphlet. "This is our new line. It's a departure from what we've been doing. You'll see that we've added a lot of moving parts and expanded the number of pieces available. We plan to add to the collection every quarter with special editions for the Christmas season."

Her gaze fell on the literature he'd given her. The photos on the slick paper electrified her.

Treewalk had recreated the town of Mystic, Connecticut, down to the tiniest detail including the harbor with its big whaling boats and tiny dories. Before she could read the information, Lee spoke again.

"On behalf of Treewalk, I'd like to ask a favor of you."

"Yes?" She peeked inside the brochure. They created a flourmill with a waterwheel that turned? Wow. And a blacksmith shop with smoke coming from the chimney.

"We'd like to introduce the Mystic series here in your store." He sat up on the edge of his chair. "We'd arrange a catered party with the media, your customers and staff, my family and business associates. We would, of course, depend on your creative input to make it a success."

"Here?" Tessa's mouth fell open. A surge of excitement shot through her. *What a great opportunity.* "Wonderful. When?"

"You'll do it? Great." He looked down at the papers. "We'd like the first weekend in November. That would give Christmas customers plenty of time to view the pieces."

She glanced at her annual wall calendar. Eight weeks away. "Sure. No problem."

They discussed various ways to display the Treewalk ceramic villages for a few minutes, then Lee stood. "I'll be in touch with more details in a week or so."

Tessa walked with him to the front door where he offered his hand.

"Thank you for your time," he said in a low voice, his

gaze meeting hers. He held her hand a fraction of a second too long then smiled when he realized it and let go.

"I'll be in touch," he repeated.

Tessa watched him climb into a red sport utility vehicle.

"He's not just good looking, he's gorgeous." Marie came to stand beside her. "Is he nice?"

"Oh, very." Tessa heard the dreamy inflection in her own voice and glanced at her friend. "He's Lilly's son. Wait till you hear what they want us to do."

"Did he ask you out?"

"Marie." Tessa groaned.

"Did you ask him out?"

"I'm not in the habit of asking salesmen out on dates."

"Hmmm." Marie's gaze followed the truck as it pulled onto the main road. "Maybe you should step outside that comfort zone of yours once in a while."

Tessa said nothing as she returned to her office, but deep inside she was a teeny, tiny bit disappointed that Lee hadn't shown any interest in her as anything more than a customer. She thought of his lingering handshake. Or had he?

A few weeks later, Marie cut through the packing tape on a box of Treewalk Mystic Village accessories and unwrapped several figurines. As she studied one closely, she exclaimed, "God almighty, Tessa, look at this." She held up a man dressed in a boat captain's garb. "It's Lee."

Tessa looked closer. Blue eyes. Dimple. Wide shoulders. Long legs. The spitting image of Lee Trenton.

"Spooky, huh?" Marie gingerly handed him to Tessa.

"No. His mother is the designer," Tessa explained. "It makes sense she'd create one in the likeness of her son."

"Well, now he's all yours." Marie laughed out loud as she reached for more pieces to unpack.

"Has he asked you for a date yet?" Joe set another box on the table and leaned on it, watching Tessa.

"No. He's shown no interest in me." To hide her

disappointment, Tessa began to position the new ceramic pieces at a quick pace, not taking time to admire each as she usually did.

"Not true, not true at all." Joe gave her a thoughtful look. "And that reminds me, you never did give me your word not to interfere."

"Tessa, I will never do anything to embarrass you or make you unhappy." He gave her an earnest look. "You know that."

"Yes, you wiley old fox, I do know that, and you still haven't given me your promise."

Joe straightened and looked toward the front door as customers entered the shop. "I promise to let magic do all the work."

Tessa stared after him, not certain she'd gotten the answer she wanted. Tessa sighed. Lee. She had never spent so much time thinking about one man in her life. He popped into her head at the oddest moments and with no apparent provocation. Then, she couldn't get him out again until she immersed herself in a mentally demanding project.

As if on cue, the front door swung open and in he strode with a box under one arm. He nodded to Marie who then tipped her head toward Tessa. Lee glanced around, grinning wide when he spotted her. He crossed the shop and stood next to her.

"I brought a few more of the accessory pieces," he said, setting the box down on a table. "I'm a little worried we won't get everything ready on time."

"We'll be ready."

"The presentation is crucial," he told her. "Since Mystic's only an hour's drive from here, a lot of your customers will be familiar with how the streets and buildings really look."

"Last week I shot three rolls of twenty-four shots." Tessa held up a fistful of photographs. "We have pictures of every inch of water front, every street, every historic building. Even the lampposts."

"I never even thought of that." He shook his head in wonder. "Great idea."

She basked in his praise and almost suggested talking further over dinner, but stopped, stymied by her old inhibitions.

Often during the days that followed, she'd look up and catch Lee looking her way. He'd smile, sending tingles up her spine.

"Honey, he's interested," whispered Marie. "I've seen the way he looks at you. Ask him out."

"Oh no. I couldn't." Heat suffused Tessa's face. But his actions did hint at something. An attraction?

But he's been coming here for eight weeks now, she reminded herself. *And he hasn't asked me out which proves I was imagining things.*

Of course, Lee's interests didn't mesh with hers. In their casual conversations he'd mentioned water skiing, boating, and camping. Tessa had never learned to swim and the only tent she'd ever been in was at her cousin's backyard wedding. She preferred lunches at small cafés, browsing through used bookstores, and observing the heavens through her telescope.

On Friday evening, after the store closed, caterers arrived with tables for food and drinks at the same time a videotaping company showed up to decide where to put their cameras.

Lee stood next to the replicated harbor, studying the layout. He turned to smile at her as she approached. "This looks so realistic."

"I have the boats propped on small plastic stands," Tessa said, moving to his side. "They're not really floating in the water, they just look that way. I put you on the deck of the whaling ship."

"Hey, I like that." He nodded his approval.

Pleased, but unnerved by his scrutiny, she moved a mariner's church an unnecessary half inch to the left. She glanced at him out of the corner of her eye and thought she detected a flash of merriment in his eyes.

"There's still more work to be done?" He turned back to the layout.

"Not more than an hour's work. The lights aren't working along that one street." Tessa pointed to a road running along the back edge of the table. "I can't get electricity to them. One of the circuits might be tripped."

Lee worked by her side for over an hour, checking the circuit breakers, running extension cords, and finally getting every light to work.

Sighing with relief, Tessa leaned against the wall behind her. On the opposite side of the room, tables with white linen tablecloths stood ready for trays of food and drink. Tripods rested in the far corner, an X marked on the floor with masking tape where the main video camera would be placed tomorrow morning. Except for Lee, herself, and Joe, who was finishing up the day's deposit, the store was empty.

"Where'd everyone go?" Tessa looked at her watch. "Holy cow, it's after midnight."

"How time flies, huh?" Lee laughed.

"You were having fun?" Joe's eyes were wide as he looked from Lee to Tessa.

"Yeah," Lee said at the same time as Tessa. They looked at each other. Her heart fluttered.

"I'll drop today's deposit at the bank," Joe said, his words sounding far away. "See you tomorrow."

As the door shut behind him, the store grew quieter. Wanting Lee to stay, Tessa scrambled for something to say.

"What did you do before you came back to work for your family?" She saw the surprise in his eyes at the question and wanted to fade out of sight, but he settled into a nearby chair and gestured for her to sit across from him.

"I design custom sailboats," he said. "I also teach people

how to sail them."

"Oh, how interesting." *That's how he got his tan,* she thought, *although it's faded some.* "Did you build them around here?"

"No, in Florida."

"I'll bet you miss that warm weather now that winter's coming." The minute she said that, Tessa wanted to sink through the floor. *It's the same sort of thing I say to my customers when I'm making small talk. He'll think I'm boring.*

"Actually, I missed winter when I lived there." He shrugged. "Every place has its charm."

A soft hum surrounded Tessa. Thinking something was wrong with the rigged electrical wiring, she jumped up and ran to the display table, Lee right behind her. She reached for the mill pump.

"I'll check the connection in the back." Lee's voice grew faint as the floor shifted beneath her feet. An odd rushing noise filled her ears. Tessa reached for the power switch, but found her arms suddenly too short. With a whoosh, the room began to move, rushing toward her in a tunnel with moving walls. The only comparison her panicked mind could make was like going into lightspeed in one of those space movies. She caught the edge of the table and held on as the wood floor withdrew and the ceiling receded into the distance. The whole experience lasted just a few seconds, then she found herself sitting in a place that looked familiar, but unreal.

Afraid to move, she shifted her eyes around, trying to get a perspective on what happened. Where was Lee?

She stood on wobbly legs, fear freezing her feet in place. For a few seconds she waited to see if something else would happen. When nothing did, she took a tentative step backward then turned and stared at the sight. The ceramic houses now looked life size.

To her left, footsteps reverberated off the buildings, growing louder as they came toward her.

"Tessa!" Lee yelled her name as he came around a street corner.

She sagged with relief. At least she wasn't alone.

"Are you all right?" He held her by the shoulders and looked her up and down.

"Fine. At least, I'm not hurt." She looked into his eyes. "You?"

"I'm okay." He turned and looked over her head. "But look at this."

Tessa turned and swallowed hard. Stretching away before them were the tables and countertops of Promises to Keep, but huge, like football fields.

"I noticed." Her words sounded faint as she nodded at the houses. "What happened?"

"I don't know." Lee reached up to touch the foot long glass lens of a street lamp. "But I used to hold this on my fingertip."

"Oh, gosh, I don't feel so good." Tessa swayed, nearly falling.

"I've got you." A strong, steady arm caught her around the shoulders. Tessa let him lead her back toward the church, slipping on the cobblestones beneath her feet. Her mind scrambled for an explanation. To her left, water tumbled down the stream they'd admired earlier. She looked up. In the dim distance, track lights beamed from a drop ceiling.

This simply could not be real.

Of course. She wanted to laugh in relief. It wasn't real. She turned to Lee. "I'm sure we'll wake up any minute."

"You think we're dreaming?" Lee turned doubtful eyes toward her.

"What other explanation is there?" She waved a hand at the room. "I don't see a beanstalk, do you?"

"Maybe we've been drugged." He narrowed his eyes. "Or hit over the head. Maybe we had an earthquake."

"Look at my store." She waved her arm at the familiar place, everything now in gigantic proportions. "I don't think an earthquake did this."

"I think the store is fine, Tessa," Lee said gently. "I think we're the ones who have changed."

"You mean we're small?" Tessa frowned at him. "I don't like this."

"Let's not panic." Lee caught her hand and turned her to face him. "People who panic cause more harm to themselves than any disaster ever could."

Tessa started to argue with him, but his calm demeanor soothed her. She drew in a shaky breath and nodded.

Lee glanced around. "We're not hurt or in any danger that I can see." He offered his arm. "Let's take a walk."

Tessa, still disoriented, willingly accepted, happy to feel his warm, solid arm under her hand.

They walked between the lovely homes, gaping at the perfection of details from a more proportional perspective.

"This is weird," Tessa muttered as she stepped around a porcelain shrub.

"Yes, it is." Lee paused to examine a cat sitting on a fence post. "But no matter what happened, we can use this experience to our advantage."

"How do you figure?" Tessa looked at him, incredulous.

"In several ways, actually." He leaned down for a closer look at the molded animal. "I can study the details of the pieces and see if they can be improved." He glanced at Tessa. "You can see if the village really looks authentic from a human viewpoint."

"Who cares if it looks authentic?" The idea struck her as ludicrous. "People aren't going to be walking these streets."

"We don't know that."

Lee's words struck home. They didn't know anything about their situation. Had this happened to other people? Would things ever return to the way they had been before?

They continued their walk up and down streets until they arrived at the harbor. Lee stopped on the crest of a stone bridge. They both rested their elbows on the railing and looked down into the water.

"Tessa, can I ask you something?"

"If it's about this," she waved at the small flotilla of boats sitting on their invisible perches, "I don't have any answers."

"No, I realize that." He cleared his throat. "This is probably not the right time or place, but Joe told me you wouldn't say no if I asked you to dinner."

The words came out in a rush, bunched together as if racing.

"Joe did?" Tessa regarded Lee with surprise.

"He and I were talking one afternoon when you were doing something in your office. I said something about you being very pretty." Lee kept his tone matter-of-fact, watching her out of the corner of his eye. "He told me to go ahead and ask you out. But I didn't."

"Why not?"

He looked startled. "Ah, well, I didn't think you dated guys like me."

"Guys like you?" she echoed, surprised. Her gaze searched his face and flickered over his stylishly cut hair. "What are you like?"

"You're probably used to guys who enjoy things like opera and playing chess." He rubbed his chin. "I like being outdoors. On the water, if possible."

"I hate chess," she protested. "And where did you get the idea I don't like the outdoors?" Tessa looked down at her satin-lined wool pants, matching jacket and silk blouse. "Okay, maybe I'm not exactly dressed to hike through the woods." She lifted her chin. "But I do own a pair of jeans."

"You're really different from women I usually date." He chuckled.

"Yes, I can imagine." Tessa's imagination worked up images of statuesque blondes in bikinis lounging on the deck of his boat.

"Don't let your imagination run away with you." He regarded her with a steady gaze. "For the most part, the ladies I've known are hard-working, like you. The difference is that they have no interest in tomorrow. We never make plans. Which is why, at age thirty, I've yet to have a lasting relationship."

"Oh." She stared at him. Then why did he want to date *her*? Heaven knows, no one could label her spontaneous. She planned everything and often far ahead of time.

"But I don't want someone who's exactly like me. I want someone different." He looked at his hands. "A woman like you, with brains, ambition, and a future, usually scares the salt out of me."

"Oh," she said again, wishing she could think of something more to say. Her hopes of going out with him vanished. She'd always tried to look competent and self-assured, even if she rarely felt that way. Now she wondered if she came across as prim and unapproachable. At least to men. At least to Lee.

"I didn't say that right." Lee sounded disgusted. He straightened up. "What I'm trying to say is I like you. You're interesting, and I want to know you better."

"Really?" Tessa's mouth fell open.

"Yes." He reached over and touched her cheek. "Working with you these last couple months has been a great experience. I've learned a lot and not just about my family's company, but about myself, too."

"All right. Sure." Tessa's heart soared.

"Come on. Let's find a place to sit down." Lee walked off the bridge to a park-like area Tessa had created with green velvet for grass.

She stared after him, still uncertain, but torn between choices. She could follow him, sit with him, talk with him, or she could fight this entire experience.

It's a no-brainer, Tessa. Go on.

She followed, falling to her knees onto the fake grass.

"This may all be a hallucination, but you know, I like it." Lee ran his hand over the luxurious fabric under him. "I could get used to a world with velvet grass."

"You like that? I wondered if it looked too rich."

"It's perfect."

"Perfect." Tessa echoed his sentiments, but realized she wasn't talking about the ceramic display.

"This must be magic." He looked at her with a half-smile as his wonder-filled words struck a chord in her heart just before they rang a bell in her head. Hadn't Joe said something about magic? She hadn't believed in fairy tales or such things since childhood. But she always wanted to.

"The question is, are we here forever?" Lee shifted on the ground and glanced over his shoulder.

His voice broke the romantic spell. She followed his gaze out over a painted railing where the variety of boats "floated" on the surface. Beyond the collection of masts Tessa caught a glimpse of store shelves that held an assortment of Colonial style ceramic homes. A vivid reminder of their dilemma.

"How deep is that water?" Lee nodded at the harbor.

"A foot or so. Even though I added food color to the water, it still had to be deep enough to camouflage the bottom, which is a plastic dishpan." She grinned when he gave her an incredulous look. "You use what you've got."

"Very creative. You've done a great job."

She squirmed under the intensity of his gaze and changed the subject. "Do you have any brothers and sisters?"

"Five younger sisters, all of whom are following in Mom's footsteps. They come up with the new ideas, my mother does the drawings, and they make the mockups. But not one of them has a head for the business end, which is where I come in." He rolled his eyes. "Having so many sisters made things interesting growing up in a house with one and a half bathrooms."

"I'll bet." Tessa laughed.

"What about you?" Lee asked. "Sisters or brothers?"

"I was an only child with lots of cousins close to my age. I had the best of both worlds, playmates and all of my parents' attention." She grinned. "Very spoiled. Very happy."

"Imagine that," Lee said. "Two people who grew up in loving homes."

"If you believe the stories in the magazines and newspapers, it's an unusual quirk of fate."

"I hope to keep beating the odds when I start my own family." He nodded once and stared out into the harbor.

A comfortable silence filled the air between them. Tessa liked sitting there with Lee. Her usual shyness with men dissolved under his easy-going manner. She felt no pressure to talk or entertain him in any way. His matter-of-fact attitude about giving up his own career for his family brought her admiration for him into sharp focus.

"There is one thing that would make this experience even more mystical." Lee's eyes grew serious.

"What?"

He leaned over and touched his lips to hers. Tessa's thoughts scattered in a whirlwind of emotions. She closed her eyes and leaned against him, slipping one arm around his neck. The kiss intensified. Lee pulled her close.

For long minutes, she savored him, the warmth of his body, the taste of his mouth. Then Lee broke the kiss.

They stared at each other.

"Tessa—" Lee stopped just as a loud roaring again filled Tessa's ears. She reached for Lee's hand and held on tight. This time, Tessa felt a strong pulling sensation as the village receded, growing smaller with the same "lightspeed" effect.

Within seconds, the store around them looked normal. They perched on the edge of the table, threatening to tip it over.

Lee stepped down to the floor and helped Tessa to her feet. She avoided his eyes as she pushed her hair behind her ears and tugged down the sleeves of her sweater.

What on earth just happened? Had it really happened? How did they return to normal?

She clasped her hands at her waist to still their trembling. Lee cleared his throat several times but didn't speak.

"I have to go home and get to bed," Tessa finally said in a shaky voice.

In self-conscious silence, they turned off the lights and locked up the store. Lee walked Tessa to her car and kissed her once more. As she drove away, she saw him in the rearview mirror, hands stuffed in his pockets, watching her.

By the time Tessa arrived at the shop the next morning, she had convinced herself that the night before was a hallucination.

Lee's truck pulled into the space next to Tessa's. He jumped out and met her at the back door.

He startled her by saying, "You were an only child with lots of cousins."

She stared at him. "You have five younger sisters."

Together they said, "It was real."

Before she could fully digest what seemed to be true, a van pulled into the parking lot. The doors flew open and a group of women, led by Mrs. Trenton, converged on the two of them. Introductions flew by Tessa, who only managed to catch one or two names, but noticed they all had the same blue eyes and winning smile as Lee.

"My sisters," he whispered in her ear.

Joe joined them and took charge of unlocking the door and turning on the inside store lights. The caterers arrived with trays of food and within minutes, Tessa lost herself in the surrounding activity.

As the day progressed, Tessa realized that they had a successful product launch on their hands. Available pieces sold out, creating a need for waiting lists. Some avid collectors indicated a desire to purchase the entire series. For a few hours, she didn't have a chance to dwell on the previous night, but a lull finally hit just after two o'clock.

She went to find Lee.

Tessa found him in her office, logging orders into his laptop computer. "You need anything?" She edged toward the desk. "Something to eat? The food's really good."

"I'll come out in a few minutes." He put his pen down and rubbed his eyes. "Have you thought about last night?"

"Constantly." She held her hands out, palms up. "I have no idea what happened." Tessa plucked a roll of cash register receipt tape from the supply shelf. "But I still think there's a logical explanation."

"I think it's magic," Lee murmured, watching her out of the corner of his eye.

"I'm not sure if I believe in magic," Tessa said.

By ten thirty that night, Promises to Keep had been emptied of customers, food, cameras, and extra display tables. Marie left with her husband, but Joe, Lee, and Tessa remained, content to sit and talk.

"I'm beat," Lee said, "but it feels good."

"I think everyone had a good time and the Mystic Village may just be Treewalk's best selling series yet." Tessa popped a chocolate candy into her mouth.

Lee nodded. "We've got back orders for just about every piece."

"Your mother is charming, by the way." Joe's eyes twinkled. "I understand she's a widow?"

Lee narrowed his eyes before answering. "Before I encourage your pursuit of her, I'd like an answer to a question I have."

"Okay." Joe waited as Lee seemed to fumble for just the right words to say.

"Do you have any idea what happened to us last night?"

"Something happened to you?" Joe cocked one eyebrow.

"We shrank until we were about this big." Lee held his thumb and forefinger about two inches apart.

"Shrank?" Joe's eyes widened. "Like in that movie where

the father shrank his kids?"

"Yes."

"Hmmm. Maybe you worked too late." Joe frowned. "Stress can cause the most fantastic hallucinations."

"Stress?" Lee gave Tessa a quick look.

"Or, maybe you just ran into a little magic," answered the clerk.

"Now Joe, we all know there's no such thing as magic." She reached over and patted his hand. "Although you do have a way of making nice things happen."

"Don't patronize me, Tessa." Joe waved a finger at her. "Magic is real."

"If you say so." She gave Lee a glance, but he simply looked amused.

"All right." Joe stood. "I'll show you. Hold on to your hats." He reached into his pocket, pulled out a fistful of something, and tossed it into the air. The room filled with sparkles.

Tessa gasped and, in the blink of an eye, she sat in the middle of a huge expanse of leather she recognized as her desk chair. The arms towered above her, the back rose high as a skyscraper. Joe, also tiny, appeared beside her.

"Whoa. Maybe you are a fairy or something," Tessa agreed, staring around her in wonder.

"You do believe me? That magic is real?" Joe asked, his face glowing.

"How could I not?" She glanced up at her desk, looming over her. "Look at that." She leaned back against the chair. "Where's Lee?"

"Over in his chair. He's fine." Joe lifted an eyebrow. "You want to be big again?"

"Please."

Joe lifted his hand, made some quirky move with the fingers, and all three returned to their full size.

"Are we going to stay this size?" Lee looked at Joe intently.

"Yes." Joe nodded. "Unless I have to step in again."

"Tessa." Lee leaned forward and caught one of her hands in his. "I think we'd better go out to dinner tomorrow night. We don't want Joe making us small again."

Tessa heart pounded as Lee pulled her up out of the chair.

"Well. Ahem. I'll be going." Joe jumped up out of his chair. He shrugged into his jacket and left the conventional way, out the back door.

Tessa barely heard the door shut behind her friend.

"So, how do you feel about us?" He pulled her into his arms and looked into her eyes. "What do you think?"

"Joe would call it magic. Pure magic," she whispered against his lips. "And I think I'm beginning to believe."

THE MAGIC OF LOVE

Su Kopil

Damon kicked the cloud he stood on, sending a white puff floating into the atmosphere. "If you're done lecturing, Uncle Elliot, I've got a delectable, little cowgirl waiting for me in Houston." He grinned at his uncle. "I'm considering letting her rope me in."

"For how long this time?" Elliot produced a cigar from thin air and stuck it between his teeth.

"A week, maybe two." He shrugged, feeling the tingling warmth in his finger a second before the small flame shot out of its tip and lit his uncle's cigar. It was the first bit of magic Uncle Elliot had taught him. At five, the word warlock meant nothing. Shooting fire from his fingertip, on the other hand... now that grabbed his attention. And despite his advanced level of powers it remained his favorite.

"And what of the girl in Wisconsin?" His uncle continued to question him.

"The relationship soured." Damon laughed.

"Enough!" Elliot thundered. His short, rotund torso elongated until he towered over Damon's lanky frame. "You've been warned, Damon. After being given ample time to prove yourself, you have failed. Your powers will be stripped from you as of this—"

"You can't! Not without the approval of the Witch's Board."

"You think they're not aware of your activities?" Elliot shook his head. "Who do you think intervened for you with that girl in Switzerland? You broke one too many hearts, Damon Lane."

Damon felt the blood drain from his face. "That was a mistake. It won't happen again."

"You're right, it won't happen again! You have lost the privilege of magic until—"

"No!" Damon tried to conjure a bottle of wine, a glass, a ball, but it was useless. Try as he might, the familiar warm tingle would not return to his finger. He felt naked. Hollow. Finally, his uncle's last words registered. "Until?"

"Until you help a mortal woman find true love. It's time you mend a heart instead of break one."

Mend a heart? How was he supposed to do that without his powers? But he knew better than to ask that question, so he asked another instead. "When?"

"Immediately. Her name is Emily Watson."

"Emily." Damon grimaced. *Humph… probably a toothless, old spinster.* "And how will you know—"

"I'll know."

Damon saw the concern behind his uncle's scowl. For all his gruffness, Damon knew his uncle cared. He'd acted as both a father figure and mentor, rescuing Damon from one scrape after another. When the occasion called for it, Uncle Elliot even fibbed to his own sister, Damon's mother, in order to spare his nephew's hide. His father never popped in long enough to learn of his son's mischievous ways.

"Remember," Elliot warned. "She must find her true love."

Elliot's voice faded, and a swirl of clouds and smoke enveloped Damon. He felt himself being lifted, his body weightless, changing shape, as his uncle's powers transported him to Salem or worse.

"Ouch!" He landed on the hard limb of an apple tree, knocking loose fruit and leaves. "A bit off on your aim, old man," he muttered, rubbing his backside.

"Ow! Is someone up there? What do you think you're doing?" A female voice squealed.

Damon glanced at the woman squinting up at him through the branches. "Sorry." He shrugged, waved his arms with a flourish, then frowned when nothing happened. "Of all the blasted luck," he grumbled. Careful to keep hold of the tree, he sought one foothold after another. "Who needs powers?" He bragged, impressed with his own prowess. Reaching with his right foot, he missed the next branch, and promptly fell to the earth.

"Are you okay?"

He heard concern in the female voice and decided to open his eyes. After all, lying on top of lumpy apples wouldn't get him his powers back. He grinned at the creamy, lush vision before him, and started to rise. "Aargh," he moaned, removing an apple from a spot no apple should be. He tossed it aside and sat up.

Her hands gingerly touched and poked his body, feeling, no doubt, for broken bones.

"And who might you be?" he asked. She smelled of honey and cream. He couldn't keep the leer from his tone or quell his rising excitement. Nor did he want to.

Seemingly satisfied he was all in one piece, she removed her hands from his body and stood.

He missed her touch and intended to rectify the situation when she answered his question.

"Emily Watson."

She may as well have tossed cold water on him. *So much for a toothless hag.* At least, his task would be much easier.

"I live in this apartment building. Who are you and what were you doing in that apple tree?" She stood, hands on hips, looking for all the world like his mother after he created some magical mischief. The difference being he had an incredible desire to kiss this woman.

"Damon Lane at your service." He performed a mock bow. "Would you believe I was searching for the juiciest, reddest apple?"

She glanced at the fallen fruit. "Considering they're all green. No! Perhaps I should call the police."

He knew a bluff when he heard one but since he'd been ordered to play matchmaker for this woman, he needed to gain her trust. Damon pulled his wallet from his pocket. Heck, even warlocks needed ID once in a blue moon. He handed her his license.

"Not a very good likeness." She gave it back to him.

He shrugged. Everyone knew warlocks didn't photograph well. "I'm better in person." He smiled. "But now you can believe I am who I say I am."

He noticed her lips twitch but her voice remained stern. "That still doesn't explain what you're doing in this courtyard. Are you a new tenant? I haven't heard of anyone moving out."

"Actually—Ouch!" A small paperback book bounced off his head and into his lap. He glanced at the title, *How to be a Good Superintendent.* Damon jerked his head up searching the tree. "Uncle Elliot!"

"Mind your manners, my boy." Elliot, looking quite comfortable sitting on a lower limb, bit into a green apple. The juice dribbled down his chin. "Mmm." He savored the flavor a moment before flashing Damon a warning look. "Remember why you're here."

"Of course, Uncle Elliot." Damon stood.

"Excuse me?" Emily looked puzzled and took a step backwards.

Damon knew she couldn't see Elliot. Not unless the old man chose to be seen. Damon knew he wouldn't do that.

"Uncle Elliot... my Uncle Elliot owns this building. I'm

sure you've met him." Damon grinned and shot a glance at his uncle. "He's taken pity on his poor nephew and hired me to be the new superintendent." He showed her the handbook.

"I've heard grumblings about a new super." She eyed him uncertainly. "It's about time. No one's ever met the owner of this building but your Uncle Elliot sure took his time finding us a new super. The last one didn't fix a thing. Half the people here have one thing or another broken in their apartments. As for me, my faucet is dripping, and my toilet keeps running and...." She glanced at the spot Uncle Elliot occupied.

Elliot still refused to show himself, and Damon knew he couldn't expect any further help from that quarter. Seems he'd gotten himself tangled up tighter than a black widow on a windy day.

"You do know how to fix things, don't you?" Emily asked.

"Yes, of course." He lied. What else could he say?

"How's tomorrow morning then, say 11:00?"

"Tomorrow?" Getting better aquatinted with Emily Watson was a given but fixing toilets definitely didn't fit into his plans. Not that he had a plan exactly.

"Apartment 7B. See you then." Her gaze drifted to the tree once more. Then she smiled at Damon and left the courtyard.

"Running toilets and dripping faucets." Damon hissed, turning back to his uncle. But the old man was gone. He felt a tap on his shoulder and jumped.

"Behind you, boy."

Damon glared at Elliot. "What do I know about plumbing? This wasn't part of the bargain."

"There is no bargain, Damon." His uncle frowned. "You're here to learn a lesson. Emily Watson's heart is in your hands. Your powers won't return until she finds her true love. Meanwhile, you have the handbook."

The handbook. Damon studied the offending paperback.

When he looked back up his uncle was gone, and he still had no earthly idea how to fix a toilet.

The next day, Damon paced the hallway outside of apartment 7B. Word spread fast about the new super in town. Tenants had been badgering him non-stop until he'd finally told them all his job didn't officially begin until Monday. That gave him two days to get his powers back. More than enough time. The only problem now was how in Aunt Tilda's broom closet was he going to make Emily Watson trust him with her heart?

He couldn't just walk into her apartment and declare himself her matchmaker, ready to drop true love into her lap. A simple love incantation would solve the problem, but unfortunately he had only his wits and his charm.

His charm. No mortal woman or witch, for that matter, could resist his boyish charm. With a grin he was sure could melt an Alaskan ice princess, Damon knocked on the door.

Emily greeted him in jeans and a T-shirt, her hair caught in a ponytail, and a cautious smile on her lips.

No stranger to gorgeous women, Damon knew Emily's simple beauty outshone the lot. He faltered, surprised by his own hesitancy. "I'm here to stop your drip, I mean, to flush your toilet."

Emily laughed. "I know what you mean. Where are your tools?"

Damon looked down, then very nearly blushed. "Oh, tools...."

"That's okay." Emily's soft hand encircled his wrist, and she pulled him inside the apartment. "You can use Tom's."

"Tom?"

"My boyfriend."

Boyfriend? Damon tried to shake off the weight that suddenly seemed to press on his chest. He should be happy. With a boyfriend in the picture his work was half done. He whistled softly under his breath while Emily rummaged through a closet.

"Here." She hauled out a large metal box. "When the last super left, Tom planned on taking care of a few problems for me, but he never got past bringing his toolbox over."

Damon stopped whistling. *What on earth was he supposed to do with all those tools?*

She led him into the kitchen and set the toolbox down with a clang on the small table.

They stared at each other.

"Well...." She averted her gaze and pushed back a stray strand of hair.

"Well?" He grinned, wondering if a quick tumble was definitely out of the question.

"The faucet." She moved next to the sink. "It's dripping."

He crossed the distance between them, leaned over until his eye was level with the tap, and pronounced, "So it is."

Her foot started to tap. He had the absurd impression she expected him to do something. He had some delectable ideas, none of which would stop a leak. Then there was Tom. Perhaps Uncle Elliot decided to go easy on him after all.

Damon returned to the toolbox.

Emily's foot stopped tapping.

He rummaged through the metal gizmos making lots of noise, assuming that would please her. It did for awhile. Then her foot started dancing again.

"Ah! Here it is." He pivoted to face Emily.

"A screwdriver?" Her brows raised.

"Exactly." Obviously the wrong choice, he turned back to the box and pulled out a contraption that looked like it could fix anything. Facing Emily once again, he took her silence as approval. He stepped back to the sink and stared at the faucet, watching each drip splash to the stainless steel basin.

"Ready?" The question was more for himself than for her.

She nodded.

The doorbell buzzed. She looked torn but, finally, on the fourth buzz, she excused herself.

Damon breathed a sigh of relief. "Uncle Elliot," he hissed.

"Uncle Elliot?"

Nothing. He was still on his own.

Leaning against the counter, he felt a lump on his backside. The handbook! Pulling it from his pocket he flipped through the pages. Faucets. Leaks. "Thank you, Uncle Elliot."

To his utter astonishment, Damon found the problem.

"You need a new washer," he told Emily when she returned. The relief on her face fueled his sense of pride. "I'll bring you a new one tomorrow. Now where's that pesky toilet?"

"Um... actually, the toilet will have to wait. There's a bit of an emergency, and I sort of volunteered your help."

Damon raised a brown. "You volunteered my help?" He didn't know whether to be flattered or annoyed.

"Yes, that was Mrs. Crump at the door. Seems her cat has gotten himself stuck in a tree, the apple tree as a matter of fact." A smile tugged at her lips. "You are the new super and since you have a way with trees... I thought...."

"You thought I'd rescue Mrs. Crump's fool cat?"

She nodded, the smile breaking free and lighting her whole face, while her eyes implored him to help.

Damon's knees grew weak. He reached for the counter for support. At that moment, he thought there was nothing he wouldn't do for this woman. Never had anyone looked at him with such faith, such hope. How could he refuse?

"You forget that I fell out of that old apple tree, practically on top of your head."

"Right." Her smile wilted. "How could I forget. I'm sorry, I shouldn't have—"

"I didn't say I wouldn't try." Damon smiled. Magic or no, how difficult could it be to rescue a cat from a tree?

Three hours later, he had stopped wondering.

"Alright you flea-bitten ball of fur, I've had enough chasing you around this dang tree." He muttered, while awkwardly balancing on an upper limb.

The cat, Sweetie, as Mrs. Crump so fondly referred to him, actually looked like an over-sized cotton ball that had been rolled one too many times in a pile of ashes.

"Can you reach him, Damon? I think he's getting tired." He recognized Emily's voice though he couldn't see her through the leaves.

"That makes two of us," he called back. "But I think I've got him now."

After several scrapes and a bruised knee, the cat now sat inches from him, calmly licking a furry paw. "Rescue my foot! I think you've been enjoying this whole mess." Damon spoke to the cat. "Playtime's over. I'm getting out of this tree, and you're coming with me whether you like it or not."

He reached for Sweetie, fully expecting the cat to leap out of reach again. Instead, his hands sunk into silky, soft fur. Damon was so surprised he nearly lost his balance. But having become rather proficient at tree climbing in the last twenty-four hours, he managed to right himself and started making his way down the tree, cat calmly tucked beneath one arm.

"Look, Mrs. Crump! Damon's got Sweetie." Emily clapped her hands.

The moment she did, Sweetie clawed her way up Damon's arm and clung to the back of his head and neck.

"Oh," Mrs. Crump fretted. "Don't hurt my sweet girl."

"Hurt your—" Damon spluttered as his feet touched the ground.

"She's fine, Mrs. Crump." Emily carefully lifted Sweetie off of Damon's head and shot him a warning look.

"There's my pretty girl," cooed the older woman. "Thank you, Mr. Lane. You've a kind heart."

"Mrs. Crump is right. Thank you, Damon." Emily said.

To Damon's delight, she reached up and kissed his cheek. "Those scratches on your neck look bad. You'd better come upstairs and let me put something on them."

"If you insist." He could think of better things to do

behind closed doors. In fact, by the time they'd reached her apartment his mind had conjured up all sorts of delicious scenarios. As he followed her inside and onto the sofa, he sternly reminded himself of why he was there in the first place. Her gentle ministrations to his neck only made matters worse until finally, he jumped off of the couch and moved across the room.

"I'm sorry. Did I hurt you?" Her eyes, a transparent green, haunted him.

"No, of course not." He waved the thought away. "I suddenly realized I'm starving. Feel like grabbing a bite to eat?" He hoped a crowd of people would help him to keep his mind on the task at hand.

"Why not." She grinned. "Give me one minute." She set the tube of ointment on the table and sprinted into the other room.

"You don't mind walking, do you?" he called.

"Not at all. It's a beautiful day," she answered from the other room.

"Good," he muttered to himself. "Since Uncle Elliot neglected to provide me with a car." He only hoped food could be found within walking distance.

Damon needn't have worried. A few short blocks and they were in the center of town. Emily fit right in with the little cafés and quaint shops. Damon found himself forgetting about his powers or lack thereof, Uncle Elliot, and even the Witches Board. For that moment in time, his world revolved solely around Emily and the way her cheeks dimpled when she smiled, the charming tales of her childhood, and the way she listened so attentively to his own stories.

When she admired another woman's bouquet of flowers, he tried to conjure some up for her. Of course, he couldn't, but his disappointment only lasted a moment. Instead, he plucked a handful of wildflowers from the side of the road when she wasn't looking, getting stung in the process. But her delighted laughter made it all worth while.

"I'm sorry about your bee sting." They stood in front of Emily's apartment door.

He laughed. "I barely felt it once you pulled the stinger out."

"Thank you again for the flowers, " she said. "They're lovely."

"My pleasure." Desire welled inside of him. He took a step back, reminding himself again of his reason for being there. Today had been a good day. Probably the best he ever had. Somehow he'd managed to gain Emily's trust. It would be foolish to risk losing it now by kissing her.

"I'll stop by tomorrow with the washer and see about that toilet."

"Right." Disappointment flashed across her face, or was he imagining it?

Before he could talk himself into seeing something that wasn't there, Damon turned, and left.

After a restless night, Damon arrived at Emily's apartment the next morning as promised. He replaced the washer and proudly showed her the leak was gone. Feeling almost eager to tackle his next project, he strode down the hallway, Tom's toolbox in hand.

He stopped short inside a small bathroom.

Emily bumped into his back. "I'm… I'm sorry." Her voice trembled.

Setting the toolbox down on the closed toilet lid, he turned towards her.

"I—I'm sorry. I'm a little distracted. Tom called just before you got here." She glanced behind her. When she turned back around, he noticed the shine in her eyes. "He… I'm supposed to meet him for lunch…. He—"

The next thing Damon knew, Emily burst into tears, and he was trapped in the tiny bathroom with no escape. He'd seen many women cry, but the waterworks usually occurred upon his walking out the door. This time he was stuck.

Damon found himself at a loss. If Uncle Elliot felt any mercy at all now would be the time to return his powers. But try as he might, he simply couldn't vanish, instead he awkwardly patted Emily's arm.

"There, there," he murmured.

Brushing the tears from her cheeks, Emily sniffed. "I don't know what's come over me. It's just that...."

"Yes?" Damon could have kicked himself for asking. Obviously, her tears had something to do with Tom. Even though it was in Damon's best interest to hear the reason, a part of him wished to remain ignorant.

Emily's gaze searched his face, and he suddenly found himself hoping he had what she was looking for.

"I think Tom is going to propose to me." She spoke softly.

"Propose? As in marriage?" Damon felt his heart slam into his chest. A moment passed.

His heartbeat steadied. This was what he wanted, needed, wasn't it? At this rate, he'd have his powers back quicker than a cauldron boils. "Congratulations. That's great." He couldn't quite get the proper note of excitement in his voice, but she didn't seem to notice.

Emily shook her head.

Damon shook his head. "No?"

A rogue tear streaked down her face. "I don't love Tom."

"But you must!" His voice was a bit too loud even for his own ears.

Emily raised an eyebrow.

"I mean, it's nerves. Everyone gets nervous at the thought of being trapped... er, stuck... I mean, together with one person the rest of their lives." He should know, having received many a proposal himself. He had to convince Emily to accept Tom's offer. It was the only way he would get his powers back. He didn't understand why, but her tears upset him. He found himself wanting to make her happy and if that meant seeing to it she married Tom, then so be it.

"I'm sure Tom's a great guy. Look at all the tools he

owns." Damon gestured to the toolbox sitting on top of the toilet.

Emily laughed.

The sound brought a rush of warmth to Damon's chest.

"He is great. It's just that…." Emily glanced at her feet. "There's no spark. He kisses me and… nothing. Do you know what I mean?"

He knew what she meant. He'd kissed women too numerous to count, and he couldn't recall a spark ever igniting. Desire, lust, yes, but not the kind of spark Emily meant.

"Sparks are overrated. Friendship and loyalty are the true signs of love." Damon repeated the words his mother recited to him over and over and again. For the first time, he felt like he understood what she'd been trying to tell him.

Emily frowned. "But I thought when a couple loves each other fireworks light the sky, so to speak." She blushed.

"Any two people can create sparks. It doesn't mean they're in love." But as he spoke the words, he couldn't seem to tear his gaze away from her lips. Their gentle curve and fullness beckoned him closer. He wanted to taste the corner, moist from a tear trail. Would he feel a spark? Would she?

It was a question he needed to discover an answer to and so his thoughts became reality when their lips touched.

He reveled in their softness, the sweet, slightly salty taste of her. She responded, her lips parting, drawing him inside of her.

He couldn't get enough. His body responded with a fierceness that shocked even him. He had to stop. But he couldn't think straight. She cast a spell on him, and he was losing control. With great difficulty, he pulled away, breaking their connection. Damon willed his body to relax but his heart, beating a rapid pace, continued to betray him.

"See," he rasped. Clearing his throat, he tried again. "Sparks but no love."

He hated the way the light in Emily's eyes dimmed. If he

was supposed to mend her heart then why did he feel like he was breaking it?

"You're right," she answered in an icy tone. "Thank you for so adequately pointing that out. Now if you'll excuse me." She backed out of the doorway. "I've got a date to prepare for."

"I'll get that drip fixed tomorrow." Damon stepped past her. A part of him wanted to take her in his arms and tell her to believe in their kiss, not his words. But that was his lust talking. The thing that had gotten him into this mess in the first place. For once he had to put a woman's heart before his own needs. He'd told her the truth. A few sparks didn't equal love.

Or did they?

"You'll be doing the right thing marrying Tom." He wasn't quite sure whom he was trying to convince.

"I know." She followed him to the door.

Anger flared in his chest. He had to stop himself from kissing her again. He wanted to show her—show himself—just how powerful a spark could be. Instead, he walked out the door.

Damon returned to his apartment or rather, the apartment he knew his uncle had so fortuitously provided, along with the bundle of cash Damon found in his pocket.

"Uncle Elliot," he hollered. "Show yourself this instant."

He waited.

Nothing.

Using all his concentration, he tried to conjure the old man before him.

Nothing.

Next, he tried to make himself disappear.

Again, nothing.

Slamming around the few pots and pans left by the last super, he paced the small kitchen. Fury at his helplessness engulfed him.

"Harmless flirtations." He spoke aloud, hoping his uncle

was listening. "What have I done that mortal men haven't been doing for ages? Is giving a woman a few hours or days of pleasure so wrong?"

He stopped pacing and stared out a dirt-streaked window. Now when he wanted to see where that pleasure would lead, he was denied. He'd told Emily two people could create sparks without love, but he wasn't sure he believed that himself. Of all the woman he dated, not once did he feel the excitement, the crush of emotions, that he felt with one kiss from Emily. For the first time in his life, he desired only one woman. The woman whose heart he'd been sent to mend.

A movement outside caught his attention.

Emily.

Witch's Board be damned! He intended to find out for himself just exactly what these new feelings were stirring inside of him.

Damon moved on instinct, racing for the door, then down the hallway. He cursed the two sets of glass doors in his way. Flinging open the last door, he rushed outside. He spotted her immediately climbing into a blue sedan. He yelled. But the door shut, and the windows were closed tight against the chill fall air.

With a wave of his arms he commanded the car to stall.

Instead, the sedan pulled away.

Cursing his lost powers, he started to run. But, he was too late.

His anger returned only to drain from him a moment later, leaving him feeling empty inside. He walked to the apple tree and sat beside its wide trunk.

He'd practically pushed Emily into the arms of another man. The wrong man. She said so herself. How could he have been so foolish—so blind. No woman, no kiss, had never caused such confusion in his heart. He only knew her a scant three days, yet he knew what he felt was more than lust. Heck, it scared him to his very soul, that is, if he had a soul. There had to be a reason Uncle Elliot chose to entrust him with Emily Watson's heart. Despite all his grumblings and lectures, the old man was the only one who had ever believed in him. Perhaps he still did.

A spark of hope lit Damon's darkness. Maybe it wasn't too late. He survived this far without his powers. He could survive awhile longer. There was no time limit on mending a heart. He still had a chance to fan the spark their kiss had ignited into a flame.

These feelings inside of him were more powerful than any magic. For the first time in his life, he cared about a woman more than himself. Powers or not, he planned on exploring those feelings and discovering to what new heights they might take him.

Then so be it. He would tell Emily the truth, and see to it that Tom, no-sparks, took a hike. His decision made, Damon settled back to wait.

"Damon. Damon." A soft feminine voice called.

Damon opened his eyes to a black star-studded sky and the vision of a beautiful woman. Sure that he must still be dreaming, he sighed, and closed his eyes.

"Damon Lane, don't you dare go back to sleep!" The voice scolded.

Something shoved him hard. He bolted upright, wide awake.

"Emily!" Surprise turned to pleasure at the sight of her, especially as the more delectable parts of his dream returned to tease him.

"What are you doing sleeping out here at this hour? You're chilled to the bone."

Pleased by her concern, he shrugged, and stood. He barely felt the cold against the heat she stirred within him. "I could ask you the same thing. What time is it?"

"Eight o'clock." She pulled her sweater closer. "If you must know, I wanted a little solitude to enjoy the stars. And you?"

"I was sleeping." He thought that was obvious.

"Fine. You don't have to tell me." She stepped away from him. "Since the courtyard is occupied, I'll go inside."

"Wait!" He caught her arm and moved in front of her.

"Why?" Her chin jutted out just enough for the moon to illuminate the soft pout on her lips.

"We have to talk." He tried to steady his hammering heart.

"Again, why? I believe you said all that needed saying after you so rudely kissed me."

"Rudely?" Damon spluttered, automatically jumping to his own defense. "I was trying to prove a point."

"And you did," she agreed. "Sparks mean nothing."

"Well, I was wrong."

"You were?" She bit her lower lip.

"Perhaps we should try again." He grinned.

"I... I don't think that will be necessary." She took a step back.

He took two steps forward. His voice deepened. "We want to be sure."

"Sure?" She repeated, her lips parting.

"Sure that there are no feelings that need exploring." His head lowered. "Just sparks, right?"

"Just sparks." Her warm breath caressed his cheek.

His mouth captured hers. He half expected her to pull away. Instead her body melted into his, causing a fire in his veins that burned to the depths of his heart. A river of emotions unleashed inside of him. He knew he must discover where they would lead him. The realization frightened him but not as much as the thought of denying himself what could be. He'd take it slow, give her time to accept who he was—what he was. But first he had to explain.

Gently, he eased his lips away from hers. Squeezing her arms, he waited for her to look at him. When her gaze finally met his, he was floored by the desire in her eyes. "Can you deny your feelings now?"

She shook her head.

"Smart girl." He smiled.

"You…." She swatted him playfully.

He chuckled, then grew serious. "There's something I need to tell you." He led her to a wrought iron bench. They sat.

He took her hands in his. There was no easy way to say it. "I'm a warlock."

She gasped and stood up. "You don't need to make ridiculous excuses. Just because we share a—spark, it doesn't mean we're bound to each other."

He caught her around the waist and pulled her back onto the bench. "It's true. I'm not making it up."

She studied him a moment, her brow wrinkled. "And I suppose you just snap your fingers and things just appear."

"Actually, pointing my finger works just fine." He gestured to illustrate knowing full well nothing would happen. But he was wrong. His arm started to tingle, and he felt a warmth in his fingertip. Suddenly a small burst of flame illuminated the night.

Emily shrieked.

Damon threw back his head and laughed, delighted to have his powers restored.

"What are you, some kind of crazy magician?" She backed away from him.

"No, I'm a warlock!" He grabbed her and kissed her.

She sat still, her eyes wide.

"This is great. No. This is better than great. Don't you see?" He wanted her to understand his excitement. He needed her to understand. "Uncle Elliot took away my powers with the approval of the Witches' Board. Not to be restored until I helped you, Emily Watson, find her true love. At first, I thought you'd be some old hag."

The shock had worn off enough so that she looked insulted. Damon took that as a good sign.

"But then I met you under this old apple tree. And I swore I'd never seen such a beautiful woman in all my life. But it's more than that." He paused, at a loss for words. "The return of my powers means there is something between us, something real."

Emily's silence worried him, but at least she hadn't left.

"This morning, I told you to marry Tom because I thought he was supposed to be your true love. I needed you to marry him so that my powers would return. After I left, I knew I was wrong. I saw you leave from my window, and I tried to catch you but I was too late. I didn't care if I never got my powers back, I wanted us to have a chance, to see where that spark would lead us."

"But your magic is back." She spoke softly.

"Yes."

"Are you saying I'm your true love?"

"I'm saying I want a chance to find out."

"But—"

"And if you would rather I not use my powers, then I won't."

"But—"

"Give us a chance, Emily. Please."

She covered his mouth with her hand. "Will you let me speak now?"

He nodded, kissing her palm before taking her hand in his own.

"What makes you so sure that I didn't say yes to Tom's proposal and that's why your power returned?"

"What?" He jumped up and started pacing. "You said yes? You told that no good, sparkless jerk, yes?" He looked at her, his anger at a boiling point. That's when he noticed her mouth twitch as though fighting a smile. He sat back down. "What did you tell Tom?"

Her grin won the battle. "I thought you'd never ask."

"Well?"

"I told him I didn't want to see him anymore at the same time he told me he wanted to see someone else."

"You mean, he never proposed?" He started to chuckle.

"Not even close." She laughed.

"So does this mean you'll give us a chance?"

Before she could answer, a swirl of colorful smoke appeared.

Emily gasped.

Damon squeezed her hand. "Don't worry. It's only my Uncle Elliot."

Elliot's rotund form appeared as the smoke dissipated.

"My dear." Elliot performed a regal bow and held his hand out to Emily.

She tentatively placed her smaller one in his.

He gave it a perfunctory kiss. "I trust my nephew is treating you well?" The old man glared at Damon.

Emily glanced at Damon before answering. "Yes. He is."

"And it pleases you to be with this impetuous warlock?"

Damon looked at Emily, eager for the answer he'd been waiting to hear.

"Yes." Emily smiled.

Damon grinned.

His uncle directed his attention back to him. "This is not exactly what the board had in mind. They are not pleased."

"But my powers. They're restored."

"A simple indulgence on my part. The girl needed convincing. The board agreed to a temporary reinstatement."

"Temporary? What do you mean?" Damon asked. "Are you saying Emily and I shouldn't be together? Because if you are Uncle Elliot, I must protest. The board cannot decide—"

"Hold on." Elliot raised his hand. "I'm not saying anything of the sort. There are extenuating circumstances that prevent me from granting the reinstatement of your powers."

"So you're not forbidding us to be together?"

"No. But your powers will not be restored for one year, at which time, the board will review your commitment to Emily. Do you have any problems with that?"

Damon could have sworn his Uncle Elliot winked. Did that mean he approved? He was almost sure of it. He grinned. "Not in the least."

"Then I will leave you two to get better acquainted." His uncle smiled, and Damon knew he was on their side. With a flourish of brilliant smoke, his uncle vanished.

A single red rose appeared in Damon's hand. He laughed and presented the rose to Emily. "I believe my uncle approves."

"I can see that he loves you, Damon." Emily breathed in the rose's fragrance.

"Don't let him hear you say that."

"Damon?" She touched his hand. "Will you be okay without your magic?"

"Honey, there is only one kind of magic this warlock needs." He cupped her face in his hands. "The magic of your love." He pressed his lips to hers and showed her just how powerful a spark could be.

ROOM AT THE INN

Tami D. Cowden

Sarah Thane peered through the wet windshield at the old hotel's sign. Between passes of the wipers, she saw the bulbs in the "VA" and "CY" end were burned out. But the flickering red "CAN" told her the inn had rooms available.

She slowed. Torrents of rain prevented a thorough inspection of The Grand Inn, but the little she could see was not encouraging. It might have been grand at one time, but peeling paint, dead flowers in window boxes, and more than one dangling shutter gave the lie to the hotel's name. The old coast road, which on the map had seemed a lovely way to view the ocean on the way to Seattle, didn't have a lot of hotels, and those she'd seen so far hadn't had any vacancies. She might have to drive for hours to find another one. This place had the advantage of looking well within her price range. Maybe her luck was finally starting to turn.

Any port in a storm. The thought brought a grimace, but she pulled into the parking lot. The sunroof in her old VW was leaking again, and she was tired of icy rainwater dripping down her neck. She stopped next to an aged jeep, the only other car in the gravel lot. Grabbing the duffel bag that contained most of her worldly goods, she dashed for the front door.

The hotel lobby carried on the exterior's image of better days gone by. Dim lighting revealed faded tapestry covering sagging cushions, copies of famous paintings hanging in dusty gilt frames, and foggy crystals swaying listlessly from a chandelier. The same musty smell that had permeated her grandmother's nursing home filled the air. Sarah suppressed a shudder and stepped up to the high desk. The lobby was silent, the only sound the drumming of the raindrops against the window. She hoped the room rates reflected the current situation, not the hotel's former glory.

No clerk stood behind the counter. She tapped on the silver dome sitting in front of a "Please Ring Bell" sign. Nothing. She tapped it again, harder. Still nothing. Exasperated, she slapped her palm down on it.

"It's broken."

Sucking in a gasp, she spun around to find the source of the deeply toned words. Her duffel bag fell from nerveless fingers. Squinting her eyes to see in the watery light given off by the dirty light fixture, she could just make out a dark form seated on an old fashioned settee.

He stood and walked toward her. This time, her gasp was not from fright. Wavy black hair fell over laughing blue eyes. Strong white teeth gleamed in a wide grin above a rakish goatee. Clad in cowboy boots, jeans, and a flannel shirt, the man exuded confident masculinity at its very best. Sarah wished she'd dressed in anything other than sweat pants and sneakers.

Of course, since most of her wardrobe had gone up in flames with the rest of her belongings and the apartment house, her only other outfit was a night gown. The thought brought heat to her cheeks as she tried to tear her gaze from the smattering of dark hair peeking from his open collar.

He stopped at her side. "There's an old guy around somewhere. His wife, too. They run the place." Cupping his hand around his mouth, he shouted toward the door behind the counter. "Hey, Mister! You've got another guest!"

With a creak worthy of the scariest of horror films, the door opened. A wizened old man wiped his hands on an apron covered with dark stains as he shuffled through the doorway. Stepping up the desk, he looked at Sarah through his bifocals and nodded.

"Evenin,' Miss. Need a room?"

"Y-yes. No. Maybe." The stains covering the front of his apron looked an awful lot like blood to her. She had to ask. "Is that—"

"Blood?" He cackled, a high, keening sound. "Sure is. Wife and I just bought a side of beef. Get the best price, if you cut your steaks yourself, you know." He tapped a red stained finger against his nose as he gave this sage advice.

"Oh." Her relieved sigh turned into a nervous giggle. Obviously, she was letting her recent run of bad luck get to her. After all, she hadn't really thought a crazed killer would put on a "Kiss the Cook" apron before dispatching his victims, had she? "Yes, I've heard that. A good idea if you have a big enough freezer."

Another high-pitched laugh. "Oh, we have a big freezer, Mabel and I do." Despite his gruesome appearance, there was something comical about the old man. "So, is it yes, no, or still maybe about the room?"

Sarah glanced at her fellow guest, who waggled his eyebrows at her. The easy camaraderie expressed in his gesture caused the tension in her shoulders to ease. "Yes, please." The softly murmured "good" as the younger man went back to his seat brought an upward tilt to her own lips.

"Good. Glad to have you."

A short form was pushed across the counter for her to fill out. A few minutes later, she was on her way up creaky stairs to find her room, an iron skeleton key in her hand. She walked right by her room at first. The nail holding the top of the number "6" had fallen out, so it look like a "9" instead.

But the key turned easily, and she pushed the door open.

No faded grandeur met her sight. While the carved plaster ceiling hinted at the former glory, the furnishings would have been considered utilitarian in a prison. A simple bed with no headboard, covered by a thin cotton spread, dominated the small space. In lieu of a closet, a huge armoire stood in one corner. A nightstand and a hard chair were the only other furnishings. A tiny alcove hid the bathroom. There wasn't even a reading lamp, just the overhead light. She was sure she wouldn't find ice or vending machines down the hall, but the price had been right.

After a few minutes trying to find a comfortable spot on the bed to read, she gave up. Carrying her book, she went out into to the corridor. The chairs in the lobby might be old, but at least they did have cushions. And reading lamps.

She shivered at the chill. The gloom pervading the place was getting to her. Or maybe her recent run of abysmal luck was taking its toll. With no job and no home, it had seemed like a good time to move on to a new life. So she'd hit the road. The great northwest had beckoned to her.

A thousand miles and a new transmission later, she still wasn't any closer to a place she'd like to call home. The rain was quite a change from her Phoenix roots. And her small savings were fast running out. At least this place was dry and wasn't costing her an arm and a leg.

Faint squeaking noises sent her scurrying quickly down the stairs. But the pleased smile of her fellow guest did much to smooth balm on her troubled soul.

"All settled in?" With a nice show of courtesy, he stood as she approached. His rich voice offered a pleasant contrast from the unwelcoming atmosphere in the small sitting area.

"Yes, I suppose so." She sat, throwing him her own wide grin as she slid her novel down between her thigh and the side of the chair. She'd much rather talk to this hunk than read the horror tale. Besides, the hotel was conducive enough to nightmares; she didn't need fiction.

"Where you headed?"

Her heart skipped a beat at the genuine interest reflected in his eyes. "Seattle. You?"

"Here and there." He held out his hand. "Tom Morris."

"Sarah Thane." His grip was warm and firm. She could feel the faintest of calluses on his fingers, suggesting he'd earned the muscles evident under the flannel the old-fashioned way. Maybe her luck was finally changing. "Pleased to meet a fellow traveler."

Over the next hour or so, she found herself pouring out her whole life story, including her impulsive decision to move to an unknown city. All the events leading up to the decision, her parent's car crash two years before, the downsizing at her company, and then the fire, the final straw. The college boys next door whose drunken indoor barbecue had burned down the apartment building had been sorry, but sorry didn't make up for a lack of renters' insurance.

"So you see, everything I own now fits into my old bug. A cross country move suddenly seemed like a good idea." She hunched her shoulders with a self-conscious laugh.

"Wow. I'm impressed by your good spirits." His eyes crinkled as he smiled his approval.

During their talk, an old woman, apparently the clerk's wife, moved the dust on the china knickknacks littering every flat surface. Between coughs, Sarah learned enough about Tom to hope "here and there" might include Seattle. She couldn't help feeling a bit of feminine satisfaction when he asked if she'd join him for dinner.

The old woman surprised them both by suddenly asking, "You folks want some supper?"

Startled, they both looked at her. Sarah asked, "You have a restaurant here?"

"No. But it's raining mighty hard out here, and the nearest diner is more than thirty miles away. She eyed them with an appraising look. "You can have some of Jim's and my stew for five dollars apiece. Pie for dessert."

Sarah resisted the impulse to ask how much dessert would cost. She looked over at Tom, hoping he'd prefer the drive. But she was disappointed.

"Stew? I love stew. Terrific."

Mabel nodded with satisfaction.

During dinner, Sarah realized how little Tom had revealed about his own history during their conversation. He steered questions from their hosts away from himself as skillfully as he had her own. Observing his ability to parry pointed inquiries, her interest was further piqued. He seemed to have some secrets. She always seemed to fall for the enigmatic kind and hoped Tom's secret didn't involve a wife and kids.

The stew was surprisingly good. There was an unusual taste to it, which Mabel claimed was cinnamon. Sarah wasn't sure, but Mabel clearly cooked better than she cleaned. And apparently prided herself on it, as she was less than pleased at Sarah's firm refusal of blueberry pie. Even when Sarah explained her allergy to berries, Mabel was unsatisfied. But Sarah was not intent on winning her hostess' approval.

She would have liked to have spent more time with Tom, but her eyes kept drifting closed. Realizing she could only make a poor impression if her head fell into the pie Mabel insisted on placing in front of her, she yawned her way through excuses and went up to bed. Her head no sooner hit the flat pillow, and she slept.

Her eyes shot open. She lay still for a moment, holding her breath, wondering what had awakened her. Her conscious mind slowly took over and awareness came. Water. Slapping rhythmically against a solid barrier. Struggling to understand, she shook her head to clear it of the last cobwebs of sleep. Her eyes grew accustomed to the darkness, but the instead of the faint outline of the plastered ceiling of her room, she saw stars. Lots of them.

Outside? But how? She tried to sit, and the surface on which she lay rocked back and forth. Her hand stretched out to steady herself, but met cold damp wood instead of the thin cotton sheets. Sarah lay back , willing herself to wake up. She just could not possibly be in a boat. She had gone to bed safely locked into her shabby little room. People didn't just wake up on rowboats floating who knows where.

But after pinching herself and blinking several times, she was still swaying gently under the stars. She supposed she should be thankful it was no longer raining. Desperately trying to come up with a reasonable explanation for her predicament, she slowly sat up.

The lack of a moon meant there was little light. She couldn't see the shore and had no idea which way land was. But that didn't matter. A quick feel around the small boat proved there were no paddles. She wasn't going anywhere.

Many miserable minutes passed as she huddled on the floor of the boat making her plans. It was cold, but not so much that she'd freeze to death. When daylight came, she would be able to see the way to shore and could swim for it.

Then she'd find out who had done this to her. And almost as important, why? Surely her few belongings weren't worth these extreme measures.

Her speculation ended as the boat suddenly pitched to one side. A dark figure with goggles appeared over the edge. She shrank back against the opposite side, terror robbing her of the breath to cry out. A dark gloved hand swept the face mask away to reveal the frogman's features.

Tom! Every tale of charming but vicious serial killers she'd ever read in tabloid papers suddenly paraded across her mind. Without thinking, she kicked out. His stifled curse at her connect with his chin brought her a fierce satisfaction. She scrambled to her knees to try to flee over the opposite side while sucking in a gulp of air to scream.

In a single smooth movement, he flipped himself into the boat and clamped a neoprene covered hand over her lips. His firm body pressed over hers to hold her down. She pushed against his chest. His free hand caught both of hers in a tight, but not painful grip. She tried to kick him off of her. He merely pressed closer, allowing her no leverage.

"Hold still. Federal agent."

Her eyes widened. She shook her head and pushed.

"I won't hurt you. I'm here to protect you." Sincerity dripped from his words, but she couldn't believe federal agents dragged women out to boats and attacked them in order to "protect" them. A silent, desperate struggle ensued.

Suddenly, a faint mechanical whirring emerged from the darkness. Sarah and Tom both stopped their battle, and looked in the direction from which the noise came. The sound increased and Sarah realized a boat was approaching.

Tom quickly lay flat against the side their boat, hiding from the newcomers. He whispered sharply "Pretend you're asleep," even as he drew a gun from a pouch at his side.

She searched his face, but instinctively closed her eyes when a sudden spotlight swept across her face. She wasn't sure why, but somehow she did believe he was there to help.

"Is the girl still drugged?" A faintly accented voice called.

"Looks like we won't have trouble hauling her aboard."

Sarah repressed a shudder. Their voices were cold and uncaring as they spoke of her being drugged. Maybe from the stew? She was now sure these men definitely were not here to help.

The approaching boat slowed. A skilled toss of a rope brought her own boat close to the other.

Suddenly, searchlights lit the area.

"Hold it right there! Federal Agents." Tom stood up straight, gun pointed toward the crew of the incoming boat. "Hands where we can see them." More frogman emerged from the sea, climbing over the sides of the boat. Within moments, what had seemed a dark empty sea was as well lit and crowded as any shopping mall.

The crew were too stunned to do anything but comply. As Sarah huddled in a blanket in one corner of the boat, Tom efficiently placed the men in handcuffs. Then he calmly spoke into a radio before turning to her.

"Are you all right, Sarah?"

She nodded dumbly. Her tongue felt thick and her head a little fuzzy. She wasn't sure if it was the after-effects of the drug or sheer astonishment at the situation in which she found herself that caused her muteness. Flashing red lights reflected in the lapping waves, and she heard men's voices coming from below. Tom tenderly helped her from the tiny rowboat onto the coast guard cruiser that pulled close.

Soon she was wrapped in a warm blanket and sitting down on a bench on the deck. Tom kneeled before her, a rueful smile curving his lips. "I guess you're wondering what this was all about, huh."

The idiocy of that question brought her out of her stupor. "No, of course not. I always wake to find myself in the middle of the ocean, surrounded by FBI agents." Considering it was pretty clear he'd saved her from a dreadful fate, she supposed she ought not to snap at him. But she did think she had the right to snap at someone, and he was the only one left.

He didn't seem to mind. "Oh, okay, then." He sat down next to her with a laugh.

She crossed her arms. Tapping her toe, she glared at his profile. After a sidelong glance, his hands went up in an admission of defeat. Winking, he murmured, "I love that sense of humor."

"Ahem," she said loudly.

"Okay. Here's the grim story. About two years ago, women started disappearing from this area. Gone without a trace. Ten of them, altogether."

One hand clasped over her mouth in revulsion. He pulled her close to him, and for the first time in she didn't know how long, she felt safe.

She also felt sick to her stomach. She whispered into his shoulder, "You mean, the side of beef…." It was too horribly disgusting. She couldn't finish but just looked at him.

"Side of beef?" Tom's eyebrows shot up in puzzlement. His eyes widened as he realized what she meant. "Oh. No, no, it's not that bad. They were selling the women to white slavers. A ship would lay anchor off the coast, and the Larsons would send the women out to it in a boat. They kept the women drugged in the hotel's broken walk-in freezer until the ship arrived. One of the women ended up in Asia and managed to escape to the American embassy. That's how we found out about the whole operation."

"Oh." White slavery was slightly better than ending up in stew, but she still felt very grateful to Tom. And she said so.

"On the contrary, we're grateful to you. We had an undercover agent on her way to pose as a traveler, but she ran off the road due to the storm. We were going to have to scrap the sting until you showed up." He stood and pulled her to her feet. "There's a nice hotel not far from here. How about a room courtesy of the federal government?"

"That would be great." She searched her brain for a nonchalant way to find out where he lived. She was about to come out and ask, but he had a question for her, instead.

"So, still heading to Seattle?"

"I guess. Why?" She pulled the blanket closer.

"Oh, it's just that I'm located in Tacoma. My sister lives there, too, and she's looking for a roommate." He looked almost shy now, as he waited for her answer.

"A roommate?"

"It's a nice place," he coaxed. "And my sister is a good cook." He winked. "I know, because she has me to supper at least once a week."

She gave him her very widest smile. After all, she'd just picked Seattle out of a hat—it might be nice to actually know someone in her new town. Especially this someone.

"Tacoma, it is."

When he gave her a pleased smile, she knew she had been right. Her luck had definitely changed for the better.

BELLE OF THE OHIO

Susan D. Brooks

Morning fog clung to the southern Ohio treetops as Calliope Stokes clambered onto a bus. Tugging a yellow historical society volunteer's vest over her white tee shirt and jeans with one hand, she carried a garment bag containing a change of clothes and her wallet in the other.

Callie smiled at the other people on the shuttle, remembering her grandmother's admonition. *If you're a stranger in a strange place, pretend you aren't.*

Having relocated to Cincinnati just three weeks ago, she barely knew the people at work much less anyone on a social basis. So, when she saw the poster recruiting volunteers for the Tall Stacks steamboat gathering, she had jumped at the chance to participate. Few sternwheelers operated on the rivers anymore and seeing so many in one place at one time would be an extraordinary experience.

Settling into a seat, she thought how neatly events fit together, bringing her to this place at this particular time. After her parent's deaths, Callie had immersed herself in her job with a marine engine parts manufacturer in Boston. She worked hard for the title of lead project engineer, but it was a stroke of luck that placed that project on the Ohio River where steamboats still cruised.

"Is this your first time volunteering at Tall Stacks?"

Callie turned to see who spoke. Across the aisle, a woman with wavy silver hair smiled.

"Yes. In fact this is my first time at the event." Callie took a butterfly clip from the pocket of her bag and secured her hair on top of her head. "They've got twenty sternwheelers and side-wheelers this year. I can't wait to see them."

The lady laughed. "I've worked the event since 1989, and I still get excited when I look over the riverbank and see them lined up." She grabbed the back of Callie's seat as the bus careened around a corner. "Whew. That driver's a wild one, isn't he? My name's Valerie."

"Mine's Calliope, but everyone calls me Callie."

"Calliope?" Valerie's eyes flew open wide. "Like the steam pipe organ?"

"Yes, exactly. When I was born, my parents let my great-grandfather, who was a riverboat pilot, choose my name." She pinned her volunteer badge to her vest. "I'm really glad his passion wasn't the steam stacks or the paddlewheel."

"Would have been hard to come up with a nickname in that case." Valerie laughed. "What's your assignment?"

"Ticket taker for the *Belle of the Ohio*." Excitement tickled every nerve as Callie spoke the name of the boat. Her Great-great Aunt Carolina had been given the same nickname years ago when her beauty and charm captivated southwestern Ohio's male population. Callie felt the coincidence an omen of good luck.

"The *Belle*, huh?" Valerie gave her an appraising look. "Hmmm."

"Oh, it will be fun," Callie insisted. "I'll be right in the thick of things."

"You've been invited to join the dinner cruise?" The woman nodded at the garment bag.

"Yes, the volunteer coordinator told me the captain

always invites the ticket collector along on the last cruise of the day. It's his way of saying thank you." Callie thought of the dark crimson silk and lace creation she'd found in a second-hand clothing store. The Victorian style made her feel regal.

"I hear the food on the *Belle* is out of this world," Valerie commented. "The new chef used to work at a five star restaurant."

"Oh, I hadn't heard that." Callie pressed one hand on her stomach. "Good thing my dress fits a little loose."

Both women laughed as the bus pulled into a parking lot near the river and stopped. Around them, people started to gather belongings as they prepared to disembark.

"Well, you'll have a nice time. And we sure are glad to have extra hands to help. Seems we never get enough volunteers." Valerie reached under her seat, retrieved a backpack, and stood. "Just don't pay any attention to the stories about Captain Walker, the commander of the *Belle*. I've met him several times, and he seems as normal as you and I."

Before Callie could ask what she meant, the crowd surged from the back of the bus, pushing Valerie toward the front door.

"Have fun, Callie!" Valerie's voice drifted back over the heads of the other passengers.

I will. She puzzled over Valerie's words, but then shook off the twinge of uneasiness as she picked up her garment bag. What could possibly happen?

Callie stood on the sloped parking lot at the Public Landing, gazing at the scene before her. A battle between joy and apprehension raged within her. She recognized this place, but she hadn't been here before today. Of course, she'd seen pictures, but the reality sent waves of trepidation shooting down her spine. Along the paved riverbank, twenty steamboats of varying sizes and shapes tugged at mooring lines that held them against the pull of the Ohio River current.

This is the right place. You'll find him here.

Callie jerked her head around, thinking someone had spoken to her, the words sounded so clear in her head. Where did that thought come from?

She shrugged off the strange feeling. Maybe she'd listened to too many of her grandfather's stories about growing up along Cincinnati's riverfront. He'd told her tales of ghosts and unexplained happenings, anecdotes peculiar to the Public Landing area. And, of course, he told her of the last days of steam-powered boats and the people who lived their lives on the moody Ohio River, a fascinating mix of scoundrels, heroes, and heroines.

Although Grandpa moved to Massachusetts after World War II, chasing his dream of being a tugboat pilot, his heart remained in Cincinnati with his ancestors, a colorful clan of river rats and socialites. He spoke most often of his Aunt Carolina, frequently telling Callie that her resemblance to his father's sister was uncanny.

"You are so much like her," he'd marvel, staring at Callie's face. "You think like her, look like her, and you even wear the same color clothing she favored, all those reds and greens."

Callie thrilled at the comparison.

"She never married and she never favored any one man over another." Grandpa had scratched his chin, as he always did when trying to catch a fleeting memory. "But now that I say that, I think it may not be true. Something tells me she got engaged once, but her fiancé' disappeared one day. I think she was in her late twenties when that happened."

But Callie didn't concern herself with Carolina's love life. Instead, she studied the hard evidence of brilliance her great-great aunt left behind. Carolina devoted her life to studying engineering and mechanics, producing seven volumes of notebooks with prototypes of newer, safer machinery for water vessels. Grandpa owned several of these books and Callie spent hours going through them, studying each drawing, memorizing each word. They were the reason she chose mechanical engineering as a career.

After her grandfather's death, Callie and three other cousins each received one of the notebooks. She chose the first volume and now it sat in her glass-enclosed bookcase, protected from dust and direct light. On rare occasions she would remove the fragile tome and leaf through the pages, amazed at the concepts illustrated inside. Ranging from practical to fanciful, they represented the broad range of a clever, analytical mind.

Callie walked along the Landing. Carolina must have spent a great deal of time here. The drawings she'd made all had careful notes indicating the date, location, and name of the boat she used as a model. Many had been in Cincinnati.

Keep looking. You'll find him.

That same voice as earlier. Again, Callie stared around her, wondering what was happening. No one's eyes looked her way; no one stood near enough for her to hear if they had spoken. Her apprehension skyrocketed.

Callie stopped at a water fountain and got a drink. The cool liquid helped her refocus on the task at hand, to find the *Belle of the Ohio.*

Other people in yellow vests hurried past her heading toward a large red and white striped canopy with a posted sign reading "Volunteer Station." Callie followed them and signed in, receiving an event schedule and a typewritten paper listing facts about the steamboat.

"This is what people are going to ask," the volunteer coordinator told her. "So we had it written down for you."

Callie glanced at the paper and continued on. Most of the information related dimensions, horsepower, and passenger capacity. All forty-eight staterooms were first class, meaning that the Belle carried fewer people in greater luxury than any of her rivals, including the famous Delta Queen.

She flipped the paper over, but the other side was blank. No tales about the Belle? No account of the crews that served her? Callie remembered Valerie's puzzling words about Captain Walker.

Those stories would be more like rumors, she decided. *Besides, I'm not here to be a tour guide.*

Still, she wished she knew more about the boat's history, if only for her own knowledge.

Callie found the *Belle* at the easternmost mooring. Rising four decks over the water, she was one of the bigger boats, as well as one of the more elaborate ones. Her brass fixtures gleamed from frequent polishing and her white paint and red trim looked fresh in the early sunlight. Along the upper promenade decks, rows of wooden chairs invited guests to relax and enjoy the view. Above the topmost level, which the info sheet listed as the Texas deck, two signature smoke stacks stretched proudly into the clear sky.

Callie stepped onto the narrow bridge leading to the boat. Halfway across, she paused to peer down into the murky water. A wavy outline reflected back as towboats passing in the main river channel sent ripples to the shore. She made a face at the stink of diesel fuel.

Not much cleaner than burning coal.

A movement in the mirrored image caught her attention. She turned, looking up toward the pilothouse. Inside, a shadowy outline of a man filled one of the windows. Callie shielded her eyes against the morning sun, trying to see him better. Was that the captain? Or the pilot? Again, vague recollections teased the corners of her mind.

Then, without warning, an unfamiliar handsome face popped into her mind followed by a wild surge of happiness. She recoiled at the sudden intrusion into her thoughts and grabbed the rope railing for support.

"Excuse me, Miss." One of the deckhands stood patiently behind her, waiting to get past. He leaned down, studying her face. "Are you all right?"

"Fine, yes, I'm fine. Sorry." Callie stepped out of the way, then turned to look for the shadow again, but whoever cast it was gone. So was the picture in her head.

She continued to the main deck of the boat and hesitated, wondering where she should put her extra clothes.

A lady wearing a suit with the ship's logo embroidered on the jacket introduced herself as the *Belle's* social director.

"Since you'll be joining us for the late dinner cruise, I'll put your bag in the captain's cabin. All of our guest cabins are full this week," she explained. "Our weeklong cruises are always sold out this time of year. When you're ready to change and freshen up, anyone of the crew can take you to it." The young woman disappeared up a set of outdoor stairs with Callie's garment bag.

For the first two hours of the event, the *Belle* opened for tours, allowing people access to all public rooms including the engine room. Callie lost track of time as she directed people, collected tickets, and rattled off facts about the *Belle*.

At ten o'clock, the tour visitors returned to shore as preparations began for the first of the hour-long river cruises. Lines of excited passengers formed along the Serpentine Wall, a cleverly disguised flood wall consisting of wide, tall steps that led from the Landing to the top of the riverbank.

As people began to cross the gangway to the boat, Callie turned to direct a customer to the stairs when she spied a tall, dark-haired man watching her from one deck above. He wore a black suit cut in a style from long ago. A hat, decorated with gold braid, shielded his eyes from the mid-morning sun.

You've found him, the inner voice said as Callie's heart filled with bliss.

But I've never seen him before. Shivers of anxiety wrapped around her unexplained happiness, pushing sanity to the forefront of her thoughts. She could not look away as he came down the steps and moved toward her. His gaze met hers, shooting tendrils of wonder up her spine. She wanted to run to him, to lose herself in his embrace.

And I don't know who he is.

Hands trembling, Callie turned back to the passengers as he came to her side.

You have a second chance. Don't let him go without you.

"Carolina?" The handsome stranger reached for her hand. Callie barely registered her great-great-aunt's name before a loud voice intruded.

"Oh! Look how he's dressed, like an old time riverboat captain. Let me get a picture!" A woman held up disposable camera and snapped a shot.

"You're the captain?" Callie asked, pushing tickets into the pockets of her vest as more visitors clamored to board.

"Yes, I'm Captain Walker."

When Valerie mentioned his name earlier, Callie had barely noticed, but now, standing beside him on the main deck of the *Belle*, it struck a deeper chord. As more people crowded around them, she couldn't take time to sort out the strange feelings. She felt his gaze on her, studying, assessing, but he remained silent except for an occasional hello to his passengers.

When everyone was on board, Callie turned to face him.

"Carolina." His gaze moved from her mouth to her eyes to her hair. He touched her cheek with his fingertips. "You finally came."

Callie stared at him, sure that she didn't know him, but just as certain that she did.

When she said nothing, he frowned. "Don't you know me?"

"No. Yes. I don't know," Callie stammered. "Have we met before?"

An expression of understanding transformed his face. "Search your memory. And don't be afraid of what you find."

When he nodded and turned to go, Callie touched his arm. "Wait."

He stopped and looked back at her, a smile teasing the corners of his mouth.

"Why do you think you know me?" she asked. "Who do you think I am?"

"You are a member of the Stokes family?"

"Yes," she stammered.

"Miss Stokes, you look like Carolina." He grinned. "The original *Belle of the Ohio*."

Callie forgot what she planned to say. "How do you know that?" she asked, not sure if she referred to him knowing her family name or her aunt's nickname.

"I'm the one who gave her the nickname," he said. "And you could be her twin sister."

"You knew her when you were a child?" Callie gaped at him as her mind scrambled for an explanation. This man couldn't be more than thirty years old.

From the topmost deck, the *Belle's* whistle wailed, drowning out all other sounds. She glanced up. Steam poured from the twin smokestacks as the boat prepared to move.

"We are leaving port," Walker explained. "And I understand you must remain here, but when I return, we will talk further." He bowed slightly and started for the stairs then turned and added, "But please, keep your mind open to any possibilities."

Callie crossed to shore and watched the *Belle* pull away. She hoped for another glimpse of the handsome, enigmatic captain, but he didn't reappear.

When the *Belle* returned after her first excursion, Captain Walker came to the gangway. She studied him from out of the corner of her eye as he approached, stunned at the intensity of her feelings at seeing him again.

"I regret that my schedule is full for the rest of the day, and I won't be able to talk with you as I would have liked," he said in a low voice. "But, I've been told that you have accepted my invitation for this evening's late dinner cruise."

"Yes," she answered. "I'm looking forward to it."

"No more than I." He nodded. "Until tonight."

Callie watched him walk away, admiring his confident bearing. But she also felt a bit giddy, too.

He must have asked the social director if I've been invited. That means he's been thinking about me.

Infused with a sudden exuberance, Callie greeted the next passenger with more enthusiasm than necessary, earning a glare from his female companion.

She smiled an apology and calmed herself, but let her mind wander as people flowed past, shoving tickets into her hand. The dinner cruise that night looked more and more intriguing.

On her lunch break, Callie wandered around the rest of the festival, stopping to buy a couple souvenirs and a bowl of chili. She sat on a low brick wall and stirred shredded cheese into the meat sauce. Valerie plunked down beside her.

"Hello again," she said. "Mind company for lunch?"

"Hi, Valerie. I'm glad to see you."

"Having fun?" The older woman bit into a bratwurst sandwich.

"Oh yes. The people are wonderful and the boat is magnificent." Callie took a bite of chili.

"Prettiest boat here or anywhere else."

Callie chewed and swallowed. "Valerie, you mentioned Captain Walker this morning on the bus. Something about stories?"

"Oh, I wouldn't give those another thought." The older woman waved her hand in dismissal. "Can't think of why I told you such a thing."

"But you didn't tell me anything, and I'd really like to know more about him."

"Well, if you want to hear, I'll tell you." Valerie took a sip of cola. "It's said that he's been captain of the *Belle* for as long as anyone can remember."

"So?" Callie shrugged.

"Honey, I'm sixty-seven years old and I remember him from when I was in grade school. He looked exactly the same as he does today." Valerie nodded for emphasis. "Some say he's a ghost."

"That's silly." Callie looked in the direction of the river.

Valerie shrugged. "Maybe so, but he refuses to talk about himself to anyone."

"It's possible that the job has passed down through the generations. And my family has told me I'm the image of my great-great aunt. We even have the same interests." Callie took another bite. "Maybe he just looks good for his age. What else?"

"That boat, the *Belle*? It's said she disappears for days at a time. Right off the river. No one can find her."

"What do the passengers say about that?" Callie couldn't keep the amusement out of her voice.

"There haven't been any on board when that happens. This is only when she's not carrying customers." Valerie snapped her fingers. "I just thought of something else I heard. The crew. They've all been with the *Belle* as long as Walker has. They don't age either."

Callie smiled as she took another bite of chili. Such stories always followed people who held themselves apart from the rest of the world. She shook her head, refusing to let rumors distort her opinion.

"But I'm getting carried away. No one really believes these stories." Valerie chuckled. "After all, they're working people. Somewhere in the world they must have Social Security numbers and bank accounts like the rest of us."

They ate in silence for the rest of the meal, listening to a bluegrass band play in the pavilion nearby. Callie swallowed the last of her food as a whistle blew in the distance. "There's the *Belle* coming back. I've got to get to the landing."

"Okay." Valerie stood and tossed her garbage into a

nearby trashcan before looking at Callie with a curious expression. "How did you know that's the *Belle's* whistle? I thought this was your first Tall Stacks."

"No one can quill a whistle like Justin Walker. It's his signature. The old time railroad men used to do it, too." Callie's words faded as she froze in her steps. How did she know his first name?

Back at the landing, Callie watched the boat return to the dock. On the top deck, a calliope puffed out the tune of "Dixie". Tourists swarmed around Captain Walker, most stopping to chat with him for a moment or two. She watched, intrigued by the way he seemed so pleased to see each and every person. Then he spotted her and lifted one hand in greeting. A knot formed in her stomach as she waved back. He was no ghost, but just who was he?

As evening came, crowds thinned, leaving couples and groups of teenagers to settle in front of band shells where bands played music ranging in style from Dixieland jazz to classical. Callie totaled her tickets for the last cruise and matched the number against a reservation roster. She turned the tickets over to the volunteer coordinator and crossed the moveable bridge to the *Belle of the Ohio*.

One of the deckhands escorted Callie to the captain's cabin where her garment bag had been hung that morning.

"The dining room is down a deck and towards the stern, Miss. You can't miss it." He smiled, ducked his head, and left.

Retrieving her toiletry case, Callie turned and stared around the room.

He keeps his clothes in that small room to the left of his desk.

The thought came out of nowhere, the same as the others had earlier today. Callie hesitated then took a step toward the door. She turned the small knob and tugged, revealing a closet with several suits on wooden hangers. *Of course, that's the closet. Any idiot would know that. Where else would you put a closet anyway?* The next door opened into a powder room. Callie washed up in the small sink and reworked her hair into a neat chignon. The dress felt cool against her skin as the fabric fell to her ankles. Donning a marcasite and pearl bracelet with matching earrings, Callie felt elegant and in tune with the atmosphere of the historic steamboat.

She pulled out a tiny beaded purse, tucked a twenty-dollar bill inside, and left to seek the dining room.

Callie followed a long corridor, descended two stairways and pushed through a mahogany door. The soft churning of the sternwheel greeted her in the warm rush of an Indian summer breeze.

She half turned to go back when a movement by the railing caught her eye. Captain Walker turned and nodded in greeting. "Good evening, Miss Stokes."

Her cares seemed to slip away as a sense of rightness, of being in the perfect place, stole over her. She savored the sensation, gazing out over the river as she stepped to Walker's side. Tiny drops of water splashed up from the giant wheel, brilliant for a moment in the moonlight, then black as they fell back into the current.

"Beautiful, isn't it?" Walker's admiring words spoke volumes.

"Oh yes. Like nothing else." Callie stole a look at him out of the corner of her eye. *He loves this as much as I do.*

The thought pleased her.

"Were you exploring the boat or looking for me?" Walker cocked an eyebrow.

"I was trying to find the dining room. I was certain that it was here." Suddenly, she felt a little foolish. How had she messed up on the simple instructions given her? She twirled the bracelet on her wrist.

His gaze shifted from her face to her nervous hand then

back. "It will be my pleasure to escort you." He moved to her side and held open the door. Callie noticed he smelled of fresh air and cigars as she passed by him into the corridor. "You were right. The first class dining room used to be here. It was moved when we added more staterooms to this deck."

"Oh." Callie, attributing this additional knowledge to the research that she'd done earlier, looked past him off the stern of the boat. The lights of Cincinnati should still have been visible, but all was dark. Even the small watercraft she noticed when boarding earlier had disappeared.

We must be further upriver than I thought.

"The move made sense, of course," Captain Walker continued. "No one pays attention to the view outside at night. Especially when the room is filled with women as lovely as you."

"Are you flirting with me, Captain?" Callie turned to him with a smile.

"I was giving you a compliment." His eyes twinkled in the dim light from the wall sconces. "But yes, I suppose I was flirting, too. A dying art, don't you think?"

"Yes, I believe you're right." Callie wondered how he'd gotten so close to her. She had to tip her chin up to look into his eyes. His chest nearly touched hers.

"Carolina was a gifted flirt."

"How could you possibly know that?" Callie's disbelief shattered her playful mood. She put her hands on her hips. "She died before I was born. And why do you think we've met before? I'm certain we haven't."

Walker's gaze moved over her, appraising. "You're more beautiful than Carolina."

"Stop that. Answer my question." She realized how she sounded when his eyes narrowed. Quietly, she added, "Please."

"I will, but you're not ready to hear the answer." He offered his arm. "After dinner, we will talk. Until then, let us enjoy the evening."

Callie started to tell him she didn't want to wait, she wanted answers now, but stopped. He was right. She wanted to relax and have fun, too. So, she set her concerns aside and laid her hand on his wrist. He felt warm, strong, and completely human. A sigh escaped her lips, drawing an amused glance from her escort.

"You should have turned left coming from my quarters, not right," Walker said. "It's easy to get turned around."

They started down a hushed, carpeted gallery, lit by brass gas wall sconces.

"Do you know anything about the *Belle's* history?" Walker asked as he led her up a stairway.

When she answered no, he proceeded to tell her a story about when her hull was built, sometime during the Civil War.

"The builder laid the keel in 1862, after he completed her sister ship, the *Whirlwind*. He enlisted that year and died at the Battle of Vicksburg. The *Belle* sat for four years, unfinished, in a small shipyard up by Marietta, Ohio. The *Whirlwind* was used for carrying troops until the end of the war, when her captain ran her aground and smashed a hole in the hull.

"My father found the *Belle* in 1866 and had her completed that year. He also raised the *Whirlwind* and put her back in service." He turned a corner and led Callie up another stairway. The low murmur of voices and an enticing mixture of roasted meat and fresh bread drifted through closed double doors.

"Thank you for bringing me here." She released his arm and smiled. "I imagine we will see each other later."

"We will see each other all night." He opened the doors and gestured for her to precede him. "I have had you assigned to my table."

Callie felt him take her elbow as she tried to quiet the turmoil in her heart. Again, that curious mix of confusion, relief, and joy flooded her veins. As they passed a waiter, she heard him say, "Good evening, Miss Stokes."

Without warning, a surge of déjà vu shifted her perspective. She'd been in this room before. She stumbled as memories overwhelmed her. Walker caught her around the waist, but Callie barely noticed. These thoughts of past events didn't belong to her. She didn't know them. Did she?

"Are you all right?" Walker held her chair then took his place on her right, leaning toward her for an answer.

"I feel like I've been here before." Her fingers traced a pattern on the linen tablecloth. "But I haven't."

A crystal wineglass caught the light from the overhead chandelier, sparkling onto the delicate blue-edged white porcelain plate emblazoned with the name of the boat. Callie clutched her hands in her lap.

This is ridiculous. How could this be so familiar?

Walker cast an enigmatic look at her before focusing on the waiter who appeared on Callie's left, flourishing a bottle of wine for the captain's approval. At Walker's nod, the steward opened the vintage and began to fill the glasses.

"Miss Carolina, would you like wine this evening?" The waiter hesitated, the bottle poised over her empty glass.

"This is Miss Stokes, Steven," Walker said. "But not Miss Carolina." He winked at her. "He gets confused sometimes. Would you like a glass of burgundy with dinner?"

Callie nodded, mute, as a white-haired gentleman across the table engaged Captain Walker in a discussion of steamboat racing.

That waiter thinks I'm my great-great aunt. She reached for her glass of water and took a big gulp. *Weird. She'd be well over a hundred years old by now.*

But I do feel like I've been here before.

Okay, if I really remember, there's a water tureen on the table by the potbelly stove. She turned and looked over her shoulder. The large silver urn sat just where she'd envisioned. She stiffened.

A lucky guess, she told herself. *But if I truly have*

memories of this boat, the silverware pattern will have a magnolia flower in the center.

Her gaze shifted to the knife on the right of her plate. A magnolia bloom dominated the design.

Walker's voice calling for everyone's attention distracted her. He lifted his glass in a toast.

"To the *Belle of the Ohio.* May time never keep us apart." He took a sip of wine and sat back down. Other guests echoed the words, cheered, and conversation resumed.

Before Callie brought her wine to her lips, a vignette played in her mind, playing in fast-forward like an early motion picture. *A young lady falls from a bridge into rushing water below. She struggles to stay above the surface, but she sinks. Then a pair of strong arms catches her and brings her to safety on board a sternwheeler. She knows the hero's name before the scene fades.*

Justin Walker.

I remember Grandpa telling me about that. She drew in a quick breath and cast about in her mind for more of the memory. *Aunt Carolina's carriage turned over during a thunderstorm. She fell into the water and was rescued by one of the river pilots.* But the rest of the details eluded her.

A waiter set a plate of sliced melon before Callie. Placing a linen napkin across her lap, Callie picked up a spoon.

"Justin," she said, without looking his way. "Your name is Justin."

"Yes." He looked pleased. "Did you remember or did someone tell you?"

"My grandfather told me, I think." Callie rubbed her temples. "Being with you seems to bring these thoughts out of hiding.

"Yes, maybe so." His expression turned thoughtful as he took a bite of fruit.

Conversation swirled around her filled with interesting snippets of life in other parts of the country. Most of the other passengers appeared to know each other, or at least be acquainted, so Callie just listened, contributing little.

She remained highly aware of Justin beside her, a charming and gracious host. He chatted easily with everyone at the table, listening and asking intelligent questions at the appropriate times. Sometimes she would look his way and find him watching her, his eyes dark with an emotion she couldn't quite name.

Her own emotions dipped and rose as if on a small sailboat in a hurricane. First, she felt so happy, so content to be near Justin. Even the *Belle* herself proved to be one big comfort zone, familiar and welcoming.

Then her sensible side kicked in and bewilderment clouded every moment. She'd never seen this place before, so she didn't trust the feeling of serenity. And, although everyone treated her with kind respect, Callie felt as though she'd stumbled onto a stage during a performance. Conversation flowed around general topics, but nothing came up about sports teams or television shows, usually safe topics for strangers to discuss. She also noticed a complete lack of personal information, no one spoke of his or her employment or families, also subjects people spoke of at length.

When the stewards came by to clear the plates, Callie decided that all in all, she enjoyed the two-hour banquet, but mixed feelings dampened her enthusiasm.

Expecting to return to port right away, the crewmembers startled her by pushing aside tables and chairs. A small brass band tuned up in one corner.

"You must do me the honor of leading the first dance." Justin stood and offered his hand to Callie.

Eyes wide, she shook her head. "I don't know how."

"You will catch on quickly." He smiled, caught her hand in his, and tugged gently.

As they approached the floor, he gave her quiet, easy-to-follow instructions. A moment later, the band launched into a stately march. Callie managed not to make too many mistakes, earning a smile of approval from her partner. The march dissolved into a quick-paced couple's dance Justin told her was named the gallop. She laughed with delight as they crossed the floor at breakneck speed.

Songs blended from one to another, masking the passage of time. Callie learned about quadrilles, performed in sets like square dances, and contras or line dances. She had several partners throughout the evening, but Justin always returned to her side for the couple dances. When the band took a well-deserved break, Justin left to check with the engineer about something. Callie slipped outside to the promenade for some fresh air.

Looking out across the shimmering, moonlit water, she marveled at how dark the night seemed far from the city. No cars traveled the river roads and no party lights glimmered on private docks. The *Belle* slipped past another steamboat moored at the foot of a hill. Callie squinted to read the name. The *Cheyenne.*

For a long while, she stared out into the darkness, enjoying the feel of the moist air on her face. Since the dancing began, she'd forgotten about her real world and the rumors related to Justin Walker. Somehow, her job and her life before today seemed far away, belonging to someone else, and memories she hadn't known before now seemed to be hers.

"I thought I'd find you out here." Justin appeared beside her and leaned down to rest both forearms on the railing. "Are you enjoying yourself?"

"Um, yes." *Except that I don't understand what's happening here.* She forced a smile. "This boat is a dream come true." She studied the backs of his hands, the veins that ran up to long, square fingers. Capable hands.

"That's how I see her, too." He patted the carved railing. "I never wanted to live any other way." Justin half-turned toward her. "I don't dare believe this is true." His eyes searched her face.

"What's true?" Callie held her breath, wondering what he meant.

"That you're here with me."

Her heart fluttered even though her head warned her he was just flirting with her. "Am I ready to hear your answer to my question about Carolina Stokes?"

"Maybe." Justin turned an appraising look on her. "How open-minded are you?"

"Very." She thought of the vision she'd had earlier, of the voice that spoke in her head. "I think."

"Do you believe that things can happen for which there's no obvious explanation?"

She hesitated. She hated to say no, because she found herself wanting to believe in magic, wanting to believe in the extraordinary.

"Let me ask you this." He straightened to his full height. "How did those people in the dining room look to you?"

"I'm not sure what you mean." Callie glanced over her shoulder toward the main cabin. "They looked perfectly normal."

"Do they?" Surprise widened his eyes. "I'm glad to hear you say that, few people have the gift of seeing past the time barrier." Walker took her hand in his. "I have one more test for you."

Curiosity burned through Callie as they returned to the stern of the boat, overlooking the paddle wheel.

"The *Belle's* turning back upriver," he said. "We'll get within ten feet of shore. Keep an eye on the embankment and watch what happens."

Callie felt the shift as the rudder turned the boat. Lights began to wink on between the shore's trees and bushes.

"Did we wake everyone up?" She glanced up and down the river where other signs of life appeared. "The *Belle* is so quiet that's hard to believe."

"No, we didn't wake everyone," Justin said. "We've made a transition."

"Transition?"

"We've returned to your day." He leaned down, looking into her eyes. "To the time of Tall Stacks."

"Returned?" Callie watched him, searching for the truth. His gaze remained steady. "Where have we been?"

"Here, near Cincinnati, and, judging from the presence of the *Cheyenne* back there, sometime between spring 1883, when she was built, and summer 1883, when she ran aground and sank." Walker stroked his chin.

Ignoring the voice in her head that said he spoke the truth, Callie shook her head. She tapped her foot. "Time travel isn't possible."

"Didn't anyone ever tell you about the *Belle?*" He didn't wait for her answer. "She's unusual. She can travel through time." He winked at her. "I've read that book by HG Wells."

"Oh, come on." Callie gestured impatiently with her hands. "Are you telling me that we've gone back in time?"

"Yes and, now that we're close to land, forward in time."

"How do you explain this boat being in my lifetime, then?" she demanded. "How can I be here?"

"Time only changes when we're out in the river's current. That's when we go back." Walker nodded at the riverbank. "If we're within twenty feet of shore, we move forward. It's the best of both worlds, really. If I need repairs or medical help, I put in to dock. Otherwise, I stay out here. The river is my home. This is where I belong."

"And you can't tell what year it is out here?" Callie waved her hand at the river.

Walker shrugged. "Not exactly, but judging from other boats, bridges, and even buildings, I can get within a couple years. I can't get a newspaper because they're all from your time. The dates advance on shore, but not out here. I haven't aged physically since this started. It's like I'm suspended in time. Like I'm waiting to complete something I began."

"Was my Aunt Carolina ever on this boat?"

"Yes. Several times." He took her hand and laced his

fingers through hers. "She loved the *Belle*."

Callie digested that statement. Could it be true she had been reincarnated? True, she had memories she'd never had before today. And true, she had feelings she'd never experienced before. She stared at Justin. She didn't want those to go away. But the whole idea was so ridiculous.

Yet she still felt like her old self. Still had memories of Boston and growing up in a loving family. And other things didn't mesh either.

"But if you're a ghost, why aren't you transparent? Why aren't the other people in the dining room transparent?" She put her hand on his arm and squeezed. "Why do you feel so real?"

"I am real. As real as you. I'm not a ghost. I simply live in a range of time that shifts unaccountably.

"And you, Miss Stokes, aren't the first to come back." He glanced at the door to the dining room. "Three others in there are like you. They came back as someone reborn. They have lived two different, but full, lives."

"Where are the other passengers? The ones from Tall Stacks?"

"In the other dining room on the Sun Deck." He nodded to the floor above them.

"Did they see the *Cheyenne*?" Callie fought her rising anxiety. So much couldn't be explained, yet he had plenty of answers. "Did they see the lights along the river reappear?"

"Some may have, but they won't give it much thought. If they find out the *Cheyenne* sank over a hundred years before tonight, they'd assume they read the name wrong or that she was reconstructed."

Callie thought the theory made sense. "Who are the people in the dining room? Are they always on the *Belle* with you?"

"They were my passengers. They were on my boat when they died." He stared down at his hands; a frown furrowed his forehead. "I've thought about this, and I believe that time isn't a straight line, but layers." He held one hand horizontally and placed the other on top. "Sometimes, a part of one layer bleeds through to the others."

"So, you can live in different times?"

"I don't know that I'm alive in the conventional sense of the word," he said.

"But how?" Her mouth went dry.

"Who knows?" He held up his hands. "There's so much I can't explain."

"Well, how did you begin this, uh, journey?"

"There was an explosion on the *Belle*. I was hit on the back of the head by something. It knocked me into the river. I remember an awful, blinding pain, cold water, and then, nothing." He closed his eyes for a moment. "I woke in a strange room with a desperate urge to get back to the *Belle*. I was halfway to the Landing before I realized I had no pain. When I touched the back of my head, I had no wound. People greeted me as if it was just another day and my presence an ordinary occurrence." He smiled ruefully. "At the Landing, I found the *Belle* intact, my old crew preparing her to go." He looked at Callie. "I can't begin to tell you how confusing that was. At the time, I thought I'd dreamed the whole episode."

His gaze never left her face. She sensed how difficult it was for him to tell her this, how much he wanted her to believe. But as the lights of modern Cincinnati popped into view, reality hit her like a bucket of cold water.

The *Belle's* whistle startled them both.

"We're returning to shore." Justin gripped the railing with both hands. Without looking at her, he asked, "Do you believe me?"

"I want to." Callie looked up as they passed under the Roebling Suspension Bridge, car lights flashing between the railings. Her jumbled emotions twisted her insides. The romantic within wanted nothing more than to believe, to stay here, with Justin, forever. But how could she be in love with him? Her mind rebelled at the idea.

"Captain Walker, excuse me, sir. You're needed on the main deck." A young deck hand grinned at them from several feet away. "We're back in Cincinnati." Justin thanked the boy and waved him away. His gaze fell on Callie, scorching her soul with its intensity. "Do you think you'd like steamboat life?"

"Oh yes. I know I would." She heard the eagerness in her own voice. "I've been on the Delta Queen for a weeklong cruise."

Justin laughed. "That's just a taste. Think you'd like a steady diet of shipboard life? Every day waking up on something that moves?"

"With you, yes," she thought then stepped back from him realizing she'd spoken out loud.

"You are bold." He sounded pleased. "I like that. It's refreshing to know what a woman really thinks."

Callie blushed under his praise. He glanced down at the main deck where the crew scurried to secure the boat. "You must tell me your given name. When I call you Miss Stokes, I think of Carolina, but you are only part her. There is another part that is more…charming."

"My name is Callie." When he looked quizzical and repeated the name, she added, "That's short for Calliope."

"How enchanting." He grinned. "I shall call you Calliope."

"I never liked anyone to call me that." She glanced down the side of the *Belle*. "But here it seems all right. Appropriate."

"I never cared much for nicknames." Justin bent low over her hand. "Now I must see to the *Belle's* departing guests. Thank you for your help today. You will return tomorrow?"

"Yes." She felt his warm breath, then his lips, touch briefly on her skin. He smiled once more, released her hand, and returned to the dining room.

Justin's touch lingered on Callie's skin. She sighed as the

Belle drew up to Cincinnati's waterfront. She had much to think about, things she needed to be alone to sort out, but she also wanted to stay with Justin Walker.

Even if he is crazy, she thought. *Or even if I am.*

Mooring lines secured, Callie headed to the captain's cabin to collect her things. She lifted her garment bag from the coat tree and turned to leave when she spied a picture on top of a built-in bureau. Funny, she hadn't noticed the wooden frame when she changed her clothing earlier that night.

She crossed the room and picked up the black and white picture. Two rows of young ladies stood around a seated woman wearing an elaborate gown and veil. Words written across the bottom read, "Until I can get one better, this poor photo will have to do. With love, now and in all days to come, Carolina."

The words echoed in Callie's head. *With love.*

She held the picture up to see if she could pick her aunt out of the group. She found her right away.

She looks just like me. Now I see for myself why my grandparents told me that. She returned the frame to the bureau top and turned to go when a stray thought halted her in her tracks.

That's why Justin is being so nice to me. He thinks I'm Carolina. He all but said so.

Callie mulled this over. Perhaps she really was Carolina to some extent, but she was herself, too.

At the gangway, Justin, locked in conversation with a passenger, didn't look up as Callie passed. In her head, she wished him a good night's sleep.

"Better hurry, the last shuttle to the parking lot is leaving in ten minutes." The volunteer coordinator touched Callie's shoulder, bringing her back to reality.

She nodded and, with one last longing glance at the *Belle*, ran for the bus.

At home, Callie prowled restlessly through the rooms of her apartment. She strove to reconcile the incredible events, the myriad of puzzles that had developed. Had it only been this morning that she caught the shuttle bus to Tall Stacks? *Maybe one day in hours, but a lifetime in emotional upheaval.*

She could not explain Justin's existence, yet she didn't doubt his reality. He sounded real, smelled real, and heaven knows he felt real when they touched. *I should sleep.* She rubbed her dry, tired eyes. *But I need to know more about the Belle and Justin.*

Her gaze fell on a box of keepsakes. Most of the contents were from Callie's high school years, but she thought there was something that belonged to her grandmother, too. She pulled everything out, scattering them on the floor, until she found a wide book that looked familiar.

Laying the fragile cloth volume on her lap, she opened the cover. Page by page, she scanned names of places, names of people. She studied dates, trying to find anything connected to Carolina, the *Belle*, or Justin Walker. She found nothing until the very last page. And there he was.

Posed in front of a background painted with a river and steamboats, Justin Walker stared at something just out of sight of the camera. Along the bottom edge, someone had written, "The Heroic Justin Walker."

Callie ran her fingertips over the image, as if she could feel the coarse wool coat or his warm skin, but the cool paper proved a poor substitute.

She searched back through the book, looking for a picture of Carolina, but found nothing. Frustrated, she replaced the book in the box. She looked around the office, seeking ideas, clues she knew weren't there.

Without warning, an image burst into her head, the sight of a steamboat with smoke roiling from windows and doors. Wooden crates, stacked around the outside of the main deck, blew out into the river as if a hurricane had formed inside the superstructure. People on the upper decks jumped into the water as passengers on lower decks stumbled from smoke-choked hallways and stood screaming as the river began to wash over their feet. Justin pushed over several crates, emptying their contents into the river. He lowered the wooden boxes into the water, then helped the ladies and children to grab hold of the splintery crates and float. Waiting rowboats snatched the survivors up and carried them to safety. Justin disappeared.

Callie watched this all happen as if from a distance, the sounds muted, and the smells faint, until the scene faded. She stood and drew several deep breaths. She'd never seen anything like that in her life. That was not a memory. At least, it wasn't her own memory.

Callie tried to swallow and found her mouth dry. She went into the kitchen and got a can of root beer from the refrigerator. After pouring the contents into a glass with some ice, she calmed down.

I'll get some rest. Maybe that will clear my head.

On the way to her bedroom, she passed the bookcase and noticed Carolina's notebook inside. Forgetting her need to sleep, she stopped, opened the doors, and removed the book.

This time, Callie saw the notes and sketches in a different light. These weren't just raw ideas, but serious attempts to introduce safer equipment on riverboats. New boilers with self-adjusting safety valves, overhead pipes that would carry pumped river water to every room on the *Belle*. Wooden flotation devices stored on every deck of the boat to be retrieved by passengers in case of emergency. Even wide wooden cradles with high sides for children and babies.

Was this Carolina's response to witnessing the explosion?

She got to the end of the book and, for the first time, noticed that the last page stuck to the back cover. Gently, she slipped a fingernail under the corner and eased the papers apart. Several yellowed newspaper clippings, two letters, and a photograph fell out onto the floor.

Callie scrutinized her aunt's picture then looked on the back. In a delicate script, she'd written, "To my beloved, on our wedding day, Carolina."

Wedding day? But they never married. Had they?

She reached for the newspaper articles next. The first recounted a tragic fire that took place in August 1883 on the *Belle*, killing over sixty people. The boat sank just fifty feet from shore as she turned to come into Cincinnati's Public Landing. A contemporary newspaper reported that a faulty boiler safety valve was to blame and boldly stated that the captain, Justin Walker, had called for more steam, pushing the engine past its limit. His body had not been located after the incident.

Justin was presumed dead.

Callie sniffed. It would be easy to place blame on a dead man.

If the valve was faulty, would anyone but the manufacturer of the valve be to blame?

Callie tried to recall her employer's position on like matters, but nothing came to mind. Parts she designed had been tested extensively before they shipped to the customer. Of course, there had been rumors of an old lawsuit that never went to court for lack of evidence.

Old law suit. Her stomach clenched.

Her company, founded in 1840, made switches and valves for nautical engines.

Frantic, she scanned the newspaper article. What company made the steam valves? No name was mentioned.

Goosebumps covered her arms. She laid the clipping upside down on the floor beside her. She'd think more about it later.

Next she found a brief account of Carolina's rescue from an overturned boat on a flooded Ohio River, copied from an old newspaper. Captain Justin Walker, in port due to the high water, heard cries for help and, without hesitation, dove into the treacherous current and pulled the young lady to safety aboard the moored *Belle*. Hand written in the margin, someone indicated that Carolina had been the victim. She and her mother remained guests on the steamboat for a week during her recovery. In dark, angry letters were the words, "Mother does not approve of Justin. Says he is common. He is not."

Callie glanced at the date of the accident. May 15, 1883. Three months before the *Belle* burned.

By comparing the handwriting to the letters on the picture, Callie realized that her Great-great Aunt Carolina had made the notes.

Fingers trembling, Callie picked up the last brief extract. The date on the top read, August 6, 1883, the day before the *Belle* was destroyed by fire. A few terse words announced the engagement of Carolina Stokes to Weston Canfield, the oldest son of a wealthy state senator. Shaken, Callie assumed that Carolina's engagement would have been to Justin.

Well, whoever this Canfield fellow was, Carolina didn't marry him.

Gently, she placed the announcement on top of the other papers and picked up one of the letters. Unfolding the two sheets, she noticed heavy creases that began to fray in the middle of the page. Undated and addressed to Carolina, this had been read over and over. She flipped to the signature line.

Forever yours, Justin.

In short sentences, he pleaded with her to marry him and become his wife. He begged her to respond right away and not let her family change her mind.

The second letter, also from Justin, coolly congratulated her on a lucrative engagement. Smears blurred some of the letters, making the words hard to read. Callie's heart ached. The smudged blots looked like dried teardrops.

She let the letter fall into her lap and leaned back against the wall. So many pieces of this puzzle remained hidden. Carolina's response to Justin's pleas were lost to time, but judging from the notebooks and the items her ancestor kept, she had not stopped caring for him.

Callie's gaze fell on the article about the fire. Nothing was said about Justin. What had happened to him? She had to know.

Toward dawn, Callie headed for the bathroom to take a quick shower. She'd scrutinized every inch of Carolina's notebook and even her grandmother's scrapbook but discovered nothing else.

Too much has happened. Too many things to sort through. Now I know why Scarlett O'Hara always said, "I'll think about that tomorrow."

She disrobed and stepped into the spray. Tipping her head back, she let the warm water roll over her skin. In the next instant, she couldn't breathe. *Icy darkness enfolded her, covering her mouth and her nose. Her eyes flew open. Murky water swirled around her, below her, and above her. Flailing her arms, she reached out but couldn't find the tiled wall. Her head bobbed up above the surface. Dark skies above. A clap of thunder. She gathered a deep breath and yelled for help before submerging again.*

Then he was there. His dear face before her in the dim water, strong arms reaching and catching her, pulling her to safety. Callie blinked and was back in her shower. Hands shaking, she turned off the faucets, and curled up in the bottom of the tub. The range of feelings, from terror to tenderness to love, fell upon her at once, leaving her trembling and unable to move for several minutes. Had that really happened? But what happened? A memory? Or a slip in time?

More unanswered questions. She dashed away the tears that rolled down her cheeks.

Why was this happening to her? She liked her life before all this happened. She liked her job, her apartment, and her new city. And sure, she missed her family and friends back home in New England, but she met people easily. But now... now everything seemed... messy. And frightening. Out of her hands. As if a silent storm blew in and the wind's name was Justin Walker.

Justin. His name alone inspired goose bumps to chase up her arms. But his presence satisfied something in her soul, an unnamed yearning she hadn't been aware of before yesterday. Somehow, he gave her a home in a world where she'd never felt lost. He gave her passion when she suffered no lack of love.

And they barely knew each other.

Or did they?

In her living room, a clock chimed four. This sound, so much a part of her everyday life, spurred her into action. Ignoring the practical advice from her brain that she hop into bed and get some rest, she did as her heart commanded.

Callie climbed out of the tub and dried herself with a fluffy towel. She applied makeup, selected earrings, and fastened a watch on her wrist. Dressed in a tunic sweater and tights, she climbed into her car, and drove to the Public Landing.

This time, hours before the scant parking was needed for disabled visitors, Callie parked in the lot and ran as fast as she could to the *Belle*. Her footfalls echoed off the Serpentine Wall, sounding in time with the beat of her heart. Was Justin still there?

Out of breath as she reached the place where the *Belle* was moored, she stopped, spying a tall shadowed form on the moveable bridge.

"You came early." Justin's voice reached her across the short expanse.

"I have some questions."

"Do you believe I'm real?" He took a step toward her.

"Yes." Callie barely heard her own voice. In her heart, the truth could no longer be denied. "Yes, I believe you."

"When you left, I realized you weren't Carolina. Not entirely, anyway." Justin remained silent a moment then said, "I thought you wouldn't return."

"But here I am." Callie searched his face in the soft light. "And Justin, I'm convinced that part of my aunt does live on in me."

"We still have some time before the rest of the crew awakens." He held out his hand. "Let's find a place to talk."

They settled on life preserver chests at the stern of the boat, away from the cabins and out of sight of the shore.

"What are your questions?" Justin leaned toward her, his smile warming the chilly morning.

"Were you engaged to Carolina?"

"Not officially. Nothing had been announced because her parents were dead set against our betrothal." He laughed bitterly. "Her mother hated me after she found out my family fought for the Confederacy. It might be hard for you to understand the emotions at that time, but the war was very, very much alive in 1883. The Stokes family fought for the Union." His jaw tightened. "Carolina's parents published an engagement announcement for their daughter and a man she barely knew, a wealthy New Yorker. They told her the alliance would benefit everyone."

"She never married him."

"I know." He ran his hand over his eyes. "I found out later, just before all this," he waved a hand at the *Belle*, "began."

"I have something that belongs to you." She pulled Carolina's picture from her purse and gave it to him.

"Thank you." He stared at the image in silence then put it in his pocket.

"Were you eloping when the *Belle* exploded?" Callie didn't know where the question came from, but she suddenly understood the truth.

He nodded. "I was putting in to the Landing to pick her up. She was there, waiting, with an absurd amount of luggage." He looked at her, eyes widening. "I'm so glad she wasn't on board. I would have killed her."

Callie laid a hand on his arm. "It was a bad valve, Justin. The fire wasn't your fault."

"Yes, technically that is true, but as captain, I was responsible for the integrity of the engine. I should have inspected everything closer."

"You couldn't have anticipated a bad machine part. Especially since it had been operational until then."

"I don't remember what I told the engineer. Maybe I did tell him more steam." He shrugged. "I don't know, but I should have put my job before my heart." He looked over his shoulder at the cabins. "So, now I take these same people up and down the rivers over and over again."

"The same passengers?" Callie puzzled over that information. "The ones from the fire? Like a penance?"

"Strange as it may seem, though, it doesn't feel like a punishment. More like a reward." He laughed lightly. "Which I don't understand. This is what I hoped Heaven would be like." Justin sobered and looked into Callie's eyes. "If you were here with me I'd be having the time of my life."

"This is confusing." Callie rubbed her temple. "But I guess I shouldn't bother to try to figure it out."

"What else do you want to know?"

"What was the name of the company that made the valves? Do you remember?"

He snorted. "How could I forget? The Belton Company. One of the surviving crewmembers tried to sue them, but the case was dismissed for lack of evidence. They couldn't find the broken part."

"I'm an engineer for Belton Valve and Switch. Last year I designed a new system of marine switches that would prevent an accidental overload of power to one circuit." Callie took a deep breath. "I think this ties in somehow to your, ah, predicament."

"What?" His head snapped around, his gaze seared her.

"What if I had to have a solution to the valve problem before we could be together? Carolina spent the rest of her life studying the mechanics of steam engines. I used some of her theories to create new equipment for the company whose poor quality control caused the fire.

"I do believe that part of me is Carolina, but I'm me, too." She heard herself speak, aware of emotions seeping through from another side of her. These feelings once belonged to Carolina, but now mingled so closely with her own that they could no longer be separated.

"You just may be right," Justin said. Then he smiled. "I'm glad you're you, Calliope, and also some of her, but what do we do?"

Callie's pragmatic side warred with the idealist in her soul. How could she dump a successful career and run off on a steamboat with a man who lived such a bizarre life? Yet how could she return to work tomorrow? How could she call on customers and face each humdrum day knowing Justin Walker sailed through time on his ship of dreams?

Simple. She couldn't.

"Why isn't it possible for me to stay with you?" With those words, she made her commitment to him and to her past.

"But it is possible." His head snapped around to look at her, his eyes reflecting the cool gray of dawn. "You'd give up your present life to stay with me here on the *Belle*?"

"I can't imagine living anywhere else anymore."

He jumped to his feet, a wide grin splitting his face. "I'll have my steward move my things to a guest cabin. You'll be comfortable in mine…." He stopped. "I could give you a few days to think it over," he suggested.

"No, I don't need a few days." She looked into the depths of his eyes and saw herself at peace. It no longer mattered if she was herself or Carolina. Her soul belonged here, no matter what name she used. "I'll go with you right now."

Justin pulled her to her feet and into his arms, relief

softening the lines around his eyes. His lips met hers and they shared a short, hard kiss.

"Do you think my presence will change things? Here on the *Belle*, I mean," Callie asked.

"Let's find out." Justin stood and helped her up. They walked to the bow and, at a signal from Justin, the crewmembers flew into action, releasing mooring lines and raising the bridge. A slight vibration warned Callie that the huge paddlewheel had started to turn.

"Now we will see what happens." Justin sounded calm and confident.

The *Belle* steamed to the middle of the river where Callie watched the shoreline blur then reform in a different shape. Cincinnati shrank to a low profile of two and three story buildings. Dozens of steamboats lined the Public Landing, but they had unfamiliar names painted on their sides.

Callie felt Justin's arms enfold her from behind, wrapping her in strength and courage. She turned to face him, trying to melt into him, be part of him. They shared another kiss, one with an increasing passion that left her breathless.

As the *Belle* passed out of sight of the city, Callie noticed that the ship had moved close to shore, traveling within several feet of the riverbank. But nothing changed. She searched for cars on the road, for airplanes in the sky, but saw none. Her heart pounded as suspicion grew in the pit of her stomach.

As they glided past a small shipyard, workers slapped paint on a brand new steamboat. The name on her side was the *Cheyenne*.

"I think we have our answer," Justin said.

Giddy with relief, she laughed. "Oh, I'm so glad."

"Are you?" His eyes sparkled in the sunlight.

"Yes," she said as something occurred to her. "And for more reasons than one. Didn't you say the Cheyenne launched a month before the *Belle* sank?"

"Yes, I guess we won't have much time together," he

commented dryly.

"But we can fix that valve." She grabbed his arm. "You won't have the fire this time."

"Of course. Of course! That's why you're here." His eyes skimmed down her body as furrows formed between his eyebrows.

"Look." He touched Callie's sleeve.

She glanced down and gasped at the long white cotton dress she now wore. Her hand flew up to find her tresses pinned up in an elaborate series of braids.

"It appears you have taken Carolina's place." He nodded at the shoreline. "We're almost scraping the riverbank." His voice, filled with quiet awe, barely reached her ears. "We should be in your time, but we're not. We didn't make a transition."

Callie's heart skipped a beat. "Maybe you had to wait for me before you could go forward again."

"And now that you're here, we've gone home. You may never return to your time."

"I've left no family behind, only a few friends and a job they will quickly fill." She snuggled closer to his chest and felt the quick tightening of his arms. "My home, my heart is here with you. And the *Belle of the Ohio*."

THE TALISMAN

Betsy Norman

Ceallaigh moved into the house because of the painting.

The inheritance from a bachelor uncle surprised her. Her parents had rarely mentioned him in the years before they died. Her last memory of a visit with Uncle Dennis was when she was a little girl riding her bike along the sidewalk in front of his house. The attic windows and broad porch created a face that smiled at her as she rode by.

She remembered squinting up to see her uncle watching from one of the attic eyes and waving. But then he was on the porch, too quickly for him to come down the three flights of stairs. The summer sun had played tricks with the heat off of the roof, Uncle Dennis would explain. He'd not been in the attic. It was no matter. Ceallaigh promised herself one day she'd live in a happy house that loved her just like her uncle's.

A fondness for older homes, and this one in particular, made her curious if there were any truth to the whimsical fantasy of her childhood that a magic house could cure her melancholy. All her life she felt as if she wore the wrong skin; a misfit lacking something she could never name.

Relationships never stuck and jobs didn't last. Would she ever feel like she belonged, like she'd come home at last? Following the lawyer for a walk-through, she climbed the stair to the attic for the first time.

"These leftover items from the auction will be hauled away," the lawyer told her, gesturing toward the various trunks and battered antiques cluttering the attic. "It's already been picked over by the dealers. Unless there's a Picasso under that no-name oil over there, you'll be out of luck." He shrugged. "Besides, it's ripped."

At the top of the stairwell, she felt her pulse trip-hammer when she saw the painting he referred to propped near the window. A life-sized image of a man. Gasping, her hand flew to the heart locket at her throat, rubbing the warm metal to calm herself. Perhaps the painting watched her when she was a little girl, and she mistook it for Uncle Dennis.

"No, no." Ceallaigh shook her head, already mesmerized by the painting. Her artist's eye caught every detail. The strokes and color textures were obviously painstakingly created to capture the very soul of the model. "That won't be necessary. There may be some hidden treasure here." Enthralled, enamored, so strong was her reaction when she saw his inviting hand held out, she had to catch her breath. Her mind filled with a longing to accept and follow wherever he led. Where did these strong feelings come from? She wondered if he was the reason that she was always drawn to the house.

Luck is relative, Ceallaigh thought, scorning the lawyer's crass dismissal of the painting. Not all value can be measured monetarily or through perfection. Some things had priceless sentimental value, like the locket she wore from her grandmother, passed down through generations. The catch was broken, and it wouldn't open, but she drew comfort from stroking the metal just the same. Maybe this painting meant a great deal to her uncle for similar reasons, despite the damage done.

The tear in the canvas stood out like a scar, awkwardly puckered and stitched back together, but failed to mar the masterpiece. She itched to fetch her palette and pigment tubes to camouflage the repair. Ceallaigh wondered if her meager talent was worthy enough to blend in with the unique shadows and dimensions.

"How soon can you move in to settle the estate?" the lawyer asked.

In this house, Ceallaigh felt as if she had finally found what she'd been longing for to fill the void of emptiness in her soul. The man in the painting beckoned her home.

"As soon as I can pack," she told him without hesitation.

During the two weeks it took her to box up her solitary lifestyle and make arrangements to move out of her apartment, the dusty canvas she'd seen in the attic formed a life of its own in her mind. She longed to step inside his world of deep moss-carpeted forest and reach for his outstretched hand. His profile teased and intrigued her; the sharp line of jaw, full mouth and rambling mahogany hair bound in a leather strip. The broad crux of his shoulders, accented by the padded gambeson of a medieval warrior and draped in brown woolen cape, were held just so, waiting, waiting. Clad in black leather boots, he stood patiently, his back slightly turned so she could not see his eyes, and his palm tilted upward for another to join him.

For whom did he wait?

Her nights spent dreaming of a two-dimensional image and fleshing him out inside her mind had come to an end as she pulled into the driveway. Ceallaigh unlocked the door to the house and ran up the three flights of steps to the walk-up attic. Breathless and excited, she was eager to touch the textured oil again. To be with *him* again. Soiled buckcloth, carelessly tossed by the lawyer over the painting as if to discount its worth, hid the picture from view.

She took a deep breath in preparation, closing her eyes and recalling her memory's version of the glade and the wandering stranger. Dreams that had animated the scene and given it tangible warmth allowed her to follow the mystery man wherever he led in their nocturnal trysts. Gingerly, her fingers took hold of the creased drop cloth and pulled it away from the frame.

There, at last. Her mind's snapshot image had captured each detail in true form. Her hands reached to caress his cloak and trace the mended scar of the canvas. Who would try to destroy such a magnificent piece of art, and who took the time to try and repair it and why? She stroked the inviting palm, lingering at his fingertips.

But wait, his eyes hadn't reflected back in shades of gray from the woven surface of the canvas before, she was certain they had been hidden from her. The curve of one shoulder dipped further, revealing more than the sparse profile.

His expression imparted yearning. A mirror image of her own emotional longing these past weeks was reflected in his gaze back at her. An eeriness crept over Ceallaigh, nape hairs rising. She felt a whispered warmth against her neck. His eyes watched too keenly, and she no longer felt as if she were alone in the attic. The faint smell of wood smoke and pine needles overtook the mustiness of the stored items.

Captivated trance-like by the stranger's gaze, Ceallaigh forced herself to look away and distance herself. To back off and escape the palpable ghostly presence surrounding her. She bolted down the stairs and slammed the door. Her breath and pulse thundered in alarm.

Nay, fear naught. A low, almost familiar, baritone filled her mind. *Come back to me.*

She turned the key, locking out the voice and the craziness that surely conjured it up. A painting, she kept repeating to herself, gripping her locket tightly for assurance. He was only a painting.

The movers arrived later that morning, and her attention shifted back to reality as she directed the delivery of her boxes and furniture. She made a point of carrying in her easels and pigment crates herself, setting them up in the bright sunroom sporting a full wall of bowed out windows. Her paintings, the computer, her father's Victrola and mother's antique jewelry box, her African violets, all these items she insisted on handling alone rather than risk damage.

Loath to accompany the men up to the attic, she asked that the boxes labeled "storage" be placed to one side opposite the items left behind from the previous owner.

"Lady, you got a draft up there." One burly mover shook his head. "Darndest thing, too, it's cold as ice e'en though today is hotter'n heck."

"Oh?" Ceallaigh shuddered in her summer tank top and rubbed her hands over her bare arms. "I didn't notice."

"Who's the mean-lookin' fella in your picture?"

"Excuse me?"

"He sure does have a terrible frown, like we're buttin' in on his space, or somethin'. Gives me the willies. You don't have much more that needs going up there, do ya?"

"No," Ceallaigh replied absently, glancing toward the stairs. "I don't think so."

"Scaredy-cat," his buddy jeered. "Afraid of some painting of a long-haired pansy? He don't look so tough to me. I'll take the last load."

While the mover carried the last of her storage boxes up the stairs, she gingerly followed behind. She had to go back up to the attic. What were they talking about? The man in the painting looked lonely, inviting, not angry. Peeking above the pocket stairwell at the picture, she saw the menacing scowl directed toward the worker. Half-turned, his hand almost looked as if it were now pointing in a commanding gesture. Was his change in position a trick of the light?

"You so bad in your pretty boy curls," the mover laughed at the painting. "I bet I could kick your butt." He dropped the final box in place, dancing and jabbing in front of the portrait in a shadow-boxers stance. Flapping one hand dismissively at the image, he turned and laughed, about to walk away, before promptly tripping and falling flat on his face.

Ceallaigh clapped a hand over her mouth to stifle her giggle. In an instant, the man's expression in the painting transformed back to the solitary longing as her gaze met the one brushed in oils. Her eyes widened in shock.

"You!" The hushed accusation barely escaped her lips. This was no trick. She'd seen him actually move, his gray eyes twinkling back at her.

The mover grunted and dusted himself off, muttering "Damn loose floorboards," before stumbling once more and toppling into a stack of boxes.

"Oh!" She jumped to assist him and cast an anxious glance at the painting, which seemed to smile back at her. "Here, let me help you." Arm firmly grasping the man's elbow to lend support, she gave another quick look to the painting to see dour repentance gleaming back. "I'm so sorry, I'll have those boards checked."

The mover flushed, obviously embarrassed at having her witness his clumsiness. "Yeah, better check 'em for missing nails. Don't trip yourself, ma'am."

"I shall endeavor to take heed of your wisdom, good sirrah," she assured him. *Where on earth had those words come from?* Her throat seized. Now the painting was manipulating her, too?

The mover looked at her strangely. "How's that?"

Ceallaigh puzzled over her own words, realizing what just came out of her mouth. "I said, I'll try not to trip."

He shucked off her assisting arm to make his way down the stairs.

A warm rush of spice-scented air embraced her, stroked her cheek and slid down both bare shoulders.

How I have waited for you. Your soul, your eyes. Stay. The masculine voice caressed her mind again.

Suppressing a shiver, Ceallaigh looked to the painting that obviously was much more than mere pigment to canvas. The strong figure faced her now, revealing the full breadth of powerful shoulders and lean waist. His palm reached further still with entreaty. She released a cagey breath before dragging her gaze upward to meet his own.

"*Lochlain....*" Recognition enchanted her and the name spilled over her lips of its own volition. "Milord, what blessed reunion is this?" Her floating steps headed toward the oil-brushed visage, arms outstretching to greet him.

"Lady, all we got left is your 'Arm-woire.'" The mover's tobacco-graveled voice trailed up from downstairs to interrupt her hypnosis.

Ceallaigh blinked away the cobwebs in her head, fighting for conscious thought. *What's happening to me?* Hands splayed desperately to hold the two-dimensional stranger, she found herself prostrate against the painting. Face-to-face she saw his eyes widen in anger at the cursed intrusion, flashing storm cloud black, making the very backdrop of the painting shadow with impending gales.

"You said you wanted to supervise this." The mover barely concealed his sarcasm. "Would you mind coming down so we can finish?"

"I... I..." Her throat fought against the gripping uncertainty. Entwined in an unseen force, she couldn't pull away. "I'll be right down," she called. Still, the clinch would not relent. Furious gray eyes engulfed her. "Please," she begged. "Let me go."

Roiling emotions of fear and fascination warred within Ceallaigh. She *knew* him. Deep in some secreted cavern of her soul, she recognized the beckoning spirit.

She stumbled away from the painting as if a puppet freed of its cross and strings. Rejection and hurt clearly written in his face, he now turned as before, half-hidden in shadow. Forcing back a sob against her fist, Ceallaigh ran for the stair and slammed the door shut in finality. This was some sort of ensorcellment aimed at claiming her sanity. She turned the key and tucked it deep in a pocket.

The movers delivered their last lot in haste, aided by Ceallaigh's uneasy guidance. Blackness like a veil shrouded the horizon, and she feared Lochlain's anger over their interruption stretched beyond the confines of the attic. She paid the men quickly, bidding them thanks and hurrying them on their way. The movers hightailed it to their truck just moments before madness and fury shredded the sky, lambasting the earth below with an onslaught of thrashing rain and hail.

Once they were gone, the bend and moan of floorboards and structure beneath the potent barrage of wind deceived her senses. She could feel the spirit two floors above roam and pace in restless agitation. Or was it her own feet wearing a rut in the bare hardwood?

She couldn't concentrate with the howl of the storm outside or the subliminal summoning to return to the attic. A wall of unpacked boxes lined the lower hall. How could she move into a possessed house? Had some medieval sorcerer cast a spell of enchantment? Who was Lochlain, and how did she come by his name? How did the painting end up in her uncle's attic?

A thought nagged at her. The lawyer called the painting a no-name oil, and yet didn't every artist draw a signature somewhere on his work? Perhaps therein she'd find a clue. Finding out the name of the artist might also tell her who the man in the painting was.

Which meant she had to go up to the attic and look.

Resigned to the task, Ceallaigh took a deep breath to fortify herself. The storm surrendered at once to a content patter, mere fingertaps against the windowpanes begging to gain entrance.

Her stocking feet mute against the steps allowed her heart to hammer all the more loudly in her ears. The latchkey clicked easily, and her wary gaze sought his once she reached the attic. His posture returned to original form, palm outturned. Close scrutiny revealed no hint of thunderous gray eyes or longing expression. He was as before, face hidden from her.

Perhaps it was a dream? But she did not recall sleeping. Chalk it off to wild imagination, then? Circling the painting, tense with anticipation, no awareness penetrated her soul. No whispering baritone implored her. No ethereal arms surrounded her. Nothing.

Her breath deflated and a puzzled furrow formed on her brow. "Lochlain?"

No answer either.

She pursed her lips and crouched low to discover what anonymous hand laid brush to canvas to create this mysterious enigma. Searching, her fingers scrubbed the textured shrubbery floor of the scene in hopes of finding a bare spot to reveal the signature. Turning the mammoth frame around, she checked the stretched edges. A brief scrawl caught her attention.

"Aha." The tattered weave nearly obliterated the brushed cursive and she struggled to make out the initials. A bold "C" or was it a "G"? Followed by a slurred "E" or maybe a "B" and a faint symbol burned into the canvas. The rest was lost in artistic expression.

She sat back on her heels. Not even a full surname to investigate. Only two vague initials. Perhaps that and the mended tear were why the dealers hadn't bothered with the portrait. She returned the frame to its initial position and studied the canvas. It wasn't an old painting, but the style and method dated the artist as non-contemporary. The texture and color came to life of their own accord, Ceallaigh admitted, and the creator's talent far surpassed her own fledgling attempts.

Sighing, exhausted, she descended the stairs to the master bedroom on the second floor and stretched out on her bare mattress. Sleep drugged her into deep unconsciousness.

Feverish dreams infested her slumber. A wild, unkempt woman buffeted a huge canvas with relentless strokes of color. The details refused to come clear. Aged hands like claws clutched the brush in desperation to complete her task before... before....

Ceallaigh awoke in a rush of breath as if an unseen hand released her nose and mouth from suffocation. The woman's face engraved itself in her mind. Those eyes, deep chips of agate consumed with a passion to reclaim what was lost, haunted her. Ceallaigh recognized the similarities to her own unusual eye coloring and high-boned features. *So familiar.* Where had she seen that woman before?

Ceallaigh thought, tried to focus, then recalled the découpage box of photographs her parents had given to her on her twenty-sixth birthday just before they died. The family tree of faces and names to cherish and pass on to the next generation, should there be one. She was an only child with no living relatives. Ceallaigh held little doubt the box holding her past would live on to contain the future. Her heart was bound by an unexplained loneliness no man could ever cure. She resigned herself to the fate that there would be no husband, no children, and no legacy of her own to pass these momentos on to. She could drop off of the face of the earth right now, and none would note her absence.

Nay, a deep inner whisper urged. *Find her and you shall find your true fate. Bring to me the Talisman.*

Ceallaigh pressed her palms to her temples to force Lochlain's mental encroachment aside. *Have I finally reached madness?*

Downstairs, she searched through the packing boxes for the one containing the family photos. Her greedy hands at last found the decorative box and sprawled its contents across the floor. The faces of her relations shifted from color to black and white, names and dates recorded for posterity across the backing. On the bottom of the box, she found an ornate graph spidering a web of fingers to link each of the names down to hers.

One name stood out from the rest: Ceallaigh Barrows, her

great-great-great aunt on her mother's side. She instinctively found the photo and recognized the woman as a younger version of the fevered artist in her dream. Staring at the photo, she blinked at the posed image and the strong resemblance to herself. Quickly leafing through the leather-bound book accompanying the photos, Ceallaigh read the brief history her mother provided from collected word of mouth accounts retold through her late grandmother.

Ceallaigh Barrows: born October 27, 1836 in Piqua, OH, died July 22, 1916. Never married. Artist of sorts. Institutionalized at Sacred Lady Hospital for delusions. Died of broken heart, so said. Her last painting and personal items distributed among family.

A prayer card fell free from the pages, the parchment tea-colored with age. Inside she found a clipping of the obituary with the address of the funeral home and hospital.

Ceallaigh forced herself to breathe evenly and absorb the information. She could easily dismiss the events as coincidental, snap the journal shut and pack the whole box up and into the attic—never to set foot up there again.

And perhaps spiral into the same delusional madness as her aunt, listening to whispering paintings and questioning her sanity.

The initials matched. Did Ceallaigh Barrows paint Lochlain? Why? A painting was specifically mentioned among her belongings. The one in the attic? What caused the rip? Was there a bewitching spirit trapped in the painting? What was the connection between Lochlain and her aunt?

"What does it all mean?" she whispered.

I need the Talisman, Ceallaigh. An adoring stroke slid down her spine. *I beseech you, my love. Seek the means to return to me and all shall be revealed.*

Ceallaigh shivered. She quickly packed an overnight bag, grabbed the ledger containing the information about her aunt and ran from the house, determined to find the answers to her questions.

"Yes, I remember Ceallaigh Barrows," the elderly woman told her. "She was a resident here when I was just a child."

At last. Ceallaigh closed her eyes and exhaled slowly, bracing herself for the interview. She'd spent the past week driving to Ohio and rooting through archives and files in the basement of the hospital where her aunt died. The nuns and nurses were helpful but couldn't provide the answers she needed to find. A tour of the rooms surfaced the link she didn't think possible. By introduction, Mary Sanders informed each and every passerby that she'd walked the halls of Sacred Lady Hospital since she was twelve. When she got on in years and it was her time to be cared for, she'd consider nowhere else to be but Sacred Lady. At age ninety-six, Mary still possessed youthful blue eyes that looked misplaced in the wrinkled and weathered face.

"How did you know her?" Ceallaigh leaned forward, pencil in hand to sketch the woman's animated features.

"Oh, let me see. My mother worked here as a charwoman, and I tagged along to carry her buckets." She tsk'd and curled one gnarled finger to her cheek, ruminating. "I only knew her a short while before she died."

"She was… an artist," Ceallaigh hesitated, not wanting to reveal too much. "I think I may have come upon one of her paintings."

"Heaven's yes, she was. Very talented, too. And messy. Your aunt's room was a trial. Paint everywhere, all the time. Even the nurses cursed under their habits at having to bathe her so frequently." Mary gave a tiny, chortling laugh. "She let me finger-paint once. I'll never forget the caning I got because of my dirty pinafore, but it was worth it," she confided. "Because in kind, she let me watch her paint *him*." A long sigh and silence.

Ceallaigh held her breath, then caught herself and reminded her heart to beat again. "Him, who?" she whispered, already knowing the answer.

"Lochlain." Mary winked and her creased brow smoothed

out in dreamy reflection. "Her love. So handsome, other-worldly and mysterious. I was infatuated, myself."

Ceallaigh tried to stifle her reaction to Mary's revelation, prodding further. "But my aunt never married. There is no record of a—"

"Oh, goodness no, dear. Not a lover in the flesh. In the past."

"But how could that be?" Ceallaigh shook her head. "My aunt was delusional," she stated. "Perhaps in her mind—"

"She was no more delusional than I am." Mary pursed her lips and sat closer. "Those starched nuns. Intolerance ruled the day back then, you see? Heaven and Hell, period. No room to consider a recycling of souls. Craziness to think it, they claimed."

"Reincarnation?"

"Yes." Mary nodded furiously. "Your aunt's soul was recycled but her lover's wasn't. Caught in limbo he was, because he couldn't accept eternity without her."

"She believed this? That she and Lochlain were lovers in another lifetime?"

Mary's crinkled face set in an enigmatic smile. "Hmm. You have your aunt's eyes, child. Such an unusual color," she mused, stroking Ceallaigh's temple. "Eyes are said to be windows to the soul. Perhaps you've inherited more than your name from her, hmmm?"

Her remark chilled Ceallaigh. Same eyes, same name. Both Lochlain and Mary hinted at something that she refused to acknowledge. She grew up believing her soul was destined to a final paradise, not handed down through untold generations.

"Your aunt's painting, the one you have, is a man, is it not?" Mary asked. "A man your heart recognizes. And that's why you're here."

"Yes," Ceallaigh confessed. "I inherited the home that's fascinated me since I was small. I found him in the attic."

"No," Mary shook her head. "Lochlain has found you, my

dear. Just as he found your aunt. Only, this time, perhaps he's not too late."

Ceallaigh shivered, fingers worrying the chain of her necklace. "He moves within the painting. Manipulates his surroundings. My words."

"You think him evil," Mary stated. "As did your aunt at first." Mary's hands fidgeted in the nest of her lap as if she harbored the same doubts of dark magic that Ceallaigh did. "Dreams plagued her." Her hollow tone spoke low. "His spirit reaching beyond the chains of physical plains. She'd fallen into despair, sleeping at his feet, weeping—"

"Why?" Ceallaigh urged her on. "Madness?"

"A madness borne of frustration. She could not produce what he asked for to reunite their souls."

"The Talisman?"

"Yes!" the older woman exclaimed. "Do you have it?"

"Does such a thing even exist?"

"Your aunt believed she knew where it was," Mary whispered sadly. "But the only belongings they allowed her to keep were the paints and brushes. She begged to return home and look for the Talisman, but they thought her mad when she told them why." Mary trembled, tears coloring her rheumy and mournful eyes.

"Did she tell you what it was, where to look?"

"Sadly, no, I cannot help you there, but you must find it or suffer the same fate. She was heartbroken, unable to go to him. The night she died, a howling storm raged, terrifying the whole ward." Mary leaned in, confiding. "I overheard your aunt's attending nurses whispering the next day about the mysterious tear in the painting. As if it tried to rip itself in despair over her death. I tried to fix it, but my clumsy stitches…." she trailed off.

"Thank you." Ceallaigh knew the painting's ability to lash out and didn't question the alleged source of the damage. Still, she didn't know what to think. "But how can I know for sure—?"

"What does your heart tell you?"

Ceallaigh's hand stilled. She could not answer. How did one put to voice the rapture her despondent soul experienced when in Lochlain's embrace?

"Go to him. Find the Talisman."

During the trip home, Ceallaigh fixated on what Mary told her. Was she destined for madness? Did she harbor deep inside her the spirit of Lochlain's former love, as her aunt had? What was the Talisman, and where could she find it? And once found, what supernatural magic did it possess? How was it used?

Her new home loomed ahead, the attic eyes watching her approach. Slow, steady, key in the lock, she opened the door. Silence pounded thick in her ears while she strained for his voice or a sign of his presence. A strange yearning to hear him, to negate the chilling fear, crept down her spine to hang heavy in her belly. When there was no greeting from Lochlain to comfort her, Ceallaigh paced the lower level.

"Help me," she whispered, not knowing what to do. Palm pressed against her forehead, she implored her long gone aunt, but again the irony reared her anxious thoughts in a circle. If she accepted Mary's tale of her aunt's reincarnated soul, were not the answers she sought from Ceallaigh Barrows, or rather, the Ceallaigh from the middle ages of Lochlain's time, within herself? She hugged her arms around her waist with eyes closed and rocked to a soundless beat to clear her mind.

A magnetic sensation tugged at her limbs. Lochlain, she knew, at last willed an audience with her. "Coming, milord," she whispered. She blinked and shook off the foreign speech as yet another subtle influence the painting thrust upon her. The word structure was too arcane for her to believe it was divine guidance from a third generation aunt.

A seizing thrill galvanized her footsteps up the stairs. She wanted to see him again, wanted to hear the truth.

Ceallaigh, have you recovered the Talisman? He faced her now, the painting animated. She could almost feel the fresh breeze from the moors, hear the gulls call as they soared above the towering castle now visible in the distance. Her heart clenched in remembrance.

"Nay." Ceallaigh swallowed. "I mean, no. Tell me where to look. What to look for?" She reached out to touch him, but only felt the canvas barrier pressing against her outstretched hand. "What will happen if I don't?"

Lochlain's breath hissed, and he fell to one knee; his chest aligned with her palm. *You must.* His spirit pulsed vibrant through the canvas, seeping brilliant warmth upward over her arm to fill her heart. *So many lifetimes have I waited for you to walk by my side once more. Come to me.*

"I don't know what to do. I don't know how—"

Seek out this symbol. Releasing the ties of his cloak, he allowed the fabric to fall loose. The firm sinew flexing, he withdrew a pewter amulet tucked beneath the gambeson. A thin strip of leather, oiled from wear, coiled through the ornate looping of the metal, which looked incomplete somehow. A piece missing.

"But I've never seen anything like this. I wouldn't know where to look."

Look inside your heart, Ceallaigh. Do you not see yourself at my right hand? The very hand that beckons you home?

Ceallaigh bowed her head and wept. He referred to the inviting gesture documented by her aunt's talented brush strokes that initially drew her like a magnet to the painting. Yes, she saw herself accepting. In her dreams and in her waking hours. Did she not will his world into three-dimension while waiting to move into the house?

"I do, milord. I crave it so." Her fingers scraped at the rough canvas, threatening to shred the fibers so that she may crawl through.

Believe. Find the Talisman so that you may reach your hand to mine and take hold. His fevered words cut through her helpless resignation.

"But I can't. I don't know what to do."

You must strive, Ceallaigh, else you perpetuate this torment evermore.

Weak and afraid, she could only sob louder. The barrage of conflicting emotions battering their way through her mind caused Ceallaigh to doubt her sanity.

Lochlain rose and removed the amulet from around his neck; the leather dangling from his fingertips as he resumed his original pose.

Ceallaigh traced the symbol, recognizing it as the same design burned into the back of the canvas. No, she frowned, not the same. Scrambling behind the frame, she searched for the fading initials to look more closely. Alternating back and forth between Lochlain's amulet and the design on the back of the canvas, she noticed an infinity symbol twined in the branded design was missing from the one wrought in pewter.

Was that the Talisman?

Wracking her brain, she poured over everything Mary had told her. Her aunt must have known what the Talisman was, but was prevented from retrieving it from her home. The painting and all of her aunt's belongings were distributed to family members per her mother's journal.

The Talisman could be anywhere!

Ceallaigh despaired. *Think, think, look inside your heart.* Bowing her head, she rubbed her brow to ease the tension.

"Her belongings were distributed to family," she muttered aloud, trying to puzzle things out. "And Mary said my aunt knew where the Talisman was, but couldn't get to it."

Frowning, she mentally sifted back through the photograph box to recall if she came across anything resembling the infinity symbol from the amulet. No. What else did she have?

Mother's antique jewelry case!

Of course, where else to hide the relic but in the safety of the locked box. Ceallaigh ran down the stairs, her feet sliding down the smooth wood slats in haste, to the bedroom closet where she stored the heirloom.

Her hands shook as she lifted it down from the shelf to place it on the floor. Kneeling, she turned the small key, half-afraid, half out of her mind in joyous anticipation. Bright baubles of brooches and ear bobs twinkled inside, but they failed to spark her interest. She rummaged through, placing each intricate piece aside to search in favor for a plain pewter-wrought looped symbol.

Emptying the case, she turned it upside down and shook hard, hoping to dislodge anything overlooked. Tears slid down her face. Her fingers stuffed into the corded satin pouches over and over again to find nothing. Scrutinizing every nook and cranny in hopes of finding a secret compartment, Ceallaigh started to cry in earnest.

"It has to be here," she sobbed. "Where else could it be?"

She pulled out the box of photographs again, scattering the contents across the downstairs foyer floor. After scanning the backs for signs of anything being attached to them, she cast aside each portrait and grabbed another. Her greedy eyes read page after page of the family journal for clues. She snatched up the picture of Ceallaigh Barrows and demanded "Where is it?"

Clutching the photo to her chest, she descended upon her father's Victrola. Dragging the albums out of their stained sleeves, scratching into the slim cabinet shelves to pull out nickels and lost paperclips, she still couldn't find anything close to resembling the symbol.

Back to the attic, her dazed mind absorbed the job lot of trunks and antiques her uncle had left behind. So much to look through. Sinking to her knees at the foot of the painting, she smoothed out her aunt's photo still caught in her fist.

"Help me," she whispered.

Ceallaigh Barrows' solemn face stared back at her. Hair caught up in a tight coil, shoulders painfully squared, her young face reflected the same lost soul Ceallaigh saw in the mirror every day. The severe black button-down blouse.

Wait. Ceallaigh squinted at the photograph, bringing it closer. A pendant flashed at her aunt's throat. Heart-shaped, just like the one—Ceallaigh gasped and clutched at her necklace. Quickly undoing the chain, she held the locket in her palm. Could it be the same one?

Her shoulders slumped. Didn't matter. She wasn't looking for a heart shape. She was looking for an infinity symbol. Burning tears clouded her vision again.

Look inside your heart, Ceallaigh, Lochlain's bass timbre made her nape hairs rise.

Ceallaigh stared at the locket. *Look inside....* The catch had always been broken, so she'd never tried before. Anticipation roiled up within her chest again. She pried a fingernail between the two halves, forcing her way inside until her nail broke. Shifting to her feet, she dug through the hodge-podge of the attic for a tool or weapon to use to wedge the locket apart. An old toolbox supplied a screwdriver. Sticking the blade inside, she twisted until the metal snapped. Her breath left her lungs in an exultant gasp.

Spreading the halves like a pearl-bearing oyster, Ceallaigh looked inside of the locket.

The Talisman!

There lay the small pewter infinity symbol, bent; the loops like wings of a tiny butterfly. Most likely the reason the locket had been sealed shut to keep the precious relic within.

Lifting the delicate symbol, she held it above one palm and ran to the painting. "Lochlain! Milord, I have found that which you seek." She held the Talisman aloft with glee.

Lochlain's image animated in response, his eyes glowing. *Bring it to me, my love, so that I may see.*

"Is it?" Ceallaigh's hopes were dashed when she reached out. The canvas still prevented her from touching him.

Aye, he breathed, his eyes closing. His voice caught in a hard swallow. *You have found the key to return you to me.* His palm sprawled outwards against the barrier. She covered his hand with her own.

"Tell me how."

You are certain? The gray light in his eyes implored her to search within herself. *You leave all you have now behind.* And what did she have to leave? Family? None were left. Friends? Lovers? Ceallaigh smiled ruefully. There were none to speak of in her life. She always knew she could vanish without a trace, and none would be the wiser.

"Nay, milord, I leave nothing behind."

A muscle in his jaw worked. His gaze devoured her, and she thrilled at the intensity he held in check. Flashes of impassioned embraces and hard, tan sinew braided with creamy limbs rushed through her mind. She knew this man. Knew his power, knew his love. Her pulse thrummed a hypnotic beat.

Come to me, Ceallaigh. The strength of his voice invaded her senses while he murmured low incantations and lifted the pewter pendant toward her.

She envisioned the completed symbol on the back of the canvas and fitted the Talisman into its rightful place. A jolt of electricity shot through her arm, radiating outward to charge her entire body. Ceallaigh cried out, her mind sucked into a vortex of lifetimes spent, spiraling backward in time. A kaleidoscope of faces, their agate eyes glazed over in the same intrinsic loneliness carried from generation to generation, swept through her vision. Her own life became null and void, as if she never truly existed until now.

"Ceallaigh." Lochlain whispered. Strong, capable hands pulled her from the trance and into a reverent embrace. "My love, how I have yearned for you, yearned for this moment to hold you in mine arms again."

Afraid to open her eyes and chase away the dream this surely was, Ceallaigh let her trembling hands explore her soulmate, cataloging each texture to memory. The formidable breadth of his shoulders, the stubble below the skin's surface of his clean-shaven jaw, his full mouth and thundering heartbeat.

Her pulse soared with joy, flooding her senses with the long elusive rhythm of peace, harmony, and belonging. She belonged with him, to him. She had loved Lochlain always and would do so for an eternity. But what if this rapture was false? A delusional trick forged out of her desperation?

"Lochlain?" Swallowing back the fear and doubt of reality, she hesitated to believe in this fantasy.

"Aye, dearling." His lips pressed feverishly against her temple and over her eyelids. "Open your eyes so that I may see your love shine once more."

Slowly, she let her gaze focus on his chest, then raised it to meet the gray assurance found in his eyes. A stifled gasp erupted from her. Could this be true? Shifting in his arms, she glanced backward to see the attic portal close behind her, then looked down, to the spongy moss below her feet.

Hunter green skirting caught her attention, and she kicked out a foot covered in supple suede booting. Taking a step backward, she smoothed her palms in amazement over the fine fabric of her gown; the leather girdle at her waist. She touched her face then her hair, loose and windswept, each curl alive in the breeze. A merry laugh bubbled up inside, spilling over as she twirled about to throw herself into Lochlain's outstretched arms.

His lusty laughter joined in as he lifted her in the air, letting her body slide back down to fit intimately against him. An ardent gleam in his eyes lent insight to his desire. Sparks ignited low in Ceallaigh's belly. She caught her hands into his thick mahogany hair and bent his mouth to hers, sipping at his kisses until an impassioned moan from Lochlain pressed her into a bolder embrace. His hand upon her breast seized an arch of her back, guiding his mouth to taste her ripe flesh until she nearly burst with anticipation.

Around her neck he draped the leather cord of the Talisman, kissing it reverently before placing the pendant at her throat. "Have care with this so that we may never be parted again."

Ceallaigh gripped the symbol hard in her palm, closing her eyes against the rush of emotion of gratitude and serenity. "I will cherish it always so that I may never be lost from you again. Take me home, milord."

Sweeping her into his arms, his long stride carried them across the Scottish moors. Ceallaigh buried her face to his throat, clutching at his shoulders as her body burned to join with his.

As if his impatience surpassed her own, Lochlain halted on a sloped foothill below the castle keep. "'Tis been too long and the journey has nigh become impossible to withstand further."

Against the tender bed of grass she lay with him, limbs entangled in an act of love that knew no bounds of time, an infinity of passion and commitment. Replete and complete, Ceallaigh's soul at last rested in its rightful place.

The lawyer glanced over the old oil he found stored in the attic of his deceased client. He couldn't bring himself to have the painting destroyed with the rest of the antiquated junk left behind, so he purchased it for himself. The rest of the lone bachelor's belongings were auctioned off because he had no family, no nieces or nephews to bequeath his meager estate to. *A lonely existence*, he thought, but perhaps it held small purpose in fate's master plan.

The painting's panoramic view of flourishing forest and distant stone structure enveloped him with an indescribable sense of calm and happiness. Like the painting represented some insurmountable victory or endless tranquility. Squinting, he could see the minute shadows of a couple linked arm in arm upon the ramparts.

He sighed in wonderment. Truly something timeless and precious must have inspired this artist to create such a Talisman for the soul.

ICE MAIDEN

Carolee Joy

The spirit called to her again, pulling her along with seductive fingers. His whisper hovered over the water, enticing her. Lily stood at the edge of the dock, teetering on a precipice of uncertainty. A chill wind tugged at her white gown and whipped her blond hair across her face.

One step more, that's all it would take. Then she would be with him at last. The dark despair shrouding her heart would be banished forever.

"Lily!"

Tom's voice proved stronger than whatever it was that called to her from the depths of the cold, dark lake. She turned, dazed, bemused and chilled to the bone.

"Are you crazy? It's thirty degrees out here! What are you doing outside in your nightgown?" Strong hands pulled her away from the water's edge. She shrank from his touch, but her husband of three years wrapped a blanket around her shoulders, then propelled her toward shore. The dock's rough, cold wood penetrated through her bare feet. She stumbled on a rough edge of planking.

She rubbed a hand across her forehead. "Why am I here?"

"That's the question I've been asking you for the past three months." Tom's voice was little more than a growl. "One of these nights, you're going to get pneumonia or fall into the lake. Either way, you're going to catch your death."

Her death. Lily shivered, as much from the macabre thought as from the damp November air. One of these nights...."You mean this isn't the first time?" She could hardly believe she'd been so foolish before, but she had no memory of ever standing in the moonlight by the water's edge while frost painted the ground white.

Yet an indefinable something pulled at her even now. Lily glanced over her shoulder. The lake rippled under the light of a three-quarter moon, whispering. Calling.

"You know damn well it's not." His words were a growl.

She huddled closer to Tom's side even though his attitude toward her was hardly more welcoming than the thought of plunging into the icy depths of Lake Superior.

Why had he developed so much disdain for her? At one time, he had been a trusted friend to her first husband, and when she became widowed, he'd been a friend to her as well.

"I don't remember," she whispered.

"I do." He scowled down at her. "And if you think I like chasing after you in the middle of the night, you're wrong."

"I'm sorry." The words emerged as a croak. What had she done to make him so angry? She could hardly be blamed for walking in her sleep. If that's what she was doing.

Words sighed through her mind again, as they had earlier that night, like the lyrics of a half-forgotten song. *For whom do you wait?* Lily cast a quick glance at her husband, but he appeared not to have heard.

Wind rustled the tops of the tall pines. She quickened her pace, stubbed her toe on a rock on the narrow path leading to the house, and lurched into him.

Tom frowned down at her. "If this doesn't stop, Lily, you're not giving me any other choice."

Her heart froze. Oh, no. No! Inwardly, she screamed in

panic. He wouldn't put her back in the hospital. She didn't think she could survive it.

No place where you can emotionally flee. The strange words pounding at her mind, Lily stifled a gasp, pulled away from Tom and ran towards the luxurious house huddled on the shore of the forbidding lake. "Leave me alone!" But she wasn't sure who she was shouting at. Footsteps pounded behind her. She felt the sharp bite of a needle in her arm, then blackness swarmed around her, stealing her away to the dark place where her dream lived.

Voices came at her from a long way off.

"I'm sorry to drag you all the way out to this forgotten place, Joseph. She's been out for two days." Tom's voice was smooth as hundred year old brandy as he addressed her lawyer. Not at all like the impatient tone he usually used on her. Tom and a visitor must be in the living room adjacent to her bedroom. Lily kept her eyes closed and drifted to the time when he had talked to her that way. Soothing. Comforting. Persuasive.

"A woman shouldn't live way out in the woods alone in this great big house. Marry me, Lily. I'll protect you. Drew would have wanted it this way."

Her first husband had drowned in a bizarre early winter storm that claimed his life and his crew on the *Ice Maiden*. Numb with grief and shock, Lily had agreed to marry the man who had been Drew's business advisor.

She knew she would never love another man with the passion she'd felt for Drew, but the isolation of the house, the depth of her loss, the need for advice, had made her believe someone reliable and solid like Tom would get her through the aching loneliness.

Unfortunately, it hadn't taken Tom long to start hounding her about the fortune Drew had left behind. When it became apparent the money was sliding off into one shaky venture after another, Lily started tucking bundles of cash away.

She could have left him, she supposed. But then the nightmares began, and after she confided them to Tom, she woke up one morning in the psychiatric ward of the hospital sixty miles to the southwest.

Joseph's brusque tones pulled her back to reality. "It won't do any good to have her sign a new will while she's still under Dr. Sorenson's care. Sound mind and all that. It would never hold water."

"Ah. Well, that is all for the best, I'm sure." Tom's voice gentled with the utmost understanding.

Lily clenched her hands under the covers and forced herself to breathe evenly.

"I was simply following her request to have it changed. It would never do if something happened to her. She still has her dead husband listed as the beneficiary! Could make for an awful mess for me after all the work I've put in here. Don't know why I should stand aside and let her greedy cousins jump in to claim a share."

"Don't blame you a bit, old man." Joseph's commiserating chuckle grated on her tense nerves. "You've done a great job keeping the place up. It could really have started to fall into disrepair after Drew's passing. There's just one thing that bothers me in all this."

Glasses clinked and Lily pictured Tom pouring another glass of very expensive Scotch into her Waterford snifters for the lawyer.

"What might that be?" Tom's voice remained genial and just the right amount of curious.

"What have you been doing with all the cash? I had a talk with your banker the other day, as you instructed. Not only is your line of credit up to the max and the house mortgaged to the hilt, he says all the cash accounts have been wiped clean."

The last thing Lily heard before the darkness snatched her back under was the sound of shattering crystal.

"Where's the money, Lily?" Tom's hands shook her, roughly bringing her back from the dream place she wanted to linger in forever. The place where she found Drew once more. The sanctuary where his love made her feel cherished and protected.

What had ever made her think she could find happiness with Tom?

Prisoner of repression....

"No!" She jerked back from his angry voice, his relentless hands shaking her, always shaking her. She scrambled from the bed and stumbled away.

"Come on, Lily." Tom turned cajoling. Coaxing. "You know I'd never hurt you, baby. I just don't like the secrets you've been keeping from me."

"What about what you've been keeping from me?" With trembling fingers, Lily held out the bottle of potent sedatives she'd found in Tom's desk. The one he usually kept locked. He'd wrongly assumed she was still in a drugged sleep long after Joseph departed. He shouldn't have left it open after he'd tried to coerce more medication down her throat.

"Or maybe it's more like what you've been forcing on me." Except for today, when she'd hid the pill beneath her tongue and spit it out after he left the room.

"Honey, you know you've been having troubles lately. I just thought if you could sleep better at night, it would help."

"I've never heard of the doctor who prescribed these." Lily flung the bottle at him when he advanced toward her. The cap fell off, strewing the floor with brightly colored capsules.

"That's because you've been too out of it lately." He made a grab for her, but Lily was quicker, darting just beyond his grasp and whirling towards the door.

Free your heart from an icebound state.

The voice was louder now, more compelling than ever before, giving her strength. And now she knew just who it belonged to.

Drew. Speaking the words of a poem he'd written for her years ago.

"Help me," she screamed.

"Oh, I'll help you, all right. Back into the hospital where you belong, crazy woman." Tom lunged, catching a handful of her gown as she dashed through the doorway.

A blast of arctic wind caught the heavy paneled door and blew it back against her husband's face. Tom grunted with pain and released her. The door slammed between them, enclosing Tom in the bedroom while Lily ran into the living room.

No way you can recreate just you and me.

Lily sobbed. She knew that now. Drew was the only man she would ever love. All this time, he had been trying to tell her she'd made a mistake by marrying Tom. Denying the inner voice had nearly cost her sanity.

No more.

Come to me, Lily.

The wind roared again, blasting down the chimney, sending sparks shooting out over the hearth where Tom had once again neglected to put the screen back in place after lighting the fire. A spark danced on the carpet. Then another. And another.

Lily grabbed the shovel leaning against the bricks and began beating the flames which began to race over the priceless Oriental rug.

Give it up, sweetheart. It doesn't matter any longer.

"Lily!" Tom staggered from the bedroom, blood streaming from his nose. "What the hell is the matter with you? What are you doing?"

Acting on impulse, adrenaline and an instinct born of fear, she swung the shovel just as he roared and dove for her. The iron smacked against the side of his head. Tom lurched and fell face first into the smoldering rug.

Don't count the moments. Run, Lily, run!

In the instant she hesitated, the couch ignited. Then the

drapes. She looked down at Tom one last time, then bolted as the house went up in flames.

The voice propelled her down the rocky path. She barely felt the cold on her bare feet, then she was standing at the end of the dock, the frigid water shimmering below her. Tears streamed down her face.

With all her heart she longed to be with Drew. But how was that possible?

Swallow icy tears. Don't deny me your love.

Lily glanced over her shoulder. The dark shape of a man lumbered from the glowing house. Tom would either kill her or have her committed permanently. Either way, her life was over.

Flames shot skyward, consuming everything she had ever possessed except the one thing that had mattered most: Drew's love. "It's all gone, Drew," she whispered. "I hid the money inside the house."

The wind answered, tugging at her gown, pulling her hair, coaxing her closer to the water's chilly depths. Drew's smile beckoned.

Lily took a deep breath and stepped off the dock. Icy water swallowed her, plastered the thin cotton to her skin and dragged her down. The pain of a thousand knives jabbed at her, consuming her.

Gather close vanished dreams. Ward off the cold. Come to me, Lily.

I never stopped loving you, Drew. The words swirled through her mind, as real as if she spoke them.

In the next instant, the cold disappeared. Soothing, dream-like warmth enveloped her as he embraced her.

Nor I, you.

She looked into Drew's eyes and saw her love reflected there. The pain and sorrow of the past three years vanished, and when her lips met his, she became his again.

Forever.

LOVE'S HYPNOTIC CURE

Susan D. Brooks

"I have a rash on my thigh, ringing in my ears, and heart palpitations." Kate Camberg steered her convertible Mustang into the company parking lot. She glanced at her friend in the passenger seat. "What else could it be but stress?"

"Maybe you should make an appointment with Jason," teased Linda, referring to their co-worker. "I hear hypnotherapy works wonders when you're under a lot of pressure."

"I can hypnotize myself, thanks," Kate replied dryly. "What I can't do is predict whether I'll have a job tomorrow." She turned off the ignition and looked down at the keys in her hand. "Maybe I should have waited to replace my old car."

"That car was an ancient ten years old. It drank oil by the gallon, the trunk wouldn't open, and the windshield leaked in every storm. Your mechanic told you the transmission was shot, didn't he?" Kate nodded and Linda dismissed her friend's concerns with a wave of her hand. "Then don't worry about it. You did right." Linda tugged the scrunchie from her hair and used her fingers to comb the strands into place. "If you're fired and feeling desperate, you could put your duplex on the market," she suggested. "It would sell overnight."

"I'd rather stop eating."

"I don't think you need to worry. Honestly, I don't think you have anything to worry about as far as the job goes." Linda looked at Kate with wide, innocent eyes. "Are you sure you're not just having a reaction to our new boss?"

"Don't be ridiculous." Kate gave her a sharp glance.

"Bennett Ames's a prize," Linda said, coming around to the front of the car. They fell into step, heading across the parking lot to the small brick building that housed the stress clinic offices. "He's got a great sense of humor, and he's smart. Besides being gorgeous, of course." She wiggled her eyebrows. "And I think he likes you."

"Not in that way." Kate sighed. "He makes me nervous."

"Can a mere man make Kate Camberg nervous?" Linda rolled her eyes. "I don't believe it."

"He could ruin my future. Wouldn't that make you nervous?" Kate opened the door and stepped into the empty lobby. "I have to admit, though, he's wonderful with the people that come here for treatment. He has a way of making each person feel important. And, by taking over the management side, he's starting to turn the clinic around."

"Yeah, but he's making the place a success by cutting people left and right," Linda reminded her, putting on the tiny telephone headset.

"I wonder where he learned about running a business? Wasn't he an artillery officer in the Marines?" When Linda nodded, Kate shook her head. "He's right, you know. We're overstaffed, and he should cut one more therapist." Her heartbeat accelerated. "But I hope it's not me."

"Well, all we can do is wait and see. Who knows what he'll decide to do?" A soft ring announced an incoming call. Linda reached for the phone and added, "But he'd be a fool to let you go."

Kate patted her friend's shoulder in thanks and headed down the hallway to her office. Absently scratching at the rash on her thigh, she plunked down in her chair and swiveled around to stare out the window

What would she do if she lost her job? Not a lot of opportunities existed in Wilmington. Especially not for a hypnotherapist. Although using hypnosis to change unwanted behaviors had gained popularity in the last few years, demand hadn't risen enough for a city the size of Wilmington to need two clinics.

And she loved this area. Loved the ocean, loved her seaside duplex. Her family, firmly ensconced in Gatlinburg, Tennessee, could not understand the attraction.

"No fresh mountain air here," announced her father on his one and only visit. Her mother and ski-bum older brother agreed, but Kate didn't care. The sea called to her, fascinating her with its endless changes. And, since becoming a certified hypnotherapist, she'd found the same satisfaction in her work. Helping people exchange their bad habits for good ones made her believe she could really make a difference in the world.

Her gaze fell on the now familiar blue Honda Accord owned by Bennett Ames. He had parked in the space furthest from the office door right outside Kate's window.

Not really what I expect an ex-Marine to drive, she thought. *I thought they were all issued souped-up Cameros or pickup trucks when they earned their commissions.*

"I learned about finance at Rice University," came a soft voice from across the room, "and about stress while I was in the Corps. I think I know enough to make decent business decisions, but I always admit when I've made a mistake."

Kate whirled at the sound. "You overheard us talking in the lobby?" Her face grew warm as Bennett Ames studied her from the doorway.

He nodded. "I was in my office."

"Oh." Kate tried to remember the exact words she had

said to Linda, but failed.

"Being in the military's not an easy life, you know." He leaned against the door jamb and crossed one leg over the other. "Lots of responsibility. A lot of time away from home."

"That's what I've heard," Kate stammered, her rebellious mind feeding her an itemized inventory of his physique. Muscular thighs under the pleated khaki trousers, slender hips, broad shoulders, firm jaw, ocean green eyes, and short, dark hair just beginning to relinquish the traditional "high and tight" Marine Corps style.

"And it's true." His tired eyes crinkled at the corners as if he fought a smile.

"Well, you can't blame me for speculating." Kate snatched her purse from the desk and threw it into a drawer, diverting herself with action. "You appeared out of nowhere, bought this place, and turned it inside out."

"Yes, I did shake things up. Had to. I bought the business to make money." He tipped his head. "Did you know that the last owner took a loss two years in a row?"

"None of us knew about any of that. Poor management?" Kate suggested.

"Too many employees, too many expenses." Bennett stepped further into the room. "And she tried to expand too quickly."

"I think Robin just wanted to help more people," Kate said, defending her former mentor. "She thought offering different services would help."

"Normally, she'd be right," he agreed. "But, when you're trying to expand your clientele with customers from local military bases, you don't add aromatherapy to the list of choices." His blue eyes now sparkled with amusement.

Kate feigned an innocent expression. "You're saying that men can't find relief in aromatherapy?"

"No, I won't say that." Bennett's lips twitched. "But you'll have a hard time getting a guy dressed in camouflage

to ask for a blend of tuberose and hyacinth to sooth him at
the end of the day."

"Oh? Then what about the female Marines? We both
know they're under more stress than the men." Kate lifted
her chin. "And probably need therapy more."

"Of course, and women are more likely to seek help, but
we need more male customers to stay in business." He
paused. "I need to talk to you about something."

Kate coughed, her throat suddenly tight. "My next client
isn't due for a half hour."

Bennett eased his long frame into a wingback recliner.

"I'm getting ready to make the final staff cuts," he began,
catching her attention again.

Kate looked down at her desk and picked up a pen,
clicking it on and off, on and off. She willed all expression
from her face. She rubbed her skirt against her rash.

"I want to find out what you offer your clients." He held
up a hand as she began to protest. "I don't want to sit in on a
session, I don't believe in that. What I'd like you to do is
have you put me through a session."

"You want me to hypnotize you?" Her mind whirled. This
man was full of surprises.

"Yes. A real program, as if I'm a paying client." He
leaned forward, hands on his knees. "It's the only fair way to
determine who will stay and who will go."

She clenched her fists, fingernails digging into her palms.
What therapy would he need? Weight loss? She noted his
lean form.

I think not.

"To stop smoking?" she asked.

"I don't smoke." He shifted in the chair. "I have trouble
sleeping. You could work up something on that."

"Insomnia? Sure." Kate swallowed hard. "When do you
want to schedule this?"

"I had Linda check your calendar. Tomorrow afternoon at
three."

"All right." Kate stared numbly at her appointment calendar.

"Write it in." Bennett stood. "Just like I'm a real customer."

Kate scribbled his name into the small space.

"I'm seeing Jason this afternoon." He flashed her a grin and walked out.

She dropped the pen and put her head in her hands. A sleeping disorder. Piece of cake. She could handle that. But could she concentrate? Could she keep her focus with so much at stake? She bit her lip. She had no choice.

That night, Kate sat on the beach behind her duplex, sipping a beer. She thought back over her conversation with Linda in the parking lot after work. They had been making plans to see a movie next week when Bennett had driven past, giving them a cheery wave. Linda again hinted that he may be interested in Kate as more than an employee.

"No way, Jose'." Kate shook her head, annoyed at the change in conversation. "And I am not interested in him."

"Why not?"

"He's my boss and an ex-Marine." Kate held up two fingers. "Two strikes."

"Kate, I've known you for what? Three years? All you've ever dated are Marines." Linda shook her head. "What's the problem with Bennett?"

"I've sworn off Marines."

"Since when?" Disbelief colored Linda's voice.

"Since last winter."

"If you mean Ron Wolford, I don't believe you," Linda declared. "Your pride took more of a blow than your heart when he dumped you. Besides, that one guy couldn't damage you enough to keep you away from the men of the Corps."

"I think I'm getting burned out on all that." Kate looked out at the ocean. "You meet a decent guy, you have some laughs, maybe get involved physically, then news comes that he's either deployed for six months or he's transferred to Camp Pendleton in California. You write letters, maybe get a few phone calls, flowers on Valentine's Day, and it's over." Kate shook her head. "I'm tired of that. Besides, I don't want to get married."

Linda had laughed out loud. "You don't have to marry anyone, honey. Just enjoy."

Kate wedged her half-empty can into the sand, laid back, and stared up at the darkening sky. The day's events rolled through her mind, leaving a trail of unanswered questions.

Would Jason's session with Bennett be more successful than hers? Jason was, after all, an ex-Marine, too. One of the guys. Would her boss feel more comfortable with him?

And how would she approach her own appointment with him? Was he audio? Did he learn by hearing? Or was he visual, processing information by sight? Maybe he was kinesthetic, learning by touch. She didn't know. She pounded her fist on the sand. She just didn't know.

When she woke, night lay full around her, stars filled the sky. Not sure what woke her, she sat up and looked around. The tide splashed water onto her feet.

Must be after midnight. She cushioned her head with her arms and smiled at the sky. *Maybe I'll just sleep out here tonight.*

"Hello, Kate." A man's voice came from behind her.

She bolted upright, grabbed her can to use as a weapon, turned, and peered into the darkness. Bennett watched her from the top of a small dune. Wearing jeans shorts and a white polo shirt, he looked good. Oh, so good.

"Been trained to defend yourself, huh?" He grinned. "Not much of a weapon, but creative."

"Uh, hi." Kate let her arm fall to her side. "What are you doing here?"

"I live up that way." He jerked a thumb toward the north end of the island. "I'm out for a walk."

He can't sleep. Was Jason unable to help him? The thought brought a stab of sympathy for Bennett. She gestured to the sand. "Have a seat. I'd offer you a beer, but this is the only one I brought."

"That's okay." He eased down next to her, knees up, arms folded around his legs. "Any kind of alcohol works against me when I try to sleep."

They sat in silence for a few minutes, watching the tide begin to recede, leaving a swath of hard-packed beach. Out on the ocean, a red blinking light marked the passage of a late-night boater.

"When did your problem with sleeping begin?" Kate looked over at Bennett.

"When I was in the Corps." He ran a hand through his hair. Pale starlight caught on the short strands. "Right before I got out."

"You were an officer?"

"Uh-huh. Artillery." He smiled. "M-198s."

"Ah," Kate nodded, "the big guns."

"Yeah." He reached down to filter a handful of sand through his fingers. "I knew who you were, you know, before we met."

"What do you mean?" Surprised, Kate felt her mouth drop open. "How?"

"You dated my roommate for a while."

"No way." She laughed out loud. "I'd have remembered someone like you." The moment the impulsive words left her lips, she faltered. "I mean, I don't remember meeting you."

"No, we didn't meet. I was in Okinawa. He sent me a picture of you and him at a dance at the O Club. You broke his heart, you know."

Kate frowned into the darkness. Whose heart had ever been hers to break? "What's your roommate's name?"

"Ron Wolford."

"Ron?" She rolled her eyes. "I'm not sure he even has a heart much less one that can be broken."

"Hmmm," Bennett said. "I think I've heard that about him before."

"That wouldn't surprise me," Kate said dryly. "Anyway, we were talking about your sleeping problem."

A long silence followed her observation. Finally, Bennett shrugged. "I decided that my goals and those of the Corps didn't mesh anymore. That was not an easy conclusion to come to."

"I imagine not." Intrigued by his candid answer, Kate shifted around so she could see him better.

"I wanted a life of my own," he continued. "One where I make the decisions, not some general in Washington. And I wanted a family." He laughed bitterly. "That's not a popular option in the Corps."

"I know." Kate's gaze met his and held. "I've heard that over and over. Most troops learn to deal with moves and long separations. Or their spouses do."

"With disastrous results sometimes." He used one finger to doodle in the sand. "I actually sought help at your clinic for a while."

"You did? I never saw you come in."

"No, Elizabeth rearranged her appointments so I could come late. It was the only time I could get away." He picked up a handful of sand and let it slip through his fingers. "She helped me to relax so I could rest. It made a difference. My mind was less foggy, I could make decisions again."

With those words, Kate understood that Bennett owed Elizabeth a debt that would be difficult to repay. The choice for the last hypnotherapist slot came down to her and Jason.

"She's one of the best," Kate agreed.

"She's a real asset to the business." He smiled. "Well, I've kept you up long enough. You won't be effective tomorrow if you don't get some rest." He brushed the sand from his feet, slipped his sneakers back on, and stood. "See you in the morning."

Kate watched his tall form disappear into the darkness.

She gathered her things and picked up the cooler. Apparently, Jason's therapy hadn't worked. Tomorrow was her turn, but she found that she wanted to help him as much as she wanted to keep her job.

Even with a full schedule, Kate's morning dragged by slowly. Wayward thoughts of Bennett on the beach crept into her mind, distracting her between clients. She had no problem concentrating as long as a customer sat in the recliner across from her. It was the chasms of time between their visits that aggravated her rash and made her heart race.

At noon, Linda poked her head into Kate's office. "Want to go out to lunch?"

Kate looked up. "I brought a sandwich." She smiled. "I have to get ready for my session with Bennett. Hey, how did last night go? Did you have fun?"

"Oh yes." Linda's mouth curved into a coy smile. "Great time." She turned as a telephone rang. "I've got to get that. I'll talk to you later."

Kate nodded and turned back to her collection of hypnosis scripts. Which one would help Bennett and ensure that she could keep her job? Maybe she could drop a hint about that in the middle of the session?

Unethical, Kate, and it wouldn't work. This guy's been through hypnosis. Just stick to what you do best.

Breathing deep to calm her pounding heart, Kate unwrapped her sandwich, looked at the whole wheat and turkey, and then stuck it back into the plastic bag. Maybe she'd be hungry later.

At precisely three o'clock Bennett strode into her office.

"I'm here." He thrust his hands into his pockets. "Shall we begin?"

"I'm ready." She waved him into a recliner. "Please, sit down. Feel free to lie back." Kate inserted a compact disk into a player. The sound of waves flowed into the room.

"Hey, like last night." Bennett smiled. "You know, I went home and slept for four hours?"

"Four hours?" Kate's professional side took over. "That's great, but we can do better than that." She sat in a chair next to his. "I've worked up a program that will help you handle any sleep disorder. Just close your eyes, relax, and believe."

"I already do believe." Bennett's gaze shifted to her. "Let's do it."

Kate pressed the PLAY button on her CD player. The sound of ocean waves breaking on the shore filled the room.

"Lean back and, when you are ready, close your eyes. Take a deep breath and feel your body relax."

She watched as Bennett settled back in the chair. His chest rose and fell several times, his shoulders relaxed, indicating his acceptance of her instructions. She glanced at her notes.

"Slow your breathing… breath evenly and deeply… relax. Step onto the beach and feel the sand between your toes. Smell the salt air as it blows in from miles across the sea. Enter the water and feel the cool liquid wash over your feet. Hear the sea gulls cry above the sound of the waves.

"Your body may feel heavy or very light. You may feel as if you are floating above the ground. Anything you feel is right for you.

"Now follow a set of stairs or an escalator leading down, deeper into a peaceful, quiet place. Stop at any floor. Enter the room there and look around. Are there logs crackling in a fireplace and bookshelves lining the walls? Or does the room have many windows that overlook a mountain stream? The right image will come to you. This is your private place. Leave the outside world behind while you are here."

Kate studied his eyes, watching for the tell-tale sign of movements behind the eyelids. This would tell her if he had achieved the alpha state, the twilight between awake and asleep; the optimum state for suggestion. If he was a visual person, he might be there already.

"You hear nothing of the outside world, nothing you don't

want to hear. You won't even hear my voice if you don't want to hear me speak."

Bennett appeared to be in a deep state of hypnosis. Now Kate began step two planting the ideas that would allow him to fall into a restful sleep each night. She lowered her voice, speaking in a measured, somewhat monotonous tone.

"Visualize the different parts of your body going to sleep. Send relaxation to your toes… to the soles of your feet… and your ankles… let your legs go limp… your knees… then your upper legs…."

Kate watched as his body reacted to her suggestions, seeming to melt into the chair. She continued sending messages about his arms, chest, and head.

"Time melts and flows around you. Allow your mind to drift where it pleases. Enjoy this state of deep relaxation."

For a second, Kate hesitated. This would be the time to hint at Bennett keeping her on the payroll. She dismissed the temptation, and the moment passed. She couldn't overcome her deep belief in the power of hypnosis. She might destroy any healing he'd experienced during the session by inserting something he didn't agree with or want to happen. She took a sip of water and continued with her original script.

"Now you have established a pattern for healthy sleep.

"When I count to ten, you will open your eyes and know that tonight you will enjoy a full night of sleep then awake refreshed in the morning.

"…nine …ten. Open your eyes… wide awake and feeling great." Kate took a deep breath and let it out slowly. The session was over.

"You've got a nice voice." Bennett opened his eyes and looked at her. "And I like the background you chose."

"Thanks." Kate bit her lip, waiting.

"And thank you. Well, I have to think a little while. I'll let you know on Monday." He stood and left her office.

Exhausted, Kate slumped in her chair. *I don't want to just sit here and wait.*

Checking that she had no more clients scheduled that afternoon, she grabbed her purse from her desk and walked out into the reception area.

"Linda? If Bennett needs me, have him call me at home, okay?"

"Oh, Kate. What happened?" Concern darkened her friend's eyes.

"Nothing, I'm just tired. I'll talk to you later." She scooted out the door and to her car. With the top down, she drove from the lot and headed up Route 17.

By the time she'd driven the long road to the island, she convinced herself that her job was history.

He should have been able to make up his mind right then. How could he not decide between Jason and I? We have totally different styles. Kate went over the session in her head again and again, stopping only when she realized that there was nothing more to do. She'd done her best.

The next day, Sunday, Linda called in the morning to talk. She didn't know Bennett's decision, but she did know he'd gone to Raleigh and wouldn't be back until evening. Kate listened to her friend chatter about her wonderful date the previous night.

"And now I've got to go because Tim's taking me to Beaufort for the day," Linda said. "I'll call you if I hear anything from Bennett."

Kate drove to Ft. Fisher and spent the day reading a Regency romance on the dunes. Hours later, she put down the book, wishing her story would end as happily as the heroine's had. Startled, she realized that she had placed Bennett in the role of the gallant British officer, out to win the hand of the lovely heroine.

When she returned home, Kate found six calls on her recorder, all within the last hour. Her breath caught in her throat as she heard Bennett's voice.

"I need to talk to you," he said.

The third, fourth, fifth, and sixth were also from Bennett, the messages all the same. He rattled off his cell phone number.

Kate dialed Bennett's number and got a busy signal. She took the cordless phone, grabbed a bottle of water from the refrigerator, and went out onto her deck. As soon as she sat down, a car pulled into her driveway and skidded to a stop. The door opened then slammed shut.

"Why didn't you return my phone calls?" Bennett's voice, although pleasant, hinted at frustration.

"I just got the messages," Kate told him and held up her handset. "I tried to call you but your phone was busy."

He climbed the stairs to the deck. "Well, I've made a decision."

Kate remained silent, fighting for control of her emotions. The familiar ringing began in her ears. The rash made it's presence known with an insistent itch.

"I slept last night," he announced, a wide grin on his handsome face. "The whole night through." He held up one hand. "I know, it may not be a permanent fix, but damn, it felt great, and I want to thank you."

Delighted, Kate opened her mouth to speak, but Bennett stopped her.

"Let me finish." He began to pace. "I've decided not to cut anyone from the staff. You're all good."

I'm not being fired? Kate felt giddy.

"I am, however, moving Jason to massage therapy because he has training in that so you'll have to pick up the slack in hypno." He paused and looked at her. "Is that okay?"

"Absolutely." She nodded. Elation rushed through her. She'd keep her job, her home, her life.

Not thinking, Kate jumped up and ran to hug him, but stopped just as she lifted her arms. Bennett's gaze caught hers, searing her with it's intensity. She stood, suspended in time, hands reaching, heart caught between reality and fantasy.

"Bennett?" Her mouth, dry, barely whispered his name.

"I think we may have something more to discuss." He leaned toward her, caught her hands, and pulled her close.

"What?" Kate felt his fingertips rub circles on the back of her hands. The ringing in her ears faded.

"I hear you like movies."

"Yes." He was going to ask her out. "Linda and I go every Tuesday. Bargain night, you know. The theater's almost empty and movies are so expensive...." Kate heard herself babbling and let the last words trail off into an embarrassed silence.

"I like empty theaters," he whispered.

"Oh." Kate had a sudden vision of the two of them snuggling in the back row like teenagers.

"May I take you to dinner first?" He moved even closer to her.

She shivered in the warm evening air as she answered. "Yes."

Bennett's smile lit the night and, when his mouth claimed hers, Kate ceased to think rationally.

This time when her heart beat a wild rhythm, it wasn't because of stress.

FANCY'S FORTVNE

Su Kopil

Dry Creek, Texas—late 1800s

Fancy's fingers pressed against the cool globe of the crystal ball. Distant laughter filtered through the canvas walls of the wagon. Earlier, she had watched the townsfolk enjoying the games and carnival food, wishing she could be a part of the group of women who chatted so easily at one table.

But she could not.

Her dark hair and skin labeled her gypsy. It did not matter that her father was white. She was an outcast, belonging fully to neither race.

People always stared, as did the young boy who sat across the wooden table from her, eagerly waiting to hear his fortune. Even the man who accompanied the boy had not taken his eyes off of her since their arrival. She had been in this part of Texas long enough to hear tell of Trace Colby, the wealthy rancher who cared for his young sibling in the absence of parents. His reserved, hard-working reputation preceded him. To Fancy's practiced eye, however, the tiny crinkle lines fanning from the corners of his smoky blue eyes told a greater truth. She wondered what the wealthy, white rancher saw when he looked at her.

Fancy smiled at the boy and put on her best showman's voice. "The ache in your stomach will disappear by night's end."

"How'd she know, Trace?" The boy asked in amazement. "How'd she know my tummy hurt?"

Trace chuckled and winked at her. "Maybe she saw those two candy apples you choked down or that sack of popcorn and bottle of sarsaparilla."

"You really saw all that in there?" The boy pointed to the ball, his eyes wide.

"Gypsies know all." Fancy shrugged non-committally. She never directly lied to her customers. The crystal ball was for show. They expected it. However, there were times, more and more often, when she saw visions of the future. Small glimpses that didn't always make sense but never failed to come true.

Other times, she would listen to the inflections in her customer's voice or look for physical evidence as she had done with the boy. She immediately noticed the stains on his shirtfront, his pale skin, and the way his hand kept moving to his stomach. Couple those signs with the carnival atmosphere outside, and her deduction was obvious.

"Your turn, Trace." The boy jumped from his chair and tugged at the man's arm.

"I think we've taken enough of the lady's time for one night, Billy." He frowned.

"Aw, don't be chicken." Billy persisted. "Ain't no other folks waiting."

Fancy knew the moment Trace gave in. His brow smoothed, and the easy humor returned to his eyes. She was not sure if his change of heart came from Billy's urging or from the lack of customers standing in line. She suspected the latter though why he cared she did not know.

Trace eased his long frame into the chair Billy had vacated and placed another coin on the table.

"If you are reluctant, the reading—"

His laughter cut her off. "There's nothing reluctant about me as my little brother can testify. In fact..." He slid the coin closer, a lazy grin on his face. "I'm mighty curious to hear if there's a raven-haired beauty in my future."

Fancy pushed the burning tallow candle to the end of the table, the small wagon suddenly feeling too warm despite the cool October air blowing through the open flap. She spied Trace Colby often in town, their gazes meeting on more than one occasion, although they had never formally met.

Despite the rush of feelings his small attentions invoked in her, she knew she had no right to believe he could be interested in her. He was a prominent citizen of Dry Creek. She was a gypsy. She would read him his fortune, and that would be the end of it.

"Very well. If you are ready?"

He nodded.

She glanced at Billy crouched by the tent flap staring outside, a ray of sun glinting off his tousled red hair. As the young will do, he'd already lost interest now that the attention no longer focused on him.

Fancy breathed deeply. The aroma of burning sweetgrass filled her senses and cleared her mind. She cupped her hands around the sides of the crystal ball and stared into its depths.

Immediately an explosion of orange and red filled her vision. She jumped. More images followed. A dark alley... an empty whiskey bottle... darkness. Then the gleam of a gun barrel flashed briefly... another explosion... Trace falling.... She wanted to cry out, but only a whimper escaped her lips. Blackness descended, then cleared. Once again she stared into the clear globe of the crystal ball.

Her heart raced. Fancy willed the images to reappear. She wanted to make sense of the fragmented pictures. That danger surrounded Trace was obvious. But what, who threatened him? Try as she might, the images would not return.

A large callused hand covered the back of hers, which still pressed against the ball. She raised her eyes to meet his questioning gaze. Concern furrowed his brow.

"Are you alright?"

His voice... the soft words, caressed her heart.

She nodded, but fear left her mouth dry.

"Tell me." His thumb stroked her wrist.

She found the movement comforting. Lowering her voice so the boy would not hear, she said, "I see danger."

"Billy?" He frowned.

She shook her head, wanting to put at ease his instinctive concern for his brother. "Not the boy. You. Danger hides in the shadows. You must return home. Do not leave your house before daybreak."

"You mean run away?" He scowled. "From what?"

"It is not safe. I cannot tell you why, but danger lurks. Please...." She squeezed his hand before slipping hers from his grasp. "Do not question. Just go."

He stared at her a full moment before scraping his chair against the wooden bed of the wagon. "The lady has talent." He laughed and stood as best he could in the cramped space.

"Trace." It was the first time she had spoken his name, and it had the effect she desired.

His attention refocused on her, surprise showing in the slight widening of his eyes.

"Please," she beseeched, "do not think my warning folly."

He rested the knuckles of one hand on the table and leaned forward so that his face stopped inches from hers. "Folly is not the word I would use. Perhaps...." His finger teased her jawline.

She drew in a sharp breath.

"Perhaps it is you who should be careful, Fancy." He closed the short distance between them. His mouth covered hers in a whisper soft kiss that left her breathless.

By the time her breathing had returned to an even pace, he was gone and Billy with him.

Fancy noticed the first stars beginning to twinkle in the darkening sky as she strolled through the now nearly deserted main square. By the sounds of merriment emanating from the saloon it would seem the more boisterous revelers continued the party there while the respectable folk returned home with their children.

Did Trace heed her warning? She pictured him ·sitting comfortably before a fire with Billy by his side. But thoughts were not visions, and so she continued to worry.

In no hurry to return to her wagon, she set the small basket of supplies she had purchased at the mercantile on one of the makeshift tables someone had neglected to remove.

"Nice night."

She started at the sound of the familiar voice. Stepping toward the shadows, she recognized Trace's lean form lounging against the trunk of a tree. Her pulse quickened with the remembrance of his lips on hers. Then fear gripped her heart.

"What are you doing here? You should be home." Realizing she sounded like a mother scolding an errant child, she started to apologize only to be cut off by his laughter.

He pushed away from the tree and stepped closer. "You don't know me very well if you think I'd run from trouble."

"I do not presume to know you at all. But I trust my visions. They are never wrong."

"Yet, you can't tell me who or what means to do me harm?"

Her gaze dropped to the ground. She shook her head. "No."

Even after Trace left earlier, she had tried to recall the vision. She wanted to put a face to the menace. But it would not come. Her restlessness and worry for a man she barely knew brought her to the mercantile to purchase items that could well have waited until morning. She had searched the near empty boardwalk and alleys, satisfying herself that nothing was amiss. And just when she thought all was well, Trace had appeared from nowhere.

"Have you noticed my frequent visits to town these past weeks?" he asked.

Her gaze sought his, but she remained quiet.

"I know you have." His teeth gleamed in the darkness, and she knew he smiled.

"Yes," she admitted.

"That wasn't an accident." His hand trailed down her arm sending a shiver through her. "You trust your visions. I trust what I feel when you're near."

What was he saying? Each time she saw him, she dreamed he would speak words like this. Yet, she dare not believe. "I'm a gypsy. You cannot have feelings for me. It… it is not allowed."

"Who says it's not allowed?" His voice deepened with annoyance. "All I see, all I've seen for weeks now, is a beautiful, independent woman. A woman whose very nearness inspires me. And you say because you're a gypsy I can't feel this?" He moved closer. His hand stroked her hair.

She barely heard his next words for the pounding in her ears. Despite the boundaries that divided them, desire streaked through her.

"Because you're a gypsy I can't kiss you like this…."

His lips touched hers, and though she wanted to resist— told herself she must resist, she found she could not. All of her strength, all of the self control that had enabled her to live alone in a society that shunned her kind, that said she didn't fit in anywhere, melted when his body pressed close to hers. How could something so pleasurable be so wrong?

Gathering strength from a reserve pool deep within herself, she managed to pull away from Trace's embrace. Casting a furtive glance across the square, she spotted two men weaving outside the saloon. Thankfully, the rest of the town remained deserted. It would not bode well for Trace to be seen kissing a gypsy.

"Please…" Her hand, seeking support, caught the rough bark of the tree. "Promise me you'll go home."

"I'll go. For you, Fancy. But this isn't over."

Unable to express either the joy or the unease his words instilled in her, she grabbed her basket of supplies and hurried off in the direction of her wagon.

Not wanting to tempt trouble, Fancy stayed to the side opposite the saloon. She fervently hoped Trace would keep his word. The night was still young and her uneasiness grew with each step she took. As much as she would like the opportunity to know Trace Colby better, the rules laid down by society denied her the chance. She could not allow the damage his reputation would sustain should the town discover he courted a gypsy. Secrecy was out of the question. She knew Trace well enough to know he would not stand for it, and her heart told her it was more than one night that he wanted.

Passing the corner bank, Fancy stepped off the boardwalk and onto the dirt-packed road. A whiff of sour whiskey assaulted her nose a second before an arm shot out of the darkness and pulled her roughly into the alley.

She opened her mouth to scream but a large hand clamped over her lips. Dropping her basket, she clawed at the hands that held her captive. Kicking behind her, she felt her foot connect with a knee.

Her captor yelped and slammed her back against the brick building. His body covered hers so that she could barely move, yet still she struggled.

"Quit fightin' gypsy! We saw you kissin' Colby."

"Yea," a second cowboy slurred. "All we want is some-a-what you been givin' Trace."

Fancy bit down hard on the hand covering her mouth until she tasted blood.

"Yeoow!" The injured cowboy swore.

Fancy screamed. Frantically seeking a way to escape, her gaze caught a glimpse of the whiskey bottle in the second cowboy's hand. Immediately the fight drained out of her, and she stopped screaming.

The whiskey bottle... the dark alley, this was her vision. She prayed Trace was safely home with Billy by now. But if not, rather than risk his life, she would suffer her captors assault in silence. Instead of calling attention to herself by screaming, she would find her own way to escape.

"That's better." The cowboy, whose hand she'd bitten, leered at her. Taking her stillness as compliance, he tore her shawl from her shoulders.

She gasped.

"You be a good gypsy, and I just might let you read my fortune later." He laughed, his comrade joining in.

Fancy could smell the man's fetid breath. Through gritted teeth, she spoke, "Let go of me, white man, or I will put a gypsy curse on your head that will render your most prized possession useless."

She felt his hold loosen slightly as he contemplated her words. Twisting to the left, she tried to free herself of him.

But the whiskey had not dulled his reactions enough, his right hand grabbed her, pulling her back. The weight of his body pinned her against the wall.

He laughed. "Then I best use what I got before it's gone. Ain't that right, Clem?"

"Wait 'til she sees you already been cursed." His friend guffawed.

Fancy closed her eyes and felt her stomach churn. Holding her breath, she waited for his lust to overtake her. Instead, she heard a sickening crunch as flesh met bone. She opened her eyes, but it was not the ruffian who stood before her. It was Trace.

"Fancy! Thank God! Are you alright? Did they—"

She shook her head. Despite her earlier bravado, her heart swelled at the sight of him.

The sotted cowboy at her feet started to rise. Trace shoved him back to the ground with a booted foot. A whiskey bottle sailed past Trace's ear and crashed against the brick wall. Fancy heard the deadly click of a hammer being drawn back. Her gaze caught the gleam of a gun barrel.

"No!" She screamed and lunged at the second man. They fell to the ground a second after the gun exploded.

"Trace!" She craned her neck in time to see Trace fall.

Footsteps pounded the hard earth. Suddenly, the alley was crammed with a knot of men.

"What's going on here?"

Fancy barely registered the tin star pinned to the man's shirt. The cowboy, whose legs had entangled with her own in the fall, shoved her aside and reached for his lost gun.

"I wouldn't do that if I were you." The Marshall held his own gun aloft and motioned for two others to take hold of the ruffians. "Trace?"

"Brett." Trace acknowledged the Marshall and started to rise.

Fancy rushed to Trace's side searching for the hole that must surely be the cause for all the blood staining his shirt. "Where are you hurt? Did the bullet pass through?"

"It's nothing Fancy." He smiled down at her. "It merely grazed my arm."

"But the blood...."

"Looks worse than it feels." He bent to retrieve her shawl and place it around her shoulders.

Despite the curious onlookers, she took comfort in his touch.

"These two were attempting to harm the lady." Trace spoke to the Marshall. "I intervened. This one fired." He pointed to the cowboy staring at his boots. "If Fancy hadn't knocked his aim off, I might not be standing here."

There was a low murmur among the crowd.

Fancy heard words like brave and only half-gypsy. She wondered what it meant.

Then a tall, lanky man stepped forward. Removing his hat from his head, he twirled it in his hands. "If it's alright with you, Miss Fancy. I'll see to it you get home safe."

An older man with a gruff voice and manner, who Fancy recognized as the proprietor of the mercantile spoke. "A woman alone on the edge of town. It's not safe. I've got a room in back of the shop. Could use an extra clerk."

Fancy didn't know what to say. He'd always welcomed her in his shop, one of the few who did, but to offer her a job? "Thank you, Mr. Potter. I'll have to think about it."

He nodded, and she detected just a hint of a smile.

"Miss Fancy?" The hat twiller offered her his arm.

"Sorry, Nate." Trace held his good arm out to Fancy. "The lady is with me."

Fancy felt a warm glow spread through her at his words. She smiled.

"Is that true, Miss?" The Marshall directed his gaze towards her.

She nodded, too full of emotion to speak.

"You doubt my word, Brett?" Trace frowned.

"Just makin' sure the lady is safe." He winked at Fancy. "See to it you get that arm looked at. 'Course the Doc's not quite feelin' himself tonight." He grinned.

"Sauced?" Trace asked.

"To put it mildly."

"I will see to Trace's arm. Already the blood is drying. The shirt is ruined." Fancy scolded.

The men laughed good-naturedly, and the crowd started to drift away.

Trace's breath tickled her ear. "Do you still fear what the town will say when I call on you?"

"No." She smiled and knew that it was true. Though it wouldn't be easy, she could honestly say she no longer feared the prospect.

"Good." He grinned as they left the alley. "And I promise never again to doubt Fancy's fortune."

ETERNAL FLAME

Betsy Norman

"Death comes for thee, Gabriel."

"Then let it come swiftly, for my will is long abandoned." With that said, Gabriel left the soothsayer in disgust. Death had come for him long ago, but mercy failed to accompany. For too long his dreams of a blinding flame provided insight to his future in hell.

The eternal reward for all vampires.

Gabriel damned Victoria for the thousandth time. When he rebuffed her sexual advances, spite and jealousy drove the immortal socialite's madness toward a cusp of vicious revenge. Victoria stole his human life and forced her own demonic existence into his veins. When she realized his heart and soul still belonged to another, that her theft only resulted in the master possession of his body, she slew his love before he could stop her.

Ayslinn....

The image haunted him still. Her lifeless body hung crucified and upside down, pure white linen gown spattered with crimson. He could still feel Ayslinn's warm blood stain his hands and face and the repugnant hunger the ferrous stench awakened within him.

Victoria's cacophony of laughter had echoed off the abandoned stone church. "Take her! Drink of your love now, Gabriel, before her rotting corpse draws scavengers worse than yourself."

Gabriel forced the horror from his mind. He could no more let Ayslinn's life force pass his lips than he could any other human. His love was stolen, and his life sentenced to immortal agony without her. Gabriel's only hope was that Ayslinn would guard well his heart and soul until his time came to burn in the hell Victoria thrust upon him.

He fed on animals to survive, perpetuating his hollow existence only until he could avenge Ayslinn's death. Once Victoria was destroyed, he'd welcome the burning flame of the sun, no doubt the omen of his dreams.

Glancing through the night alleys, his preternatural senses reached out their tendriled search for his nemesis. Gabriel allowed no rest for the malicious bitch, tracking her constantly. He trapped her once, but the bloodlust of retribution made him impatient and careless. Her escape cost him centuries. She went underground, making it impossible for him to find her.

Until now.

News of her re-emergence traveled to his ears. Victoria foolishly flaunted her location, daring him to seek her out. Practically issued an invitation engraved in blood.

Gabriel accepted.

He grew weary of the torturous dreams and begged a deaf God to grant him release before casting him to Hades. The purgatory of a scorching banishment from the purity of Ayslinn's memory forever tormented his every thought. That there was no hope for the reunion of their souls in the afterlife dissolved his tenacious hate into despair.

So often his mind slipped into peaceful oblivion at dawn with his last thoughts of their time together.

Gabriel, Ayslinn called to his subconscious, and his heart soared eagerly into the past when her touch was still warm with life.

The lilting rhapsody of her laughter spun around him like a sheer veil, coloring his vision in shades of sapphire and topaz.

"*Gabriel.*" His name was a sonnet on her lips of peach blossom, calling, teasing him by hiding, galvanizing his body into action to find the whimsical muse who captivated him.

"Have care, my love, for when I find you shall I seek reward for your game." In a sun-dappled meadow, the air hazy with dandelion down and butterfly wing, he searched for her as he sliced through tall grasses and blooms.

"And I most eager to reward you, milord." Ayslinn's giggles gave way to shrieks of surprise when he caught her about the waist and twirled her above his head.

"Then give me my due, as my patience flees when I look upon your face and eyes, and I am overcome by my desire."

He loved her then. The soft haven of perfumed earth and moss often served as their trysting place. A marriage bed made of one soul's commitment to another, without legal or ecclesial sanction nor band of gold. Away from jealous eyes and disapproving patriarchs. A love forbidden and thus kept concealed.

Blinded to the prospect of Victoria's deceit in his desperation to save Ayslinn, he laid down his life so that his lover might live. Immortality was a small price to pay when faced with even a fraction of mortality without Ayslinn.

Victoria's threats of exposure forced his hand. She wanted him as her own. Gabriel's life in exchange for sparing the angelic Ayslinn.

"You give your word she will remain unharmed?" Gabriel's hands banded about Victoria's throat in futile human effort to subdue her supernatural strength.

Her throaty laughter seduced his panicked mind. Her long, slim fingers slid over the alabaster skin of her breast, cold, bloodless, perfectly sculpted into eternal youth. The hand rested where the heart no longer beat. "I give you my solemn oath, Gabriel."

He forfeited his life force in a carnal bath of blood and lust. The feral tearing at his throat provoked his instincts to survive, thrust her away, but the relentless pull of her mouth, the dizzying kiss, deflated his will into feeble unconsciousness.

"You are mine now, Gabriel," Victoria hissed into his ear, the words snaking into his blank mind while his veins thinned and emptied, begging for the life stolen from them. "Drink, my sweet angel of death."

Victoria slit her breast, ripe now with his own blood, and bid him nurse to appease the ravenous, repulsive hunger that shred his gullet in twain. The irony of her perfume steeped into his numbing brain as he bent his head. Lilies of the valley, beauteous to behold, deadly to consume. The final act of surrender that would enslave him to her and save Ayslinn.

What a fool he was to believe her.

Each evening upon arising from the corpse-like sleep, the cruel, cycloptic eye of the moon squatted in the sky, mocking his naiveté.

No more!

Tonight, he would find Victoria and seek retaliation for her murderous lies. He would mourn Ayslinn for an eternity in hell, but he refused to exist as some bloodless demon on earth any longer.

Prostrating himself for the last time atop Ayslinn's grave, he moved his lips in the only prayer allowed him. "Forgive me, my love. My heart, my soul, were meant for you."

Teeth bared, he cared naught for the startled pedestrians he left in his wake through the city. Victoria had taken up residence on the fringe of affluent society. Her location was close enough to harmonize with the opulent denizens of the east side, and yet able to attract hopefuls eager to ingratiate themselves. These were the ones she preyed upon. Gabriel knew her agenda well.

Victoria's mansion loomed ahead like a sinister old man, shoulders hunched against the chill. The flicker of light showed only through the lower level and the corridor of blazing lamps lining the lane. A thrush of high-pitched party voices and music assaulted his driven senses.

"A welcoming committee, is it bruja?" Gabriel ground out through gritted teeth, slanting his stride to the outskirts of the ornamental topiary edging the lawn. A sharp tang of evergreen and sandalwood thinned his nostrils, decreased his ability to hone in on Victoria's scent. Relying on his vision, his gaze pierced through the litter of mortals to pinpoint her minions. A harem of well-cut men mingled through the crowd to patrol the surroundings.

How to get past them?

Gabriel scouted along the creek gully dipping through the north end of the property. Poorly lit, a grotto curved upwards from the stream, the water sluicing over the connected bridge, slumped with age. Agile and sleek, he cleared the mottled wall and hid within its maze. In moments he followed the circuitous path up to a rock garden flanking a lower patio. He could easily blend in with the partygoers but couldn't guarantee word of his arrival would go unnoted long enough for him to locate Victoria.

Silently, he remained still as marble within the cloaking embrace of the shadowed grotto. His gaze scaled the ivy-choked walls of the manor to the upper landing. Breath quickening, nostrils flaring at the swift inhale of the cloying lily bouquet of her scent, Gabriel knew Victoria was near.

In one rapid movement, his muscles bunched and lunged, landing soundlessly atop the balcony. He moved so quickly, none save the keenly attentive servants would have borne witness. Discovery was inevitable now, but he still had time. Even if her men saw him, they'd hesitate to alarm the guests and make the main course skittish.

Closing his eyes, he fought the hypnotic hum Victoria's nearness created in his mind. The magnetic pull of master to slave. She was so close; Gabriel grappled with the feral hunger surging through his lifeless veins, the salivating thrust of his fangs.

Ayslinn, give me strength, my love.

He needed to concentrate, focus his energies for this final battle of retribution. To summon up the strength to slay Victoria and say goodbye to this mortal realm forever. Goodbye to Ayslinn, for surely hell would rob him of his most precious memories.

The French doors stood slightly ajar. Opaque, crimson velvet drapes crisscrossed in front to obliterate any light daring to seek entrance. Ducking carefully within the jet-black room, Garbriel's sight instantly adjusted and strip-searched the inner sanctum of Victoria's chambers. There, in the corner in a blood red damask wingback, she sat regal and serene.

"Gabriel, my heart," she cooed. "So eager to visit my boudoir you chose an unconventional path?" She waved off the attending servants.

"Your claim is false, Lady, to lay it so vainly. My heart belongs to Ayslinn and always shall."

A subtle ripple creased her brow, smoothed instantly with self-assurance and retort. "She may have the empty shell, then, for I have already drained its contents for my own."

Outwardly stoic, Gabriel clenched at the reminder.

"Tut, tut, my dark angel, have you no reply to that?" Calm, her heart-shaped face tilted coquettishly, mouth forming a moue. "No, I suppose there's no denying my possession, is there?" Rising, lithe as midnight, she took mincing steps toward him. "You're pale, Gabriel." One red-lacquered talon sliced open her lower lip. "Wouldn't you like a taste?"

He swallowed hard against his enslaved will. Resistance to the siren of his master's blood became a tangible enemy, doubling his gut in wrenching pain, begging him to capitulate. He forced himself to wall off the abhorrent craving, to physically push her away.

"Nay," he choked out.

"Fool. If I wish it so, you *will* feed." Victoria batted away his grip, her dominance outweighing his inner skirmish to withstand the lure of her blood. "And once you're drunk with my essence, you'll lay with me as lover and give penance for your insolent attempt to destroy me. Please me well before sunrise, and I may consider forgiveness. Fail, and yours will be a fiery demise."

"Never, bruja." He spat. How ironic her threat. Gabriel felt the leaden weakness her presence affected on him. He knew his resolve would crumble, had to, for his plan to go forth, but to betray his love inflicted excruciating agony to his soul.

Ayslinn, I beg you forgive me.

"Drink," Victoria commanded, this time viciously forcing his mouth to her throat. The bouquet of her lily-white skin and the salty clot of blood engulfed him.

He tore at the cold flesh, her husky laughter inflaming his shame and degradation. Like a dog, she led him to tumble on the bed, her hands clawing at his clothes. He was, indeed, intoxicated, his mind a zombie to her desires, his body grown turgid from the rush of her blood.

A searing pain howled through his brain as she sunk her fangs into his chest to reclaim her life force, reiterate her dominion over his will. Mounting him, Victoria completed the rape, crying out triumphant over his helpless surrender.

Gabriel felt his soul weep in anguish, trapped while she defiled his body. So different than the intricate quiver of rapture he experienced in Ayslinn's adoring embrace.

"How glorious you are, my pet." Victoria purred, sated and smug. She lolled to one side, gloating over her conquest while Gabriel's flesh recoiled from her possessive touch.

He wanted to flee, escape this route to destiny, and warp back to the moment of error when his judgement was unclear, and he trusted a demon to save an angel.

Death comes for thee, Gabriel.

The soothsayer's words slithered into his unconscious and a crescendo of fear gripped him. Was he not already dead? Stricken down not when Victoria stole his will, but when she desecrated his love? What further horror awaited him?

Ayslinn, a thousand times I would die again, if only I were spared a measure of comfort from thy forgiveness.

Fear for his mortal soul held little consequence in comparison to the lamented failure of Ayslinn's love and trust in his returned devotion.

How I do love thee, you may never know.

Though his body betrayed their union, Gabriel knew in his heart, he remained steadfast. This knowledge renewed his spirit to attain his goal and face his fate.

The air in the cloistered room grew warm and claustrophobic. He feigned the relaxation that claimed Victoria as she braided her limbs into his within the closed canopy bed. His body and mind warded off the lethargy of dawn which would hypnotize his mind toward a corpselike slumber.

Reserving energy, Gabriel concentrated on forcing his brain to remain alert until Victoria succumbed, yet blanking his thoughts so that she could not read them.

"Sleep, pet. There's no escaping me." Victoria kissed him. The deliberate gesture illustrated her confidence in his acquiescence. He knew he must act compliant, but he could not refute the bile in his throat when her lips claimed his. Sighing, she withdrew into the rigid posture of undead repose.

"Oh, but there is, bruja. Escape… and death."

With lightening speed and precision, Gabriel hauled Victoria over one shoulder to drag her from the bed, slashing aside the protective drapery. Her shrieks of outrage and fury deafened the tranquil haze of dawn surrounding the manor in vain. None would risk their own skin to rise to her aid once the sun rose.

"Traitor!" All fang and razor-sharp talons, Victoria sliced his back to ribbons. The pain incited his rapid movements to hurl her through the open French doors and drop the latch. Gasping for breath, he leaned his back against the doors, palms splayed across the glass to reinforce the barricade.

Victoria thrashed against the frame, hands busting through the squares of glass to claw at Gabriel. The sliver of shadow from the roof sash afforded her minute protection. Each frenzied movement whipped her flesh with sunbeams, the puffs of spontaneous flames invoking shrill cries of terror.

"Let me in!" she commanded over and over again as the sun rose higher. The French doors were all but shards of kindling and shattered glass beneath her desperate attempts to gain entry. Flailing madly, she finally broke through. Gabriel struggled to catch her wrists as she bludgeoned him maniacally with all her might.

Death comes for thee, Gabriel, his mind hissed.

"Then let it come swiftly, for my will is long abandoned!" he roared, tackling Victoria to the outdoor balcony.

Searing torment blanketed his flesh. Victoria's howls as her body burst into flames echoed a fiery death knell through his brain. The acrid stench of her demise clogged his nostrils. Stumbling away, he fell to his knees, raising charred arms and gaze heavenward, sacrificing himself to the sun and God and Ayslinn.

"Farewell, my love."

The pain turned to numb apathy as the flames consumed his mortal shell in preparation to feast upon his soul for eternity. The blinding omen of his dreams at last became reality. His consciousness embraced the deadly light while his flesh was reduced to ash. His spirit rising from the rubble, he awaited the harrowing spiral to hell.

Gabriel.

How cruel, he thought, that Satan should summon him in his lover's voice.

Gabriel, arise. Come home to me, love.

He refused to believe the evil ruse. "Nay, reveal thyself, or is this my everlasting torment to endure?" Already his agony began. The precious memories he thought would be vanquished would instead be used to torture him.

Gabriel wept as an image of Ayslinn descended to welcome him with ethereal arms, gossamer robes as white as a dove's breast, an aura of purity surrounding her, nearly blinding him with her beauty. "Your torment is over, as is mine own while parted from thee. Here lies the haven for thy soul, Gabriel, as I have sheltered it in wait for thy return."

The sweet lyric of her voice beckoned, while his dizzy mind strived to ferret out the truth. "Ayslinn?"

"Aye, love, 'tis no illusion."

"I had thought you lost to me forever."

"Nay, only my mortal self. My heart and soul have always belonged to you, as you have given yours to me. The arduous journey to reclaim them is over. Come to me now."

"I am not worthy. I have betrayed thee—"

"Shhhh." A slim finger silenced his lips. "Never. For I have always basked in the strength of your love. No physical act ever diminished the faithfulness of your heart, and so there is none to forgive."

Her words struck to his core. There was no further denial he could debate. Even in his darkest hour with Victoria, Gabriel had remained loyal in his heart's allegiance with Ayslinn. Had he truly been spared by love?

Absolution bathed his spirit, filling him with ecstasy. Swept into her angelic embrace, Gabriel again experienced the joy and peace found in the glow of Ayslinn's devotion. Entwined, the rush of ascent intensified the glorious reunion as she led him heavenward to his final reward.

The eternal flame, the omen of his dreams, was not the fiery torture of damnation, but the warmth of his inextinguishable love for Ayslinn.

Ayslinn. The keeper of his heart, his soul, his salvation.

THE FINAL CONTRACT

Tami D. Cowden

Serena watched as her target opened the driver's door to his classic T-Bird. He slid behind the wheel with his usual leonine grace. After the barest adjustment of his rear view mirror, he peeled the car away from the curb and entered traffic. She silently counted to four, then followed in her own BMW.

Amazing, the way the man managed to do everything so well. He wove through the traffic easily, with never a sudden brake nor quick acceleration, but his driving ability was the least of it. His walk, his voice, his charm, the game of pick-up basketball he started with some down and out teenagers. And the meal he had purchased each of them afterwards.

It was a shame he had to die.

She had never been so tempted to fail before. But business was business. After all, she had a reputation to protect. Besides, this job would be her last. One last job, and the Company would let her walk away. No strings, no trip back to prison to serve out a sentence for a crime they'd framed her for in the first place. She'd finally have her freedom.

Still, if ever a man deserved to live just for what he was,

for the sheer pleasure he gave a woman who simply watched him, Malcolm MacDougal was the man.

Of course, if the merry chase on which he'd led her so far indicated anything, it was that this contract was not going to be easy to fill. MacDougal—Mac, as she'd begun to call him in her head—had yet to give her a single opening. When he wasn't whizzing around in that cool car of his, he was in very public places, surrounded by crowds. Even if she were willing to risk witnesses, she'd not take the chance of harming someone else. The business was dirty enough without bringing others into it.

And trying for him at home was out of the question, too. The security staff at his apartment building could teach a few things to the folks at Fort Knox. In fact, when the job was over, she just might look into moving there. Just in case the Company changed its mind.

Her musing on the future came to a sudden halt as she realized her prey had suddenly sped up to make an intersection just before the amber light switched to red. But the drivers in the two cars she'd kept between them clearly didn't have the same sense of urgency he did. She was stuck craning her neck to see his car continue down the street.

His taillights flashed against the growing dusk as he braked for a turn. Into the park? This might be her chance! Her fingers drummed impatiently against the steering wheel as she waited for the light to change. One hand reached into her purse for her Ruger.

The cold steel touch felt like the icy fingers that closed around her heart all too often these days. The Company would surely see that this had to be her last job. She was letting herself get sentimental. Or was she getting soft?

It was that touch of sadness she saw reflected in his eyes that made her regret his contract. The brief glimpses she had into a soul that seemed as tormented as her own.

But he undoubtedly deserved to die. The Company could only be bothered by the highest level of targets. Whatever

Mac seemed, he had to be a major scumbag. Probably the leader of major drug cartel or something.

Anyway, he was just another target. Nothing to her. Just her final contract.

Malcolm slowed just enough so the woman on his tail would see him make the turn into the park. The time had come to confront his shadow—and, he hoped, finish up with the Company once and for all. Just this one last contract, and he could walk away, they'd said.

Yeah, and he had some beachfront property in Kansas to offer anyone who believed that line.

He parked near the lake, in a spot he knew well. A flick of his fingers against the latch opened his brief case. The cardboard silhouette figure he'd stuffed inside began to unfold. He propped it against the driver's window, and then slipped out the passenger door, and around into the thick stand of trees. A quick glance satisfied him that the cardboard figure was convincing. From behind the cover of a tree, he kept his eyes on the road.

When her car became visible, he saw it slow almost imperceptibly, then continue past the trees in which he had hidden. He knew she'd park a half mile or so down, and then make her way back on foot. He turned his attention to the woods behind him.

He didn't have long to wait. She was definitely careful, but the sturdy boots she wore weren't meant for stealthy walking through dry autumn leaves.

As he expected, the woman stopped only a few feet from his hiding place, at exactly the spot he would have chosen in her position. He'd been right. This one was good, better than all the rest. She just might be his ticket out of this hell.

She used both hands to raise the gun, its silencer giving it an eerily elongated look beneath the shadows of the trees. The gun lowered once, but suddenly she raised it, took careful aim, and fired at the silhouette. The sharp crack as the car window gave way offered testimony of the accuracy of her aim. Her gun lowered to her side, and she turned. Tears ran down her cheeks, and a jagged sob escaped her lips.

He had not expected the remorse. It only strengthened his own resolve.

He knew the moment she saw him. Saw the .45 he aimed directly between her brows. In that moment, emotion flashed across her face. Relief? Joy?

With his left hand, he first gently wiped the tears from her face, and then took her Ruger and threw it a few yards away. With his right hand, he kept his own weapon steady. "They told you this would be your last job, right?"

Her eyes widened, and then narrowed as understanding of the Company's betrayal hit. Her chin jutted up, and her breath quickened, but she showed no fear. "I guess they weren't lying."

He smiled. Defiant humor? She was definitely the one. "They were lying, but we can make their promises come true. Together." He took a risk and lowered the gun. "Truce?"

She stared back at him for a moment, then nodded. "Truce."

After only a second's hesitation, he holstered his gun. "Okay, here's the plan."

Four days later, Serena lounged lazily on the hotel bed. Flicking through the channels, she stopped at a news report.

"...the drivers of the two cars continued to exchange gun fire for more than a mile." Jerky video taken from a traffic helicopter showed her BMW chasing Mac's T-Bird. A lengthy stand of trees hid the cars from view for nearly a minute, and then they reappeared. "As you can see, both vehicles crashed through the barrier blocking a bridge under repair and plunged into the water." The camera zoomed in on the half-submerged cars, the water rushing around them.

"Authorities do not believe either driver survived. Divers continue to search for the bodies, but experts say the current probably sent them down river, and very possibly out into the gulf. They hold out little hope of finding them."

The television view switched back to the genial anchors in the studio. The woman smiled broadly and spoke to her colleague. "Bob, they recovered several weapons from the vehicles. The police speculate that the parties involved here were either rival drug dealers, or perhaps gang members."

Serena switched the television off and gave the first carefree laugh she could remember in years.

"I must say, you are taking your demise very well." Mac handed her a flute of champagne before settling next to her. His hand traveled along her thigh, leaving trails of tingly warmth.

Amazing how he did everything so well. She snuggled closer to the man who'd proven all she had imagined and more. "At least we went out with a bang."

"More like a splash! Too bad about the cars, though." He grinned back at her and waggled his eyebrows. The haunted look was still in his eyes, but much fainter.

She understood. She'd never be completely free from what the Company had forced her to become. But with every minute she spent in freedom, with every minute she spent with Mac, she moved farther from the woman she had been for too long. She laced her fingers in his. Holding his gaze, she leaned close for a kiss. "Who cares about stupid cars?"

His head shook. "Not me." He gave her a gentle kiss in return.

Peace settled within her. Together, they would make the journey back to the light.

SWEETBRIAR INN

Su Kopil

This story is dedicated to my grandmother, Margaret Elizabeth Dunlap, who shared her love of roses and gardening with me.

Devon Cates steered her '69 Mustang off the country road onto a long drive shaded by enormous live oaks dripping with Spanish moss. The lush gardens and wide expanse of lawn could only be described as breathtaking. Yet, it was nothing compared to the columned plantation house with the enormous wrap around porch gleaming in the morning sun. Obviously, someone took pains to care for the old place despite the resident ghost said to roam its halls. Devon doubted the existence of this ghost she'd been sent to report on, or any ghost for that matter. But the prospect of a little R & R lured her like nothing else could.

Maneuvering the car into an empty parking space, Devon pulled her suitcase and canvas overnight bag from the backseat. A silver-haired couple waved to her from the porch. The plaid-shirted man hefted himself out of the rocking chair and ambled down the steps toward her.

Devon couldn't help but smile. The pair matched the picturesque inn perfectly. Yes. She definitely would enjoy this weekend away from the bustling city, the stressful office, and, most especially, the plastic men.

"Good morning." Devon handed her suitcase into the owner's outstretched hand. "The Inn is beautiful!"

"It is something," he agreed.

She followed him up brick steps to the wide front porch. "I'm Devon Cates from the Lansing Observer."

"Roy," he said, setting her suitcase on the painted wooden planks. "This here is my wife, Joan."

The petite woman stopped rocking and smiled. "You must be the reporter Jack told us about."

"Yes." She had talked to someone named Jack on the phone.

"Can I pour you a glass of sweet tea?" Joan reached for a clean glass and the half-filled pitcher sitting on the table next to her.

"That would be nice. Thank you." She accepted the refreshment. The cool liquid soothed her parched throat. "This is good… different."

"It's the mint," Joan said. "Around back is an herb garden. Jack likes to flavor the teas."

So Jack worked in the kitchen and answered the phones. "It's delicious but, if you don't mind, I'd really like to get settled in my room."

The couple glanced at each other. Roy let out a deep belly laugh. Joan smiled.

"What's so funny?" The screen door squeaked open and a man in jeans and a cotton shirt stepped onto the porch.

Devon's glance faltered on the devilish dimples flashing in a near perfect face. She hoped this man wasn't a guest. Unearthing an imaginary ghost would provide enough frustration without battling a distraction as tempting as him.

"I believe Miss Cates here thinks we own the Sweetbriar," Joan supplied.

Devon pivoted toward the woman. "You don't?"

Joan shook her head. "We stay often enough but, no, we're guests."

"Then who does?"

The couple nodded towards the man standing in the doorway.

Devon felt the heat creep into her cheeks. Her instincts weren't usually so off. As a reporter she couldn't afford them to be. Turning, she met his amused gaze.

"Jack Garrett at your service." He held out his hand.

"Devon... Devon Cates," she managed, feeling the strength behind his gentle grasp. A jolt similar to static electricity from a TV screen shook her. They stood; their hands locked a fraction too long. Had he felt it too? Finally, he released her.

"Ah, yes, the reporter. Welcome to the Sweetbriar. If you'll excuse us." He winked at the couple. "I'm sure Devon would like to see her room." Grabbing her suitcase and overnight bag in one hand, he held the door for her.

Devon stepped over the threshold into a spacious foyer of polished wood. From the gleaming floorboards, to the dark luster of the antique furnishings, to the serpentine balustrade, the house breathed simple elegance.

Jack headed for the stairs. Devon followed.

"I'm sorry we didn't get a chance to talk more on the phone." He slowed his pace until she caught up to him. "However, you did say you were coming to do a story about Rose."

"Rose?" Devon couldn't help but notice she only reached his shoulder. The fact made her feel petitely feminine.

"That's what the guests call our ghost. The lucky few who are favored with a nightly visit often find a rose on their pillow in the morning."

Devon raised her right brow.

"A non-believer I see." He laughed, stopping before a door at the end of the hallway.

"Nothing against the Sweetbriar," Devon said. "I don't believe ghosts exist anywhere. Like love at first sight. It just isn't real." She averted her gaze from Jack's knowing smile, suddenly feeling uncomfortable. Now why had she picked that particular analogy?

"Then you would be an odd choice for this assignment, no?"

"Yes, well...."

"No one else wanted it?"

His directness was unnerving. "No one else was available and, well, I... I needed a vacation." She hadn't meant to say that. Something about him drew her out. Perhaps it was his own forthrightness.

"I see." He pushed open the door.

She wondered if she'd hurt his feelings, then chastised herself for being ridiculous.

"I'll leave you to get settled. Come down when you're ready, and we can talk." He set her bags on the floor and started to back out of the room. "I hope you don't mind. They say this was Rose's room when she lived here. I thought you would like that. For research purposes." He flashed her a grin, then softly closed the door.

Devon warily surveyed her surroundings. Aside from the absence of a TV or stereo, she found nothing out of the ordinary. A four-poster bed with what appeared to be an antique quilt filled the room along with two dressers with a matching nightstand. Everywhere she looked there were flowers. Roses delicately climbed the wallpaper, single blossoms hung in frames on the wall, even the curtains sported bountiful bouquets. Relaxing her shoulders, she let out a sigh. Ghosts existed in fanciful imaginations. She wouldn't allow a well-placed suggestion from Jack to take root in hers.

Lifting her suitcase onto the bed, she started unpacking. She would gather enough information to write an article about the Sweetbriar, and let the readers decide if they believed in the legend of Rose. Her mind set, she finished putting away her belongings, fixed her hair and makeup, and went in search of her host.

She found him in the kitchen. A tray of sandwiches, tomato salad, and a pitcher of iced tea sat on one counter.

"There you are." He smiled. "I thought you might be hungry."

"Starved actually. Where are the other guests?" She hadn't noticed anyone in the halls on her way down.

"Exploring, shopping. There's quite a lot to do in the area." He picked up the tray and headed for a side door. "The terrace is cool this time of day."

"Sounds lovely." She wondered if he was this gracious to all his guests or if he was hoping for a good write up. She'd like to think it was the former.

Several glass-topped tables were set up on the brick terrace. Jack set the tray on a smaller, cozier one. He held a chair out for her before seating himself.

She tilted her head as though the angle would afford her a better perspective of the man.

"What? Did I do something wrong?" he asked.

"No. It's just that I'm not used to a man with manners. Men in the city seem to have forgotten how to treat a woman." She glanced at his face to see if he would laugh at her. He did not.

His expression was serious when he replied, "A lady should be treated with respect."

Her heart thrummed in her ears. She felt a quickening of desire for this man she barely knew.

As though sensing her discomfort, he drew her attention to something else.

"I hope you don't mind herbs in your salad. Some basil, chives, and marjoram fresh from the garden."

"No, Joan told me about the tea." She noticed the curving beds surrounding the terrace. "Are these your herb gardens? They're beautiful."

"With the cooler weather coming, most of it is going to seed. But I dry enough to see us through the winter. I'll show you around after we eat." His dark gaze sought hers. "Would you like that?"

Though a simple question, she felt it held some importance to him. "Yes," she answered. "Very much." A tremor of anticipation raced along her spine. What was the matter with her? She glanced at the table, the terrace, the gardens, anywhere but at him while he served the meal. She was here for a story and, hopefully, some rest. The way her pulse hammered in her neck, it felt like she'd just run a marathon. She'd been around handsome men before. The city was full of them. It must be stress. A relaxing afternoon out in the fresh air would do wonders for her.

They ate in a companionable silence, enjoying the bird songs and the gentle breeze. Jack made her laugh by mimicking a mockingbird call so well a curious female perched close by for a moment before taking flight.

"The food was delicious. Thank you." Devon started stacking the dirty dishes on the tray.

"I'll get it later." Jack placed his hand on hers.

The plate she held clattered to the table. "I'm sorry, my finger slipped in a spot of mayonnaise." She quickly wiped her hand on a napkin so he wouldn't catch her lie.

When he didn't respond, she glanced up. His brows drew together. A strange look shadowed his eyes. Had he felt it? That almost electric current that passed between them when their hands touched? The same as when they shook hands earlier, only stronger. Ridiculous! She dismissed the notion. If she weren't careful, she'd be spouting poetry and swooning in the man's arms.

"Shall we take that walk then?" She hoped her voice didn't sound as strained to him as it did in her own ears.

They strolled along cobblestone paths. Jack pointed out different herbs explaining their uses. They came upon a rose garden. Devon inhaled the sweet perfume. Pulling a small scissors from his jeans pocket, Jack snipped a large pink rose and handed it to her.

"This garden is almost as old as the house." Jack shoved the scissors back in his pocket. "They say Rose tended it herself, filling the house with sweet blooms." He glanced at her. "Some say she still takes a cutting from time to time."

"Tell me about her." Careful not to let the thorns catch her fingers, Devon twirled the rose in her hand

"There's not much to tell. The few records available mention a woman, Rose Thorndike, who once lived here. She'd been engaged to marry but for some unknown reason broke the engagement. She lived here alone, never marrying, until her death in 1862. Those are the facts." Jack shrugged.

"And the legend?"

He chuckled. "Legend has it that Rose broke her engagement after reading a letter telling of her fiancé's infidelity. She broke the engagement but never recovered. They say she regretted her choice to believe written accusations instead of her lover's profession of love. Because she didn't believe, she lost her chance at true love."

Devon smiled. "That seems a harmless interpretation of the truth. So when did the rumors of her roaming the Sweetbriar begin?"

"About forty years ago. My parents ran the inn at the time. A young woman spent the week as a guest. Night after night my parents heard her crying in her room. Finally, my mother could stand it no more, and she asked the woman what ailed her. Apparently, the woman had become the object of pity among her family and friends. At age twenty-six, they'd convinced her she would never marry or raise a family. The next night a vision of a woman in a flowing gown appeared in her room. No words were spoken. The young woman assumed it had been a dream. She awoke to find a fresh rose on her pillow. The next day, a handsome bachelor checked in. The two were married, on these very grounds, six months later. Since then, legend has it, if a guest discovers a rose on her pillow true love is sure to follow."

Needing time to digest Jack's story, Devon walked towards a small pond. Undoubtedly, parts of the tale were true becoming stretched and romanticized over the years. What bothered her was her own overwhelming desire to believe the story. As a reporter, she'd always based her life on facts, pure and simple. To consider doing otherwise left her shaken and unsure.

"Devon?" She hadn't heard him come up behind her. Nor did she expect to find him standing so close when she turned around. She could smell the scent of roses on the breeze.

He parted his lips, and she noticed how full they were. She saw him hesitate, then his fingers touched her hair. A chill danced along her skin. Without meaning to, her body swayed closer to his. The next moment, his lips were on hers, soft, exploring, teasing her with a barely restrained passion.

Desire flooded her. She gave in to his kiss, pressing closer, her hand tangled in his thick hair. Sanity nagged at her. She pushed it away. What she felt was anything but sane. It insisted. She relented. And in that moment of indecision, Jack must have felt her hesitancy.

He broke their connection.

She felt an immediate loss, a darkening much like a light dimming, revealing only cold shadows. She shivered.

"I'm sorry." He ran a hand through his hair. "I don't know what came over me. You're a guest. I never should have—"

"It's okay. You don't need to explain. I felt it too."

His gaze searched hers, but he said nothing. Instead, he guided her back towards the house.

When they reached the terrace, she asked, "What you told me, back there in the garden, about the young woman. Are there any other stories like that?"

"A few here and there over the years. Sometimes Rose doesn't appear for years. Then suddenly a guest will find a rose on her pillow."

"How long has it been since her last visit?"

"Five, maybe, six years."

"And have you ever seen her?"

"No." He shook his head, his gaze clouding. "She's only shown herself to women."

Devon felt him withdraw. Did he hope to find a rose on his pillow in hopes true love would follow? She fought the urge to reach out to him. Instead, she thanked him for the lunch and hurried inside. At the rate she was going Jack Garrett would have her believing in ghosts and the possibility of love at first sight.

The rest of the evening passed quickly. Devon only had the opportunity to talk to one young couple who had come to the inn hoping to see a ghost. Though disappointed not to have seen the legendary Rose, they claimed to love the Sweetbriar and would return again.

The inn didn't provide dinner for guests, only breakfast and an occasional lunch. But Jack invited her to join him in the kitchen for a light meal. She thought of feigning a headache until she realized how silly that sounded. She'd been attracted to handsome men before and hadn't felt the need to run and hide. She refused to start now just because this particular man made her feel things, think things, that shook the very core of her being.

Dinner had been awkward at first but soon they fell into an easy banter. Jack described the area and its history. He offered to show her the sights the next day to which she eagerly agreed.

It wasn't until they brought their mugs of tea onto the porch that the awkwardness returned. Night enveloped them in an inky cloak save for the soft glow of a quarter moon. He sat in a rocking chair, she in the porch swing. Yet, the distance between them seemed miles.

A thick tension pulsated in the air. The silence stretched uncomfortably. Finally, Jack rose and stood before her.

"May I?" he asked.

"Certainly." She slid over making room for him on the wicker swing.

He watched her for a moment as though unsure where to start. His nearness heated the cool night air. Finally, he asked, "Remember earlier when you said you didn't believe in love at first sight?"

"I still don't." Despite what her body felt, her mind refused to believe such a thing was possible, just as ghosts were an impossibility.

"What if you're wrong?"

"I'm not."

"Never?"

"Not about this."

He sighed, and she heard exasperation in it. "So you live your life looking only at the facts, refusing to believe anything that can't be explained in a nice, tidy package."

"And you, I suppose, believe in Santa Claus, the Easter Bunny, fairytales, and ghosts?" He'd put her on the defensive, and she didn't like it.

"Yes."

"Yes, what?" She wasn't following him.

"Yes, I believe in ghosts."

"Even though you never saw one."

"Even though I never saw one." He agreed. "At least, I'm open to the possibility of these things. You shut the door without even looking at what's inside. I feel sorry for you."

"Sorry for me?" she spluttered. "Because I'm pragmatic?"

He stood. "Because if you're not careful, you'll end up like Rose." He walked towards the screen door and opened it. "Oh, by the way," he paused, "that couple I told you about who married six months after Rose's visit?"

"Yes?"

"You met them yesterday."

She gasped. "Joan and Roy?"

"The same. Goodnight, Devon." The door banged shut behind him.

Later, Devon lay in the large four poster bed with the quilt pulled up to her chin. Jack's words kept echoing in her head. *"If you're not careful, you'll end up like Rose."*

What was that supposed to mean? She'd become a ghost? The thought made her frown in the darkness. Ridiculous! There was no such thing. Then what did he mean? He'd said Rose lost her one chance at true love because she believed in what she thought were the facts and not her lover. Well, she didn't have a lover and she didn't plan on getting one anytime soon. Yet, her traitorous body warmed at the thought of Jack lying in bed next to her.

She rolled over, punching her pillow, and willed her body to relax. Eventually, she fell into an uneasy sleep where dreams of Jack and a ghost named Rose haunted her rest.

Devon awoke in a cold sweat. Sunlight filtered through the window curtains. She bolted upright throwing back the covers. She searched the bed looking under the pillows and on the floor. No fresh rose. She breathed a sigh of relief. It was only a dream. There'd been no ghostly visit in the middle of the night. The thought cheered her considerably. All of Jack's talk had her doubting what she knew was true all along. No more. She would talk to Joan and Roy. Surely they could offer a logical explanation of the rumors surrounding the Sweetbriar.

By the time she finished dressing and joined Jack downstairs, the rest of the guests had already started their day. One group had checked out, the young couple she'd talked with yesterday left for the beach, and Joan and Roy had embarked on a day of shopping. She had no choice but to wait to talk to the older couple.

True to his word, Jack produced an itinerary while she grabbed a quick bite to eat. He made no mention of the night before and neither did she.

"Of course, we don't have to follow this to the letter." He chuckled, handing her the list. But I thought it would give you an idea of what's around for your article. I've got my part time help coming in so we've got the whole day. Unless you'd rather I didn't accompany you."

She brushed his concern aside, aware of the disappointment deflating her spirits at the thought of their not spending the day together. "Of course, you must go. I couldn't begin to read your writing." She joked, gesturing to the itinerary and his illegible scrawl.

His answering smile and nod sent a thrill of anticipation through her.

They spent a glorious day riding bikes though a historic village, collecting shells at the beach, eating at an outdoor café, and seeing the sights. Devon sampled her first southern fried crabcakes and loved them. Night had already descended by the time they returned to the Sweetbriar, exhausted but happy. Jack walked her to the foot of the stairs.

"I've got to check on a few things, but I wanted to thank you for today." He smiled at her, the same smile that had made her heart beat faster all day.

"I'm the one who should be thanking you. Do all reporters get such special treatment?" she teased.

"Only you." His expression grew serious.

She thought he would kiss her. She wanted to feel his lips pressed against hers, wanted a chance to quench the desire he so easily kindled within her.

He bent his head, placing a chaste kiss on her cheek. "Goodnight, Devon," he whispered. "Sweet dreams." He turned from her, heading back toward the kitchen.

Disappointment slowed her steps as she climbed the stairs to her room. Jack had been the perfect gentleman all day while her thoughts and emotions ran rampant. If she didn't know better, she'd think she was falling in love with him. But that wasn't possible. Not after knowing someone for only two days. Or was it?

Despite her exhaustion, sleep eluded her. When she finally dozed off it seemed only moments before she woke again. Bleary eyed, she rolled over to read the clock on the nightstand.

"Ouch!" Something sharp cut into her arm. Fumbling in the dark, she managed to switch the lamp on. It took her a moment to adjust to the bright light.

"Oh, my...." Lying on the edge of her bed was a fresh red rose. She shivered, glancing nervously around the dark room and the even darker shadows lurking in the corners. "But, I didn't see any ghost—"

A soft thud sounded in the hallway.

"Jack." She scrambled out of bed, careful not to crush the rose, and headed for the door. Opening it, she peered into the dim hallway. She recognized the silhouette of a man heading for the stairs. "Jack!" She called just above a whisper.

He turned and slowly walked toward her. "I'm sorry. I didn't mean to wake you. I couldn't sleep. I thought if I could—"

"I know what you thought, and it was sweet." She couldn't hold back her feelings any longer. Flinging her arms around him, her lips sought his in a kiss she hoped would never end.

But it did, all too soon, when he gently pushed her away from him. She saw his frown in the darkness. "I don't understand," he said. "What was sweet?"

"You don't have to pretend." She smiled. "I know you put the rose on my pillow. That's why you were sneaking away just now. You hoped I would think it was from Rose."

"Devon, I ...." He shook his head.

"Jack?" A chill raced up her spine. "Jack, tell me you left the rose."

"I came up here hoping you would be awake. I needed to talk to you. I needed to convince you—Then I saw your light go on, and I chickened out." He took her hands in his. "But, I swear, I didn't leave a rose on your pillow."

"But, if you didn't, then...." Her voice trailed off as a soft glow filled the hallway. They both turned as one towards the window at the end of the hall. A faint image of a woman appeared. Through her Devon could see the outline of the window and the stars in the night sky. The woman smiled and nodded, as though at a job well done.

"Don't go, Rose." Jack took a step forward. But when he did the image faded and only the window stared back at them.

"Rose," Devon breathed. "I can't believe you saw her, too. I thought only women could."

"Who knows why ghosts do what they do?"

She heard the awe in his voice. She laughed nervously, then grew serious. "So I guess ghosts really do exist...."

Jack took her in his arms, holding her against him. She felt his warm breath in her ear and heard him whisper, "And so does love at first sight."

She smiled against his shoulder. She didn't need facts this time to know it was true.

AGAINST THE WIND

Carolee Joy

Hayley could just about swear she saw the stallion sculpture move in the moonlight.

Impossible. She turned away from the window and her view of the larger-than-life bronze mustangs in the plaza below her seventh floor office. What was it her mother had said? Oh, yeah. Hallucinations typically indicate a reaction to stress.

If that were true, the men in white coats had better prepare a padded cell for her. On the extended plan. She was actually beginning to think she would someday be caught up with her work and be able to return to a semblance of a normal life. Talk about fantasies. She returned her attention to the occupancy reports spread across her desk.

"Hayley?" The slightly twangy tones of her assistant's voice floated over the intercom.

"Yes, Tabitha."

"I'm leaving for the day. Is there anything else you needed?"

"Just dinner." *And a long, long sleep.* She tapped her pencil against the desk blotter.

"The deli downstairs is still open if you'd like me to order you up a sandwich."

"No, thanks. I'll probably get more done if I take a break first." Hayley said goodbye and returned to the printout of an electronic spreadsheet. There must be a reason why so many tenants were moving out of the deluxe office spaces. Sure, there was a lot of competition in the market now, but Mustang Towers boasted several amenities other complexes couldn't begin to offer.

She'd rent space simply because of the horse sculpture, but other people probably weren't into art, or horses, as much as she was to be able to be able to appreciate it. Tabitha claimed the statue's realistic pose of mustangs splashing through a creek on the cobblestones made them look like real horses frozen in place.

She tossed the pencil to the desk and retrieved her purse. No sense stewing over it on an empty stomach. A short time later, a stuffed baked potato in front of her, Hayley sat in the café by a window facing the plaza. From here, the mustangs looked even more lifelike. If she didn't know better, she would think she saw the nostrils flare on the lead stallion.

She turned away from the window and scanned an article in her marketing magazine only to be drawn back to the mustangs by the uncanny sensation she was being watched.

But except for the sculpture, the courtyard was deserted. A white grocery bag floated in the wind, scudding along the cobblestones, then soaring up only to drift back down to the ground. *Forget about the horses.* Closing her eyes, she counted to ten, then opened them and determinedly dug into her chili and cheese potato.

Back in her office she pored over the reports and ran another computer analysis of the financial information the staff accountants had prepared for her. As vice-president of marketing, it was her responsibility to see why the management firm was losing money and tenants, then to suggest possible solutions. She rose and stretched to ease the kink in her back, then stood by the floor to ceiling window and looked down into the courtyard.

How odd. From up here, the mustangs looked as if they were in a different formation than they had been while she ate supper. She pressed her fingers against her temples. *Stop it!* She was letting her fascination with the new sculpture interfere with her work. If she kept this up, she'd be here all night, and that was no way to prepare for the important meeting in the morning.

She started to turn away when another thought occurred to her. Why not take another short break, stroll around the courtyard for a few minutes, and clear her head? That should put these ridiculous notions to rest.

A few minutes later, she stood at the building entrance looking out towards the bronze herd, their likeness caught in what would be a thundering gallop. If they were real.

If, if, if. How could a logical woman such as herself be so caught up in a fantasy?

Footsteps echoing on the brick, she walked slowly to the center of the courtyard and stopped directly in front of the horses. If they were real, she'd be on the brink of being stampeded.

She smiled. Lucky for her they weren't alive.

The lead stallion's nostrils flared.

Hayley stifled a gasp. No, no. She didn't see what she thought she just saw. It was impossible. The horses were cold, unmoving bronze castings.

Suddenly, the urge to stroke the satiny coat was overpowering. Hayley took one step forward, then another until her outstretched hand touched the stallion's nose. How lifelike he was, she could almost feel him breathing against the palm of her hand.

What would it be like to ride such a magnificent animal? If he were real, she hastily clarified. She missed the horses she'd grown up with. After she left home to attend college, her parents had sold them off, one by one, but it shouldn't matter. Ten years later, she certainly didn't have time for a hobby as consuming as keeping horses.

An overwhelming urge to ride swept over her. She glanced around to make sure she was still alone. Nothing but shadows and silence accompanied her. Feeling as giddy as a child, she kicked off her pumps, hiked up the skirt of her conservative suit and boosted herself up onto the stallion's slippery back. For a moment, she could only grin, half-embarrassed, half-pleased by her impulsive act.

The horse shuddered beneath her, head rearing back, one hoof pawing at the ground. Hayley's shriek lodged in her throat as the stallion reared slightly, nearly unseating her. He turned his head, as if to make certain he hadn't lost her, then began to canter.

Clutching a handful of mane in her shaking hands, she squeezed her knees against his side in a vain attempt to guide him. The stallion ignored her efforts at control. However this was happening, he apparently wasn't about to take any suggestions from her!

Hooves clattered along the cobblestones as they moved further and further away from where she feared she'd left her sanity. Exhilaration overpowering her fears, Hayley glanced back. Mustang Towers, a few windows illuminated as the cleaning crew made their midnight rounds, presided over a herd of sculpted stallions gleaming in the moonlight.

But now one horse was missing.

She bent low over the stallion's neck, adjusting for the rhythm of his long stride. Wind tore at the clip taming her shoulder length hair. Reaching up, she yanked it free, letting the tawny waves fly, giving herself up completely to the crazy moment of unreality.

Hours later, Hayley woke in her poster bed, her memory of how she'd ended up there fuzzy, as if she'd been indulging in a bottomless margarita glass at Rosita's Cantina. A soft spring breeze fluttered the curtains, letting a pale glow from the streetlight below briefly illuminate her room.

And the bronzed skin of the naked man next to her. She shrieked and scooted up against the headboard, the sheet clutched up over her bare breasts. Lord, what had been in that chili? She most certainly was hallucinating now. The last thing she remembered was the wild ride on the mustang all the way to her house, a half mile away from Mustang Towers. She also remembered feeding the stallion, a hastily concocted mixture of oatmeal and apples, before she had stumbled to her bed and fallen into a dreamless sleep.

"It was delicious," he said, as if reading her mind. "Although I really would rather have a steak, medium rare."

"Nooooo," her voice emerged as a frightened squeak. She groped for the bedside lamp, hoping light would chase this dream, this apparition out of her bed and out of her mind.

He intercepted her trembling fingers and brought them to his lips, the motion immediately sending calm spreading through her. Peace, and a dangerously intoxicating languor.

"Who are you?" she whispered as he began to lavish kisses on her fingertips, her hands, then moved slowly up the inside of her arm.

"Chad Harrington." He let his tongue trail from the sensitive skin above her elbow up to her shoulder. "At least, I used to be."

She cupped his face in her hands. Dark brown eyes gazed solemnly back at her. Shoulder length chestnut hair tumbled back from a breathtakingly handsome face. "You're the sculptor. You did the Mustang castings." She recognized him from the advance publicity shots she'd seen advertising the dedication of the sculpture slated for two days from now.

"As I said, I used to be. Now," he shrugged, then bent his head to suck on the sensitive area at the juncture of her shoulder and throat, making her shiver with delicious anticipation. "I don't know what I'm supposed to be. Or how long this fantasy will last."

"Fantasy?" Again, her voice emerged as a squeak.

"Hmmm." He kissed his way up her throat, nibbled on her earlobe, then pulled her closer until she felt the hot, hardness of his flesh press against her thigh. "I've been watching you, Hayley Wilder. Why did it take you so long to touch me?"

"I don't know," she whispered, wondering why she had hesitated even for a heartbeat as her hands skimmed along the taut muscles of his perfectly sculpted chest.

Chad's hand cupped her breast, his forefinger and thumb gently toying with the nipple, then moving lower, down over her abdomen and between her legs. She gasped and arched her hips toward him as his fingers parted her and began a rhythmic stroking. Whatever kind of crazy dream this was, she didn't want to wake, didn't want it to end until the lonely coldness which surrounded her heart thawed, at least a little.

Chad's forefinger dipped inside, and the warmth shot through her, sending her rocking against his hand, dragging little whimpery pleas from her throat. Looking as dazed as she felt, he slid his knee between her thighs, easing her legs apart and hovered above her, the tip of his erection branding her with heat and sending her close to the edge.

She didn't understand at all how this was possible, if she was awake or dreaming, but she didn't care. All she wanted was for him to complete her.

The next moment, he was buried inside her, his face pressed against her neck, his breathing harsh and ragged.

"I thought I was a dead man, and I must be, for I am surely in heaven."

If she was dreaming, then she hoped she stayed asleep for a long, long time. She tugged his mouth to hers and kissed him. Mouths mating in unison with their joining, she cupped his buttocks and pulled him deeper inside until his soul wrapped around hers and took her with him to paradise.

Bright sunshine spilled across her face, startling her into instant wakefulness accompanied by the shrill ring of the bedside telephone. She bolted upright. What a night. What a

...dream. It was all just a dream, or else why would she be sleeping alone like she always did?

She groped for the phone, knocking a partially full water goblet over onto her black satin pajama top lying in a crumpled heap on the floor.

Wait a minute... on the floor? She didn't have time to ponder the significance of that before Tabitha's concerned voice filled her ear.

"Hayley. The board is due to arrive any minute, and Mr. Redding is about to have a hemorrhage wondering why you're not here yet. What happened?"

Hayley cautiously settled back against the pillow. "What do you mean?"

"You always leave your office so organized and right now it looks like the aftermath of a paper bomb. Mr. Redding wants those reports and even I can't find them. He's having a fit about being sure the meeting is over before that sculptor gets here this afternoon."

Closing her eyes, she rubbed her forehead and took a deep breath. "I must have brought them home with me. I'll fax them over and be there in plenty of time before Mr. Harrington," she stumbled over the name as the dream of Chad's hands exploring her shattered her concentration, "shows up. And if I'm not, take him out for a cappuccino or something."

"Okay, I'll do my best to stall them. Hayley," Tabitha sounded hesitant before she continued. "Are you all right? You sound... well, very fuzzy."

She felt as muffled around the edges as the inside strand of wool on a ball of yarn. "Just tired, I guess. I worked pretty late."

Hayley hung up and considered what she knew for sure had happened last night. She'd had dinner, then returned to her office. She'd worked long and hard on the reports, in preparation for the meeting. Then she must have driven home, had a glass of wine and overreacted to it, and fallen into bed and into some incredible dreams.

That was it, then. Just a dream. It would definitely make it a little difficult to look Mr. Harrington in the eyes, though. She slid from bed, put on the silky robe lying at the foot and tied the sash as she walked to the window to look out at her backyard. The sight below made her feel as if she had stepped into an elevator shaft without checking to see if the car was there.

A bronze statue of a galloping mustang presided over the middle of her back yard. Right next to the hot tub.

Moments later, she stood beside it, running shaking hands over the cool figure. She may have dreamed riding it, fantasized about Chad, but that didn't explain how the statue came to be in her possession.

Not knowing what else to do, she draped a drop cloth over the statue to hide him from view in case any of her neighbors happened to look over at her yard. Then she faxed the reports, showered and dressed, horrified to discover she had a faint love bite on her neck.

Great. Really nice way to present a professional image to the board. She put on a high collared blouse and tried not to think about it. Maybe it was a spider bite. It could have happened while she slept.

The next hurdle came when she discovered her car wasn't in the garage. But maybe that explained the whole thing better than anything else could. She'd stopped off at Rosita's Cantina for a drink, decided she shouldn't drive home and had called a cab.

Except that she never stopped for drinks on the way home from work unless she was meeting a colleague. She never had more than one. Never. Still, what other explanation could there be?

But there was no way she could explain how one of the treasured mustangs had ended up in her back yard.

Or how the lead stallion could have vanished from the sculpture at Mustang Towers, either, she realized as the cab pulled up in front of the building. Had anyone noticed it was gone? Her unease increasing, she paid the cabbie and made her way to her office.

She found Mr. Redding finishing up the board meeting. He glowered at her a moment but said nothing. A short time later, everyone disbursed with promises to return for the cocktail reception honoring Mr. Harrington.

"I trust you slept well?" Mr. Redding sat back in his chair and steepled his fingers, his gaze taking in every detail of her appearance.

Hayley, stifling the urge to pull her blouse collar up higher, rose and began gathering up her papers. "I apologize for being late, Mr. Redding. It won't happen again." She stepped away from the table and started to walk around behind him, but his hand on her arm stopped her.

"I'm just concerned about you, that's all. You've been working harder than anyone towards making this building a success. Put all that aside for the next couple of days. I want you to concentrate instead on making Mr. Harrington welcome."

Again, the mention of the sculptor's name sent a delicious shiver through her. The papers trembled in her hand, but she fought to overcome it. "Thank you, Mr. Redding. I'll do my best to make him feel at home." Turning, she scurried off before dream remembrances ruffled her composure any further.

"Tabitha," she said when she got to her office. "Do the mustangs look any different to you today?"

Her assistant joined her at the window. "Of course not. Why would they?"

"No reason." Hayley swallowed. Strange how no one seemed to notice that the prized exhibit was now one mustang short.

Neither had anyone commented about the pair of red pumps by one of the remaining sets of bronze hoofs, either.

Was everyone crazy or was she alone in her madness?

Making an excuse to Tabitha that sounded as flimsy as wet tissue, Hayley hurried to the courtyard to retrieve her shoes. Bending low, feeling like an idiot, she had to squeeze between two sets of legs to reach her pumps and bumped her head several times in the process. Straightening, the shoes clutched to her chest, she turned to find a man standing behind her.

Chad Harrington.

"That's not what is meant by "shoeing" the horse." His lips quirked in a smile, but it was clearly an effort for him. She looked up into the coldest, most lifeless eyes she'd ever seen.

"Mr. Harrington." She extended her hand and gave him a polite smile. "I'm Hayley Wilder. It's nice to meet you."

This man wasn't Chad! His eyes were as chilling as black ice. His lips weren't as full, his hair lacked the vibrancy of the man in her "dream", and his face didn't hold the compassion and tenderness it had last night.

What was she thinking about? It had all been a dream. She stifled a feeling of repulsion from the feel of his hand in hers and gently eased her fingers from his. She had to force herself not to wipe her palm against her linen skirt.

"Not planning a little bareback riding, are you?"

The question should have been a joke, but the hardness in his voice sent a frisson of fear shooting up her spine. Next he'd be asking her where the lead stallion was. How could she even attempt to explain?

Summoning all her poise, she gestured playfully at him. "They certainly do look life-like. One could almost imagine them stretched out in full gallop, their manes flying free in the breeze."

His expression relaxed a bit, but his eyes remained as cold and hard as the bronze statues. "That's what I do, capture the living into something more... permanent."

The threat in his words was unmistakable. Forcing herself to overcome her unease, Hayley moved away from the mustangs and indicated for him to follow. "If you'll come with me, I'll take you to Mr. Redding's office now." Strange how the man didn't even notice one of his own sculptures was missing. What if this man wasn't really Chad Harrington?

Somehow she made it through the rest of the day and the endless media interviews, lunch, a cocktail party, a lavish dinner hosted in the sculptor's honor and a wrap-up session afterwards in Mr. Redding's office. At least her boss was pleased. All the publicity surrounding Harrington's visit was free advertising bound to impact the success of Mustang Towers.

The moon shone brightly as she made her way home, half-excited, half-terrified of what'd find there: man? beast? or a very huge bronze statue?

She was unprepared for the depth of her disappointment when she went into the backyard and the statue was still there, sporting the drop cloth just as she'd left it. Maybe she could explain away everything as a dream, but that still didn't answer how the statue came to be in her yard. How was she going to put it back where it belonged before anyone noticed? Or maybe, since no one had yet, it wasn't really here, and she was hallucinating.

She tugged on the cloth, her breath catching in her throat as the bronze-sculptured sinew of the horse was slowly revealed. He was gorgeous. No wonder Mr. Harrington was so cold and lifeless. He put his soul into his art.

Trembling, she stretched out her hand and let it smooth over the unyielding muzzle. Closing her eyes, she laid her cheek against the cool surface. So beautiful, so inanimate.

So warm and alive.

This time she felt the change as it occurred. One minute, lifeless sculpture, the next a living, breathing stallion of incomparable beauty. He whinnied.

Hayley stepped back, not sure if she should run or faint. "Oh my God. Are you real?" The horse nodded his head up and down vigorously. She stroked the velvety texture of his nose, then smoothed her hands down his coat. "Are you hungry, boy?" It was a sign of her insanity, she guessed, that had sent her to the feed store late afternoon, but now she was glad.

Once fed, the horse pranced restlessly around her small yard. Of course, he needed to be exercised. The thought of riding the magnificent animal again filled her with excitement, but this time she wasn't going to ruin a perfectly good suit. She changed into jeans, tee-shirt and sneakers and went back outside.

Moments later she was astride him, bent low over his neck as he conquered the neighborhood fences and sped through the night. The wind blew past her face, fresh, exhilarating, making her fear and inhibitions no more substantial than the air filling her lungs.

When she awoke, the bedside clock read two a.m. Just like last night, only unlike the night before she was completely alone.

Or was she? Suddenly, she became aware of the sound of someone else's breathing. Right next to her.

Stifling a cry, she started to scoot away when the man's arm shot out and circled her waist, pulling her up tightly against his hard, naked flesh.

"You didn't by any chance happen to pick up a steak at the market, did you?" Chad's smooth voice rumbled with a laugh.

"How did you get here?" She ceased struggling as she recognized that just like last night, he meant her no harm and her traitorous body began to respond to him as he stroked and caressed her.

He propped himself on his elbow and gazed down at her, one finger lightly tracing the contours of her face. "What do you mean?"

She frowned. "One minute I'm racing against the wind on the back of a stallion, the next thing I know I'm waking up as if from a dream, only you're here, so it must still be a dream."

"This is no dream," he murmured, lowering his head to kiss her. His tongue plunged deep inside her mouth, stroking her, making her senses swim as her body went soft and pliant with readiness.

She ached to hold him inside, she yearned for the chance to be with him in the light of day, in the heat of the night and always.

When he claimed her, she felt as if the world fell away and nothing existed except for this moment, this man, and the joining that again made her heart feel whole.

Just before dawn, she held him tightly, her cheek pressed against the perfection of his muscled chest, and listened as he told a story of jealousy and rage. A curse so pervasive it had forced one man's soul into exile while an entity of evil took over his body.

It had all started with Chad's African wildlife sculptures and a photo safari gone terribly awry when the group stumbled upon a secret gathering of shaman.

He stroked her hair as he described the beauty of Africa so vividly she could almost feel the wind rippling through tall grass and see the graceful zebras and cheetahs as Chad captured them on film.

"The shaman believe you trap the soul of the animal inside when you sculpt its physical likeness."

She considered that for several moments. "But in this case, he cursed you to be trapped inside your best creation. Who is that walking around inside of *your* body?"

"The shaman who died when the confrontation turned into a full-scale skirmish. He blamed me for disrupting their ceremony and desecrating their secret shrine."

She made little circles on his skin as she tried to sort through what he had said and make sense of it. "How did he do it? What would he do if he knew you still lived on some plane? And most importantly, how do we reclaim your life?"

"You'll help me?" His gaze was earnest and hopeful, as if he hadn't been certain she would believe him enough to try and save him.

She took a deep breath and forced herself to recognize the possibility that once his spirit was free, she might never see him again. "I'll help you. Even if it means we won't be together."

"But we will. I swear it."

She cradled his face in her hands and searched his gaze. "I know you believe that. I want to believe it, too. But we can't be sure what will happen once things have been restored the way they should be."

He closed his eyes and bowed his head. "Once he is cast out, I am certain my spirit will be able to return. His will go to its final resting place."

She pondered everything he had told her. "And you get one shot at this, right?"

"A full moon night when the moon turns red. Only then do I have a chance of reclaiming my life. Tomorrow night. The dedication ceremony for the mustangs."

Hayley fought to contain her nervous restlessness all through the next day as the media circus and Mr. Redding's endless publicity parade put her in constant company with Chad Harrington. One thing she knew for certain, if the real Chad was able to make the spirit switch, she would know it immediately. This man's gaze was dead, almost reptilian. And there was no mistaking his aura of evil, she felt it every time his glance flicked her way.

Convincing Mr. Redding to use the rare eclipse to showcase the dramatic dedication ceremony took some fast talking on her part, but Hayley managed to get his approval on her final plans. If only she could be certain the shaman wouldn't figure out what was going to happen until it was too late, she'd be able to take a relaxed breath.

The moon couldn't rise fast enough to suit her.

Shortly after sunset, the band began playing. Soft clouds drifted across the sky, turning Hayley's stomach into a knot of anxiety. What if the weather didn't cooperate? If it started to rain, they'd have to move the ceremony indoors. But worse, if the moon refused to show itself, Chad's plan wouldn't work.

She couldn't bear to think of the consequences of that. Chad's soul trapped forever inside a cold, lifeless statue. She pushed the thought away. This would work. It had to.

As Chad suggested, Hayley enlisted Tabitha's cooperation to keep the sculptor occupied so he wouldn't become suspicious that he was being engineered into a specific spot for the ceremony. This would allow Hayley the chance to slip away and return the mustang to the plaza.

Just as Chad had claimed, the minute the moon began to rise, Hayley's soft touch on his muzzle brought the cold bronze to warm, rippling life. She threw her arms around the stallion's neck and closed her eyes.

"Chad, if you're in there, please know that the past two nights have been the best of my life. Please make this work. I can't bear the thought of never seeing you again."

The stallion tossed his head as if in agreement, but it was as if he needed her to say more. She knew what she wanted to say, that somehow in the magic after midnight she'd fallen in love with her dream lover, but she couldn't force the words past the constriction in her throat.

Taking a deep breath, she mounted him and stroked her hand against his coat. "Ride like the wind, Chad. Ride the wind back to me."

The stallion's long legs ate up the distance between Hayley's house and Mustang Towers. She bent low over his neck and prayed the timing was right. Would the moon be there when they needed it?

They reached the plaza just as the sky began to darken with the eclipse. Mr. Redding's voice boomed over the PA as he recounted the story of the sculpture's commissioning, the background of the sculptor and the exquisite detail of his creation.

Now, Hayley, go now. Chad's voice seemed to echo inside her mind. She gripped her knees against his sides, and they leaped the hedge. Hoofs clattered against the cobblestones as they landed. The moon became completely dark. "When the blood moon begins to turn white again, that's my only window," Chad had told her.

The shaman, Tabitha on one side, Mr. Redding on the other whirled to face Hayley charging on the stallion. The crowd seemed to freeze as if time stood still. "Now, Hayley, now," she murmured.

As she rode across the plaza, the shaman, an expression of rage and fear on his face, grabbed Tabitha by the forearms and held her in front of him as a shield. Hayley's heart faltered. No! How could she sacrifice her friend to save a dream? She tugged desperately on the stallion's mane, but to no avail. He continued his thunderous race toward his nemesis.

Moonlight began to touch the edges of the plaza. Tabitha ground her foot on top of the shaman's booted foot, wrenched herself away, fell, and rolled to the side at the exact instant the stallion's feet left the ground.

The mustang sailed at the shaman. Thunder rumbled. The horse's hoofs hit the shaman square in the chest. Hayley flew through the air, falling, falling. A sharp pain in her head turned the sky completely white.

Lying flat on her back, she blinked as the murmur of shocked and curious voices rose around her.

"She fainted," someone shouted. "They both did!"

Hayley struggled to a sitting position. Eyes closed, Chad lay utterly still.

No! He had to be alive, it had to have worked. What was wrong with these people? Couldn't they see he needed help immediately?

She crawled to his side. Gripping his hand, she searched

frantically for a pulse, then pressed her ear against his heart. *Breathe, Chad, breathe!*

Tears streaming down her face, she covered his mouth with hers, trying to force air into his lungs as she alternately pumped on his chest. "I love you, Chad, please don't die," she whispered, over and over. "I love you."

"Then let me take a breath," he gasped, struggling away from her efforts to resuscitate him, wrapping his arms around her and pulling her close instead. "Just let me catch my breath."

"Oh, Chad." Hayley sagged against him. "Is it really you?"

Slowly he stood, then extended his hand and helped her to her feet. "You tell me."

She searched his face. Gone were the cold lifeless eyes of the shaman. In their place were the warm brown eyes of her dream man. She reached up and touched the vibrant hair tumbling to his shoulders. Her fingers traced the warm fullness of his lips. "Yes," she whispered. "It's you, my love."

"Are you both all right? Shall we call for help?" Mr. Redding and Tabitha spoke at the same time.

"We're fine, Mr. Redding." Hayley couldn't tear her gaze from Chad's as he bent and pressed a kiss to her mouth.

From behind her, Mr. Redding cleared his throat. "Shall we get on with it, then?"

"Yes, let's," Chad murmured, kissing her eyelids, her face, then capturing her lips. "We have a lifetime to get started on. And Hayley? I love you, too."

As the band began to play, the moon shook off the last vestiges of the eclipse. White light filled the plaza and gleamed off the bronze sculptures of a thundering herd of mustangs, the lead stallion quietly, permanently, braced against the wind.

ABOUT THE AUTHORS

SUSAN D. BROOKS loves to weave historical facts into her writing, which gives her an excuse to spend time visiting historical sites and researching obscure incidents from the past. Although much of what she learns doesn't make it into the pages of her published work, she feels richer for knowing more about the people who molded the foundation of today's world. She has written non-fiction articles and short stories for several online publications. Currently, she is working on a three-book historical romance series and stories for the upcoming anthologies LOVE SIZZLES and LOVE BELIEVES. Susan lives and writes in the heartland of America with her real life hero, her adorable son, and her two canine companions.

TAMI D. COWDEN always wanted to be a writer but practiced law for ten years before pursuing her dream beginning in 1997. Since then, her articles and short stories have appeared in national and online publications. Tami has won awards for her short stories, including the 1997 Individual Achievement in Fiction Award from American Mensa, Ltd. A double finalist in RWA's prestigious Golden Heart contest in 2000, Tami won the gold in the traditional category. She is co-author of THE COMPLETE WRITER'S GUIDE TO HEROES AND HEROINES, a guide to the 16 heroic literary archetypes. Tami has presented programs at the 1999 and 2000 RWA National Conferences, and at writing workshops around the country. She has taught writing at the University of Colorado and currently teaches at the University of Denver. She is now working toward at Masters in English with an emphasis in teaching writing. Write to Tami at Tami@tamicowden.com, and visit her website at www.tamicowden.com.

CAROLEE JOY is an award-winning author of romantic suspense, paranormal and contemporary romances. SECRET LEGACY, available from Starlight Writer Publications, won a Golden Quill for Best Romantic Suspense and was nominated for Best First Book. BY AN ELDRITCH SEA, from Authorlink Press, was a Golden Heart Finalist. WILD ANGEL has been nominated for numerous awards, including the Golden Quill, Rising Star 2000, and the Bookseller's Best. Look for the sequel, WILD FIRE AND ICE CREAM, from Authorlink Press Fall 2000. Other new releases include RELENTLESS SHADOW and CARELESS WHISPER, from Starlight Writer Publications. More of her short stories will be included in LOVE SIZZLES, Spring 2001, and LOVE BELIEVES, Fall 2001, from Dream Street Prose. She loves to hear from readers and hopes they will visit her websites at www.caroleejoy.com and at The Romance Club www.theromanceclub.com/authors/caroleejoy/default.htm

SU KOPIL believes dreams can come true. Although constantly seeking new venues to express her creativity, including woodworking, painting, and gardening, writing has always remained her primary focus. Her earliest inspirations run the gamut from Harriet the Spy to Bilbo Baggins to Hercule Poirot. A multi-published writer, Su's articles, interviews, and short stories have appeared in online and print publications. She is the editor of Yellow Sticky Notes, a print magazine for readers and writers, and a contributing editor to SPIN the journal of World Romance Writers. A native of New Jersey, Su lives on three acres in the rural southeast with her husband, two dogs, Timberwolf and Sage, and their ferret, Lakota. Su loves when her email box is bulging with letters from readers. You can reach her at: SuKopil@aol.com. Her webpage with free newsletter, contest, links, and more can be found at: http://members.aol.com/sukopil

BETSY NORMAN is a former accountant turned at-home mom with over thirty short stories and two monthly humor columns to her credit. She maintains her sanity and sense of whimsy through creative outlets such as writing, cake decorating and crafts. Blessed with three lively children and a husband who endearingly encourages her to "sell those books" whenever she suggests they re-do the kitchen or basement, Betsy relies on defying gravity to juggle home and career successfully. After ten years of marriage to her "Nordic Prince," Betsy believes in love at first sight, and invites you to share your true love stories with her. Please visit her home page at:
 http://members.aol.com/bgreaney/page1.htm   or   email: BGreaney@aol.com.

CHARLOTTE SHRECK BURNS most recent literary honor includes the Directors' Award from Ozark Creative Writers. When she isn't writing, Charlotte helps her husband host their Bed and Breakfast, The Country Rose, in Lancaster, Texas. Look for more of Charlotte's work in 121 NORTH, a collection of short stories from the North Texas Professional Writers Association available through Authorlink Press, www.authorlink.net or from any major bookseller.

Hot reading for summer!

Take a walk on the wild side with LOVE SIZZLES,
available Spring 2001.

Let love make you a believer!

LOVE BELIEVES, Fall 2001, a collection
of holiday and magical love stories.

Also from Dream Street Prose

House of Hearts

Madi Ryan Lee

Chapter One

A strong breeze chilled what was left of the bright afternoon. Rita Taggart shivered. She was a long way from home and the hot lethargic days that marked late summer in Fort Worth, Texas. She parked her Chevy four by four, then dialed the phone and waited for someone to answer. A two hundred-year-old oak spread its branches over the end of the paved road, the leaves chattering against the rushing wind. She rolled up the window and listened to the faraway telephone ring again and again....

On the fourth ring, the recorder kicked in. "You have reached 555-2710. Leave your name and number and a short message at the beep and someone will return your call."

The slightly insolent drawl finished and Rita cleared her throat in an attempt to sound confident.

"Hi. It's just me. Guess you're up to your neck in a bubble bath or I'd be talking to you by now and not the machine. Just wanted you to know the Jimmy acted like a perfect gentleman and we both arrived intact. The local chapter of the Historical Preservation Society has arranged for me to stay at Hartley House and I have a new phone—" the miracle of modern electronic wizardry cut off in mid-word, leaving Rita speaking to the dial tone "—number." She stared at the tiny digital handset, continuing the conversation in a less officious tone. "Well, it's been nice chatting with you, Mother. And by the way, happy birthday to you, too."

Rita liked some distance between her and her mother

when it came to the one thing they had in common but the thought of being nearly two thousand miles from family and friends today left her feeling a little lonely.

A shower of leaves pelted the windshield as she gazed straight ahead down the rough roadway, and thoughts of her mother disappeared in her eagerness to see Hartley House. An educated guess said at least forty acres of unkempt ground sprawled between her and the pre-Civil War mansion. Caught within the dark prison of the woods, lanky shrubs stretched skyward in search of the sun, their pale leaves fluttering in the fading light as they beckoned her forward. Rita put the Jimmy in gear and eased around a pothole roughly the shape and size of Indiana. The rest of the drive was hardly better.

It was apparent from the hot house architecture planted sporadically down the road behind her that the cream of Maryland, Virginia—and possibly Washington, DC's—elite had spent the past one hundred years migrating into the countryside. But none of the modern mansions could match the tattered splendor of the house at the end of the gravel road. The truck moved slowly along under a high roof of thatched tree limbs and emerged to climb a slight rise.

Twilight softened the ravages of time across the face of Hartley House but nothing could disguise the harsh scars of bricked up windows on the first floor.

As Rita got out and walked toward the porch, gravel crunched underfoot and the wind whipped hair across her mouth and eyes. Recently acquired knowledge of the southernmost tip of the Delmarva Peninsula reminded her they could have stormy weather here anytime, either from Chesapeake Bay to the West or the North Atlantic. Right now neither idea appealed.

Rita glanced at her watch. She was late.

And no one was there to meet her.